DRAGON MATES

BOOKS 1 - 3

J.K. HARPER

DAZZLED | THRILLED | BURNED

ABOUT THIS BOOK

DAZZLED

She is the key to his treasure

Seduction. Mystery. And treachery...

A billionaire dragon shifter on a desperate hunt. The fated mate who can save him. Sizzling attraction binds Sebastian and Lacey—but time is about to run out for them.

THRILLED

She is either his salvation—or his destruction

Passion. Secrets. And danger...

Devastating loss haunts water dragon shifter Kai Long—until he meets spirited underwater archeologist Gabi Santos. But she has a terrible secret. The kind that can wreck any chance for true love...forever.

BURNED

Beauty and the beast...with dragons!

Heat. Intrigue. And magic...

Fate brought damaged fire dragon shifter Ash and warrior-hearted book conservator Teagan together, but their love may be a double-edged sword...

DAZZLED

She is the key to his treasure—but only if she can unlock his heart in time

1

As usual, traffic on Sunset was a tangled bitch. Lacey Whitman took another long sip of her only vice, a thoroughly decadent caramel macchiato. She allowed herself to have one every weekday morning. On occasion she even had whipped cream added to it, such as this morning.

Pure heaven.

"The sonar images tell me that it's just the right size, so it really might have been the Santa Maria." The excited voice spilled out from Lacey's car speakers as she idled on the backed-up thoroughfare. "It's killing me to have to wait until Saturday to go down there, but the currents are still stirring up too much sediment from the ocean floor because of that storm off Baja. We won't be able to see much until it settles down."

The voice of Lacey's best friend, Gabi, rang out with its usual wild rush of adrenaline-fueled excitement. Lacey sighed to herself. What could she say? Gabi was a total badass who lived life out loud and in vibrant color. While Lacey and her best friend both adored ancient things and preserving cultural history, the similarities pretty much ended there. Gabi preserved the past by literally diving into oceans to save it.

Lacey preserved the past by curating objects in the museum she worked at, safe and sound on dry land.

A badass Lacey definitely was not.

"I'm totally psyched for you, Gabs," she said sincerely. "I'm also totally psyched that I'm not going to be the one down there." Lacey shuddered. "I swear, you're the bravest person I've ever met."

Gabi's rich laughter filled the car. "Tons of people go diving. I told you a million times it's completely safe as long as you get training and then go with people who know what they're doing. Like me."

Yeah, well, Gabi could say that. She was an underwater archaeologist who'd been in love with all things ocean practically since she was born. Lacey did not share that gene.

"Well, I can't wait for you to find out what's down there," she said, tapping her fingers on the wheel of her unmoving car as she frowned at the long line of similarly unmoving vehicles ahead of her. "I really hope it's something that's going to get you a killer new byline in one of the big journals. That would really get your name out there."

Gabi snorted. "Yeah, right. I'm still clawing my way up that ladder. The likelihood of me making a really big find right now is about the same as the likelihood of, oh, I don't know," and her voice suddenly became teasing. "You maybe finally acting on your baser instincts and jumping that blazing hot hunk of a boss of yours?"

Lacey, mid-sip on her macchiato, nearly choked.

Yes, the man in question was a wildly hot specimen of pure manliness. Yes, she hadn't seen any action in, oh, about an ice age or so. But there was one major problem with Gabi's vision.

"Yes," Lacey said when she could speak again, still coughing a bit, "my *boss*. Remember that part? Not a smart move. I'm in the same boat you are, Gabs." She rolled her eyes at the car speakers, even though her friend couldn't see her.

"I'm lucky to have this job, and I'm still clawing my way up the ladder too. Last thing I need to do is throw it all away by sleeping with my boss. Besides, he's not even my direct boss," she added, breathing a sigh of relief as her car finally started inching forward. "He's my boss's boss's boss. He hardly knows I'm female, anyway. We're professionals," she added with a haughty sniff, ignoring the tingle in her lady bits that always happened whenever she thought of him.

Truth be told, Sebastian Antonio Bernal was wildly sexy. In fact, the man was sexier than sin. Lacey would be lying to herself if she didn't admit that every time she was alone with him in her wing of the museum, examining an artifact or discussing the display of her big upcoming exhibit, she had to internally rein herself in because his mere presence really was a little bit of an aphrodisiac. Seriously, all she had to do was look at the man to feel a wave of heat roar through her body. His looks on top of his intelligence, his charm, and the dark broodiness that she somehow sensed covered a deep pain that he wasn't willing to share publicly always tended to make Lacey feel sort of protective toward him.

Which was really stupid, considering that he was so rich he could probably buy the entire world fifteen times over without batting an eyelash. He didn't need anyone protecting him. Especially not some not-famous, not-rich, definitely not-sexy girl from the hinterlands of Moreno Valley.

Gabi sputtered with laughter again. "Please. You're a bombshell. You try to hide it under those prim librarian clothes and that pulled back hair bun, but you are a genuine, one hundred percent, total babe." Gabi's voice sounded so certain that Lacey almost believed her. Almost. "Trust me, Sebastian Bernal can see that about you. Everyone knows he's a ladies' man to beat all ladies' men. I'm actually totally shocked he hasn't hit on you yet."

"Maybe that's because he can literally have his pick of the

world's most beautiful, most famous, most wealthy, most interesting women?" Lacey said pointedly.

Sebastian Antonio Bernal was definitely the stuff female wet dreams were made of. A very masculine six foot two, his tousled dark hair, mahogany brown eyes so dark they were nearly black, gorgeous body that regularly graced magazine covers, witty charm, tremendous power, and of course vast amounts of wealth put him on every magazine's world's most eligible bachelors list every single year without fail. Then again, it seemed that Sebastian Bernal had no intention of ever marrying, let alone settling on only one partner for more than a day or two at a time. Nearly all the photos snapped of him by the gossip rags showed a beautiful woman, sometimes even two, hanging off his arm as they went into fancy restaurants, gallery openings, award ceremony after-parties, and other such events around the planet that seemed typical to the lives of the rich and famous.

No, decidedly ordinary Lacey Whitman, whose geeky passions were old California history and cultural artifacts, wasn't exactly in the same league. Sure, she knew he appreciated her work. Actually, they both really enjoyed the Californios history niche that was her specialty. Sebastian himself was from the remaining extant Californio family, descended from a long lineage of Spanish people who had settled in the Golden State centuries before. It was no secret that he was very proud of his heritage.

Lacey had routine conversations with him about it, because it was her own speciality. All their conversations were work related, of course. Naturally, every discussion always had been purely professional. Theirs was strictly a business relationship. Definitely.

Well.

Maybe, just maybe, she'd had that one wild fantasy about him that one night—oh, who was she kidding. It had been nearly every single night for the past year since she'd been hired—when she'd been tossing and turning, unable to get to sleep because she couldn't stop thinking about his mouth. But really. The man was hotter than hot. She was female, after all. Even a celibate-but-not-by-choice girl who worked about seventy hours a week had needs. Even if the only answer to those needs was the bright pink battery-operated pal that lived in her bedside drawer.

But god. The man's mouth. Just his mouth could make an angel sin.

Okay, fine. As the line of cars finally began rolling down the street, Lacey let the truth smack its way out of her logical brain. Sebastian totally hit on her every single time they were alone. He wanted into her pants and he didn't hide it. She was some kind of challenge to him. He probably saw her as a conquest, just like he seemed to view every woman.

So far, she'd resisted the smoldering looks, the playful banter, and the outrageously gorgeous if almost savagely inaccessible face that promised her a night of passion like none other she'd ever experienced. Not that she'd ever experienced a decent night of passion. But she was pretty sure that if she ever caved, Sebastian Bernal would be the man to give it to her. In delicious, decadent spades.

"It's just business, Gabi," she said out loud, speeding down Sunset at a whopping eight miles per hour. Even though she twinged a tiny bit at that inaccuracy, she still kept the flirtation between her and one of the world's richest men to herself because she knew her well-meaning best friend would hound her into acting on it. But no way could she jeopardize her career that way. She'd worked too hard for it.

"I know he appreciates me for my mind, because that's what I was hired for." She ignored Gabi's mutter about her other assets being part of the package he'd hired as well. "Besides, I don't think he plays in his own sandbox. There are plenty of cute young interns and other types at the center. I've never heard even the faintest rumor of anything happening between him and any of them."

Gabi's exasperated sigh was followed by an equally expressive raspberry. Lacey smiled despite herself. Her bestie wasn't one for mincing words. "Lacey, seriously. You're hot," Lacey snorted at that, but Gabi ignored her and plowed on, "you're funny, you're brilliant, and you both share the same passion for an obscure yet important part of the state's history. A history that also means an awful lot to him personally. You're even fluent in Spanish, too. Don't you get it? You're perfect for him!"

Gabi's voice was filled with a sureness that made Lacey roll her eyes again.

"Trust me, girl, Sebastian Bernal has definitely noticed you. But you're probably right," Gabi added nonchalantly. "He doesn't want to mess up a good professional thing by bumping and dumping you just like he does with all his other women."

This time, Lacey laughed out loud. "Bumping and dumping? That's terrible, Gabs. And I don't think he's like that."

"Oh, no?" Gabi shot back. "Then why do all the magazines always show him with a new girl practically every freaking night of the week? It's because he hasn't found what he needs, Lacey." Her voice dropped to a more serious register. "He bumps 'em and he dumps 'em, because they're not what he's looking for," she ended on a dramatic whisper.

"Now you sound like a song." Lacey smiled at her friend's exuberant belief in Lacey's marketability.

"I'm right," Gabi insisted. "Trust me, I have a sense for these things and you know it."

Something flickered through Lacey at that. Gabi definitely had an uncanny knack for knowing which of her friends should get together in a serious way. She always joked that it was a mysterious legacy of her indigenous heritage. Whatever it was, it was real. If Gabi thought Sebastian was the one for Lacey—

Stop it, she commanded herself as she shifted the car into

8

second gear while balancing her macchiato in the hand that rested on the steering wheel. Just thinking about him brought a irrepressible tingle to her body.

"Maybe," was all she said out loud, though. Gabi snorted at that.

Lacey sighed to herself but didn't respond. For crying out loud, her panties were a little damp as it was, just thinking about the man. If she didn't change the subject now, she wouldn't be able to focus for the rest of the very long day she had planned at the museum that was her home away from home. The museum that of course bore the name of the very person she really needed to stop thinking about in such a totally carnal way: Sebastian Antonio Bernal, world's sexiest, playboy-iest, darkest, most unavailable man, who headlined her dirtiest dreams every single night.

2

The world fell away as Sebastian Bernal spread his coal black dragon wings and took flight. Beneath him, the sparkling bright lights of the city rapidly fell away as he beat his wings on the downdraft and headed south toward Los Angeles.

As he rose higher and higher, eager to get above the trapped scents of smog and fuel and all the other mingled smells of the bustling metropolitan city, he reflexively tightened his claws around the heavy object he held in them. It almost but not quite threatened to spill from his firm grasp.

He held a priceless treasure. It invigorated him more than almost anything in the world to once again have a piece of his own family's secret legacy. As a dragon shifter, this was what he lived for. As a man, this was what kept him intellectually stimulated and satisfied.

As a dragon whose personally priceless gold hoard had been diminished since before his own birth, it literally saved him.

His wings still beat steadily as he finally rose high enough in the sky to take deep breaths that weren't tainted with the nasty, toxic fumes that seem to encircle the entire globe. Sebastian's heart still raced with leftover adrenaline from having made another expensive deal on the shady black market of the underground shifter world.

"I'm letting you have that at a steal, Bernal," the mocking, oily voice echoed in his head. Sebastian's teeth tightly gnashed together with the anger that also still fueled him. "That's a sweet item I've had in my possession for about fifty years now. The only reason I'm letting you get away with it is because I know you're the only one of us who could afford what it's worth. That, and you're good at bargaining."

That statement had been the only truthful thing the other shifter, a low-life, if also rich and powerful, dragon named Malcolm Kerberos, had said all evening. Most dragon shifters were quite well-off. The old tales about dragons liking to hoard their gold were true. Even so, Sebastian Bernal stood out not only in the dragon shifter world but the entire planet. The Bernal empire was a household name, and Sebastian's net worth was known worldwide.

That brought out not only the shady crooks who wanted to shake him down for as many pennies as they could rattle out of his pockets for their pathetic trinkets, but also the big-time dealers like Malcolm, whose stolen dragon treasures were priceless.

Sebastian's enormous wealth also brought out a fair amount of female gold diggers. Letting the tiniest bit of irritated flame trickle out from a corner of his mouth at the ugly memories, Sebastian shook his head once to clear it. The thieving female shifter who'd managed to worm her way into his affections was an enormous, thoroughly regrettable mistake of his past. Thinking of her now would only enrage him.

The gold diggers didn't matter. Once badly burned, a thousand times shy. He was never letting another woman get close to him again. As for the shady dealers in antiquities black market? Well. Sebastian had his own way of dealing with them. Pretending to be shady himself, at least in the shifter world, had retrieved him many of the utterly priceless treasures that were worth far more than he had ever paid for them.

But Sebastian Bernal was too smart to let anyone know just how important the item he now held in his massive claws was to him. All the dealers in the booming black-market trade that stretched across all corners of the globe might know that Sebastian Bernal had money, and that he was just as willing to acquire interesting artifacts as the rest of them.

But not a single one of them knew the true provenance of the specific artifacts for which he searched with relentless intensity: family heirlooms that had been stolen from his ancestral estate over one hundred years ago. They were priceless in more ways than one, and Sebastian didn't dare let any shifter know the truth about them. Not even his curator at the Californio Rancho, the small but popular side wing at the world-class Bernal Center that was his pride and joy, knew how personally important these objects were to him.

Especially not that particular curator. Sebastian rumbled deep inside just at the thought of her. Layers of glowing golden hair that she tightly bound up every single day. Insanely luscious curves that she kept well hidden beneath appropriately professional, if occasionally somewhat dowdy, attire that befitted an up-and-coming young museum curator. Blue eyes that snapped with intelligence and often trembled on the edge of laughter. Those stunning eyes often lit brightly with her passion for the exact same artifacts that Sebastian held most dear to his heart: the legacies of his own Californio background, a mostly long-dead history that existed today in the same former glory and wealth in only one family in the entire state.

The dragon shifter Bernal family.

To which Sebastian was the sole heir.

Naturally, no one outside the shifter world knew the Bernals were from an ancient line of shifters, hailing originally from Europe before their move across an ocean centuries ago.

No, the human world simply thought the Bernal family had been the only one to ride out the vibrant past and epic downfall of the lavish wealth and holdings of the the golden state's Californio culture that slowly collapsed over a hundred years before. The Bernals had continued on with all their riches because of the one secret weapon no humans would ever know: they could shift into dragons, walk among the populace as human, and enjoy long, literally very rich lives.

Lacey Whitman appreciated Sebastian's Californio past nearly as much as he did, and it wasn't even her own past. For that alone, he'd be somewhat intrigued by the woman. Throw in her stunning curves, brilliant mind, and an indefinable something he couldn't quite decipher, and he was being driven half crazy by her.

The rumbling boom of a passing jet made Sebastian tighten his ear flaps more closely to his head as he soared on, the land beneath him now punctuated by larger dark patches as he flew southward, away from San Francisco towards the ceaseless lights of Los Angeles. The magical abilities of dragons to cloak themselves when flying had made sure that when the world turned modern, shifters in their dragon forms not only could not be seen by the naked eye, they also could not be picked up by radar and other modern marvels.

Being a dragon shifter was a damned good life.

Alone with his thoughts for the several hours it took him to fly over the somewhat dim heartland of the state, Sebastian was almost startled when the enormous glow of brightness over the L.A. basin appeared in the distance, so lost had he been in his own thoughts. Feeling utterly refreshed by the flight, he soared and swooped in a few playful patterns, basking in the strong feel of his wings and the powerful dragon body whose shape he took as often as he could.

He zoomed down closer to the earth as he soared over the bulge of the Grapevine, the unending stream of lights going up and down the interstate below him making him snort as usual at that exceedingly slow mode of transport. Surging close to the ocean, he spared a glance out over its darkness, idly wondering if any of the water dragons were out and about in the late night, cavorting in the waves. Sebastian himself was a classic dragon, which meant that while he could breathe fire, he could also swim quite well. But in general, he found swimming in the ocean distasteful. It didn't call to him nearly as much as it did water dragons, and he couldn't stay down in the depths for nearly as long as they could.

Turning his gaze back over the city, he banked down hard toward the gleaming white buildings of the Bernal Center, which came into view as he approached. They remained guarded with their special, and very expensive, dark sky-friendly lights every single night of the year. Sebastian's personal crowning jewel of the Bernal Center housed several hundred million dollars worth of priceless antiquities, art, and traveling displays. Their security was of utmost importance to him and the board.

Soaring down to his private landing spot—not that anyone else knew that it was a landing spot—on top of the building that housed his personal office, he touched down with much lighter grace than anyone would suppose from seeing such an enormous creature. It was actually a bit tricky this time, as he held the object in his front claws and couldn't use them for balancing as he usually did. Yet it was a simple enough matter to use his back legs and massive tail to calibrate his nearly soundless landing.

Smiling to himself, Sebastian carefully released the huge gold treasure to the ground, stepped back, and thought of his human form in vivid detail. He pictured himself in the power suit he'd worn to the meeting with Malcolm, calling up his humanity with an ease born of long practice. In half a heartbeat, Sebastian stood on two legs, clothed in the suit and skin of a man.

He strode to the door that led inside the building, entered

his private code, and swung the door open on silent hinges. Intending only to retrieve one necessary item from his office before flying farther south to the sanctuary of his family's ancestral, private hacienda, he strode with deliberate steps down the quiet hallway. A faint sound, however, caught his hearing, which was still highly attuned due to the recent change from his much more sensitive dragon self. Halting, he flicked a glance at the security cameras, then back down the hallway.

Someone unexpected was in the building. It wasn't an intruder. That was impossible. He paid an exorbitant sum for round-the-clock security at the Bernal Center. No one, not even another dragon shifter, could get in unnoticed. No, somebody who belonged here was working very late. Sebastian had left San Francisco at 10p.m., and it was now well past two in the morning.

A-ha.

With a sudden grin pulling up one side of his mouth, he knew exactly who was down the hallway. A certain gorgeous, utterly brilliant curator that he'd been more than lucky to snag for the Center her first year out of grad school.

Well, now. This should be interesting. The irresistible call of the chase he'd felt since the very moment he'd met the woman he knew was here now, working very late, prompted him to change direction to head toward the Californio Rancho wing instead.

He was about to startle the very luscious, very challenging, utterly absorbing Lacey Whitman.

3

Lacey swiped at her eyes with the back of her hand, willing away the fatigue. She had a new exhibit opening this weekend. An exhibit she'd been named lead curator on, which meant it was a Really Big Deal. Everything had to look perfect. She definitely was clawing her way up the ladder, just as she'd said to Gabi. In her case, clawing meant setting up fantastic exhibits that resonated with the viewers. That gave them a sense of connection to people long gone, people who had the same dreams and desires and longings as anyone alive today.

Taking a deep breath, she plunged back into it. What was sleep, anyway, when she was riding the fast-moving comet of her career?

She made one more tiny adjustment to the far corner of the exhibit she'd been fussing with for the past twenty minutes, then stepped back to examine it with a critical eye. No, she still had the lighting just a bit wrong. Or maybe it was that she had forgotten to add something else that needed to be in there? Yes, something was missing. A small, almost inconsequential piece that nevertheless would bring it all together. A tiny thing that was key.

She had no idea what it was.

Perhaps she just needed a broader view. It was a large exhibit, taking up half of the Californio Rancho room in the Sepulveda Gallery. She took another step back, then one more —and smacked directly into something hard, hot, and unyielding.

"Oh!" Starting forward as if she'd touched a live wire, Lacey spun around. "Oh," she said again, this time her voice much lower. Nearly a whisper, but for the little catch in her throat as she stared at the one person she didn't want to see in the middle of the night.

Sebastian Bernal stood there, dressed in a suit that fit him like a glove, his face freshly shaven, power screaming out from every pore. Power, and that crazy-hot sex appeal that drove her wild every time she was near him.

Lacey swallowed. No matter how many times she saw him, no matter what she said to Gabi, this man had this effect on her. The effect of making her forget pretty much everything in the world, even to the point of forgetting what her own name was.

The low rumble of his voice shimmied through her very bones, igniting something warm deep inside her. "Working late again, Ms. Whitman," Sebastian added, pinning her with the look that always seemed to promise a long, luscious night of worshipping her body. Well, in her dreams, at least.

He never called her by her first name. Even though she'd asked him to do that many times, given his status as her superior several times over.

She didn't want him to call her by her first name just because she wanted to hear what it would sound like on his lips, of course. Definitely not. Nope.

Swallowing again because her throat suddenly seemed ridiculously dry, she said, "Of course I am, Mr. Bernal. This exhibit is very important, and it opens in just a few days. And for the last time," she added without thinking, "you can call me Lacey. Especially when no one else is around. Oh!"

Her and her idiot mouth again. A dark fire slowly lit in his eyes when she said that, which only added to the warmth definitely spreading out from somewhere well below her belly.

Mirth? He was enjoying playing with her. Wait a darned minute now. "That's not what I meant," she said, narrowing her eyes at him just a bit and taking another healthy step backward. Being this close to him was dangerous. Something crackled off of him. The fire she always sensed within him, coupled with the low, rolling desire that seemed to pulse out every time she was near him.

A wild, reckless energy between them that as always threatened to topple her sideways. That would be just the professional image she kept trying to impress upon him. Struggling to keep herself from doing anything else idiotic, Lacey stood her ground as she tried to gather her thoughts.

He raised his eyebrows. It was such a small gesture, but it transformed his already ridiculously stunning face from that of a gorgeous devil to that of a sinfully dangerous angel. Ah, what had she been thinking about?

Dazed, she just stared at him, struggling to hold onto her own thoughts. Something about wanting to toss her panties onto the ground and let him do whatever the hell he wanted to her, right?

Wait a minute. No, that's not what she wanted to think. Dammit. Just being around him completely fried her brain.

"So, when nobody else is around, I can definitely call you," and here, Sebastian leaned forward just a bit, close enough that Lacey's pulse stampeded in her throat, "Lacey?" He stroked her name as he said it. His voice curved around it, tasting it, savoring the sound of it in his mouth.

Holy shit. He'd just addressed her by her first name. Or maybe she'd fallen asleep at her desk and was now just dreaming?

Lacey knew her jaw was unhinging slightly, but there was nothing she could do about it. His dark, sun-kissed skin, the charcoal black hair, a small bit of which just started to trace one eyebrow, his unbelievably stern yet incredibly tempting lips. And his eyes. For the millionth time, she thought to herself that she'd never seen eyes quite like his. Dark, velvet brown with a touch of some sort of flickering fire deep within them, right now they sported a dusky umber tone lit with flecks of jade green that drew her in and made her breath shorten.

Dammit. Every single time? Really? This was ridiculous. She was an adult. She was a professional. She had a Ph.D, for crying out loud. She refused to react this way just because of the way the man said her name.

He'd said her name.

Sebastian's gorgeous eyes examined her as her brain raced with her confused thoughts. "Hmmm," he murmured.

Holy shit. Were her—was she—yes. Her panties were getting damp. Like, really damp. Dear god.

Quick. She had to think of something. Earth to brain. "So," she frantically grasped for the first thing that might make the slightest bit of sense. "I, uh, there's something not quite right about this exhibit." Exhibit. Yes. She was a curator. A bright, rising star in the museum world. Right. Taking another step back and turning to gesture at the exhibit, she managed to say in her usual smooth voice, "I can't figure it out. Something's missing. Maybe you can help me?"

Lacey looked at the exhibit as she spoke, trying desperately to tamp down his intoxicating scent of bright bergamot and sage, and something indefinable that reminded her of a wild, primeval forest dusted with cedar. Then, dear god, Sebastian took a step in her direction, stopping literally only inches from her.

Swooning was a word that had always struck her as something completely ridiculous that only the dumbest romance novels would ever actually use.

Right now, Lacey was definitely about to swoon as the full force of Sebastian's presence, his enthralling scent that was making her crazy with the desire to do something completely insane, like *kiss the man,* bombarded her with relentless intent.

"Ms. Whitman." His voice was pure silk. Divine, soft, luxurious silk. "I am more than ready to help you in any way you please."

4

S ebastian watched Lacey carefully as he spoke, assessing her reaction to his words. Her glorious indigo eyes widened, then darkened even more. He also caught her nostrils flaring just a bit, although she tried to hide her response to him. To his scent, which was capturing her more surely than any snare he could ever have set for the confounding, utterly absorbing woman.

Satisfaction rippled through him as well. She was attracted to him. No question about it. His dragon roared in approval, urging him to turn the few inches it would take to lightly grasp her chin in his hand, tip her beautiful face up to his, and ravage those sweet, soft lips that tantalized him every time he came near her. That had tantalized him since he'd first met her a year ago.

Sanity prevailed. One thing Sebastian never, ever did was play with his own employees. It was a shame, because he'd certainly met some beauties who worked for various aspects of the global Bernal corporate empire, but he'd always held firm. That was a potential route to legal disaster. Besides, he spent a fair amount of his time in Los Angeles, which teemed with a veritable explosion of buxom starlets and wannabes who were more than thrilled to be his companion for a night. He didn't need to dally with his staff when the most beautiful, willing girls in the world flocked to this sunny landscape.

Even so, he couldn't help it. Lacey's luscious pink lips tormented him. Every time he flirted with her, she would catch her lower lip in her teeth, nibbling a bit in her consternation.

It always made him harder than granite.

"All you have to do," he added in a low, seductive voice, "is ask me."

Lacey stared back at him. Sebastian's gaze involuntarily flew to her throat as she swallowed. The delicate muscles there, flexing with nervous response, caught his breath in his own throat. Being this close to her threatened to overwhelm him. It urged him to do to her all the things he had fantasized about since the moment he'd met her just under a year ago. To want to smooth his fingers along her skin, listening as her breath hitched and her glorious, utterly enticing female scent deepened as her arousal came to the surface.

Yet rationally, he knew this was merely a temporary game to distract him from his goal of repatriating the entirety of his gold hoard. Lacey was a beautiful bauble, and an extremely intelligent one at that, but nothing more. Even though his dragon kept insisting that Lacey was his, Sebastian knew better. He had been heartlessly betrayed by a woman once before. It didn't matter how damned enthralling this one was. She was just like the rest of them. Not to be actually trusted.

Ever.

"I'm sorry, Mr. Bernal." She flicked a glance at him as she said that, clearly indicating that they were back into formal name territory again despite the fact that he had luxuriated over the sound of her first name mere moments before. "I, ah, don't know what to say."

Sebastian gave a quick shrug before he abruptly stepped into the exhibit itself, eliciting a gasp from Lacey. Striding into its center, he turned his attention to a gorgeous, leather-bound journal that rested atop a classic table that would be found in the fancy ranchos of the elite class of the time, nearly one hundred and fifty years ago. A quill pen rested beside its open pages, seemingly ready to be taken up to record the day's events. Carefully, he opened it in the middle. Large and heavy enough for the pages to lay flat, the journal settled against the table as if made to be there. The pages, made of thick paper, were slightly ink-stained in places. But a colorful little painting on one of them to lent a richness to the scene that was, in fact, perfect.

"Here," he said. "This is what's missing. An invitation to read about the treasures of my family's history."

He looked back at her, raising an eyebrow as he made his own silent invitation.

LACEY FELT ALL the air in the room seem to suck out sideways as Sebastian pinned her with his dark eyes. Standing there in the middle of the exhibit, his entrance into which had been both heedless yet exceedingly careful not to disturb anything, he looked like some sort of ancient king, surrounded by power and ready to blast fire or something.

Swallowing, she sternly told her brain to stop being fanciful, resume its usual function, and answer the man like the professional she was. "Oh, yes. That does actually work really well." Her voice, which usually obeyed her, was steady. "It's a beautiful little painting. It adds just the right amount of intimacy to the scene."

Oh, for crying out loud. Her cheeks flamed as he looked at her with that knowing smile turning his face into genuine sinful angel again.

"I knew you were a good hire, Ms. Whitman." His voice practically purred. "Tell me, are you still happy to be working here?"

The rapid-fire change of conversational direction made Lacey blink. "Of course I am. It's a dream to work at the Bernal Center. Everyone in the field wants to be here. There's nowhere I'd rather be," she added softly.

One of those moments, tight as a wire and crackling with restrained electricity, snapped between them again. The kind of moment that made Lacey forget her name, forget the world, and feel like she should just throw herself at the man. She felt her own breath shorten as she stared at him, wondering if she could literally drown in the dark chocolate of his eyes and the purely sensual promise they held.

No, not a smidgen of attraction between the two of them. Strictly a professional relationship.

Right.

"Excellent. I'm leaving for Madrid later today," he added in another rapid change of direction, as casually as a normal human being would announce they were headed to the beach that afternoon. "Business will keep me there for several days, but I will be back in time for the opening on Saturday. I'll look forward to seeing you then, Ms. Whitman. I know you'll have everything under control."

Stepping away from the journal and the table, he looked at Lacey. She felt herself swirling into the depths of his fascinating eyes as the tingling bits of her body told her in no uncertain terms that she wasn't really in control at all. Oh, wait. No, he meant the exhibit. She would be in control of the exhibit. The one she was standing in right now. Of course.

"Absolutely, Mr. Bernal." Her voice didn't even shake as she answered him. That had always been one of her face-saving little quirks in life—her voice never betrayed her nerves, not even when she'd been defending her bold, unprecedented dissertation in grad school. The one that her advisors had thought was either brilliant or a disgrace.

The one that had gotten her noticed by Sebastian Bernal and led her to this very moment. This moment of genuinely wet heat between her legs as one of the richest men in the world, one of the biggest playboys, and definitely the most mysteriously intriguing man she'd ever met, stared at her with eyes filled with a dark promise of sensuous fulfillment that teased her dreams every night.

The sort of fulfillment that would only get her heart broken and make her lose her beloved job in the best case scenario.

Tipping her chin up and forcing herself to look as accomplished and in control as she could at 2a.m. after a long, exhausting day, she said, "Have a good trip. I'll see you Saturday night."

The faintest etching of a grin shadowed his lips. "You will indeed." He turned and began to stride back down the hallway, then paused and swung back to her. "Oh, and Ms. Whitman?"

"Yes?" Her heart thumped like the dumb thing it was as his broad shoulders filled her vision again.

"Wear something to match your curves. I'd very much enjoy seeing them on display as well."

Unable to stop herself because it was late and she was both tired and caught off-guard, Lacey gaped at him.

"You don't show them off nearly as much as you should." His gaze, still that of the world-renowned Casanova he was, took a leisurely track of her body from head to toe and back again. "Good night, Ms. Whitman."

With that, he left for real, taking all the air in the room with him and leaving Lacey almost gasping from the innuendo.

Head ping-ponging, Lacey gave up on staying any later. Time to go home. To her lonely bed—and, she knew without a doubt, some seriously sexy thoughts about the powerful, and powerfully hot, man who'd totally soaked her panties again, without even touching her.

5

Sebastian crossed his arms as he waited for Ash's response. His expectations were not disappointed.

"Damn, Sebastian." Ash gave a low whistle as he shook his head in admiration. "You've been very busy these last several years, haven't you?"

Satisfied, Sebastian nodded as he reverently reached out to stroke the gold piece closest to them. A hefty gold cross bedecked with sparkling, colorful gems, it had been a gift from Queen Isabella of Spain to the Bernal family back in the 17th century. Sebastian's great-grandfather many times removed was one of those exploring the New World for the glory of Spain. Of course, neither his queen or anyone else knew that as a dragon shifter, he had quite an advantage over most of the other explorers of the time. In her gratitude for all that Sebastian's many times removed ancestor had done for the crown, the queen had bestowed many riches upon the Bernal family during her reign.

Riches that had been stolen amidst ugly bloodshed in the very early 1900s during what was the darkest period of the Bernal family lineage. Yet Sebastian had managed to repatriate many of the stolen artifacts since, including the sizable cross that he'd manage to buy back from Malcolm Kerberos in San Francisco the other night. It pained him to use part of his own fortune to pay for his own family's belongings, but he'd made a vow to his parents before their untimely deaths that he would do everything in his power to get back the precious items that were not merely dazzling pieces of gold so desired by most dragons.

These objects were imbued with a power far deeper than that. The loss of which power had led to his parents' subsequent weakening and slow, painful deaths when Sebastian was barely out of childhood.

If he didn't recover the entire Bernal hoard, Sebastian himself was in danger of the same fate.

"It's tough being an undercover agent," he said, earning a chuckle from his still enamored best friend, who was taking visual catalog of the rest of the carefully displayed items in Sebastian's most private, secure room at his family's ancestral hacienda well south of L.A. "But it's been worth it. You understand why."

Ash nodded, his expression going grave. As fire dragon shifters, Ash Connolly's family was just as old and powerful as Sebastian's. The ethnic lineage was quite different, however. Ash was of pure Irish ancestry, although his particular branch of the family had called America their home for well over a century now.

One only had to look at the right-hand side of Ash's face, which even in the presence of his best friend he kept carefully turned away, to see how well Ash understood the true power of a dragon's private hoard. Or rather, what the loss of that hoard could mean. Ugly, misshapen scars ran from his scalp down his neck to disappear under his shirt. Sebastian knew perfectly well that the burn scars ran all the way down the entire side of his friend's body. He had been there during the horrific event that had scarred Ash for life. It was an event that insured Ash would have a reminder for the rest of his days that some choices were, indeed, worse than others.

"Well," Ash said, his lighter tone indicating a change in the direction of the conversation, "I'm suitably impressed. How many more artifacts to go?"

"Only one more." Sebastian's voice was grim.

Ash glanced at Sebastian, his left eyebrow raising even though the right eyebrow couldn't follow suit. "I had no idea you were so close. Do you have any idea where it is?"

Sebastian shook his head. "No. Well, I have a suspicion that bastard Malcolm Kerberos knows something about it." His expression darkened again at the thought of the under-handed, truly evil dragon shifter who pretty much ruled Northern California. "I've tried to sniff it out of him the past several years, but of course I can't appear too interested. That will set off his alarm bells. He'd either figure it out, or demand a price so outrageous it could actually bankrupt me."

Ash snorted. "Not sure that would ever be possible, Seb." He used Sebastian's childhood nickname, which made Sebastian roll his eyes. Ash and the hacienda caretakers, who had raised Sebastian after his parents died, were the only ones in the world ever allowed to call him that without fear of reprisal. "He's got to know perfectly well that you have hidden accounts around the world, just like every dragon shifter. You're worth a hell of a lot more than anyone truly realizes." He gave his friend a shrewd look at that, shaking his head as a half grin pulled up the working side of his face.

True enough. All dragon shifters used human-run bank accounts for various reasons, most commonly so they could blend in with the ways of the modern world. But there were shifter-only run firms at which no human could ever open an account. Those firms housed the true wealth of all dragons. Excepting, of course, the private hoards each dragon kept securely locked away at some locale or other. Ancient habits died hard, not to mention the reasons for the actual power behind the legendary keeping of gold by dragons.

"True," Sebastian admitted. "Even so, I just can't afford for him to get suspicious at this point. If he figures it out, he'll be able to destroy me."

A long, grim silence stretched between the two as they quietly surveyed Sebastian's secret hoard. Then Ash shrugged. "For all his wily ways, you're a hell of a lot smarter than that bastard, Sebastian. And more patient. So. How's the nightlife going lately?" He wagged his eyebrow up and down in a lascivious manner, causing Sebastian to chuckle.

Clapping his hand on his friend's back, Sebastian gestured towards the door. They exited, and he very carefully set the wards that made it secure against any shifter before they headed out to the sweeping veranda that encircled the stunning hacienda that had housed the Bernal family since the late 1700s. "I have a hell of a nightlife. Gold aplenty to gaze upon, the company that allows me to pursue my passions, wine, women, and song every night, and not a care in the world. It's a dragon's life, right?"

Ash laughed, although there was the slightest wistful undertone that caught Sebastian's sympathy every time. Ash had been a hell of a handsome guy before his disfigurement. Ever since then, even though his massive wealth would still make him a catch for many women, Ash had shunned all female company. He kept himself fairly hidden away from the entire world. Many dragons had solitary lives anyway. Ash seemed to be somewhat content with his lot. Even so, Sebastian knew his friend craved genuine female company. The kind that would never judge him.

Sebastian knew better, though. He'd experienced the worst of women. They all judged, and they easily found him lacking. It had taught him to never trust them except strictly in bed.

Thoughts of a tousled mass of golden blonde hair,

sparkling blue eyes, and teasing, luscious curves that tormented his dreams every night, even when he was with other women, surged to the surface. He felt his dragon rumble deep inside him again, but he sternly forced it down. Never again.

"Indeed it is," Ash said agreeably, gazing out over the sprawling, vast lands of the Bernal estate. "Still playing the field of an endless parade of Hollywood beauties?"

Sebastian chuckled as they seated themselves on the spacious cedar wood Adirondack chairs on the veranda. He poured them each a brandy from his private collection. "You know it." Even to his own ears, his voice sounded overly cheerful. He caught Ash's inquisitive glance but ignored it. "New lady every night. That's all the silly things are good for."

"I happen to know you have some very brilliant women working for you, Sebastian." Ash's voice sharpened. "Don't pretend to be a jerk around me. I know you better than that."

Taking a long sniff of the enticing aroma from the hundred-year-old brandy, Sebastian shrugged in feigned nonchalance. "For me personally, that's all they're good for." Ignoring his dragon's disagreeing rumble deep inside, he took a long, luxurious sip of the brandy, holding it in his mouth as the rich taste exploded across his tongue. "A willing woman at night, and a good brandy with my best friend on my day off. Oh, fine," he snapped with some exasperation as Ash still eyeballed him. "Of course there are brilliant women working for me. There are brilliant women in the world, and there are definitely many women out there who are good for far more than a night's tumble. I acknowledge that. But not for me."

Another slightly uncomfortable beat passed before Ash said, point-blank as usual, "They're not all like Melusine."

Just hearing that wretched name was enough to make Sebastian grind his teeth.

Folding his arms across his chest, Ash went on, "She was a

truly nasty piece of work. You just haven't met a good woman yet. The right one."

"Oh, spare me that crap." Sebastian glared at his brandy. "Not every shifter meets his mate. I neither want nor need one of those."

Ash stayed silent for a moment. He wasn't in a position to argue that particular point, in any case. Yet, observant as always, he pressed on with the one thing Sebastian couldn't deny. "Fine. But what about that one who works for you? The one you tell me understands the family history? The one you hired because of her, and I quote," and here Ash emphasized with actual finger air quotes, "'brilliant mind as well as sharp grasp of the nuances of how the historical legacy left by my ancestors' people continues to shape this state today'?"

Sebastian frowned. He'd said precisely those words in a *New York Times* article from last year that had announced Lacey's new position at the Center. "You and that photographic memory of yours are really a pain in the ass sometimes, you know that?"

Ash shrugged. "Could be. But really, it's why you keep me around. So you don't forget anything. Besides," he added, giving Sebastian a searching look, "you gushed about her a bit more than you usually do about hires who are somewhat down the hierarchy. She's not even a department head. It was pretty easy to tell you were more interested in her than you wanted anyone to actually realize."

Just thinking about Lacey and her genuine love for his own family's history, let alone those luscious curves, was again enough to derail Sebastian's thoughts momentarily. He had to get that woman into bed. It had never taken him this long before. Then again, he did respect the fact that he didn't want to lose her as a valuable employee of the Bernal Center.

If only she wasn't so damned beautiful. So damned enticing in a way he still couldn't fully explain. "Well," he growled, battling away the thoughts of her, "you're wrong."

Ash laughed, taking another sip of his brandy. "Fine, my friend. Whatever you say. So," he added, knowing Sebastian well enough to understand that while he'd made his point, the subject wouldn't go any farther at the moment, "Madrid later today?"

"Yes." Eager to move the conversation away from the vexing, utterly captivating woman he couldn't seem to keep off his mind, Sebastian thankfully grabbed the opportunity to move the talk away from her and her highly distracting, exquisite existence.

6

Lacey awoke from a deep sleep to the sound of her phone chirping at her. She ignored it for a moment before suddenly snapping up her head, trying to focus her bleary eyes on the arms of the beautiful old clock nestled atop the desk across from her bed. It was just before 11a.m. She didn't feel completely rested despite the late hour. Then again, she hadn't gotten home until three in the morning from her final nitpicking at the exhibit. Glancing at her phone, she frowned at the flashing *PRIVATE* on its face. It kept ringing. Suddenly fearful one of the higher-ups at the museum was calling to tell her something terrible had happened, she lunged at it, swiping her finger across the screen to answer.

"This is Lacey Whitman," she said in a voice that sounded nothing at all like one belonging to someone who'd just woken up moments before. She'd always had the ability to sound cultured and in control at almost any moment, even if that wasn't remotely close to the truth.

"Hello." The deep, dark rumbling voice on the line made every single female thing Lacey had clench in a delighted quiver. Sebastian. She hadn't seen or spoken to him since the other night. Just thinking about their interaction now intensified the warm flush sweeping through her body.

"Did I wake you?" The caress of his voice through the telephone was like a rich molasses flowing over Lacey's skin. Despite the heat the mere sound of his voice sent through her body, a cool shiver of excitement rippled through her as well.

"Of course not," she lied through her teeth. "The exhibit opening is tonight. I'm—in the middle of last minute preparations." She rolled her eyes at herself as she glanced down at her rumpled bed, in which she lay wearing nothing more than a tank top and a cute pair of boy shorts.

"Somehow, I don't think that's quite the case at the moment." His knowing tone made the thrilled shivers intensify. "I know you were at the museum extremely late again last night. I'm also enjoying thinking about you possibly just waking up right now. Imagining you in your bed."

Was the man a mindreader? Lacey swallowed hard as she thought of Sebastian thinking of her in bed. "Mr. Bernal," she began, voice still steady and cool despite the leap of her pulse.

"Sebastian," he said. His voice dropped another notch, sounding both serious and devilishly teasing at once. "You want me to call you Lacey, you must call me Sebastian. Especially when we are alone at the moment, so to speak." His voice lowered even more, teasing her very nerve endings. "I'm bringing something back from Madrid for you."

A long, charged moment filled with crackling energy held space between them. Lacey caught her breath as a dozen thoughts rattled around her head at once. Suddenly, Sebastian's low laugh filled her ear.

"Don't get too excited, Lacey." Despite his words, his tone wrapped around her name again in a way that pretty much made her legs shake, even though she was still lying down. "It's something related to work. I think you will very much appreciate it. It's a token of my thanks for the excellent work you have done for the Center so far."

"Oh." Why did she feel so disappointed in that very sensible answer? She was the one worried about him coming onto her. About his playboy reputation. About her own job security. She wanted this to just be professional, right? "Well, I look forward to seeing what it is."

Another short, deep laugh. "Good. I do very much look forward to seeing you this evening, Lacey. You've done an outstanding job on the exhibit. I want to see you shine on its opening night."

Her skin prickled again, this time with a combination of desire as well as a rush of gratitude at his sincere approval. Knowing that she had done well not just for her own sense of accomplishment, for the museum's glory, or even just for one of the last living descendants of an ancient line, but for Sebastian himself, filled her with a heady sort of pride.

"I'll see you this evening, Lacey," he added again in the deep rumble of his voice. It somehow managed to reach through the phone, drop straight between Lacey's legs, and nuzzle her right there, causing a sensation of heavy softness that was achingly aware of how badly it wanted to be touched. To be really touched—by him.

Swallowing as she squirmed slightly on her bed, Lacey managed to utter a crisp goodbye before he hung up. Wide-awake now despite the few hours of sleep she had managed to grab, she lay in her bed with her thoughts still awhirl. Her body shivered from the delirious non-touch of his voice.

Just as she was about to motivate herself to swing her feet to the floor and get going, her phone buzzed again. She glanced at it and saw an email from a dealer she often had been in touch with over the past year. The subject line of "New Californio piece needs authentication" had her sitting up straight in bed and opening the email to read. A private client the dealer often worked with had a piece he wanted to authenticate before he decided how and to whom to sell it. The dealer would be in Los Angeles early the following week.

Would Lacey possibly be available to help him authenticate the item? He was fairly certain it was genuine, but being as she was one of the few up-and-coming experts in the field, he really wanted her to have a look at it herself.

Heart thumping with the excitement she always had at the prospect of a new find, she quickly answered him with a suggested date and time he could meet her at the office the following week.

Feeling energized by the sudden multitude of happenings, between the opening that evening, Sebastian's unexpected call and his even more unexpected news that he was bringing her something from his travel abroad, and the usual thrill of potential discovery about something new in her field, Lacey got up and readied herself for the day. She felt high with the adrenaline of everything.

Especially, she had to admit, the tingling charge that came with the thoughts of seeing a certain dark pair of smoldering eyes. And his mouth. The mouth that kept promising it would do dark, wicked, delicious things to her, no matter how much she told herself that wasn't what she wanted.

Right.

SEBASTIAN LEANED SLIGHTLY FORWARD in his chair, tenting his fingers beneath his chin as he examined one of the several monitors on his desk. The security cameras in the room of the opening practically buzzed with the excitement that saturated the exhibit hall. People milled around in controlled little bursts, taking their time as they went through the exhibit in small clusters. Chatting with one another, although he couldn't hear the sounds, staring intently at various aspects of the exhibit, enjoying the background music that played tunes that would have been popular at the time, and the open bar that flowed in the corner not only made this an incredibly enticing scene, they made it a perfect one. Lacey had outdone herself with this exhibit opening.

She herself stood at the center of all the high energy, beautifully dressed up for the occasion. Lacey wasn't one of those women who was completely self obsessed, always wearing the latest fashions. Yet although she was careful to downplay her assets during regular work hours, she apparently had had no problems dressing up tonight to show off her curves—as he'd requested. Tonight, she about had Sebastian's brain already wrapped in knots. He hadn't even seen her in person yet, as he didn't want to steal her thunder. The second he stepped into the gallery, attention would shift from Lacey to him. Her immediate supervisor had, under Sebastian's casual yet unyielding suggestion, allowed Lacey to spearhead this entire exhibit on her own. Sebastian had trusted her to do a fine job, and she had. He wanted her to get the glory for it that she could. His presence would distract people. He wasn't actually at the Bernal Center all that often, as he was generally too busy running a worldwide corporation to spend much time in any single place—not to mention his relentless pursuit of the last pieces of his scattered gold hoard.

Of course, during the past year he'd begun to spend more and more time here. Despite his own insistence that women were playthings to be had, enjoyed, and set loose so as to allow the next one to come along, he couldn't deny even to himself that Lacey was in a different class. Deep inside, his dragon rumbled again with that irritating conviction that Lacey was his. That she, and she only, belonged to him.

That she was his *mate*.

Setting his jaw as he battled his own self, Sebastian shook his head. He refused to believe that. But he also knew the reason he was so interested in her was more than the beauty of which she was mostly unaware, and usually kept buttoned up. It was her interest in the same field that fascinated him. It was, yes, her mind, as well as her charm, her wits, and that odd *something* that just drew him again and again to her.

His dragon roared again, frustrated and eager to get out. Frowning, Sebastian forced it down. No. Lacey was brilliant, she was intriguing, she wasn't interested in him in that fake, breathless way so many women were, and he always found himself somewhat relaxed around her. Yet for all that, she was a woman. As such, he would never trust her. None of them were to be trusted.

Then why had he brought her the gift from Madrid?

Well, damn it. Because he knew that she alone among all women would appreciate it. He also simply wanted her to have it. To be as dazzled by small piece of his own treasure hoard as he was. It was ridiculous, and something he would not admit to anyone else alive. His dragon rumbling with immediate triumph deep inside him, Sebastian reached for the small, beautifully wrapped package on his desk and gently placed it into his jacket pocket. With a final glance at the monitors, he left his office to head downstairs and see the fascinating woman in person.

And tonight, he vowed, to finally taste her sweet lips.

7

"**Y**our work ethic and passion for the subject have paid off tonight, Lacey." The voice of Lacey's immediate boss, who stood next to Lacey as they both watched the swirling excitement and enjoyment of the capacity crowd in the room, held admiration and, she was sure, no small amount of relief at the opening's success.

"Thank you. I'm just thrilled everyone's enjoying it. Honestly, it does help that Mr. Bernal is well known. It's got people pretty excited about this part of California's history. I couldn't have done it without him." Lacey might be a history geek, but she was a geek with dreams and goals. Now she could mark this off her bucket list: her first successful exhibit as lead curator. It felt amazing. The crush of people in the room, examining the exhibit, talking animatedly, laughing and discussing and experiencing that which she had poured her entire heart and soul into, was an aphrodisiac like none other.

Except the one man who was driving her wild. Lacey could practically feel the change in the atmosphere a split-second before a new voice joined the conversation.

"I'll take that as high praise from you, Ms. Whitman."

Lacey turned her head as Sebastian stepped to her side. "You did an excellent job."

Lacey pushed down the sizzle that seem to happen every single time Sebastian came near her. Hearing his voice that morning had set her nerves into a tingling delight of anticipation all day long.

"Thank you." Before she could continue, though, Sebastian inclined his head at her boss.

"I need a word with Ms. Whitman." He didn't need to say anything else. People obeyed Sebastian Bernal every time he opened his mouth. Nodding and smiling, Lacey's boss melted off into the crowd to mingle.

Immediately flustered with excitement and a fresh dose of nerves, Lacey almost swayed on her feet with the effort to not flee after her boss. But Sebastian, who clearly was observant, said in his dark honey-laced voice, "I've been watching on the monitors. You're in your element here."

That brought Lacey up short. "You were watching on the security monitors? That's a bit high-handed even for you, don't you think?" Before she began working here, Lacey never in her life would have dreamed that she would ever dare address the man who owned what seemed like half the world in such a manner. But this was the effect he had upon her. He turned her upside down, inside out, made the craziest things come out of her mouth. What was more, she felt relatively comfortable doing it.

"It's my prerogative. Besides, I do like to keep an eye on all my treasures." He looked right at her as he said that. Lacey flushed, buzzed by her proximity to him.

Just about everything female in her body wanted to fling herself at him and cry, Yes, absolutely! Yes, I'm a treasure. Keep me. Heck, just take me.

The modern, feminist part of her brain naturally wanted to slug him for referring to her as a treasure. As if she were merely a possession. Undecided as to which move would be worse, she simply froze in place, once again caught by the dark promise in the way he looked at her.

"I need to circulate a bit," he said. "But before I do that, I want to give you the gift I brought back from Madrid. Please come with me to the courtyard."

He gestured with one hand toward the large south doors that led to the enclosed courtyard, also called a *placita*, outside the exhibit hall, much like one an actual hacienda would have. Both intrigued by what he might have brought her, as well as once again battling with herself and her own knee-jerk response to just say, Yes, sir, no problem, sir, Lacey simply let herself walk in the direction he indicated.

The courtyard, a welcoming space on nice days, was empty of people at the moment. Lacey stepped out into it with an abrupt sensation of relief. She'd been loving the energy inside, but it was a little taxing.

Sebastian pulled a small, beautifully wrapped package from the pocket of his outrageously expensive jacket and extended it toward her. Very careful not to let her fingers graze his hand as she took it from him, certain that would cause one of those white-hot sparks to flare again between them, Lacey was surprised by how heavy the small box was. Glancing up at him, finding her composure again at least in her voice, said, "All the way from Madrid, really?"

That cocky, sexy grin came over his face again. "Indeed. It's very respectable, I assure you. Please, go ahead."

Despite the casualness of his tone, she could see something on his face, or maybe just in his stance, that said this little gift was more than that. He really wanted to see her reaction when she opened it. "All right," she murmured, untying the beautiful little ribbon around the heavy ivory-colored wrapping paper that covered the little box. It was only slightly longer than her hand, and barely as wide. When she took off the lid and moved the delicate tissue paper inside to reveal what it held, she couldn't stifle a gasp.

Gold, rubies, and emeralds sparkled up at her from inside the box, almost seeming to shoot off light. The heavy little gold cross was exquisitely crafted, its stylized markings immediately signaling to her its 17th-century Spanish origins. A sinuous little dragon curled around the arms behind the backbone of the cross, small rubies for its eyes, emeralds creating sparkling tips along its serrated spine. She instantly recognized Sebastian's family crest.

Tearing her gaze away to look up at him, she said, "It's stunning! Obviously it's a replica," which was something her training had immediately noted, not to mention the fact it was simply too new looking to be truly old artifact, "but of what? Your family crest, I know that. But I've never seen this cross before. Is it from the private collection?"

She was perfectly well aware that Sebastian was a private collector. The entire world knew that. And while many many of his family's heirlooms were actually in permanent exhibits at the Bernal Center, she knew some items deemed too personally precious were kept at his ancestral family home south of the city. She only had ever seen pictures of those items, though. Much as Sebastian enjoyed her interest in the entire Californio history as well as his family's personal background, she knew he hadn't shared everything with her. Although it disheartened the scholar in her, she reluctantly supposed she understood his reasons. It wasn't like her own family had heirlooms. They weren't those kind of people. But she did have a simple gold ring that had belonged to her great-grandmother that she cherished. It wasn't really worth anything, but she certainly would never part with it. Nor would she ever have been willing to have it displayed for the public's avaricious eye if it were worth anything from a historical standpoint.

Yes, some things were to be held close to one's heart. Sebastian Bernal felt the same way, she thought as she studied him studying her reaction. Despite his outrageously overt comments around her, the way the papers and gossip rags liked to make him into a flamboyant character, the swaggering ladies' man, she'd sensed there were some dark secrets Sebastian would never share with the world.

The original cross of the tiny one she now held in her hand was definitely one of those secrets.

He allowed a small smile play on his lips he answered her. "Yes. It's a replica of an item I managed to retrieve for the family holdings recently. It'd been missing for years."

Lacey nodded, looking back down at the beautiful cross in her hand as she hefted its weight. Sebastian had alluded a few times in recent months that his family had had some personal belongings that had somehow been lost or misplaced, possibly even stolen, she surmised, many years ago. That was one of the reasons she'd interested him when she'd applied for the job in the first place. Her connections to people in all corners of the small niche of history that interested them both was something that could help in finding those items.

"'There's a card in there with information about it," he said. The dark tickle of his presence played along Lacey's senses. "And there's a note from me in there as well."

The timbre of his voice shivered through her as she looked up at him again. Mouth feeling suddenly dry, she glanced back down. Carefully lifting out the bed of soft cotton material the cross had nestled upon, she found a card of heavy, expensive stock beneath it.

In silence, she read what the card said about the cross. Although a replica, it was one-of-a-kind, itself a copy of a piece that was also truly unique. The original cross had been ordered made by Queen Isabella of Spain for the Bernal family as thanks for a man Lacey knew was Sebastian's many times removed great-grandfather. The date on which the replica had been completed, which was only a few days earlier, was stamped on the bottom.

"And there's another piece of paper in there as well," Sebastian said quietly.

His heady scent, like that of a primeval forest, swirled through her, somehow mingling with her focused appreciation of the stunning little piece. Lacey tried not to fumble with the box, her heart seemed to be doing some sort of tap dance in her chest due to what she knew was the ever-present, undeniable energy crackling back and forth between her and Sebastian. She pulled out a small, creamy piece of paper and opened it to see it emblazoned with Sebastian's family crest and name at the top. Flicking her eyes up at him once, she looked back down to read it out loud.

Lacey,

This cross was a treasure to the Bernal family for centuries. It has recently come home again, which is something I know you will appreciate due to your fervent desire to keep history as it should be for everyone. I wanted you to have it as a memento in your own piece of history about this era that means so much to us both.

It is my hope that you will display this cross in your own personal treasure collection, wherever that may be, and think of me every time you see it.

Warmest regards,

Sebastian Antonio Bernal

It was true, what people said. The noise emanating into the courtyard from inside the exhibit hall fell away as Lacey looked back up to find Sebastian still watching her. His gaze was direct. Self-confident. Utterly absorbed in her. A bubble that seemed to thrum with excitement and a growing fire encircled them both, effectively cutting off the rest of the world. Lacey felt her own breath slip and shorten as Sebastian looked at her with an intent she hadn't yet seen.

An intent that caught her off-guard with its power, its enticement. With its smoldering promise of something she knew with more and more certainty that she wanted to experience, whatever that might be.

8

S ebastian had every intention of mingling with the guests at the exhibit. He felt quite a few glances aimed his way when he finally stepped into the room. His presence had been well noted by those in attendance. Yet he'd been so eager to see Lacey's response to the small gift he brought her that he'd planned to mingle for a short time before getting her all to himself again.

That wasn't going to happen. As his dragon roared somewhere in the back of his head, adrenaline and an icy fire raced up and down his body as he and Lacey seemed locked together in a little sliver of their own space.

As if no one and nothing else existed in the entire world.

She was an absolute knockout tonight in the pretty outfit she had chosen to wear. The muted teal and turquoise colors accentuated the blue of her eyes, highlighted the elation of the moment that was present on her face and every line of her body. He was well aware that was because of the occasion, not because he was standing there and just had handed her part of a piece of his own history. Even so, Sebastian felt his usual tightly controlled reason leaving him.

He needed this woman.

Right now.

It was driving him absolutely insane to not finally kiss those lips that been torturing him for the past year. She was an employee, she was someone he genuinely enjoyed relaxing with, she momentarily took him away from the daily sickening sense that his powers were ebbing just a little bit more. Something in her revitalized him.

He desperately wanted a drink of it right now. His dragon roared inside, urging him closer to Lacey's delicate sweetness.

"I'm glad you like it," he said. He took a step closer to her. The flush that rose over her collarbones, swept up her neck, was graceful. It sent his own pulse skyrocketing. "I wanted you to have something that was very specific to the Californio history, in honor of tonight's exhibit." Another step closer. "To my family." Another short stride, and he was close enough that her intoxicating scent rippled over him. "To me."

The soft shadows reaching across the courtyard slipped over her shoulder as she turned her face up toward him. Barely half a foot separated them. He could actually see her pulse vibrating in her throat. Her sweet scent enveloped him. Never in his life had he waited so long for a woman. He was about to explode if he couldn't touch her soon.

Without asking, he knew she wanted it to. Even so, he kept his movements slow and deliberate. Gently, he reached out with the back of a single finger to carefully tuck one slight strand that had fallen out of her usual severe bun to tip down in front of one ear. When his finger touched her skin, Sebastian knew he was about to finally taste her lips.

Lacey's sharp inhalation of breath was slightly wobbly. It was the first time he'd ever heard her voice lose the composure that usually held, and she hadn't even said anything yet. Emboldened by her blossoming of her scent, by the soft, sweet promise of her body, by the knowledge that he had finally gotten through her defenses with his small gift, he turned his hand around so his palm could cup the side of her face. He let his fingers gently curve around the back side of her neck, stroking the skin there.

Lacey's eyes half closed and she pulled in another shaky breath. Her lips slightly parted, and she leaned toward him just a bit. His attuned senses picked up her rapid pulse, which he could sense beating delicately in her throat.

It was too much. "Lacey," Sebastian said, his voice ripping out of him in a deep groan. "I know you want this. Unless," he forced himself to add, suddenly and oddly terrified at her potential answer, "I've totally misread the signals here?"

The beautiful flush on her face was extending lightly beneath the mid cut of the dress where her breasts swelled so temptingly. Shaking her head, she answered in low voice, "No. You haven't misread anything." Her eyes deepening to that rich sapphire color that had captured his interest the first day he met her, she added in more husky tones, "Lead the way. Sebastian."

His name on her lips, tentative yet clearly enchanted by the sound of it, shot white heat through his body. Lacey's palms smoothed against his chest, one of them already beginning to rove up to his neck. First cautiously, then with more confidence, she caressed his skin there with her fingers, bringing another approving rumble from him. Her other hand drifted lower until it found his nipple. Pausing for a long moment, clearly bolstering her confidence, she gently circled her fingers over the sensitive nub

With a soft little "Mmm," her delight in how it hardened tightened his balls. The sensation of her small fingers touching him through his dress shirt was so pleasurable it startled him into a small gasp. She paused at that, pulling her head back and slightly fluttering open her eyes to look at him. But he shook his head at her, murmuring, "No. Don't stop."

In answer, her mouth curved up in just a hint of a smile. She reached her hands out to his chest, placing her fingers on him. First tentatively, then with more certainty, she felt the planes of his chest beneath his jacket and shirt. Even through the clothing, he could feel the heat of her hands burning down to his skin. His entire body trembling with an excitement that went well beyond what even he had imagined, Sebastian gently pulled her face towards his even as he dipped his head down toward her.

Finally claiming her soft, luscious lips with his.

The taste and sensation of soft petals, her natural scent of lilies and creamy cloves and raindrops, seemed to infuse Sebastian's every molecule with a succulent blast. Her lips moved against his with a sensuality he hadn't quite expected but yet which did not surprise him. Swallowing another groan, he lightly held her face with both hands as he allowed himself to feast upon her mouth.

Lacey tasted exactly how he imagined. Only better.

Running one hand down to the small of her back, keeping the other curled behind her head, he pressed her close to him. The lush promise of her body that had been teasing him was even more sumptuous than he had dreamed during many restless nights of imagining her softness beneath him. Murmuring against her lips, he let the curve of his fingers drop down a little farther to touch the soft roundness of her delicious ass.

Lacey gasped against his mouth in surprise, but she didn't pull away. Instead, she pressed closer to him, pushing her hips against him in a way that caused his vision to darken with intense desire.

"Like this so far?" His dragon rumbled through his voice, lending a fiery edge to it.

She nodded against him. The tiny, breathless little moans he could feel dropping from her lips into his mouth excited him even more.

"Good. I don't think I could've waited another minute." Sebastian let his tongue explored Lacey's mouth, the intense heat and openness with which she welcomed him getting him harder than solid oak.

She murmured something unintelligible against his lips, but he thought it was *Me, either.*

The world faded away into a soft black explosion of velvet, punctuated with shooting stars, engulfed as he was in the soft, warm feel of Lacey's curves beneath his hands. Her lush body pressed against his with as much if not more fervent desire.

Mid-kiss, the craziest vision of him flying as his dragon while Lacey rode fearlessly on his back, laughing with sheer joy, shot through his mind. It startled him so much he broke their contact, pulling back and opening his eyes to look at her. Her eyelashes fluttered open, her plush mouth a darker red from where his lips had been tenderly yet firmly savaging hers.

That was a careless moment of confusion. Although he fully intended to have Lacey, she would never know about his dragon side. That was something he would never trust to tell her. To cover up his momentary confusion, he said the first thing that popped into his head, aching and raw in its indisputably sensuous desire.

"There will be more of this, I promise." His voice was raw. Slightly ragged from kissing her, his breath still coming fast. "You will want to feel my touch, Lacey. My fingers on your skin. Stroking, traveling along your body, dipping into every curve and rounding over every soft swell. And you won't want me to stop."

She swallowed hard, her eyes shadowing into a blue so dark they seemed almost purple. Just as she opened her mouth to reply, the sound of a small group of people tumbling out into the courtyard made her retreat away from him.

Silently Sebastian swore. He reached for her, but the fragile, exhilarating moment had been shattered.

"I—we can't," she said, taking a step back. Her fingers lifted up to her lips, feeling them as if they still burned. A deep breath. Another step back.

Damn it all.

Lacey shook her head. Her chest was heaving, and he

knew, he *knew* she felt the undeniable attraction between them, but her professional walls were well up again. "I have to get back inside," she finally said. She looked at him for a long moment before she wrenched her gaze away.

It took every ounce of self-control Sebastian had not to reach out and stop her as she left.

9

When the alarm buzzed on her phone, Lacey pushed her chair back from the desk, stretched her arms over her head, and luxuriated in a back-cracking stretch. She was working on an article about the exhibit. Since naturally the topic interested her intensely, she sometimes could find herself looking up a few hours later, stiff from sitting in the same position for so long. She'd learned back in grad school to set timers to make sure she got up every hour to move around a little bit and hopefully not drop dead of a heart attack from her sedentary lifestyle twenty years hence.

As she slowly brought her arms back down in front of her, fingers interlaced, leaning over in a forward bend, her eye caught the glitter of the little gold cross on her desk. Originally she thought she would take the cross home. Yet she was here the center so much more often. It also just made sense for the item to be in the building that housed so many objects from the same field.

Besides, not that she was observant, but a beautiful Catholic cross up on the wall at the apartment, in her bedroom, would make her feel pretty darn guilty whenever she had her very explicit imaginings about Sebastian. And she'd definitely had those, every single night, since the night of the exhibit opening.

Even though she hadn't spoken to him since then.

Well, she had made herself fairly clear, hadn't she? Like an idiot who apparently planned to be sex-deprived for the rest of her life.

That kiss had torched every rational thought in her head, setting off a chain reaction of thoughts that just wouldn't stop. Thoughts such as that she was just another conquest to him.

But surely, the small gift meant he was interested in her more than that, right? Not that that mattered, because he was Sebastian Bernal. Owner of the Bernal Center, world-renowned billionaire philanthropist, heartbreaking playboy of the Western world, and probably the Eastern world too now that she thought about it.

Besides, she didn't have time for something like that.

"Something like what?" Gabi had, naturally, been beside herself with excitement when Lacey had called her the day after the gallery opening to confess that she shamelessly had macked on Sebastian. "It's just going to be a fling, girl. That's what a guy like Sebastian Bernal is good for. You know I've been telling you forever that you need a good, old-fashioned fling. Sex, fun, nothing else." Laughter burbled under Gabi's words. "He's assured you a bunch of times it's not going to affect your job. Lacey, normally I would never say this about a guy who's in charge, but I believe him. He loves what you bring to the Center."

Well, so did Lacey. Which was why she had backed away from him the other night. Sebastian Bernal was far too danger-ous, with those chocolatey eyes and that provocative smile. She had to keep a grip on herself and her senses. It was a good thing Gabi was gone now, over on Catalina to begin the dive that she been looking forward to. It was still being put off another couple of days because the storm was still stirring up sediment on the ocean floor. Lacey's feisty bestie playfully would be pushing Lacey at Sebastian so hard, she knew she'd be hard pressed to keep resisting.

Unfortunately, tonight would be another test of her personal fortitude.

Sebastian had recently decided to have the museum host fancy events here. Tonight was one of several initial runs of wedding ceremonies before the Center would be opening to the public for weddings and other events beginning in the fall.

Lacey had been conscripted into attendance months ago when it was discovered the bride and groom enjoyed her area of expertise. She was actually kind of excited to be able to attend, but for one thing.

Sebastian would be there as well. The groom hailed from an important old Angeleno family that apparently socialized with Sebastian on occasion.

She would have to see him again. So soon after the other night. This time, she vowed, she would *not* fall for his charming lines. His come-hither expression. His utterly kissable, delectable, wildly talented mouth that could—

No. She needed to stop that line of thinking immediately. She had a paper to write and two meetings before the wedding began. Dealing with her overheated body once again wasn't going to help matters.

A few hours later, so engrossed was she in the words she was trying to write on the screen that when someone knocked at her door, Lacey about jumped out of her skin. She whacked her knee on the underside of her desk, causing her to growl an unimaginative curse, as her mother would call it.

One of the Center interns poked his head in.

"Yes?" she said, smiling as she massaged her knee.

"Sorry, Lacey. Your appointment's here early."

The dealer, here with the artifact he'd emailed her about. "Send him in," she said, getting out of her chair just as he walked into her office.

"Lacey! So good to see you again," he said, stepping

forward with a smile and his outstretched hand. "It's been, what? Since you were up in the Bay Area at that history conference over the winter, right?" Mark, whose antiquities shop was in Oakland, liked to keep up with all the latest goings-on in the state's historical world.

Lacey smiled at him. "Hi, Mark," she said, shaking his hand. Mark Edwards was a well-known dealer in the field with whom Lacey had always enjoyed working. "I can't believe it's been that long. What do you have for me?"

Mark smiled as he slung a large brown leather satchel from his shoulder and settled it on the little side table close to the door. In his fifties or thereabouts, he'd always kind of reminded Lacey of her dad, if her father had ever been remotely interested in history.

"First, I have something for you from the collector." Mark said. "A gift. Specifically for you, he instructed."

That startled Lacey. "For me? I don't even know him."

Mark shrugged as he rustled around inside his satchel for second before pulling out a small, black cloth bag. Glancing at Lacey's desk, he chuckled. Lacey followed his gaze and also laughed. Varying little cloth bags of different sizes and colors were scattered about the desk. Well, she worked and practically lived in the museum, and she was a curator. People sent her objects all the time.

None, of course, like the beautiful cross that Sebastian had given her.

"He's actually followed your career ever since you came to the center," Mark said. "You know how a lot of these collectors are. They don't want the general public to know about them."

Lacey nodded, resigned to the realities of her field.

"You mean he sometimes buys things of questionable provenance," she said in a flat tone.

Mark shrugged. "I don't ask where everything comes from when my clients tell me about them. Although you know perfectly well," his tone sharpened a slight bit, "that I only deal on the up and up."

Lacey nodded. Mark Edwards was highly respected in the field, based on a spotless career spanning thirty years. He was thoroughly vetted. No object that he ever dealt in, whether to sell or to buy, would be sourced off the black market. However, not all of his clients believed in the same thing. He didn't care about their personal ethics, as long as nothing that was illegal came into his possession.

"Anyway," Mark continued, "he told me he's appreciated you sharing details about the Californio era with me, which I then passed on to him, during this past year. It's helped him to make some good decisions for some purchases. At any rate, he said he came across this piece and immediately thought of you. Now, Lacey," and Mark looked at her carefully. "It is genuine. I've examined the papers myself. I'm certain the provenance is authentic and totally legal. However, I can't trace the chain all the way back. That's why he wants you to have it as a gift. There's no money exchanging hands in this transaction."

"I see." Lacey paused for a long moment. Mark was trying to tell her, without stating it in bald terms, that he couldn't be certain that the piece had not at some point in its life been traded under murkier circumstances.

Her curiosity was too much, however. Twisting her lips just slightly, she held out her hand. Gently, Mark handed over the little bag. Lacey upended it to gently shake out a small gold hairpin.

A miniature dazzle of gold and jewels glittered at her, almost seeming to pulse in her hand with its bright energy. "Oh, it's gorgeous!" Lacey lifted her hand closer to her face so she could carefully inspect the object. It was small, shaped like some sort of mythical creature that seemed to be half-chimera, half-dragon, encrusted with faceted emeralds and rubies. A tiny figure rode it, defiantly waving a spear overhead. Two little bumps on the chest indicated the figure was female.

"It's definitely of Spanish origin," she said, utterly enraptured by the artisan work of the piece. She admired it from all angles, carefully turning it over in her hands. Her scholarly training took over as she examined it. "Late sixteenth century." She looked up at Mark. "Did he tell you anything more about it?"

"He said he didn't know much about it himself." Mark shrugged again. "He just said something about it being a beautiful piece for a beautiful woman." Although the words were teasing, Mark's tone was a bit wary.

Lacey cast him a curious glance. "You don't sound as if I should take that as a compliment."

Looking slightly uncomfortable, Mark said, "Look. He's been a good client. Always pays me well to find him what he wants, doesn't give me trouble, and never passes objects of dubious origin my way. Well," he sighed, looking at the hairpin, "at least not of immediately dubious origin. He's just got a bit of a, mm, a sort of threatening air about him." Mark flapped his hand, curling up a lip in slight distaste. "He's just not the type for someone as nice as you, Lacey."

Mark beamed at Lacey, reminding her yet again of a doting father figure. Laughing, she said, "Well, then, I guess it's a good thing I don't know his name."

Rolling the beautiful little hairpin in her fingers, once again feeling an almost tangible sense of connection to it, she gently placed it back in its little bag and turned to Mark again.

"Now, let's take a look at the piece you want me to authenticate," she said with a smile. Mark nodded as he turned back to his satchel, already starting in about the item's history.

Hopefully, this would provide hours of focused work. Hopefully, it would distract her from the coming evening spent once again in Sebastian's presence. The dark, tingling, ridiculously arousing presence of a man who was driving her insane.

Right.

10

Doing his damnedest to focus on the conversation with the groom's father and new father-in-law, Sebastian nodded and chuckled at appropriate intervals. They were both important, generous friends of the Bernal Center, as well as men he had socialized with at various events for years now. As such, he owed them the courtesy of his attention.

But Lacey's glorious, delighted laughter kept catching his attuned ear instead, blowing his concentration. Between her laughter, her enticing scent, and the frisson of smoldering attraction between them, all his senses were wire tight.

Finally, after a last round of sincere congratulations and once more thanking them for their continued devotion to the museum, Sebastian gracefully excused himself with the excuse that he needed to circulate and be sure that everything was running smoothly. He barely registered their enthusiastic thanks for the private use of the venue as he turned to locate the burning, vexing focus of his unquenchable desire.

His dragon was going to be the death of him where this woman was concerned. The wild, ceaseless insistence that he get close to her, bury himself in her, taste all her succulent treasures and keep them to himself, was driving him half insane.

Just tonight, he silently swore his head. *One night to truly scratch this itch, get it out of my system, and move on.*

Nodding and smiling as he easily sidestepped small clusters of excited, happy wedding goers, Sebastian maneuvered his way across the marble floors of the great rotunda, heading with unerring accuracy to the sound of Lacey's low, sweet voice. Her exquisite scent pulled him along as it teased at him, urging him forward as if she tugged him toward her with a heated, sensuous leash.

There. His dragon rumbled with possessive pride. Lacey, his private obsession despite his own avowed wariness of all things female. The sexy yet classy dress she wore for the festivities hugged her curves in silky panels of pale pink rose and soft, burnished copper. A stylish silk bolero jacket just clung to her arms and shoulders, emphasizing the beautiful tapering down to her waist where the form-fitting dress accentuated the luscious hips he'd been longing to get ahold of.

Sebastian felt his cock stir as he headed her way, the fire of his dragon inside blazing with an inexorable arousal. Yet this also felt different than mere physical ardor needing to be assuaged by whatever willing, un-clingy woman he could find. The swell of Lacey's breasts that he could see as she half turned and gestured to the display hanging from the ceiling of the rotunda snared him with their soft, enticing invitation to stroke and hold and lick and nibble.

Yes. The unbearably gorgeous woman would be the death of him. Unless he could get her alone in the next two minutes.

Sebastian easily covered the last few steps to reach her side. The guests she spoke to noted his arrival, some smiling in flattering greeting while others looked simply awed that he approached them. Whether in dragon form or human, Sebastian Bernal always garnered tremendous respect.

Alerted by the glances in his direction, Lacey cut herself

off mid-sentence and swung around to look at him. The immediate light flush that heated her cheeks told him she, too, felt the attraction between them. "Mr. Bernal," she said, smiling that professional smile despite the pink in her face. "I was just explaining the history of how the museum acquired several of the pieces here in the rotunda."

Was it just him, or did she sound a shade close to breathless? Sebastian's dragon rumbled in satisfaction. He liked it.

"I trust you all are enjoying the evening. We're delighted to be able to host the wedding of the decade." Sebastian made sure his smile included everyone there, even though every piece of his being was attuned so closely to Lacey for a split-second he literally wondered if he was leaning toward her.

"Oh, it's such an amazing setting for the ceremony, Mr. Bernal," one of the women in the group said, brazenly practicing what she apparently thought was her most seductive smile on him. "It was incredibly generous of you to allow the Harringtons to hold it here."

The woman literally lowered her head so she could look up at Sebastian from beneath her eyelashes. It made her look drunk and idiotic. Sharply curbing the desire to tell her to find some other rich fool to hook her avaricious claws into, he awarded her his best gallant smile and thanked her for attending. The woman's cooing gush of appreciation nearly made him lose his patience. Masking his irritation, he turned to Lacey.

The unmistakable heated flare of Lacey's interest tickled at him. His dragon pushed at him to claim her and drag her off to his lair. Forcefully shoving down his baser instincts, Sebastian merely said, "Please, everyone, keep enjoying the center. The bar is open, and the docents are present for more private tours and to answer any questions anyone may have. I hope you enjoy the rest of the evening. Now, Ms. Whitman," he said, turning decisively to Lacey. "The bride and groom have a few specific questions about your area of expertise. I need to steal you away. The rest of you will have to excuse us." He smiled, executing a gentlemanly bow to the group. The woman who wanted more of his attention glared daggers at Lacey as Sebastian turned his back on them, putting his hand on the small of Lacey's back to guide her away.

And that sort of response was why this encounter with Lacey would be only for one night. Women were like that. He didn't need the drama. His dragon angrily muttered at him that Lacey was nothing like the others. Since his dragon side had been the one to get him into trouble before, Sebastian ignored it. Lacey was female. Enough said. This was a one-time thing. It was merely to thoroughly satisfy the promise of the tempestuous, steamy kiss they'd shared the other night before being interrupted.

He fully intended that this time, he and Lacey would enjoy one another's bodies with no disturbances. Besides which, if his desire was thwarted once again, he was likely to blast the museum with a frustrated, red-hot breath that would literally burn it down.

He doubted the board would in any way appreciate that.

As he whisked them both away, Lacey's rich voice teased his senses as she said in a skeptical tone, still a little breathier than usual, "I saw the bride and groom not ten minutes ago hiding behind the statue of Ixchel. They were making out like they were teenagers instead of a newly married couple." She shot a sidelong glance at him as he maneuvered them toward the hallway to the administrative offices. "I highly doubt they want a private tour right now. A private room seems more like it."

The gorgeous laughter that flipped him inside out rippled beneath her words. Her hip bumped against his as she gently sidestepped another small group of people. From the swiftness with which she moved away from him after that happened, not to mention the tantalizing spike in her sweet arousal that he could smell, told him she was putting on an act for everyone as well.

"No, they don't," he admitted without shame as he steered her away from the rotunda to the corridor that led to his office, nodding at the security guard who blocked anyone from attempting to explore into that part of the center as they swept past. "But I certainly need a private room with you."

She half halted, causing his hand on her back to slide closer to her waist as the momentum carried him past her for a step or two. He looked down at her as she came to a complete stop, allowing the full scope of his interest to show on his face as he gently stroked his fingers just above the front of her hip bone. Lacey inhaled sharply at that, her gorgeous indigo eyes widening as she looked at him. Her masses of blonde hair, caught up in some fancy hairdo, just begged to be let down to flow around her shoulders.

Sebastian tried to bite back a groan at the thought, but she must have caught it. She swallowed hard, her pulse leaping beneath the soft skin of her neck in a way that made him want to lick her there.

To claim her.

Damn his insistent, primitive-minded dragon. *Only sex,* he reminded himself roughly. This was only about having sex with this amazing, gorgeous woman that he couldn't get his mind off of. No claiming would be involved.

The faster they could get to said sex, the easier it would be to control his increasingly unruly dragon side.

Forcing himself to still touch her with only his hand on her waist, he said in a tone so low it was close to the sound of his dragon growling, "I suggest you keep walking with me. Because if you don't keep moving, my sweet beauty, I'm going to push you up against the wall in this hallway and kiss you until you can't think straight. And since we're still in view of the rotunda, I don't think that's a very good idea. Do you?"

SEBASTIAN'S POINT blank suggestion sent shock waves through Lacey. Mouth suddenly dry, she attempted to swallow, then licked her lips. His intense gaze shot straight to her lips. Then he looked back into her eyes, and she nearly swallowed her tongue. His expression hadn't changed, but the heated waves of energy rolling off of him and washing over her had. The hallway seemed charged with crackling fire that raced through her, leaving her nerve endings alight. His provocative, presumptuous, extremely arousing words from the other night echoed in her head.

You will want to feel my touch, Lacey. My fingers on your skin. Stroking, traveling along your body, dipping into every curve and rounding over every soft swell. And you won't want me to stop.

She looked back up at him now, almost instantly wishing she hadn't. Something was changing in his eyes. The green flecks seemed more pronounced. Brighter, somehow. The sheer desire that sizzled between them—it was palpable. Like a living thing. As if he was calling to her, driving her toward him with some sort of indomitable force. A force she really, really wanted to give into, despite her rational side contending that this was only the road to emotional danger and professional madness.

"I've been watching you all evening. Wanting you." The liquefying deep bass of his voice quickened her breathing despite her attempts to control her ridiculously aroused body. "And I always get what I want."

That self-assured note managed to shake Lacey back to a semblance of her usual strong self. "Oh, really, Mr. Bernal? Always?"

She really didn't mean for that to be a leading question. But the sudden blast of hunger in his eyes, and what she could swear was a deepening intensity of his addictive scent bathing her in his outrageously primitive pheromones, clearly told her she'd just thrown down the gauntlet.

"Yes, Ms. Whitman." He prowled closer, trapping her with his stunning eyes. "I do in fact always get what I want."

"Is that a fact." Her voice sounded like she was panting a bit, darn it. Not exactly like the cultured, professional employee she strove to be. "And what exactly is it you want right now?"

Another step, and his face was inches away from hers. Her rational side instinctively battling for control over the body that desperately wanted to find out exactly what it was he wanted to have, she could hardly breathe as his proximity struck a match to the hot flicker of sheer lust she'd been attempting to douse all evening.

"I thought I made that clear the other night, Lacey. I want you." The sheer male possessiveness in his tone sent a knee-knocking shiver racing through her. "I want to taste you. To touch you. To hear what your voice will sound like when you can't say anything other than my name."

With each descriptive word he said, Lacey's brain cells promptly fell over and played dead. Acutely aware of the pulse banging in her throat, which she knew he noticed because his eyes strayed to it with an expression she couldn't quite decipher, and her rapid breathing that she just couldn't seem to control, she tried one last weak plea for rationality. "We—we already discussed this. You're my employer. You hold a position of power over me. This isn't something either one of us can do."

She sounded thoroughly unconvincing even to herself.

"Oh, yes, it is." His hot breath brushed over her cheek as he added in a whisper, "No consequences for either of us. I promise that. And no regrets. Just stolen pleasure as I bend you over that desk of mine, as I've been fantasizing about doing all evening."

Oh. My.

Well, in that case, all her protests about propriety were really unnecessary.

"That...sounds just lovely," she said like an absolute idiot, her libido roaring through her like an out-of-control freight train.

"Excellent," he replied, his lips just grazing her ear before turning and hustling them toward his office.

Lacey struggled not to topple over as Sebastian propelled her down the wide hallway. Her every sense surged within her, electrifying her body to the point that it felt almost painful. As he strode alongside her in his ridiculously gorgeous tailored suit, the formal vest and tie matching the soft umber tones of her own fancy dress, she could absolutely understand why nearly every woman at the ceremony had been sliding glances at the man like they wanted him to lick them like they were ice cream.

She was pretty sure he'd just promised he was about to do that to her right now.

They reached his sumptuous office in record time, Sebastian barely pausing to press his hand against the small, tasteful security panel beside the door. The panel lit up as his handprint registered, the door slid open, and the dark, fierce, wildly alluring man gently yet firmly escorted her in. The door whooshed shut behind them, encasing them in a sudden bubble of utter stillness as the faint sounds of the reception snapped off into silence.

"It's so quiet in here." Lacey suddenly felt nervous again, like she was about to be gauche or awkward. "Is it always this quiet?"

Sebastian finally released her waist from the hot embrace of his hand. It felt like a wrenching coldness when he stepped away. Lacey couldn't help the little sound of protest. Instantly stopping, Sebastian gave her a long, scrutinizing look. His eyes seemed brighter than ever, much more green than usual. They captivated her with their light.

"Soundproof," he murmured. His hands went to his tie, loosening it enough that he could undo it completely, slipping it from his neck in a mesmerizing action. "And fireproof," now he shrugged out of his jacket as her mouth slowly began to drop, "waterproof," button by button, he undid the gorgeous vest and let it fall to the floor in a crumple of expensive tailoring, "and bomb-proof."

His long, strong fingers went to the buttons of his white, button-down formal shirt, undoing each one with a slow deliberateness that jacked up Lacey's heart rate to what she thought might be similar to that of a rabbit's. Staring at the gorgeous man stripping in front of her, Lacey blinked and swayed as the blinding heat rushed through her again. Her limbs felt heavy with desire yet electrified at the same time.

"I have extremely valuable items in here that do not have the luxury of round-the-clock guards as do the main premises," he murmured. "This room is the most secure non-public space on the entire grounds. Lacey," he added in low, aching tone. His voice positively feasted on her first name, rolling it around in his mouth as if he could taste it. Then he reached the last button the shirt. With a rough tug, he pulled it off and tossed it to the floor.

Oh. My. God.

Sebastian Bernal was a thing of utter male perfection. Sculpted abs, pecs with taut nipples that just screamed for her hands to reach out and touch, a six-pack to die for, and muscled arms that turned her on to a degree she hadn't realized was possible.

Feeling wobbly and beautifully lightheaded, Lacey took a step back, then another. Right into the wall beside the door. Sebastian came closer, that gorgeous, hard body wreaking complete havoc with her generally well-ordered mind. She knew her mouth was hanging wide open. That she was breathing so fast she feared she might pop the zipper on the back of the dress.

"I—wow," she managed to get out. It was lucky that by this point she was so hazed by lust that she couldn't be embarrassed by her shallow, definitely gauche appreciation. "Mr. Bernal, I didn't—"

Her voice caught in her throat when he reached out his arm to place a hand on the wall next to her head and leaned in close to her. She felt that damn swooning thing about to happen again, only this time, her resistance to it was failing. His half-naked proximity to her pretty much short-circuited everything in her brain while also bringing everything in her body roaring to a fiery, wild awareness of itself that she had never before felt.

His voice, low and soft but still commanding, washed over her. "I know the way I can make you feel is undeniable. You proved that to me the other night." With his other hand, he reached out and very gently touched his finger to her cheek, slowly drawing it down to her jawline just beneath her lower lip. Lacey trembled from head to toe, the furnace of heat centered between her legs spreading to every other part of her body as his finger began to trace the outline of her lip. A tremor of need shivered its way through her as she barely restrained a moan.

"And I know that I want you so badly I can hardly think." His voice roughened with his desire. "I can't get you out of my head. These lips," slowly, the thumb tracing her lip edged into the corner of her mouth, where it carefully, gently ran along the inside of her lower lip, "your skin," his other fingers reached around to cup the other side of her face, "the way you smell like lilies, and sweet oranges, and rainfall in the spring."

Lacey's skin raced in uncontrollable pleasure where he touched her. She knew all reason was about to leave her. The wild glint in his eye made a promise to her that she desperately wanted to agree to. He slowly ran his hand down to her neck, causing a stampede of tingles throughout her entire body, then back up again to her cheek.

She was still supposed to be noting their professional relationship, though, she thought vaguely. Something like that, yes?

"Mr. Bernal," she began in a whisper.

He shook his head. "Sebastian." Hearing him say his own name in that low, dark voice filled with need had Lacey swaying on her feet again. "When we are alone, my name is Sebastian. Isn't that right?"

Oh, holy.... She was done for.

"Sebastian," she tried out, her voice seeming loud in the still room. "Sebastian," she said again, more slowly. Oh, yes. She really liked saying his name.

But there was something else she should be thinking of. Ah. Right. "The security cameras."

One corner of his mouth very slowly edged up into a dangerous, thoroughly panty-wetting grin. Lacey swallowed as her pulse slammed to some primal tempo she could almost hear in her head.

"This will not be recorded, Lacey." His voice was practically a growl. "I already had both the cameras in the hallway and this office turned off."

Lusty haze somewhat clearing, she lowered her eyebrows. "Really? You were that sure of my response?" Despite her challenge, her voice was uneven from her ragged breathing.

His thumb dragged along her bottom lip again, very gently pulling it out. Lacey's breath whooshed out of her completely. She suddenly didn't give a damn if they were cameras zoomed in on them from every angle.

"I was sure of the fact that you want me as badly as I want you." The molten words kissed the air by her ears, sending scorching little darts straight down between her wobbly legs. "I was sure of the fact that neither of us would want there to ever be any sort of public evidence of what happens here. This is between you and me, Lacey. This" and he said the word so fiercely the little hairs on the back of her neck stood up, "is ours. We belong to no one else." He seemed almost surprised by his own vehemence, but the desire wafting from him didn't lessen one iota.

We. That word snagged on Lacey's remaining rational consciousness, but she pushed it away. Sizzles were zipping throughout her body. Sebastian still gently held her lip in his fingers, although not a single other part of him touched her. Gently releasing her lip, he put his entire hand beneath her chin to gently tip it up. He was easily half a foot taller than her, and so broad in the shoulders she literally couldn't see behind him.

It made her feel—protected.

Possessed.

"Lacey." His hazel-green eyes seemed even brighter now, as if he were lit from within by the same fire she felt crackling inside her. Desperate to get out and explode into white hot flames. "Say my name again. I need to hear you say my name again."

His other hand moved off the wall and slipped behind her head, his fingers very gently threading through her hair. Heart thumping erratically, body primed to an attention that she instinctively knew he would know exactly how to soothe, Lacey nodded. She sighed out, "Sebastian. This may be the craziest thing I've ever done, but yes. I want this," she whispered, reaching up to curve her hands up behind his neck.

A groan ripped out of him. The sound was so filled with sheer relief that Lacey's knees actually did buckle. He caught her up and gently crushed her to his chest, murmuring back, "As you wish, my sexy as hell beauty," before finally, thank god, taking her lips with his own in a ravaging kiss that knocked her sideways and inside out with the intensity of it.

She was definitely a goner.

S ebastian's thoughts turned into fiery, nonsensical bolts of stunned blankness as his lips touched Lacey's. Her sweet, decadent taste exploded in his mouth. He didn't have to ask how aroused she was. The pliable sensation of her body as she pressed her exquisite breasts into his chest, the heat he could feel pulsing off her, told him she was already wet for him.

Waiting for him to touch her everywhere.

He pulled back just enough to murmur, "Not wasting another second." With that, he easily hoisted her up into his arms despite her small gasp of surprise, heading straight to his enormous dark cherry oak desk. Setting her gently onto the edge of it, he stepped back from. Her eyes were wide, that gorgeous flush still coloring her features, as she watched him quickly shuck off every single last bit of clothing.

Stepping away from his pants, he let her take a long look. He was completely hard, his cock boldly jutting away from his body. Lacey's mouth, plump and luscious from the rough kiss he laid upon it, was open.

"Holy...wow," was all she seemed able to manage. The

dark marine of her eyes fixated on his cock, which both amused and pleased him tremendously.

"This is what you've created in me tonight. This is how you've been making me feel, Lacey." His voice was low. Utterly honest. He felt his dragon beating at his mind with his wings, demanding to swoop in and claim her. Jaw tightening as he fought himself, Sebastian forced himself to stand still for Lacey's gratifyingly fascinated inspection.

Slowly, so slowly, she looked back up, letting her gaze travel in leisurely, utterly appreciative manner along his body all the way back up to his eyes.

Sebastian felt something lurch oddly inside him at the sudden gravity in her stare. The utter seriousness he saw there was balanced with a reverence for not only him, but this moment. Eyes locked together, a very long beat passed, then another, with the two of them not saying a word as something deep, wild, and genuine leaped between them.

Inside, Sebastian's dragon struggled for release.

Barely restraining himself, Sebastian managed to step to her side without simply ripping off her clothes and feasting on her lusciousness. Her captivating scent, inches away, threatened to overwhelm him. Quietly, he ordered, "Take your clothes off, Lacey. I want to see that gorgeous body of yours as naked as mine."

She inhaled hard at that. By the rapid pulse he could sense throbbing in her neck, he knew sheer arousal roared through her as much as it did him. With only slightly shaking hands, she obeyed. Within moments, her very pretty dress lay in a neat pile on the desk, topped by her outrageously sexy pale pink bra and panties. Almost shyly, she looked back up at him. The luminous depths of her eyes caught at him again, tugging him down into something deep that might drown him if he wasn't careful.

Voice rough, he said, "You're stunning, Lacey. Now. Turn around and hold onto the desk."

That clearly took her off guard. Her eyes widened. "I—what?" Even so, he heard the ragged cadence beneath her words. A deep craving still brimmed there, blazing with heat.

Then her tongue slipped out, just touching one corner of her mouth as she stared at him in flustered yet still obvious arousal. Sebastian's control slipped over the edge. "I had a vision of bending you over my desk, beautiful." His voice slipped into the same raggedness as hers. "If you don't want to do that, we won't. But something," and he leaned forward just enough to slide his tongue up her neck, eliciting a gasping little cry, "tells me you sure as hell want to do exactly that."

Half panting now, Lacey looked at him for a long moment. Then, very slowly but with absolute certainty in her movements, she turned around so that her beautiful ass pushed against him as she leaned herself forward over his desk, bending from her waist. Turning her head to one side, she rested her cheek on the gleaming dark blood-red surface, looking at him with a sensual, increasingly excited gaze that invited him in. Tendrils of blonde hair curled onto her neck from the upsweep hairdo still pinned to her head.

Very carefully, Sebastian reached down to the thick, shiny mass and loosened the pins until all her hair fell free, flowing down. He brushed it all to one side, then slowly slid one hand from the base of her neck all the way down her bare back, lightly running his fingers over the bumps of her spine. Accompanied by the uneven breaths and eager little sounds coming low from her throat, he let his fingers reach the soft roundness of Lacey's ass, open before him without shame or fear.

Vulnerable. Willing.

His.

Even more carefully, still slowly, he dipped a finger down the soft crack, curving around her lusciously plump ass until he found the wet, welcoming heat of the sweet pussy he so desperately craved. She was already soaked, just as ready for him as he was for her. He was so damned hard he thought he might injure something if he didn't get inside her soon.

"Oh, god, yes." The breath hissed out of Lacey as Sebastian's finger delved deep inside her, curling in and out in a beckoning motion. A crass word slipped out of her in a long, keening moan as he inserted a second finger, feeling inside her lush softness as if he'd never before touched a woman there. "Please," she panted, thrusting back against him. "Please yes, just like that. Sebastian, please," and she proceeded to tell him in a low, sexy growl just how she wanted it.

Somehow, he'd known it would be like this with her. Hot, dirty, and unflinchingly honest.

Leaning down so that his breath would tickle against her ear, he murmured, "I like hearing your pretty little mouth talk like that, Lacey. Now," and he reached down with his other hand to gently urge her to spread her legs open, which she did so quickly it made a satisfied smile flash across his face, "let's see what I can do here."

Grasping her full, graceful hips with both hands, he paused for another moment just to look at her face. Still nestled against the smooth surface of the desk, it was flushed. Her teeth clamped down on her lower lip, about making his head spin with how damned erotic that looked. Those dark blue eyes of hers, now a blueberry-black shade from her arousal, tracked his as he reached down to position himself right at her beautifully plumped out pink folds. Feeling his dragon roaring through him, Sebastian watched her face as he slowly slid his aching hard cock deep inside her.

"Ah," she gasped, pushing back hard against him so that the base of his shaft snugged right up against her. Her fingers clenched hard on the deep edges of the heavy desk, her back bowing into an unintentionally seductive little curve as she pressed her hips back against his.

It was just about the sexiest thing Sebastian had ever seen in his life. His hands clutched her hips so tightly where they fused together he thought he might be hurting her, but her eyes were still latched on his, wide and vulnerable yet also heavy with longing. "Lacey," he groaned, fighting the deep unfurling inside he knew was his dragon.

Desperate to get out. To surge forth and claim this woman.

She moved her hips just slightly, his name tumbling off her lips again in a fierce, impatient whimper, and he was lost. Something hot and rich and dark moved through him, gaining force and power as it unleashed savage emotions that shattered his control over himself.

Possession. Yearning. Tenderness. Primitive desire. The unstoppable need to thrust into her again and again.

To drive himself so deeply into her that he would mark her as his, and his alone.

His thinking brain pretty much shut down. Operating from a place of untamed urgency that blasted through him like a dragon in wild, elated flight, Sebastian plunged his thick, aching cock into her slick heat. Lacey met him each time, even when he slammed into her so hard he thought he might slide them both across the massive desk. Her eyes still on his, face flushed to a rosy glow, she fought to keep her eyelids from fluttering shut as she panted from her beautifully open mouth.

"Sebastian." Her voice, throaty and uninhibited, whispered over him like a thousand tiny shimmering wings, leaving goose bumps in their wake as he tightly held onto her. "Sebastian!" she screamed, still looking at him even though he could tell she was about to fracture apart and tumble over the edge.

White-hot lightning crackled and seared through him as everything important in the world suddenly coalesced into this one single moment with this one single woman. "Yes," he growled back, hearing his dragon's deep bass shudder through his own voice. "With you. Lacey, yes, Lacey!" he shouted, watching her face tense and stretch into sheer ecstasy as her sweet inner muscles abruptly convulsed around him.

His voice was a hoarse, guttural yell as he exploded inside

her, Lacey shuddering around him at the same time as she gasped and keened. He never once dropped the scorching gaze they held with one another despite feeling like his eyes might roll back in his head from the gorgeous, powerful force of his release with her.

Still caught in the orgasm, feeling Lacey shake against him as she half-cried his name in whimpering sobs of bliss, Sebastian dropped his weight onto her, bringing his lips to her neck. Unable to stop himself, he felt the ancient power rise in him with a rush of exultant triumph.

His thrilled, defiantly roaring dragon side made him bend his head down.

Opening his mouth to send superheated breath onto her delicate neck.

Etching a shadow of his name into her skin, her bones, her soul, with the fire of his heart.

Claiming this woman, and only this woman, as being irrevocably his.

Damn the consequences.

1 2

Even though small, the plane was the most luxurious one Lacey had ever been on in her entire life. Seated on a chair that was plusher than any couch she'd ever owned and could probably fit three people, she felt a bit like a princess in a fairytale. A confused princess, but a princess nevertheless.

"Mr. Bernal will be here any minute, Ms. Whitman. Would you like something to drink? We have coffee, tea, a variety of sodas, spirits, wine, beer. Water, milk, juice. Really, just about anything you'd like." The flight attendant smiled at Lacey and she hovered beside her, discreet yet clearly ready to jump at Lacey's every command. The wide aisle, which really wasn't an aisle so much as it was a living room space, the private plane, the very attentive attendant, all meant that Lacey was trying to not get too freaked out at it all.

Oh, and then there was the mind-blowing sex last night. She definitely was trying to not freak out at that, either.

"No, thank you," she said to the attendant. "I'm fine. But thank you."

The attendant smiled at her, murmured something about calling her any moment she wanted anything, and walked away. Lacey knew she sounded like an idiot. She was positive the flight attendant was perfectly well aware that Lacey had never in her life been surrounded by the trappings of the rich, richer, and very richest in the world.

Apparently, things changed once you had a wild night of passion with a sexy billionaire. Just the thought of it brought a rush of heat to her cheeks again. She placed her palms against her face, trying to cool it.

She had had wild, crazy, deeply satisfying, thoroughly dirty sex with Sebastian Bernal all last night. In his office, for crying out loud. Bent over his desk, for even more crying out loud.

And she'd loved every single, deliciously erotic moment of it.

Afterward, he'd gathered her in his arms, leaning himself back on the desk so he could hold her close to him. He been silent for such a long time that she'd been convinced he had come to his senses, realized pursuing her had been a terrible mistake, and was trying to decide how to fire her.

Instead, he stroked her hair with his hand, fingers gently tangling in it, and whispered, "This has changed everything, Lacey. You have no idea. I'm not even sure exactly how to tell you."

The usual certainty, even cockiness, had been in his tone. But the faintest bit of doubt, or perhaps surprise, dusted the edges of his words. She hadn't really known how to respond except to nod her head against his chest. Lacey herself struggled to come to terms with not only the way he'd made her body soar in a way that never had happened before, but that she knew, deep down, that there'd been an unshakable, undeniable connection between them at the height of the ecstasy.

There had been a *moment*. She didn't know what it meant. She just knew it had happened.

She gazed out the plane's small window at the buildings beyond the small private runway where the plane idled as it waited for its owner. Last night, she had felt caught in a dream state. Sebastian had hovered over her the rest of the evening when they returned to the wedding reception, even when he wasn't literally beside her. She could somehow sense him, even from across the room, like a sheltering presence around her. Watching over her. She'd felt completely protected.

Cherished.

Although he wanted to drive her back to her apartment after the extravagant reception was over, she laughed it off. She'd brought her own car to work that day, after all. He'd admonished her to let him know the second she walked in the door so he knew she was safe.

She hadn't needed to, because he'd called her not fifteen minutes after she walked in the door.

And then there been the—yes.

There been the phone sex, late last night.

She turned her palms around so the cooler backs of her hands rested against her cheeks, which flamed anew with the memory. She'd never had phone sex in her life. It seemed like she never done a lot of things. Just hearing his voice on the phone had almost been enough to incite another orgasm. She'd been incredibly grateful that Gabi wasn't home.

Then this morning, shortly after 8a.m., Sebastian had called again. The low, sexy growl of his good morning in her ear had tightened her nipples and brought a blazing smile to her face. Then he asked what her plans were for the day. When she'd sleepily answered that she meant to come in to the Center for a few hours to finish up some details on the exhibit notes, he chuckled.

"Lacey, I more than understand ambition and drive. But you have proved yourself a thousand times over. It's also Sunday. You're allowed to take the day off. In fact, I mandate it."

She'd laughed at that, even as she had to admit it would be pretty nice to not tack on another five hours toward what had already been an 80-hour workweek. Sebastian had continued, "I want to take you somewhere today, Lacey. To show you something. You will allow me the pleasure of being in my company the entire day?"

Well, no, she wasn't about to deny him that. Not after the most insane night of her life.

So here she was. On Sebastian's private small plane, not to be confused with the company's private jet, which was parked at another hangar at the small, corporate airport. She was waiting for him to get on the plane so they could make the short flight to his family's hacienda, which was down south almost to San Diego.

Lacey had to admit that even without the prospect of spending the day in the company of the sexiest man on the planet, the man she would swear whose heart she'd glimpsed last night, she would've been thrilled to go to the ancestral home of the Bernal family. That was one place that was strictly off-limits to media scrutiny. Of course, that never had stopped photographers from taking airborne pictures of it over the years, especially recently with the invention of drones. Although she heard that those tended to mysteriously disappear every time they got over the estate. Sebastian always said that if people wanted to know about his family and his cultural legacy, they could go to Bernal Center. That was what it was for. His ancestral home was not open to the public scrutiny. End of story.

From both a professional and personal standpoint, Lacey was elated at the thought of getting to see the stunning place in person.

A small commotion at the front of the plane drew her eyes. Sebastian appeared in the doorway, nodding at the captain and flight attendant who stood at the front of the plane, before striding down the open expanse toward Lacey.

Holy...

She swallowed. She'd last seen the man less than twelve

hours before, had come on command just from his voice alone through the phone no fewer than three times last night, and talked to him again this morning. Even so, she wasn't prepared for the huge rush of both emotions and physical sensations that torpedoed through her as she saw his stunning self in the flesh again.

"Good morning, Lacey. Thank you for joining me."

The rich darkness of his voice floated around Lacey, seeming to fill the very air with the sheer magnitude of his presence. He stepped up to her and bent down to brush her lips with his. Just the thrill of that little touch blasted through her, reigniting the nerve endings that had been thoroughly played with and satiated the night before.

Clearly, she was ready to go again.

All her usual calm control shot to hell, she blushed for about the millionth time since last night. Sebastian noted it, chuckling as he dropped into the seat across from her with the elegant ease of a lifetime born of wealth, power, and the obvious certainty that he knew his place and his worth in the world. Lacey stared at him for a long moment, almost unaware of the rumble of the plane as it started to taxi for take off, ignoring the pilot's voice over the intercom.

"So," Sebastian said, settling back into his seat as the plane took off, "There is a room full of personal family antiquities at the hacienda that I particularly wish to show you."

Lacey made herself smile at him. "I really can't wait," she said, meaning it.

This was Sebastian Bernal seated across from her. Sebastian, who had touched her more intimately than any man had since her first year in grad school, who was known to millions worldwide, who was more than her boss a few times removed. Looking at him in the morning light coming into the windows on either side of the plane, the reality of the situation hit her yet again. One of the world's richest men was about to whisk her off to his family's estate, a place it was well known no one was allowed to see. No women, in particular.

She swallowed hard again. She was doing what here, exactly?

Because clearly the man was a mind reader, Sebastian smiled at her, reaching out his hand to stroke her just above one knee. The tingles that shot up from that place to land straight on the most aroused bundle of nerve endings in her entire body tucked between her legs made Lacey jump a little. A lazy half grin tugged up Sebastian's mouth as he watched her.

"You look stunning this morning." His expression left no doubt that his words were sincere. "I very much look forward to you seeing the hacienda. All my favorite treasures are there."

That last sentence seemed to amuse him more than it should have, confusing her yet again. He was such a gorgeous enigma. The world knew him, yet it didn't. She felt like she knew him, she'd gotten fairly close to him in the past year, and last night had been a stunning explosion of the simmering tension between them.

But at the same time there was so much about him she didn't know. He smiled easily for the cameras, awing just about everyone he came into contact with from the magnificence of his presence alone. Yet she'd always known all that glitz and glamour hid a darkness. Or some sort of loss. The fact that he was letting her in, even just a little bit, was overwhelming.

It was also, she sternly reminded herself even as his fingers began to stroke little circles on the skin of her thighs, sending more thrilling chills shooting up her legs, par for the course. She couldn't let herself believe it was anything otherwise. Sebastian liked women. He enjoyed the chase, and while he knew that she enjoyed the history of his family and legacy as much as he did, she couldn't let herself believe it was anything more than that. Lacey was determined that she was going to enjoy this for what it was, and not read too much into it, intense moment last night notwithstanding.

Right? Yes. Dammit, yes. Smiling back at him, she relaxed as much as she could for the flight carrying her to Sebastian's home.

13

Nothing in Lacey's wildest dreams could've prepared her for the reality of Sebastian's hacienda. First, there was the private airstrip. Second, there was the luxuriously decked out SUV waiting for them when they landed, the driver of which was standing beside the vehicle as the plane touched down and they exited. He went straight to Sebastian, nodding and smiling and saying a greeting in Spanish. Turning to Lacey, the man started to greet her in English. Smiling, she responded in Spanish, much to his surprised delight. He introduced himself as Ricardo, an enormous grin splitting his face. Glancing at Sebastian, he raised his eyebrows in some sort of signal that Lacey didn't bother to try deciphering. She was too busy staring open-mouthed at the gorgeous setting around them.

Sebastian had told her some details about the hacienda on the short flight down. Set in the middle of over one thousand acres, which he said was but a small fraction of what the family had owned when they first settled the area in the 1700s, it was filled with rolling hills, views of the ocean to the west, and a sense of secure privacy that one almost could never find in crowded Southern California. The quick ride up to the hacienda barely gave her time to prepare for it, either.

As she stepped out of the car, eyes fastened on the sprawling, gorgeous building in front of her, Lacey knew she must look like a little kid meeting Santa Claus for the first time. It was a hacienda in the same way that wealthy people would refer to their mansion as a cottage, she thought in a daze as Sebastian took her arm and gently escorted her up the walkway.

"Do you like it?" He paused as Ricardo opened the huge, beautiful wooden doors that led to a courtyard encircling the outside of the actual home.

Literally unable to speak, Lacey nodded. Okay. Her head was officially spinning. Her life had undergone a complete three-sixty in about half a day. If she said anything else right now, she would sound like a total idiot.

Much better to just nod, follow the man, and see what would happen next.

His hands gently pressing on the small of her back, sending warmth there as if they were heated brands, Sebastian gently guided her along the walkway of beautiful flagstones that led up to the actual doors to the house. The door had already opened, and a smiling woman about the same age as Ricardo waited to greet them. Her smile was so infectious, and so genuinely filled with love as she looked at Sebastian, Lacey immediately sensed that these employees were perhaps the closest thing to family that Sebastian actually had.

And that second, her heart melted a little bit more.

No. No, no no. She couldn't let that happen.

Right?

Hanging plant holders drooped colorful, fully blooming spring flowers at varied intervals around the spacious courtyard, which in this most authentic of haciendas should really be called a *placita*. A large center fountain, featuring a stone dragon that spat water in a graceful arc out of his mouth as his wings unfurled to either side with more water streams coming out of the tips, was inviting and cool in the warm morning air. The entire setting was graceful, open, breezy, quietly screaming wealth and elegance from every corner. The windows up on the second floor of the hacienda, bracketed by flung open shutters on either side, were recessed deep into the adobe walls.

"Sebastian," she breathed as she looked around, "it's the most beautiful place I've ever seen."

Lacey knew the main hacienda, and in fact the entire rancho, was constructed of the original building that first had been erected in the late 18th century. Obviously there would be modern updates. All the best that billions of dollars could buy. Although she was reasonably familiar with the trappings of wealth after having worked at the Center for a year now, and having been in Sebastian's presence so often for nearly as long, the sight here was wildly thrilling in a way she hadn't expected.

This place was genuine. It wasn't just something that she had created an exhibit for at the museum, or seen in the pages of a history book, or in glossy photos splashed across the magazines that she sometimes furtively glanced at when in line at the grocery store, every time she saw one boasting Sebastian on its cover. No, this was real because it was Sebastian's actual home. She knew he didn't get to spend as much time in it as he'd prefer. Yet she also knew from everything she'd ever read, from every casual mention he'd made in her presence, that it was what he considered his most personal, protected sanctuary against the sometimes prying world.

It was only when Sebastian's appreciative laughter whispered through the heavy, fragrant air that she realized she had stopped in the middle of the *placita*, simply astounded by its graceful beauty.

"I'm glad you like it," he said. His eyes were still hidden behind sunglasses, but she knew he was looking right at her because she could feel the delicious prickles tiptoeing up and down her body. "It fits you."

Before she could even open her mouth to ask what that meant, he gestured toward the door and the small, older woman standing there, whose face still crinkled up with smiles as she waved them both inside. "If I know Maria, she spent all morning baking some exquisite delicacies for us." Sebastian stretched out his hand toward Lacey. "Come inside. You'll need a midmorning snack to fortify yourself for the things in there that I want to show you."

Feeling still dazed, Lacey made her feet move again. She entered the hacienda, smiling as the woman, Maria, greeted her in enthusiastic, accented English. Once again, Lacey spoke Spanish in return, inviting yet another startled expression as well as that odd glance towards Sebastian.

To Lacey's even greater surprise, the woman then suddenly stepped forward to throw her arms around Lacey, welcoming her even more effusively. It felt natural to hug her back, catching Sebastian's momentarily unguarded expression as she glanced at him. His own surprise, mingled with satisfaction and a clear sense of ease at being in his ancestral home, played along the edges of something deeper.

Something that again felt like she was a deeply cherished possession. Although it should have made her feel strange, like she was an object, it didn't at all. Instead, the sensation of being utterly protected, totally safe, wrapped itself around her.

"Yes, I have many delicacies prepared for your arrival," Maria said in Spanish, urging Lacey inside the beautiful building. She immediately led them both to a side room, upon which a small table was indeed piled high with baked goods and cool drinks.

"Eat. Eat, eat, eat. Señor Sebastian has told us he will be sharing some of the family's most beautiful treasures with you today." If possible, Maria's smile widened more at that. "He tells us you are a historian. I know that means you will take hours looking at it all. You'll need your strength."

The positively maternal smile Maria awarded first Sebastian, then Lacey, reinforced Lacey's thought that this woman had been an important part of Sebastian's life growing up. Like everyone, Lacey knew that his parents had died from some sort of mysterious wasting disease when he was young. She guessed Maria and Ricardo had assisted in raising him.

Her heart thumped hard in sympathy as she abruptly pictured a young, orphaned Sebastian.

Hungrier than she thought she would be because of the excited butterflies that had insisted on fluttering around inside her since last night, Lacey enjoyed the outstandingly good snacks and the tall, cool raspberry lemonades that Maria brought out to them as well. Delicate little lemon cakes, almond tarts, sweet cinnamon-dusted churros, and more were all prettily displayed on small trays and plates on the table.

Maria's kindness, Sebastian's evident relaxation inside this house, and the high of the pheromones from her multiple incredible releases the night before all served to put Lacey at ease even within the grandeur of this stunning home.

When they finally had their fill, both assuring Maria how tasty everything had been, Sebastian stood up and again reached his hand out to Lacey. She took it, unable to stop the burble of delighted laughter as he gently tugged her up from her chair and pulled her toward the hallway. Seeing him so wondrously excited to be showing off his home to her was delightfully infectious.

"Get ready to be dazzled," he said. His smile was alight with a mixture of anticipation, excitement, and that wild, strange something she could never put her finger on. The indefinable mystery that always seemed to surround him, calling to her like the most tantalizing scent in the world. "Come. Follow me."

With that, he led her toward the beautiful, tall set of

double wooden doors at the end of the long hallway. Stopping to fiddle with the security panel on the side, he opened the doors and gestured her in, watching her face the entire time.

SEBASTIAN FELT intertwined thoughts and emotions racing around inside him as he opened the doors to his family's treasure room for Lacey to see. As little as twenty-four hours ago, the thought of doing this would have been an impossibility for him.

Never again did he think he would've trusted another woman to see the incomplete source of his remaining power, not to mention the sanctity of everything that his family had held sacred during the many centuries of their existence. The implications the night before were still undeniable, even in the broad light of this day, the early morning hours of which he had to admit he questioned whether or not he'd dreamed the entire thing.

But the beautiful impossibility was true. Lacey was his mate. The one woman in the world intended for him. He hadn't even had a chance to tell Ash about it yet, but he rather dreaded that. Ash would tease him mercilessly about it all the rest of their days.

As his mate, Sebastian could genuinely trust Lacey in a way he'd never believed possible after the hideous betrayal by Melusine years ago. With tentative hope, he allowed joy to begin flooding through his heart. His dragon bugled again deep inside him with satisfaction and triumph as Lacey walked into his private treasure lair.

As gratifyingly as when she had seen him naked the night before, Lacey gasped in pure shock as the brightness of the riches inside the room were revealed.

"Holy shit! You weren't kidding when you said you're going

to show me your family's treasure room." Her beautiful eyes were huge. "I thought you meant that metaphorically."

Sebastian stepped through the wide doorway into the room, waving for her to come in as well. Slowly following him in, Lacey took in the items of the room with a keen expression. She was looking now with the eyes of a professionally trained historian. With another gasp, she suddenly darted to one of the small statues displayed on an altar tucked into one corner. Then a painting, then another statue, then jewelry displayed on beautifully handcrafted old boxes, seemingly lit from within by their own brilliance.

"Sebastian, this is—I can't even say." Her voice was a whisper. "It's spectacular."

He smiled. "I know. It is beyond precious to me."

As she explored the room, first carefully but soon with a growing excitement that lent more quickness to her moves, Sebastian simply stood back, taking it all in. Those gorgeous legs of hers flashed out from beneath the pretty little skirt she wore. The memory of licking her up one thigh then back down the other hardened him slightly, as did the deeply satisfying joy of watching his true mate flit from one object in the room to another, blending into their shining allure with her own incredible beauty.

She dazzled him just as much as anything else in the room. Even more.

The realization struck him so suddenly that he almost staggered. Glad she couldn't see him, her back to him as she bent down over another small gold statue, babbling with excitement about its provenance, Sebastian took a deep breath as he abruptly understood the truth of what having a mate actually meant.

Lacey truly was one of his treasures as well. As his mate, she literally completed him. She added to the source of his personal powers, bringing him to true fulfillment and richness. She gave him a depth of strength he vaguely recalled from his childhood, when the combined power of the family was stronger, even though it had been already weakening enough that it would soon kill his parents.

He had to tell Lacey the truth of his legacy. She already recognized the importance of dragon symbols to his family, that was no secret. What he'd learned of her in the past year was that she was sensible, thoughtful. Logical, yet not rigid.

She would not be able to argue when she saw him shift into his dragon shape before her very eyes. Dragon-human pairings as true mates were actually not uncommon. Even so, he planned to broach the subject delicately.

She turned to gaze at a painting on the wall, her sweet, citrusy scent wafting over to him again. Drawn to it, he stepped up behind her, easily fitting his arms around her sides to clasp his hands in front of her waist. She inhaled sharply as he did that, then relaxed back against him as he'd hoped.

"You like this," he said, more statement that question, dipping his face onto the top of her head to drink in her smell even more deeply. "My personal collection."

She nodded, the hairs of her loose ponytail tickling against his throat.

"Yes." An entire novel's worth of explanation rested in her voice with that single word. "Yes. It's beyond stunning. Sebastian," she said, gently turning herself around his arms to look at up at him, wrapping her own hands behind his neck, her entire face thrilled. "Thank you so much for sharing this with me. I didn't really know what to expect when you said you wanted to bring me down here," she admitted. "This is behind any of my wildest imaginings. And I really do understand why you wouldn't want anyone else in the world to see this."

As she looked up at him, her expression was so sincere, so full of understanding, that he felt something inside him lurch with renewed awareness. Everyone from his parents, from Maria and Ricardo, from every mated dragon he'd ever known —they all had been right.

Once a dragon met his mate, and claimed her, not only would he know it was the real thing, it would completely change his perception of the entire world.

"You have no idea how much it means to me to hear that, Lacey," he said in a bare whisper, gently lifting one of her hands from his neck to kiss the back of it. Her eyes darkened a shade when he did that, her breath vibrating in her throat. "I know you want to take your time looking at everything in here. We have all day. I can answer any question you have. Then I'll give you a tour of the estate before we have dinner on the *placita* this evening. I'm positive Maria has an absolute feast prepared for us."

Sebastian felt his breath catch in his throat as Lacey looked at him with her glorious, enchanted eyes, the promise of a different kind of hunger in her gaze. The wild snap of his dark, primal desire for her swept through him, but he restrained himself.

Smiling, Sebastian claimed her mouth in a brief kiss, knowing that later, he would also feast on the delicacies offered by his most lovely mate.

14

After about five solid minutes of staring in awe at the shower in her room, which was literally the size of her and Gabi's entire apartment, Lacey finally stepped into it and enjoyed the most luxurious bathing experience of her entire life.

Adjacent to her room on the second floor of the hacienda, right around the corner from Sebastian's room, her shower room opened up even more with a floor-to-ceiling window at one end, which looked out into the miniature chaparral forest of pinyons and junipers directly outside. Maria had assured her that not only could no one see in because of the secure glass design, there would be no one out there anyway. The entire estate was extremely secure and well guarded. Lacey had lifted her eyebrows a little bit at the words "well guarded." But Maria offered no further explanation, so she didn't press.

To be honest, although Sebastian's treasure room had been a pinnacle experience of not only her career but her entire life so far—well, with the exception of the previous night with the man himself—and she had approached it with professional hat placed firmly on head, part of her was still squeaking and gibbering and jumping up and down in wild excitement. She felt somewhat like a little girl who had just been told that unicorns and flying ponies were not only real, but that she was getting some of her very own.

Of course she'd known Sebastian was insanely wealthy. Yet to actually see that wealth, in person, to see how easily and casually he lived that life, was another thing entirely.

There was no question he was thrilled she was here. There was no question that he was excited to show it off, and he was definitely into her. She couldn't deny that. It was all just overwhelming. And it kept messing with her firm instructions to herself to not get her hopes up.

Biting her lip, she finished getting ready for dinner. Midspringtime in Southern California meant the temperatures this night promised to not dip below 65 degrees. It was still about 80 right now, making her very glad she'd brought along the simple yet pretty, short evening dress in her overnight bag. Realizing how much Sebastian enjoyed her body, enjoyed looking at her, and appreciated her as a woman had bolstered her own confidence in how she decided to dress around him.

She felt pretty damned sexy, to be honest.

As she somewhat nervously primped in the bathroom's elegant mirror, she remembered how he'd bent her over his desk and had his deliciously decadent way with her last night. The mirror reflected the slight pink staining her cheeks as she fussed with her hair. Holding up her hair with one hand, she reached her other into the small toiletries bag she'd brought with her, rifling through it.

Aha. Her hand closed around the beautiful little hairpin the dealer, Mark Edwards, had brought her from his client. She thought Sebastian might enjoy the extra effort she'd taken in wearing something from their mutually beloved Californio era to dinner at his historic Californio hacienda that evening. After she clipped up her hair, topping it off with the hairpin nestled deep inside the mass of it, she took a step back from the mirror to scrutinize herself from every angle.

Wow. She had to admit it. She looked kind of—hot.

"You're a total babe, girl," Gabi's laughing voice teased in her head.

Thinking of her friend, Lacey picked up her cell and shot off a quick text to her. She hadn't heard from Gabi since her friend had gone back out to the island, but that wasn't uncommon. Gabi worked hard, not to mention she generally took time for some crazy, adventurous personal fun out there as well. Lacey didn't really expect to hear from her again until she got home, whenever that might be.

Even so, she couldn't help but snap a quick picture of her full body in the mirror, vamping for the camera. She sent it to Gabi with the words, *OK! You win! Yes, I'm a hot babe. Ha. You'll never guess where I am. Lots to tell you later XOXO Lacey*

After another fortifying breath, Lacey left the room. She managed to navigate her way downstairs to the gorgeous inner *placita* of the hacienda. Stepping outside, she gasped for the bazillionth time that day, now at the magical scene set before her. Luminarias, beautiful lights that traditionally were candles situated in pretty little brown paper bags weighed down with sand, decorated the courtyard in beautiful patterns, including stars, crosses, and something that took a long moment of puzzling as she tried to decipher what it was.

She stood there staring at it when her neck subtly prickled with a delighted realization. Sebastian was behind her.

"Step back a little bit more, and up." His deep voice murmured close to her ear as he leaned forward and dropped a kiss on her bare neck, sending a shiver down her body. "Here, up these little steps."

She stepped back with him, up onto the low, unrailed balcony that extended down the courtyard, then turned around and looked again. "Oh, wow. It's amazing. Did Maria set that up?"

Sebastian shook his head, admiring the sight with just as

much appreciation. "No, Ricardo. I asked him to make that special pattern."

The largest cluster of luminarias made the outline of a dragon in flight, stretching across the width of the courtyard. Right at the center of it was a small table for two, romantically set up, just waiting for them to be seated. "After you, my lady," Sebastian said, as he sketched her a half bow. The luminarias cast enough light for her to see the smile on his face, the seriousness of his dark eyes as he took her hand to lead her to the table.

It was a feast indeed. Exquisitely delicious food, opulent wine, and Lacey's increasing awareness of Sebastian's very male presence across the little table from her made it the most magical meal she'd ever had. By the time dessert was presented, she felt so giddy from the glasses of ruby red wine and the intensity in Sebastian's eyes that she thought she could possibly levitate out of her chair.

As Maria was leaving the table after serving their dessert, Sebastian called to her in a low voice, "Give us our privacy, please, Maria."

Lacey barely heard Maria's affirmative reply, so lost was she in Sebastian's eyes.

"Have a bite of your dessert with a sip of your wine." His voice sent another quiver through her legs. The heat was rising, coiling deep in her belly and spreading throughout her.

"It's a very special, slightly spicy chocolate dessert. It pairs perfectly with the wine. Particularly," he added in a low, seductive tone, "when you have the flavor of both on your tongue at the same time."

Lacey almost swallowed her own tongue at the innuendo behind his words.

Sebastian Bernal was definitely, positively, absolutely the most erotic man she'd ever met in her life. She was flooded with another beautifully wet warmth between her legs just from his voice. Keeping her gaze locked on his, which reminded her of the wild intensity of their union the night before, she dipped her fork into the dessert, lifted a small bite to her mouth, took a taste. Almost moaning as the hot sweetness blossomed across her tongue, she then raised the wine glass and took a sip.

Just as he'd said, the mingled tastes in her mouth were pretty much—okay, she was going to think it. They created an orgasm in her mouth. What did some people call it—a foodgasm. Yes. The way he was looking at her, she was about to have a real orgasm on top of it as well.

"Lacey," Sebastian growled, pushing his chair back from the table. "I can't let you finish that dessert on your own."

Lacey swallowed the bite of chocolate and the splash of wine. Heart banging inside her, she watched as he stood up to slowly, deliberately stalk around the table to her side.

"I want to taste everything at once." His voice had a deep, almost feral note to it. "May I?"

Mouth opening as she began to breathe faster, completely uncertain of what he was asking but definitely more than eager to allow it, Lacey nodded her head. She was well past the point of trusting her usually controlled voice. She knew it would come out a strangled gasp if she even tried to speak.

Gently, although with a restrained urgency that told her he was holding himself back by sheer force of will alone, Sebastian reached for Lacey's dessert plate. "Come," he said, turning and walking to one of the comfortably padded cedar wood lounge chairs set at the far, shadowy edges of the *placita*. "Bring your wineglass with you."

Legs trembling so much she wasn't certain she wouldn't fall on her face as she followed him, Lacey obeyed. The sheer thrill of simply doing what he asked her to, trusting him without question, made her moan out loud.

At the chair, Sebastian turned to her and said in a low voice, "Lie down on it. I want full access to your own delicious treats."

Lacey was pretty sure she was about to hyperventilate. Not taking her eyes off his, she somehow backed herself to the chair, reaching behind to feel for it so she wouldn't land on her ass on the burgundy red paving stones of the *placita,* and sank into it.

Sebastian stood there, controlled power screaming from every inch of his muscled body, just watching her. She scooted herself back until she was nestled into the chair, legs stretched out in front of her. Sebastian smiled, something so marveling, so appreciative, breaking across his face that Lacey felt light-headed along with the potential hyperventilation.

Was he going to...? Did he want her to...?

"Are you wearing anything under that dress of yours?" His voice was a dark, sinuous glide of desire that stroked up against Lacey's senses.

Mute, she nodded. Damn. Apparently she hadn't got the memo that she wasn't supposed to wear underpants to dinner.

"Open those beautiful legs of yours. I need to see you." Sebastian never took his eyes off her as he spoke, though she caught a glimpse of his pulse pounding hard in his throat where the luminarias cast it into light.

Shaking with the wild anticipation of what was about to come, Lacey did exactly as he asked. She felt absolutely no trepidation about baring herself in front of him. She felt utterly safe. Right now, she would do anything in the world he asked and not even bat an eyelash.

So suddenly she hardly saw him move, Sebastian leaped down, reached out his hand, and easily ripped away the flimsy, pretty little underpants that were all that kept her freshly shaved pussy from his view. Before she could even gasp, he rested the upper half of his body on the chair, nestled his head between her legs, and took a long, luxurious lick.

At that, Lacey couldn't stop the small, whimpering scream that burst out of her throat. Flinging her head back against the softness of the chair, her fingers clenched so hard around the wine stem she still held she wondered if she was about to break it. Yet she was past caring, because his tongue was licking, flicking, tasting, swirling, dipping into her to drink deeply of her juices.

Then he pulled back, murmuring a highly appreciative "Mmm" as he did so. Reaching down to her dessert plate that he'd set beside the chair, he scooped up a bit of the chocolate into his mouth. "Your wine," he said, gesturing at the glass she still held in her hand.

Trembling a little, Lacey handed the glass to him. He didn't try to take it, though, but simply inclined his head toward it to sip. She tipped it a bit at the edges of his lips, watching with tense anticipation as his took a sip into his mouth. He swirled the flavors together before swallowing, holding Lacey's eyes with his own the entire time.

"Oh," she whispered, enthralled. She felt so heavy between her legs, so plump and filled with need, she knew she would burst almost the second he touched her there again.

Giving her a smoldering glance, Sebastian lowered his head back between her legs, licking and sucking and swirling his tongue into her.

Without any more stimulation than that, Lacey tumbled straight off the edge into a burbling little orgasm that caught her by surprise, leaving her mouth half open in another, this time silent, cry, her head still flung back against the chair, her free hand gripping its wooden armrest.

Sebastian didn't stop his ministrations until the final quiver left Lacey's body, allowing her finally to flop down on the chair, her ragged gasps filling the soft night air. When one last, soft touch of his tongue caused her to jump, now so super sensitized down there that the feeling was too much, he sensed it and pulled back. Moving his way up the chair, his face hovered near hers as he whispered, "Open your eyes and look at me."

She did, feeling so gorgeously spent that it was an effort.

Keeping his eyes open and locked on hers, Sebastian gently kissed her. His mouth tasted like her, the chocolate, the wine, his own dark, edgy self. It all threatened to tumble her over the glorious edge again, eager and willing for the beautiful, soaring fall.

They kissed for long, lazy moments, during which Lacey absently thought she was incredibly glad he'd asked Maria to give them privacy. His hands came up and worked their way into her hair, his eyes still holding hers, letting her sink into the beautiful, welcoming depths that made her feel so safe.

Finding the pins that held up her hair, Sebastian carefully, so as not to pull any strands, worked them out one by one, setting them onto the flat wooden armrest of the chair. Lacey helped by lifting her head to give him slightly better access. When his hands found the large, gold hairpin, he smiled. "One last barrier to seeing your gorgeous hair spread around your face and shoulders. I want to see your face again when you come, Lacey." His tone was so serious, she caught her breath. "It's incredibly beautiful. It turns me on so much I almost feel as if I'll pass out."

A little too eagerly, she said, "Oh, I like the sound of that."

As laughter slightly crinkled the corners of his eyes, Sebastian finally pulled out the hairpin, casually glancing at it as he set it down on the armrest of the chair. Just as suddenly, all expression wiped clean from his face.

Lacey abruptly felt the air freeze between them.

Sebastian stared at the hairpin, his face paling in the flickering lights of the luminarias and the moon dancing far above. Slowly, he pushed himself back, away from Lacey, until he was standing again, the hairpin still in one hand.

"What?" she asked, dread tickling at her with cold fingers. "What's wrong?"

She sat up, nervously smoothing her dress back over herself. She suddenly felt completely exposed. Vulnerable.

And somehow, for some reason, in the wrong. "Sebastian, what's going on? You look—"

He sliced the air with a sharp whip of his hand, instantly silencing her. When he finally dragged his gaze back up from small, golden hairpiece, Lacey felt like she'd been punched in the stomach. The look on his face as he stared at her was filled with rage, disgust.

Pure loathing.

He suddenly seemed twice as big, as if he was expanding. As if he was taking up more space than any man should. She almost could feel the fury pouring off of him, stabbing her like angry little knives. Unable to move beneath his vicious glare, Lacey stayed where she was, hardly breathing.

"You traitorous bitch," he said, his voice filled with an awful, aching rancor—and the sharp bite of pain.

The venom of his tone, let alone the ugly word he flung at her, made Lacey recoil in sudden terror and renewed shock. He looked like he wanted to rip her apart with his bare hands.

Shaking the hairpin at her as well as his head in disbelief, he snapped, "So this is why I thought you were my mate. *This* is why I felt close to you. You had the last piece of my family's gold hoard with you. It wasn't you. You're just like *her*." The expression on his face was an awful mix of bewilderment and fury. "You care nothing about me, and only about my wealth. My power."

His rage, mingled with a horrendous, savage pain, cut right through her. She could almost feel the hurt. She opened her mouth to answer with something, anything, but he kept talking.

"Malcolm sent you here, didn't he?" Sebastian barked out a bitter laugh. "He is so determined to bring me down, he must have offered you a lot of money."

Lacey still couldn't move.

"Tell me, Ms. Whitman"—the way he sneered her formal name made tears spring to Lacey's eyes as she stared at the man who not moments before had stroked her to ecstasy in such a way that she had begun to realize she was seriously, actually falling for him—"how much did he offer you to do this? I'm sure you're set up for life now. Tell me the truth, Ms. Whitman. How much did that filthy bastard pay you off to destroy me completely?"

15

———————

Sebastian thought his head might explode from the cacophony of thoughts and rage pounding through it. He felt his dragon side wanting to take over, wanting to lash out, leap into the air in wild flight, beat his wings against the sky. bugle out utter rage at being betrayed yet again.

He knew he was terrifying Lacey, but he couldn't care. She had the last piece missing from his hoard in her possession. The last piece he'd needed to bring back his powers in full, nestled into her golden hair just as she had wormed her way into his heart.

Like a duplicitous viper. The thought of how she, along with Malcolm, must've laughed at him as they plotted out this new way to bring him down made what had been the tentative unfurling of his withered heart snap shut again with such fury that it literally hurt.

Horrible pain stabbed through his chest, making it almost hard to breathe. The only way to deal with it was rage.

"Answer me," his voice growled. His voice came dark and low with the strength of his despairing dragon behind it.

Still cowering in the chair, eyes enormous and filled with

tears, Lacey—no, Ms. Whitman, he snapped to himself, that lash of pain striking him again—shook her head. "I have no idea what you're talking about," she said, her voice wavering along with the tears that dropped from her eyes. "I don't understand a single word you just said." Her voice whispered as she stared at him.

Sebastian roared, "Yes, you do! You joined forces with Malcolm Kerberos to help him finally destroy the last living member of the Bernal family, making him the most powerful dragon shifter!" Rage made his voice lash through the air. "It's what he's always wanted."

Bitter laughter ringed his words again despite Lacey's continued shaking of her head. "Tell me, did you enjoy planning this little trick? Did you laugh every time we talked at the museum, every time you strung me along into believing that you actually cared about my family's heritage?" He ignored the pure shock on Lacey's face. "That you might actually have cared about me?" He let the last word hiss out of him, less by deliberation and more because he could barely control his own voice.

"I don't—" Lacey began in a whisper, her voice trembling, but Sebastian cut her off again.

He forced out his darkest thought next. "And then, of course, there is your collusion with Melusine." He spat the name in such disgust that Lacey literally recoiled. "She told you exactly how to get close to me, did she not? She *trained* you perfectly on every last detail of how to betray me. Just as she once did to me as well."

Sebastian let the damning words hang between them in all their wretchedness. Lacey's pale face swam like a blank white canvas in front of him, her expression nervous. Terrified.

Like that of one caught out in a lie.

His dragon ricocheted around his head, demanding to be set free. Pain blossomed in his hand where he squeezed the hairpin so tightly the little golden wings of the metal dragon dug into his palm.

Sebastian felt like nothing more than a walking, talking, living being made up of sheer pain.

Running footsteps interrupted him. The door to the court-yard was flung open, Ricardo and then Maria racing out. Maria, ever the mother willing to scold him, began to open her mouth, a look of shock on her face, but Ricardo gently shushed her. Quietly he said, "Señor Sebastian, is everything okay?"

Lacey's hiccuping cries dropped into the little silence that followed. Before Sebastian could answer, Ricardo added, "I was just coming to get you anyway, sir. There is someone at the door to see you." Casting a glance at Lacey, Ricardo looked back at Sebastian with a worried expression. "We tried to discourage him, but he is very insistent that he speak to you immediately. I truly believe he is someone," and by the slight emphasis on that word, Sebastian knew that Ricardo meant whoever it was at the door was another dragon shifter, "you must speak to."

Another uncomfortable little silence held them, although by the way Maria's eyes snapped at him, he knew full well they'd both heard him yelling at Lacey. Maria obviously didn't agree with that. Well, she was like any mother would be, even to a child that never literally had been her own. She had been brought up to believe that no man should ever yell at a woman. She certainly wasn't willing to stand for Sebastian doing that.

"I will see to it," he said, not even bothering to glance at Ms. Whitman again as he pocketed the hairpin and strode toward the door leading into the main house. "Keep an eye on her and don't let her leave," he threw over his shoulder at Ricardo, brushing past them. He ignored Maria's furious glare.

Sebastian let rage and a sour, infuriatingly helpless pain drive his steps through the hacienda to the front. Thoroughly on guard but also knowing he was so angry that if there was the slightest hint of any danger when he opened the door he would not hesitate to launch a deadly attack, he flung open the double doors of the outer courtyard with more force and perhaps a bit more dramatic flair than was strictly necessary. Yet he knew who would be there. An appearance of brute strength was necessary.

Malcolm Kerberos, supercilious smile and knowing grin rolled into one plastered across his face, stood outside. "Well. I see you got my small token of affection."

Gritting his jaw, clenching his fists at his side as he still battled his newly enraged dragon to keep from bursting forth through him so he could rend the bastard's face with his claws, Sebastian forced as much deadly quiet in his voice as he could. "You knew all along, didn't you. You knew I was looking for the missing pieces of my hoard."

Malcolm's smile only widened, his entire expression one of such triumph that Sebastian longed to simply smash him across the face and be done with it. However, that wasn't quite how things worked in the shifter world. There were rules. Regulations. Constant one-upmanship for control, coupled with a dragon shifter's native tendency toward unrestrained outbursts, had millennia ago dictated an ironclad set of rules that bound them all. Sebastian could no more attack the man on his own doorstep than Malcolm could attack him right now, either.

But if Malcolm attempted to enter Sebastian's house and do harm, then of course Sebastian could do everything he needed in order to protect himself and those within. Yet Malcolm was far too smart for that. In fact, his slippery, conniving ways had become far more clear to Sebastian in the past few minutes than ever before.

Forcing himself to count to ten while he took long, quiet breaths in through his nose and slowly exhaled them out his mouth, Sebastian managed his temper as best he could before he answered. "Very well. So you finally realized what I was searching for. What you didn't realize, however, was that the hairpin was the last piece of my hoard." He gave Malcolm a challenging look. "My powers will be coming back in full force. There is nothing you can do to stop that now."

To his surprise, Malcolm laughed, waving off Sebastian's words as if they meant nothing. "You're right. Partially." His oily voice made the words sound vile. "I had no real idea that you were searching for your hoard. Not until, of course, Melusine came to me and told me what was going on."

Sebastian willed his face to stay extremely still at the name of his former, horribly double-crossing lover. The same sort of woman Lacey Whitman had turned out to be, he thought. Hideous pain stabbed him in his chest again at the realization of how he been duped once more by a woman.

Never again.

Forcing his impassivity, he sought to regain control of the conversation.

"It was certainly a very clever tactic, using Ms. Whitman as your mule." Sebastian kept his tone level as he spoke. "I can assure you she played her part very well. But you'll never be able to fool me again, Malcolm. Not by sending another woman my way."

At Sebastian's words, however, Malcolm's eyebrows raised. The slow, mocking grin slid over his face again. "Really? Is that how it is." He studied Sebastian closely for long moments, fingers idly twisting a large golden sapphire ring on his right hand. Sebastian gave it a quick glance, knowing that it was likely one small piece of Malcolm's own hoard. "You have just given me some very intriguing information, Bernal. Do you realize that?"

Sebastian frowned. "You're speaking in riddles. Spit it out."

But Malcolm was already backing away from the house, shaking his head and making a little tsk-tsk sound. "Oh, Bernal.

You disappoint me. Men's hearts are so easy to deceive, are they not? Especially the heart of a man who clearly has found his mate." Malcolm's face was a study in sickening triumph. "The true treasure of a dragon. The only part of his treasure that truly matters to him."

Malcolm's eyes flicked to the hacienda, a more calculating expression spreading across his face. Then he glanced back at Sebastian, whose blood suddenly ran cold at the ruthlessness he saw there.

"Catch me if you can, Bernal," Malcolm Kerberos hissed, his dragon already echoing through his voice. "Because I am indeed fleeing with more of your treasure."

Quicker than breath, Malcolm shifted into his dragon. Large, scaly, his color a putrid purplish-green-black color that surely must reflect the ugliness of his own soul, Malcolm shot straight into the air with a powerful push off from his hind legs, his large wings unfurling and flapping loudly as he launched himself into the sky.

He twisted and headed straight over the center of the hacienda.

Directly toward the open *placita* in the middle, where Sebastian had just left Lacey.

His mate. His only true treasure.

A long moment of disbelieving shock, horror, and sick fury at himself held Sebastian motionless until his body caught up to his brain's sudden, frantic screaming. He pivoted on one foot and raced back into the hacienda, heedlessly charging down the hallways.

"Lacey!" Her name tore out of his throat in a frantic cry as he careened down the hall. He had yelled at her so cruelly, accusing her of betraying him. Pain punched him in the gut as he ran. The hallways of his enormous home had never felt so ridiculously long before.

A sudden, wrenching scream from ahead of him propelled him along faster, cursing the fact that he couldn't turn into his dragon in his own house, since he would be too large. He heard Maria's and Ricardo's cries as well. Then there was another long, terrified scream from Lacey that slowly grew more distant before it trailed off into the ether above the house.

Malcolm had taken her.

16

Still shaking, Lacey didn't move from the chair as Sebastian stormed away from the courtyard. His words still slapped her, the feeling nearly as stunning as if she'd been physically assaulted. Muttering in an outraged tone, Maria bustled down the few steps and swept over to Lacey.

"He's behaving like a big baboon, that one!" Maria said, speaking in Spanish so fast she seemed to hardly take a breath between words. "We could hear him yelling from the other side of the house. I don't know what he said to you and I don't care." Maria reached down to brush off Lacey's arms as if she were covered in something. "He had no cause to raise his voice to you. None."

Still traumatized and confused, Lacey shook her head. "I didn't even know what he was talking about. One moment we were—I mean, we—"

Maria nodded her head, a small smile on her face managing to break through her outrage. "Yes, chica. I know. He has true feelings for you. We know it. You are his—well." Maria looked back at Ricardo, who still stood on the steps by the courtyard's entry way. "You are his," she ended simply, her voice suddenly very tender.

Lacey shook her head, feeling only slightly comforted by having the maternal older woman's hands still lightly holding her shoulders. "I don't think so." Still dazed, she babbled. "He took a hairpin out of my hair, it was a gift from someone I don't even know. Then he just started screaming that I had betrayed him. Something about someone named Malcolm? And a woman, something—I can't remember. And then..." She trailed off before whispering in a jagged tone, "He asked me how I much was paid off in order to—to betray him."

Maria looked across the courtyard again at Ricardo. Concern flickered over both their faces. Lacey stared from one to the other, suddenly feeling chilled again. "What? What is it?"

Very slowly, Maria asked, looking at her again, "A hairpin? What kind of a hairpin? Tell us what it looks like."

Haltingly, still befuddled by the ricochet of emotions slamming around her body, Lacey gave a brief description of the hairpin. Both Ricardo and Maria turned pale, Maria's eyes widening with something that also looked like hope as she exchanged yet another mysterious glance with Ricardo.

"You said someone gave it to you? When was this? Who was it?" Maria asked gently, kneeling down beside Lacey, holding her hands and gently massaging them as if to encourage her to talk more.

Lacey shrugged helplessly. "That's the thing. I have no idea. The dealer I often work with, an antiquities dealer, he brought it to me the other day. He said it was a gift for me from one of his clients. Sebastian found it in my hair. That's when he began yelling about how I betrayed him." She shivered again at the memory of his sudden, towering rage. A rage lined with some sort of agonized pain. "That I knew all along about his treasure. What on earth was he talking about? What is going on?"

As Maria drew breath to answer, the sudden sound of enormous wings flapping in the dark skittered around the courtyard. A huge breeze sprang up, toppling over luminarias, sweeping the remains of the dessert and wine onto the ground to break against the flagstones, making Lacey's hair and dress swirl around her. Maria screamed as Ricardo yelled, both of them looking up into the sky with terror.

Wild-eyed, heart threatening to leap out of her chest, Lacey followed their gazes and looked overhead.

A dragon hovered overhead, flapping its wings in the open space above the *placita*.

A dragon. Like the creature of myth. The beast of legend.

A freaking dragon.

A real, live, giant-headed, clawed feet, long-tailed, scaled dragon with glowing eyes was in the air above them.

A for-real, actual dragon was hovering in the sky above her head.

And he was brutally ugly, and terrifying.

Lacey stopped breathing, her mind splintering in at least seventeen different directions as the mouth of the creature opened in an angry bellow, followed by a blast of actual flame. She vaguely heard a shout from somewhere inside the house, heard Maria and Ricardo screaming at the winged beast in the sky above her, but she couldn't really pay attention to any of it.

Slowly, the dragon was lowering itself through the air. Its giant claws reached for her, though she was still so frozen in place she literally couldn't move. Enormous feet with deadly claws curved around her, scooping her up, curling closed over her. Then they lifted her into the air.

Lacey's voice finally caught up to her shrieking mind. She screamed, loudly, over and over again, as utter shock and terror engulfed everything in her body.

With a whooshing rush, the enormous creature flapped its wings again as it yanked her up into the sky. The earth fell away beneath her, the hacienda suddenly spinning away and becoming small.

So terrorized was she that she barely heard the horrified screams of Ricardo and Maria. Or the long, heartrending yell that she knew was Sebastian's voice.

A bellowing cry that spiraled up from the ground as she was yanked away into the night: *"Lacey!"*

ALL THE CONFUSED thoughts of the last several moments fell away from Sebastian's mind, replaced by a singular focus.

His mate had just been taken by Malcolm.

He had to save her.

Ignoring Maria's and Ricardo's horrified cries, Sebastian shifted into his dragon shape so quickly, taking off into the air with such a monumental thrust of his hind legs and whoosh of his wings, he knew he must have knocked them both to the ground. Sending a mental apology, he opened his mouth to loose an immense roar as he streaked through the air after the other dragon who just had stolen his mate.

His true treasure. The only treasure he finally, truly understood was what he wanted, needed, and should never once have doubted.

Malcolm Kerberos had played him for a fool, just as Melusine had years ago. Even though he didn't know all the pieces, Malcolm clearly had orchestrated this like a chess master.

The irrational thought that this also wasn't quite the way Sebastian had envisioned Lacey discovering the truth about his dual life as a dragon shifter raced through his head. But there was no use worrying about that now.

First, he had to get her back.

Streaking into the warm, dark air of the late spring night, Sebastian zeroed in on his target. Although no human nor any modern equipments could sense the two dragons zipping through the sky, Sebastian had no problems whatsoever keeping Malcolm in his sights. Malcolm might be crafty, and very quick to take advantage of an unexpected situation, but he was no match for a dragon as large and strong as Sebastian.

Or a dragon whose mate's life was being threatened.

Within a scant mile, Sebastian caught up. Unsure of what Malcolm would do, but knowing that he wouldn't want to harm Lacey because she was the key to still controlling Sebastian, Sebastian turned in a double-barreled roll. He slammed his shoulder into Malcolm's hindquarters, throwing the other dragon off his trajectory and sending him likewise tumbling through the air.

Lacey's renewed, terrified screams from where she was locked in the cage of Malcolm's grip pierced more daggers into Sebastian's heart. Sheer desperation made him dive at Malcolm again, knocking into him from the other side.

Again, and again.

Malcolm kept flying. As he bobbled and wove, he occasionally turned his head to roar flame out at Sebastian. Sebastian roared back at him, although since Malcolm was a fire dragon, his flame was far more potent that Sebastian's. But Sebastian had the advantage of being larger and stronger, since he was a classic dragon.

He was also fueled by desperation.

Suddenly, Malcolm banked hard to the left. He dove down toward the ground, pulling up at the last second to shoot straight up back in the air. Lacey's screams abated. Sebastian's heart seized as he wondered if she had fainted, or even worse, at the looping, abrupt aerial acrobatics.

Having to sharply adjust his own course, he lost some time, but quickly caught up again. Reaching forward with his head, he clamped onto Malcolm's tail with the sharp teeth. Malcolm's shriek rent the air. He twisted around to glare at Sebastian.

Desperation lent a surge of strength that Sebastian never

could have found otherwise. Gathering every last bit of his reserves, he bellowed a gout of flame so enormous it blasted him backward as it left his mouth, tumbling him head over heels so that he couldn't see if it struck his target.

But although he couldn't see, he could hear. The high-pitched, petrifying shriek of agony told him his aim had been true. The flame had caught Malcolm in the face, exactly as Sebastian had hoped.

He righted his spiraling fall through the air, swooping up just in time to see Malcolm's charred body falling like a stone to the ground.

Also just in time to see a small shape, golden hair flashing in the dark, tumbling out of Malcolm's dying grasp.

Limp, seemingly boneless, Lacey's body plummeted straight toward the earth.

U nleashing a frantic bellow of horror, Sebastian banked and dove after Lacey's falling shape, his heart beating so fast with fear he was half afraid it would implode inside his body.

About fifty feet from the earth, he got close enough to thrust his own front feet beneath Lacey, claws open, so she could land with a thump in the safety of his grasp.

Terrified, Sebastian beat his wings on the back draft to gently lower himself to earth, somewhere on the vast sprawl of his estate. Carefully, he lowered his front legs to the ground, gently opening his claws to set her down. She lolled on the ground, unmoving.

Sebastian bellowed again, the panicked boom of his denial shaking the grasses and small trees.

Lacey's head moved from side to side. Her hands twitched.

Sebastian felt a colossal burst of relief.

Blinking her eyes open, Lacey stared at the sky for a long moment before carefully pushing herself up onto her hands, shoving tangled strands of her blonde hair away from her eyes. She looked up to find Sebastian staring at her. Going utterly motionless in the way he recognized all prey animals as doing when faced with a predator, fear exploded again across her face.

Right. He was still in his dragon shape.

Cursing at himself, Sebastian sharply thought of his human self, shifting back in an instant. As he appeared in front of her on two legs, Lacey's mouth unhinged, her eyes going so big in her face he could hardly see anything but her eyeballs.

"Lacey! Are you hurt? Did he hurt you?" Sebastian rushed toward her, dropping to the ground at her side.

Lacey flinched back, still staring at him with wide eyes. "You were—did I just see—I'm crazy, aren't I," she whispered, voice stricken.

In the distance, Sebastian caught the sound of an engine. Glancing up, he saw headlights probably a few miles away.

Ricardo and Maria, who, unlike normal humans, would have been able to see and hear the dragons clearly. They were coming this way. Relief washed through him.

"You're not crazy. Lacey, I'm so sorry. I never meant for you to find out this way. This isn't exactly what I wanted to have happen when I had you come down here," he finished in a bleak tone.

He could smell the acrid blast of her fear, mingling with the beautiful scent he normally associated with her. Apparently she did have a strong mind, though, because her voice was reasonably steady when she spoke again. Even so, it still sounded as blanched as her face.

"Are you sure I'm not crazy? Is there some sort of reasonable explanation for all of this?" She waved a shaking hand around in the air.

Sebastian felt his heart beat so hard with mingled relief and renewed trepidation at her reaction that he could feel it pumping his own blood. "Yes, there is. But first, tell me. You're not hurt, are you? He didn't hurt you?"

Slowly, taking a moment to assess things, Lacey shook her head. Her eyes were still fixed on him, their traumatized expression a far cry from her glorious passion earlier. "No, I'm okay. I thought I was going to have a heart attack when I was falling, but I'm okay." She sounded slightly surprised by that.

A long moment held them, filled only with the sounds of crickets and the slight rustle of the grasses.

"Sebastian," she went on in an even more steady voice, "you need to tell me the truth right now. Because I'm not sure I can believe what just happened. Except...that it happened." She laughed, but there was a gasp in it.

He drew breath to answer, but she continued as if she didn't notice.

"I've been trained to believe in things that I can see, touch, smell, hear. And," here she swallowed audibly, "I know that I saw a—a dragon. And I could smell the smoke from the fire that came out of his mouth. I could feel his claws, and his front —paws, I guess, when he grabbed me. And then there was you."

Her voice lowered to a whisper again as she stared at Sebastian, shaking her head. "I just saw you appear right now. There was an enormous dragon, and then—there was you."

She fell silent, clearly having exhausted her ability to further explain the situation on her own. Instead, she waited for him to tell her what was going on.

Trusting him to tell her the truth. Trusting him in a way that he hadn't trusted her.

Sebastian felt like the worst man on the face of the planet. He took a deep breath, raking his fingers through his hair. Still watching him with wary eyes, Lacey managed to stand up, swaying only a little. Sebastian automatically stepped forward to help her, but she flinched again and shook her head. The night was more than warm enough for her to still be wearing the pretty little dress she'd changed into for dinner—how long ago that now seemed—yet she also looked oddly vulnerable, standing there, alone, in the empty swell of landscape somewhere on his family's property.

Sebastian's vision, still enhanced from having been his dragon so recently, could see her clearly enough in the moonlight. She didn't have a scratch on her, although her hair was a wildly tangled mass tumbling over her shoulders. He also saw that her legs, while supporting her, trembled.

He wanted to catch her up in his arms, stroke her shining hair, reassure her that everything was okay.

That he had her. That she was safe.

That he had made a dreadful, awful error in judgment earlier. One born of his own incredible distrust in women. One born of his own blind arrogance and stupidity.

A look at Lacey's face now said that his being able to touch her again anytime soon was not a remote possibility. Briefly shutting his eyes, he took another breath before opening them to look straight at her as he answered.

"You are very certainly not crazy. I wanted to tell you. I meant to tell you soon." He snorted out a self-deprecating laugh. "In truth, I actually planned to tell you this evening. After we dined. I certainly had no intention of this manner being your introduction to the truth of my world."

"And what exactly," she said slowly, watching him closely, "is that truth?"

He searched her face for any signs of the beautifully open, thoroughly desirous woman who'd been so in the moment with him earlier, literally so open to him.

The only expression she wore now was one of pure wariness.

"Lacey," he tried again, uncharacteristically fumbling for the right words. Blowing out a sharp breath, he opted for a blunt delivery. "I am—my family is from a very long, very old family of dragon shifters. We have the ability to shapeshift from human to dragon and back again." He shrugged as he said it, slightly opening his palms to underline the truth of that statement. "What you saw tonight is real. There are creatures far outside the realm of normal human understanding who roam this world."

Very quietly, he added, "I am one of them."

His words dropped into silence. The slight breeze rustled again, whispering through the dry grasses, in the branches of the nearby pinyon trees, ruffling Lacey's dress around her thighs. The crickets hummed a background harmony to the scene, while in the distance a great horned owl let out its distinctive hooting cry.

The sound of the car engine carried to them as well. Lacey's head jerked as she snapped her eyes in that direction, clearly alarmed.

"It's Ricardo and Maria," Sebastian hastened to assure her.

He felt sick at the nervousness he could sense winging through her body. "They're coming to find us."

Slowly, Lacey dragged her eyes back toward him. Although his enhanced vision was slowly dimming back to his human range, Sebastian could still see her face clearly enough. Her eyes were shadowed. Her face was a pale blotch beneath the fiery golden mane of her hair. After another long moment during which the increasing rumble of the car engine and the quiet background saw of the crickets were the only noises, she said, "They know."

It was a statement more than a question. Sebastian nodded. "Yes."

Lacey nodded her own head, very slowly, her teeth catching up her lower lip as her eyes left his again to gaze somewhere in the distance. He sensed her brain frantically attempting to process everything. He stayed quiet, leaving her alone to grapple with what he knew to her was a wild truth, even though it half destroyed him to do that.

In just a few more moments, the lights of the SUV found them, slashing a brightness across Lacey's face that made her squint and throw her hand up over her eyes. The headlights immediately cut, leaving only the parking lights on. The car idled to a stop, a door opening and slamming before the engine was even cut. Hurried footsteps sounded behind him. Without needing to look, Sebastian knew it was Maria, with Ricardo close at her heels.

Maria swept past him, not even deigning to give him a glance, but she drew up short just before she reached Lacey. "It's okay," the older woman said, speaking English. Sebastian sensed that Maria knew Lacey needed as much connection to her normal reality in the moment as possible. "You're not hurt?"

Ricardo pulled up beside Sebastian, giving him a single, searching glance. Sebastian tightened his jaw and didn't return it. There was a heavy sigh, the faint touch of a hand on his shoulder, and retreat. Sebastian knew Ricardo and Maria had the greatest esteem and love for him, having raised him practically like he was their own child since his parents' death when he was so young. Ricardo also knew it was up to Sebastian to salvage the situation.

"No," Lacey said in a faint tone. "No, I'm not hurt." Her eyes, more visible now in the added orangey glow of the SUV's parking lights, blinked as she focused on Maria. She looked at Ricardo, then back at Maria, then to Sebastian again. Carefully, as if sounding out every word in her head before speaking it aloud, she said, "So, apparently Sebastian is a dragon. A dragon—shifter." She stumbled over the term. "And you both know that, right?"

It was so quiet that Sebastian could hear Ricardo swallow beside him, could feel the tenseness coming off of Maria. The one thing ingrained in each member of the few human families in the world who knew the truth about shifters was that speaking about that truth was never to be done. Ever.

Sebastian realized that Maria and Ricardo had recognized that Lacey was his mate the second she walked through the door, thus knowing that one day she would have to know the truth about his dual existence. Even so, answering her question in the affirmative was something that went so against everything they'd each known since the day they were born that he could literally feel Maria struggle to speak.

Finally, Maria sighed. She tilted her head the slightest bit back in Sebastian's direction before she very gently said, "Yes. We know this thing. We have always known."

Lacey nodded in a jerky motion. Her lingering nervousness was still so evident that Sebastian trembled as he forced himself to stand still. To not go to her and gather her in his arms, soothing her, stroking her hair, assuring her everything would be okay. To have to stay back from her, because she feared him.

Damn it all to hell. Never would he have imagined this incredible day ending in such disaster.

In a voice that was regaining the cool composure he usually associated with her, Lacey said, "I want to see it again. I need to see it again." She looked at Sebastian, her legs now as steady as her voice. "You need to show me again. You need to— change into a dragon. Sh-shift," she stumbled over the word. "In front of me, and them." She tipped her chin at Maria and Ricardo. Firming her voice even more, she said, "Sebastian. I need to see you turn into a dragon."

Silence settled again. Sebastian could smell the dry, soothingly familiar scents of his home. The sharp tang of Lacey's nervousness interlaced with her soft floral scent that tugged at him with longing. The breeze rumpled his hair, gently wafted Lacey's dress again. He nodded. "Of course."

Stepping back from them all, he gave space for his dragon to come forth. During this entire exchange, his human side had still been so in tune with his dragon that he'd only been aware of himself as Sebastian. As one single being. Now, he allowed the human part of him to fall away as he pictured his dragon form, letting it ripple and flow over him somewhat more slowly than usual. Through the change, although her figure wavered and blurred for a brief moment as his eyes went from human to dragon, he kept his gaze upon Lacey. Assessing. Watching.

Enormous, truly blacker than the night around them, making himself hunker down on the earth so he looked perhaps a tiny bit smaller, Sebastian took on his dragon form in front of Lacey.

His beautiful mate. The mate he hoped with all his heart he wasn't about to lose.

18

I t took all of Lacey's willpower to not flee screaming into the night as Sebastian did exactly what she had asked him to do and turned into an enormous black dragon in front of her eyes.

Her entire body thrummed with what she knew was her sympathetic nervous system as it very sympathetically flooded her highly alarmed self with chemicals. Chemicals that strongly suggested she fall back on the good old human standby of madly bolting in the opposite direction when in the face of danger.

Yet this wasn't actually danger.

This was Sebastian.

There was no way she could deny it. The man who'd touched her, stroked her, laughed with her, talked with her, captured her heart during the past year, was an honest-to-god, definitely real, freaking gigantic *dragon*. As in, the creature of myth and legend.

Her mind wobbled again with the shocking truth of it.

Taking another deep breath, Lacey made herself stand still and examine Sebastian as best she could in the soft darkness. He was huge. Long, even with his tail curved forward and wrapped in front of his front legs. Interestingly, he still smelled like Sebastian. Like the primitive depths of the forest, scattered with hints of a deliciously spicy musk.

As she watched, he carefully lowered his head to the ground, snaking it forward at the end of his long neck until the massive jaws rested only a few feet from where she stood.

To be honest, if it hadn't been for Maria and Ricardo standing nearby, watching him as calmly as if they'd seen him turn into a dragon hundreds of times before—which, she realized, they probably had—in all likelihood she would've given in to her body's frantic instincts and blindly vamoosed into the dark.

Yet something else deep within her also knew without a doubt that this was Sebastian. She could sense the connection between them, that electricity that snapped and sizzled every time she was around him. Despite her shocked reaction of fear, at the same time she knew on a level deep down that this giant creature wouldn't hurt her. In fact, she sensed that it would do anything to protect her.

He would do anything to protect her.

Slowly, she took a step forward. Then another. When she was close enough to him that if he turned the enormous snout just an inch, he could've knocked her over, he held himself so still that only the sound of his breathing and an odd sort of rumble from deep within him emerged. Lacey reached out her hand to the side of his face. She braced herself for cold, possibly slimy scales, similar to what she had felt while she was being carried by the other, horrible dragon. To her surprise, the dark black hide she touched now was not only soft but warm. Even hot.

Emboldened, she stroked the ridge on the side of his face, beneath his eye, on the top of his head, to the side of the fearsome looking spikes that proudly jutted out of it. The rumbling sound came from him again, and he very lightly pressed his head into her hand. It was almost like an enormous cat purring.

Lacey completely faced his side and placed her other hand on him, leaning in slightly to sniff his hide, even though she felt slightly ridiculous doing so. But really, the smell was so much of the decadent, dizzying scent she associated with Sebastian, only times ten, that she couldn't help herself.

This enormous, stunning creature was Sebastian. There was no doubt about it.

Bit by bit, she felt herself relaxing. It was real.

There were such things as dragon shifters in the world.

The parts of her brain that had stopped thinking now were slowly spitting out puzzle pieces that clicked into place. The Bernal family's association with dragons, such as on their crest. All the dragon-shaped items that come across her way during the past year of studying the Californio culture and Sebastian's own personal legacy. The paintings, pendants, statues of dragons. The extraordinary treasure room in the hacienda. The man's own luxurious, powerful, bordering-the-edge-of-deadly presence that propelled him through this world in a blast of wealth, intensity, planet-wide desire.

Yes, it all made a crazy sense now.

After a last inhale of the cedar-y, dark spiced pine scent of his hide, Lacey stepped back again. She couldn't quite see the color of his eyes in the darkness, but she could see the gleam as one of them regarded her, slowly blinking once or twice during the long moments of her observation.

Finally, she quietly said, "Okay. Can you change back?"

Before she could take another breath, his huge shape shimmered, disappearing into the fully clothed, still fully sexy man she knew was Sebastian Bernal. Lacey swallowed as she held her ground. He simply stood there, watching her with a calm yet careful expression. Waiting for her to make the next move. He'd shown her everything.

There was something else she needed to know, though.

One more thing, which her brain still questioned even though it was teetering on the verge of a total powering down in the face of everything that had happened in the past—she could hardly believe it—twenty minutes or so.

She kept her gaze firmly on his as she said, "You said something about someone named Mel—Mela—Meli—" she fought to remember the unusual name.

Tightness flickered across Sebastian's jaw, but he nodded. "Melusine." The way her name dropped flat off his tongue, like a burning hot coal flung away, told Lacey whoever the woman was, she wasn't a good memory.

"Okay. Why did you think I know her? Why did you"— dang it, her voice was shaking again—"accuse me of *colluding* with her? I've never even heard of her before tonight."

Sebastian closed his eyes, then opened them. Lacey's breath caught at his expression. A turmoil of emotions raged across it. The most prominent one was burning shame.

"Lacey." His voice was a stark whisper, but it was as steady as his gaze. "The words I said to you were inexcusable. They were terrible, cruel, and truly vile. I am deeply sorry I said those things. I am also sorry that I could even think you would ever betray me like that." His breath shuddered into him in a deep inhale. "I have nothing but my own ego to blame. She was a woman I allowed to get close to me. One I thought actually cared for me."

Something almost like a deep, rumbling growl rolled beneath his words. Like the sound an angry dragon might make. Fascinated despite the craziness of the whole situation, Lacey kept quiet and waited for him to go on.

"She led me on in thinking that it was me she cared for, but in actuality it was my wealth. Specifically, my dragon wealth. A hoard, we call it." Sebastian's black hair gleamed beneath the moonlight. "She found someone who would buy my treasures from her for a fortune."

At that, Lacey burst out, "Your treasures? But that's stealing. She planned to steal from you so she could profit for herself?" She couldn't keep the outrage from her voice.

Almost tiredly now, as if he had turned over that sort of trust-breaking, heartbreaking thievery in his mind many times, Sebastian nodded. "Indeed. Melusine came from the dragon world, so she well knew the true value of our treasures. She planned from the beginning to dupe me. But it wasn't until she met Malcolm that her plan really fell into place. He had already stolen many of my family's treasures, long ago." His voice darkened again. "She took bits and pieces of my hoard and had Malcolm sell them for vast sums of money. They made the perfect pair. Until I finally realized her duplicity and threw her out."

Oh. "She—she was living here?" Lacey swallowed as the magnitude of what Sebastian had been through became even more clear.

Maria, who still stood beside Lacey, put a comforting hand on her back.

"Yes. It was how she knew about my treasure and could pilfer it. I had allowed her access to my treasure room because I trusted her." The stark coldness of Sebastian's voice said everything.

"Sebastian," Lacey whispered, stricken for him. "I am so sorry. That explains why you—"

But he shook his head. Pride mingled with regret and that deep remorse still present. "No. I allowed my history with her to cloud my judgment with you, even though I knew you were nothing like her. I would not give you the benefit of the doubt earlier, when I saw the hairpin."

It clicked for her then. "The hairpin. I got it from a dealer I often work with. He told me it came from a major dealer in San Francisco. So that was—Malcolm, you called him?"

Sebastian's features were a study in marbled beauty in the moonlit night air. "Yes. And he originally got it from me. Stole it, to be more accurate. Why he gave it to you—well." He shrugged. "That, I do not know."

To Lacey's surprise, and obviously Sebastian's as well, Maria spoke up in a severe tone. "He did it to play a game with you, Señor Sebastian. He is a terrible monster. That is no secret." She nodded, thinning her lips in displeasure and crossing her arms over her chest. "He was very angry that his plan to steal and sell all the Bernal treasure was ruined time and again. All bullies are easy to anger. I think he wanted to make you pay somehow."

After a beat of startled silence, Sebastian nodded. "And I did." The regret shivered through his voice. He looked directly at Lacey again. "I have paid, indeed. By almost losing you."

His words were whispered away by the light breeze. This time, the resulting silence was much longer. The crickets whirred, the owl gently called, and Lacey's mind swirled around as it tried to make sense of everything she'd abruptly learned. It was shocking, thrilling, and preposterous all at once. But she knew, with a soul-deep understanding she couldn't explain but simply accepted, that every single thing she'd just experienced and been told was true.

Frankly, she also knew it was too much for her to handle with any measure of rationale right now.

Very quietly, she said, "I believe everything, Sebastian. And it's all complicated and—and I just want to go home right now." She smiled a little at him, but exhaustion and what she knew had to be some shock combined to make her entire body heavy, her mind beginning to blank out. "I'm sorry, but I just can't process all this right now. Take me home? Please?" But she didn't direct the last part at Sebastian. Instead, she gave a pleading look toward Maria and Ricardo.

There was another short, almost pained silence while they clearly waited for Sebastian's answer. By the tightness on Maria's face, Lacey guessed the older woman would have some sharp words for Sebastian later on. But Sebastian just nodded, murmuring that he would call the pilot to meet them at the plane. His jaw set again as Lacey watched him literally tuck away the pain inside him.

It broke her heart to see. Yet she had to get out of there and just be by herself for a while. Her brain was going to melt down completely if she didn't.

As Maria put her arms around Lacey's waist and gently guided her to the vehicle, Sebastian stepped forward as if to join them. Lacey stopped, shaking her head. She felt almost dizzy as the last bits of leftover adrenaline drained from her body. She had to just get out of here and lie down. At home, by herself.

"I'm so sorry," she whispered to him. "I feel terrible saying this, but I can't. I just want them to take me. Please, Sebastian. Please understand. I really do believe you, but I can't deal with this right now."

With that, she turned and got into the car, closely followed by Maria and, somewhat more slowly, Ricardo. As he pulled away, Ricardo flipped the lights back on.

Sebastian stood in their glare, watching with an expressionless face as Lacey left him.

19

F or the first time in her life, Lacey missed work the next morning. She called in sick, which made her feel vaguely guilty. Her justification was that she *was* sick. Sick to her heart, at least. While she was fairly sure now, after a long, hard sleep, that she wasn't sick in her mind, there was still a vague possibility that she really had dreamed the entire past day. Either way, it would be impossible for her to function at the place owned by the man who had ripped her soul into fifty different pieces.

Gabi still wasn't home, and she hadn't answered Lacey's last text. Really, though, she wasn't even sure what she would say to her best friend.

Hi. So, I had head-banging, world-shaking, life-changing sex with the hottest man on the planet, he took me to his private family ancestral home, showed it off to me, let me into his secret treasure room which I'm pretty sure is literally worth more than Fort Knox, wined me, dined me, and then, oh yeah. This other guy showed up, turned into a dragon, carried me away, dropped me, at which point my sexy man, who was also apparently a dragon, swooped in and saved me. Like, he flew in to save me, because he was, you know, a dragon. The kind with wings that can fly. So I didn't die, but I may have lost my mind. How was your day?

Nope, not so much.

She had to think about it for a while before she could talk to her closest friend in the world about the situation. As for anyone else, absolutely not. Not her parents, who would definitely think she'd lost her mind. She had been so immersed in her grad school network during the last several years that Gabi was the only one with whom she felt truly comfortable sharing information.

Apparently, she wasn't supposed to do that anyway. Because, right. Dragon shifters weren't supposed to exist. No one could know about them. At least, that's what Maria had told her when they drove back to the plane.

The only thing she could really do was shove everything aside and take a break to be certain her mind didn't snap after all.

So she did. She watched TV, but it made her feel like her brain was being dumbed down way too much into a pathetically sheeplike idiocy, so she shut it off.

She decided to go to the beach. Yet when she got there, the sight of all the happy, oblivious families making sand castles and splashing in the waves that rolled up onto shore was so bizarrely normal that she couldn't stand it.

She tried bookstore browsing, going to the other museums in town, even taking a drive up the Angeles Crest Highway to get above the murk of the city and clear her head. As it turned out, being so alone with her thoughts on the winding highway in the mountains was too eerie, so she turned around and just went back to her empty apartment.

Sebastian called once.

Just hearing his deep voice sent that sweet arousal through her body, despite the reality of the situation. But she needed first to be sure of two things.

One, that she could regain her own equilibrium after the chaotic events.

Two, even more importantly, was that she was grappling with the stark fact that she was actually in love with a man who could become a dragon.

"I can't yet," she whispered on the phone to him, before gently ending the call.

He didn't try to reach her again, which was almost more painful than anything that had happened yet.

Midweek, Lacey returned to work after surreptitiously checking on Sebastian's whereabouts. According to the assistant in his office when Lacey called, he was in Europe on business till the end of the week. Lacey hung up without leaving her name. She threw herself back into her work with a frenzied passion that reminded her of her grad school days.

It was hard because everywhere she turned at the Center, she was reminded of him.

She felt a deep yearning for him that she just couldn't shake. He'd said something about her being his mate. She wasn't quite sure she understood what that meant, but she also knew on some deep, primal level it had something to do with her unshakeable knowledge that she was connected to him in a way that went beyond the eroticism, beyond the simple, easy conversation they shared when they were together.

Frankly, being away from him even though by her own choice sliced at her heart more than she would have thought possible after such a short time of realizing the depth of the connection between them.

On Friday, as she left her office fairly late in the evening, her cell phone rang with a number marked *PRIVATE*. Biting her lip, she stared at it for a long moment before steeling herself and answering. To her half disappointment, a female voice answered her tentative greeting.

"Lacey? It's Maria. Maria from Señor Sebastian's household." The woman's voice was hesitant, but Lacey could hear the determination beneath it. "May I say something to you?"

Lacey, who had just gotten into her car in the parking garage, nodded dumbly at the phone before saying, "Yes. Of course."

Without preamble, Maria went on. "I know you do not understand everything. It is expected. But you must know, this is genuine from him." Her voice strengthened. "You have his heart, Lacey. He's a very hard man to know and to love, but he will protect you to the end of your days. He will never forgive himself for how cruelly he yelled at you, but that was only his own pain talking."

Lacey sighed. "I understand that. It all made sense," she added softly. Staring through her windshield at the soft spring rain that was beginning to slide down over the openings of the parking structure, she added, "I forgive him, if that helps. I just —I still don't know what to do with this. I truly can't make sense of it."

In a firm yet kind voice, Maria replied, "You will. See here now, he would kill me if he knew his mamacita had called you."

Despite herself, Lacey had to laugh a little bit.

"But," Maria went on, "I called not just for him. I called for you, too."

Lacey sat motionless as she listened.

"The moment you walked into the house, Lacey, I could see it." Conviction rang through Maria's voice. "You love him just as much as he loves you. Don't lose that just because you don't understand everything. True love is very rare in this world. You were very, very lucky to have found such a thing as your mate."

Her mate. Slowly, the word had begun to seep into her consciousness. She was Sebastian's mate.

Did that mean that he also was hers?

As she drove home, Maria's words bounced around Lacey's

head. The closer she got to the apartment, the more the events of the week and her own churning thoughts since then finally settled inside her.

It was true. Never in her life would she have thought that she, Lacey Whitman from not the wrong side of the tracks but definitely not the right side of town, would achieve as much as she had, with her education and her career. Just thinking of Sebastian, his masculine scent, incredible presence, the amazing trust he had shared with her by letting her into the deepest sanctity of his home which he was his heart, solidified everything in one flashing moment.

Sure, it was crazy. But it was true.

The man she loved was a dragon. A dragon with a past, a dragon who'd been deeply hurt, a dragon who was powerful and vulnerable and utterly stunning all at once.

And she could handle it.

As lightness suddenly buoyed her, she pulled into a parking space at home and darted up the stairs to her door. The first real smile she'd managed in a week spread across her face as she suddenly realized she couldn't wait for him to come back from his current travels so she could tell him that she was the one who was actually the fool.

But at the top of the stairs leading to the outside door of her building, she stopped short, staring.

Sebastian waited for her. Tall, lean, exuding his inexorable power, he peeled away from where he'd been leaning on the wall beside the door and stepped toward her.

Lacey's breath caught his dark, spicy scent as it reached her, sparking that little electric snap she felt every time she was near him. His face was open. Vulnerable. More raw than she'd ever seen it before.

She felt abruptly tongue-tied with shyness.

He was here. Sebastian had showed up at her humble little apartment, by himself. Lacey opened her mouth but literally didn't know what to say. He stared back at her, just as silent.

Finally gathering some of her wits about her, she simply said, "Do you want to come in?"

He nodded, the motion sending a coal black strand of hair sliding across his forehead. Lacey swallowed hard, opened the door, and gestured for him to come in. Once inside, they stood in the little living room the front door opened up to, still staring at each other. Lacey felt a brief flicker of embarrassment at how tiny and not particularly interesting, although quite clean, her apartment was in comparison to his elegant hacienda.

But Sebastian didn't seem to notice anything except her. He swallowed and licked his lips, but didn't say anything.

With a stunning jolt, Lacey realized that Sebastian Antonio Bernal, world-famous billionaire, self-assured mogul, and also apparently badass dragon shifter, was nervous.

Because of her.

The realization blasted her with such a sense of wonder, her lips suddenly curved up. She let her purse and her soft leather work briefcase slide down her arms to land gently on the ground, and took a step toward him. Another step, then she suddenly stopped cold again.

Tears were shimmering in Sebastian's gorgeous, velvety black-brown eyes. Though unshed, they were there. An expression of equal wonder bracketed his face. Finally, he spoke, his voice just barely dipping into a ragged edge.

"Lacey. There are so many things I need to tell you. So many things I want to share with you. It all begins by trusting you, implicitly."

The rawness on his face, the vulnerability, made her heart thump out of rhythm.

His voice was soft. "You are the treasure of my heart. My beautiful, amazing treasure of a mate." Sebastian blinked as he said that, his smile growing even bigger. "I think I knew that from the first moment I saw you. You dazzled me even then, but I didn't know what to do with it."

Lacey took another step toward him, tendrils of pure joy starting to dance through her body. "Sebastian, you don't have to say anything else," she said just before he opened his mouth again. "I don't understand it either, but you're right. In fact," and she suddenly felt wetness pooling in her eyes and thickening her tongue, "I think you're actually *my* treasure. I want nothing more than to be able to spend the rest of our lives together, discovering together what exactly that means."

With a groan that rumbled through Lacey from head to toe, Sebastian closed the gap between them, put his arms around her, and captured her lips with his in a long, deep kiss that melted away the rest of the world.

He pulled back just enough to trace her cheek with his finger as he said in that deep, wildly sexy voice, "This is only the beginning, Lacey. Thank you," he whispered, his voice filled with intense conviction.

"But you aren't simply my mate, Lacey," Sebastian added. He pulled back to suddenly, gracefully drop to one knee.

Lacey's hands clapped over her mouth as she stared at him, although she could feel her smile breaking out from behind her fingertips.

"I am also hopeful you will do me enormous honor of becoming my wife." Sebastian held up a small black velvet box, which he opened.

Lacey gasped through her fingers. Really, at this point she should be used to gorgeous golden objects sparkling in her eyes every time she was around Sebastian. But this one was exceptional. A stunning diamond set into the gold band caught the light with its facets. Nodding her head, she sputtered out, "Yes, yes, yes!"

Through a new barrage of overjoyed tears, she reached her hand out for him to take. First, though, he gently pulled the ring from the box, and lifted it toward her to she could see it more closely.

"Look into it," he said, the brilliant smile on his face she was sure matching the one on hers. "Tell me what you see."

Lacey peered at it, blinking furiously to clear the tears from her eyes. Deep within the facets of the diamond, she could see the beautiful, shadowed outline of a dragon's head.

"Yes," she said, then almost impatiently thrust forward her ring finger for him to slip the ring on it, which he did with a new bout of joyous, free laughter. "Yes, Sebastian. My very own dragon shifter treasure."

The End

Thank you for reading *Dazzled!* Lacey and Sebastian were really interesting to write about, and they were a great way for me to start exploring their fascinating world.

What's next for the **Dragon Mates**? Kai & Gabi's story in ***THRILLED.*** Turn the page to read it.

THRILLED

Loss froze his heart. She is either his salvation—or his total destruction

1

Gabriela Santos stretched her arms straight overhead, tipped her face up to the gloriously perfect day, and let out a yodeling war whoop.

"This is awesome!" She yipped and howled again, head flung back in joy. "This is officially the best day of my entire life!"

Laughter rippled out behind her as the crew chuckled at her antics. They were used to Gabi's crazy ways by now. She was never actually crazy on the job. No, she worked damn hard and pulled her weight as much as any of them. She was very, very good at what she did.

But there was one thing Gabi did better than her beloved job. She lived her whole life in the most exuberant manner she could, taking no prisoners and enjoying every single second of it. She and the crew had worked together for several years now, since her grad school days. Watching her standing on the deck, clad in a dive suit from the waist down and a sensible yet still cute swim tank on top, screaming her head off into the breeze and laughing like a banshee, was nothing new for them.

Besides. California University's maritime archaeology department, the jokingly self-dubbed Ancients Quest Explo-

139

ration Team, had just made one of the biggest discoveries of the century. Nobody blamed her for being excited. She simply channeled the energy of the entire team.

"Okay, Gabs. New memory card is in. We're all set." Everson Booth, the shrewd leader of the exploration team as well as Gabi's boss and mentor, flashed her a thumbs up as he handed her the underwater camera she'd been using to record their major find.

Stupidly, she hadn't paid attention to the memory card before she and her dive partner went down on their first dive that morning. After the initial overwhelming shock and joy that their suspicions had been correct, that the surprisingly intact remains of the Santa Maria were nestled atop ocean ledges many nautical miles distant from where history had always insisted the shipwreck had occurred, she'd been so fascinated as she took picture after picture that it had practically devastated her when the *memory card full* message started flashing.

She was usually more prepared than not, but she'd been too excited this morning. Everyone had. She and her dive partner, Shane, had had to come back up to the boat so she could get a new memory card. At least they'd used the time well. An impromptu, thoroughly ridiculous dance of overjoyed excitement had gripped the entire crew for several minutes once Gabi and Shane got back on board. They mightily entertained a few seagulls who watched their antics with cocked heads and quizzical expressions.

"Definitely ready," she answered Everson with a grin. She was always ready to go back into the hidden depths of the Pacific Ocean.

And continue filming. Her smile practically ripped her face in two as she wrestled the top part of her dive suit back on, zipping up and donning her mask and tank.

Everson, a seasoned oceanic explorer who had been a second father figure and definitely a strong shoulder to lean on for Gabi during the stressful past few months, smiled. Then he put a bit of steel into his voice as he admonished both her and Shane. "Take it easy down there. You guys are excited. Take a deep breath first, and remember to follow protocol. No mistakes, no problems just because we're excited." Raising his head, he cast the rest of the crew a firm look. "The rest of you too. Focus on your job, record the data, and pay attention. Liesl," he added, tipping his chin at the willowy blonde, "keep a sharp eye out. The last thing we need is visitors."

Liesl nodded solemnly from her lookout post at the research vessel's prow as Gabi got her mask and tank appropriately situated with the help of one of the crew members. The Santa Maria was the holy grail for underwater archaeologists and commercial treasure hunters the world over. After she'd sunk in 1702, legends about the vast fortune in gold and jewels she'd carried with her to the bottom of the sea had persisted throughout the centuries. Careful research by many people over the years confirmed a genuine treasure had been lost with her. Modern estimates conservatively put the value at around $200 million.

As of today, Ancients Quest had first dibs on the massive find. Even so, they needed to keep this tightly under wraps until they were ready to make an official announcement to the world. There were definitely some unethical modern treasure hunters out there who would swoop in and take it for themselves if they so much as got a whiff of the site location before the team could accurately catalogue the basics of their find, then announce it to the world.

From this point onward, it was a race against the clock.

Pushing away the deep twinge of guilt that stabbed Gabi at the deadly seriousness in Everson's voice, she gave her equipment a final check before exchanging a thumbs up with Shane as a signal to one another and the crew that they were ready to go back down. Seating herself on the low edge of the boat, she gracefully flipped herself backward into the cool embrace of the ocean. Moments later, Shane plunged in near her.

As she entered the water, Gabi pushed away all thoughts except two. One, she was part of the team that had just made one of the biggest discoveries in nautical history. Two, she was back in her favorite place on the planet. The ocean.

She began her descent back down to the shipwreck just fifty feet below, glancing over at Shane's bubbled form as he did the same. Gabi allowed the usual goosebumps of joy to wash through her body. She'd been a daredevil and a thrill seeker since she was a toddler, creating many premature gray hairs for her parents as she grew up.

But nothing compared to the wild, electrifying charge of deep sea diving. There was an entire world beneath the waves. A world few ever actually got to experience. The exploration, the knowledge that she walked a tightrope of potential disaster if anything should go wrong with her equipment, her crew, or the environment, fueled Gabi like nothing else.

Yeah, it was a little sick. But it was also the only way she felt truly alive anymore.

"This is the best!" she said to Shane over the voice communication built into their expensive, university-owned helmets.

He nodded as they headed down, his flippers propelling him through the water as easily as Gabi's. "Best damn thing in the world," he said. "Well, second best. You know me. I'm a dog."

Gabi laughed, buoyed by the waters, the rush of the hunt for antiquities, the sheer truth to what he'd said. "You and me both, buddy."

Shane shook his head, though she could tell he chuckled too. He and Gabi were both affectionately known as the hound dogs of the crew. The two of them had never hooked up with each other, partially because neither was attracted to the other and partially because they both knew that would be the death knell of a smoothly operating dive. And, of course, because

Everson had only half-jokingly threatened them both with bodily harm if they even thought about it. But they sure had a hell of a lot of fun comparing notes with one another the days following the casual hookups.

A hookup was the only thing Gabi would ever allow in her life again. Her ex-husband was a sad bastard who'd proved to her that serious relationships were for fools only. She didn't much care that her very Catholic family was pretty sure she was going to go straight to hell if she never got married again.

This was her damn life, and she liked it.

Well. She did care what her *abuela,* her grandmother, thought. Despite her intentions as she'd entered the water that she would focus only on the moment, another quick emotion stabbed at her for a moment. Paralyzing fear and worry for her grandmother. Setting her jaw, she shoved all other thoughts away again. Time to work.

As they reached the stunning old shipwreck, Gabi's breath caught again as it loomed up before them through the murk of the seawater. Listing to one side, half caught in a shallow, narrow underwater canyon, the Santa Maria was in startlingly good shape. The centuries in salt water had done some damage, but it was far less than most ships of her age. The original mechanism for the sinking, as Gabi and Shane had discovered on their earlier dive that morning, was a gaping wound low on the side of the ship that neatly went in one side and out the other.

Nautical history had always said that the Santa Maria had sunk during a violent storm. But their find threw that accepted thesis into question. It looked as if the ship actually had been attacked by pirates instead. That made sense, of course. If pirates had made an attempt to nab the ship and its loot, but then inadvertently sunk the ship and not been able to retrieve any of its treasures themselves, they certainly wouldn't have wanted the knowledge of their own poor sea battle skills to get around. They probably simply sailed away and never said a word of it to anyone.

Leaving the Santa Maria lost in her watery grave for so long.

Gabi and Shane hadn't seen any evidence yet of the deceased sailors, although she was prepared for the sight of bones when they started to explore the interior more. The enormous holes from what presumably was a cannonball meant that she would have sunk far too quickly for there to have been any survivors. While it was possible that some of the crew had escaped in lifeboats, history had never recorded the comments of any of them. Without a doubt, most if not all of them had been trapped and gone down with the ship.

It was a terrifying death. Yet the thought of it didn't frighten Gabi in the least. She'd been born with some sort of crazy immunity against the fears that kept so many people trapped in unexplored lives. She pretty much preferred to live on the reckless edge of danger, because nine point nine times out of ten, she went into situations well-prepared enough to know when she needed to stop pushing and just get the hell out.

Gabi was a big fan of keeping herself alive in order to enjoy yet another day on the wild edge of adventure.

As they approached the beautiful hulk, slowing their smooth pace in the fairly still waters, Shane said into the helmet's mic, "Circling to the east, begin recording now." His words carried not only to Gabi, but to the crew above as he flicked on the recording switch. He was the official recorder on this dive. Gabi's words could be heard only by herself and Shane, as the recording device on the boat could only effectively capture one dive helmet mic at a time.

Shane swam to the left of Gabi, his own camera up and recording both video and audio that were transmitting back to the crew on the boat far above them. He began cataloging what he saw as he went along, his voice moving into the cadence of official notation. Gabi slowly drifted her way along the edge of the boat on its western side.

She reached out her fingers, encased in her suit's glove because the cool Pacific water was too cold for her bare skin. Very gently, she touched the side of the ship. Barnacled, substantially sized for the era, its presence poured into Gabi's soul that usual rush of both adrenaline and certainty.

This was exactly what she was meant to be doing with her life. She was literally and figuratively in her element right now. It was a high almost better than sex.

Okay, fine. It was a high better than pretty much any sex of her life, even though she'd had some pretty epic experiences. But no guy could top this sort of rush, no matter how talented he was in the bedroom. This was her ambrosia.

Tilting her camera up, Gabi continued to drift along the side of the ship, gently propelling herself away from it again so she could capture more of it with her camera. There had been a bright scatter of coins over the sea ledges beside the ship that she'd noticed almost immediately during their first dive.

It almost certainly meant the complete treasure was still within the ship. The team had to be rigorously scientific about this and carefully record everything. Gabi had never been well blessed with patience. It was half killing her right now to be thoroughly professional and not just dive straight into the enormous hole inside of the ship and start looking for the gold and jewels.

Although it was something most of her crew mates didn't share, she'd always secretly been thrilled by the actual treasure hunting part of underwater archaeology almost as much as by her desire to preserve history for future generations.

Actual treasure hunters weren't very well-regarded in the academic world. As a teaching assistant and associate managing director of the university's exploration laboratory on Catalina Island just off the coastline of Los Angeles, Gabi had a hell of an image to upkeep. Swallowing hard against the surge of conflicting images and thoughts that once again managed to briefly shove themselves past her control, she quietly floated along, occasionally paddling her suit's fins as she recorded the ship.

A glint of something catching the light shimmering down through the darkening water beneath her drew her gaze downward. Widening her eyes, she flippered herself down to a small shelf just beside the listing hull of the ship. Something small glinted there, tucked beneath waving, glassy green fronds of giant kelp. Reaching out to the ledge, Gabi felt around beneath the fronds until her hand closed around a small object about the size of a half dollar, but considerably heavier. Bringing her closed fist up to her face, she uncurled her fingers.

A brightly sparkling gold nugget lay in the gloved palm of her hand.

"Wow," she breathed. As a trained scientist, she looked critically at the gold nugget, wondering about its provenance and historical significance with a dispassionate eye. As a girl who'd been fascinated by old tales of high seas battles over fortunes from faraway lands that her grandmother had told her in vivid detail throughout her childhood, however, she had to admit to a very unprofessional kick of excitement at the sight.

And as a person who was out of options, desperate to do anything that would save the life of someone she loved, a thrill of huge relief mingled with jittery, queasy nerves shocked through her at the knowledge of what she was about to do.

"What's up?" Shane's voice was clear through the helmet's speakers.

"I think I found a piece of the treasure the Santa Maria carried."

Shane's low whistle sounded in her ears. The Santa Maria's lost treasure was legendary. It was also the main reason the research crew was keeping their expedition on the down-low.

Gabi's chest constricted as she gazed at the small piece of

both fortune and history in her hand. Firmly, she pushed aside her doubts. Her team might never forgive her, but her own conscience would.

"I'm cataloging," she said. Her camera, however, hung down by her side. Glancing up to be sure no one watched her, even though she knew Shane was on the other side of the ship, she very carefully slipped the shining little chunk into the inside of her glove before resolutely turning her back on the place she'd found it. Leaving it undocumented. Unrecorded. And as far as anyone on earth knew, untouched.

She felt sick. It went against every single thing Gabi believed in. Every single thing she'd been trained in as a protector of the past. Every single piece of paper she'd signed prior to joining this crew.

It was also crucial proof she needed in order to save the one person in the world who meant more to Gabi than life itself. The one for whom she would do anything in world. Even jeopardize her own morals and her career.

Forcing down her emotional upset, Gabi slowly swam back to the ship, the nugget making a sharp, accusing lump against her finger where it was hidden in her glove.

2

Kai Long barreled through the water, diving far down into the black depths, then using powerful strokes of his wings and tail to catapult himself back up to the lightening surface of the ocean. He shot straight up out of the water, closing his eyes against the brightness of the sun glancing across the open miles of ocean as he spread his wings out into a soaring dive through the air before gracefully curving into an arc back downward. Pinioning his wings against him, he dove back into the gorgeous, salty depths.

He could feel his gold, calling to him with ever-increasing strength as he got closer to it. Its presence infused him with a magnetic energy and awareness that would sustain him for weeks.

It was nothing like the actual strength he should be at, though.

As he sliced back down into the coolness of the water, startling a pod of dolphins and narrowly missing the flank of a killer whale, Kai shook his head once, hard. The memory of his true power faded every day. What he experienced now every time he was near his hoard seemed to him to be just as potent as it had once been. Yet intellectually, he knew better. He wasn't at full strength. He never would be until he could finally figure out how to break the death spell that encased the mingled hoard that had once belonged to both him and his mate.

A tiny shard of pain bit at him as he thought of her. It was much fainter than it used to be. But it was still there. Opening his mouth, he unleashed a bellow of sheer rage and frustration. It reverberated throughout the water. Entire schools of nearby fish turned as one and fled into the distance as the sea's most incredible predator raced through it, throwing all those damned emotions into the depths so they would leave him be.

So they would allow him the blissful luxury of being unable to feel anything at all.

Mouth still open in a terrifying grimace, Kai swooped down into the blackening depths that few creatures could withstand. Yet the pressure hardly bothered him. Water dragons were made for this environment. This place was his natural home.

Several moments more through the darkness, then he turned and swam upward. Toward the surface of the ocean, where light came through again. His dragon form actually had an excellent mix of vision as well as sonar that helped him navigate in the deepest, darkest depths of the sea. But his treasure was located in more shallow waters. Besides, the land was going to start angling up again in a moment.

As he followed the contours of the underwater valleys and canyons, some of them more sizable than the largest ones upon dry land found anywhere on earth, he felt the sweet nothingness surround him with its soothing balm of quietude and peace.

After another round of yelling with his brother that morning on the phone—yelling *by* his brother, really, who just got more and more incensed as Kai stayed calm and non-reactive on the other end of the line—he'd known he needed this trip to visit his hoard. It had been nearly a month, because he'd just spent the past several weeks in Hawaii. Hence the reason for his brother being all pissed off at him anyway.

When Kai was in Hawaii, his brother expected him to do some work for the family company, Long Worldwide Shipping. The fact that Kai had unequivocally reminded his brother that he no longer held a controlling share in the company nor any job title nor any position on the board, so he didn't have to do a damn thing about it, had definitely not helped matters in soothing over the chasm that had developed between him and his arrogantly bossy older sibling during the past five years.

As the feeling of nothingness threatened to dissipate at thoughts of his brother, Kai banked hard to the left, spun in a circular torpedo motion—and nearly crashed into a great white shark.

He instinctively flung open his enormous wings and dragged his giant front claws through the water to slow his motion. As the water exploded around him into millions of shattering ripples of seawater, briefly obscuring his vision, Kai opened his mouth in a fearsome dragon version of a smile.

Hell, yeah, he muttered deep in his mind.

Sharks were always fun to play with. He carried extra pent-up steam around with him today anyway, after that phone call. A good underwater brawl would expend some of his energy. This shark was enormous, easily a thirty-footer. She wasn't looking to hurt Kai, and he knew it. He was the apex predator of the ocean anyway. Nor would he really hurt her. A little pretend game of hunter and hunted, though? No problem. He often played with the ocean's denizens, always leaving both parties unscathed.

But as the water settled and Kai's vision returned to its normal excellent acuity far beneath the waves, he immediately changed his mind. Damn it. The shark was injured. A large hook stuck out of her mouth. He also now saw she had an awkwardness of motion that meant she was in no shape to play, let alone defend her life if Kai had actually meant to attack.

Kai swore with savage abandon inside against the most terrible parts of humanity that existed on this miserable planet. The terrible kinds of people that thought nothing of harming every single creature in it, including this shark that was protected by law against being fished in these waters. Very slowly, he unfurled his wings all the way while gently curving his claws toward and below the shark as he gave a light snap of his tail to smoothly and quickly propel himself toward the creature.

Being a shark, the most feared animal in the oceans that humans, at least, knew about, not to mention that sharks just weren't possessed of high intelligence, the creature didn't react as Kai's far larger dragon shape drew near and caught it up with his powerful front legs and claws. Kai instantly sensed how weak she actually was as well, clearly to do with the blood loss streaming in a diffused reddish cloud now visible in the settling water.

Damn. Even if he could remove the hook, the shark was liable to either bleed out or attract other sharks that wouldn't think twice about chomping down on their fellow creature. They would finish off what an illegal human hunter hadn't quite been able to do.

Kai paused for a bare moment to consider the options. Before he even finished his thought process, he pulled his front legs close to his body, cradled the injured shark close to his chest, and shot off due east.

Straight for his underwater gold hoard, twenty nautical miles away. His slowly waning powers would be more acute when he was near it. That way, he could give the shark a fighting chance.

The only chance she would have.

Moments later, as he neared the shipwreck, Kai felt the compelling draw of his hoard reach out to him through the water. Like a slow but powerfully rolling tide, it eased along the currents to surround and fill him with strength. With clarity.

And with the limited yet genuine power to heal.

The broken yet mostly intact hull of the ship that housed Kai's treasure hoard came into view through the brightening gloom of the rippling blue-greens of the water. As he blasted closer toward the old wreck, he anticipated the incoming swell of energy that would carry him through the next month. Giving him more time to figure out how to break the spell and be able to receive the full powers that his gold gave him.

First, though, he had a wounded creature to help. Hovering in the water, his wings fluttering just a bit to keep him in one spot as his tail gently swayed to buoy him against the calm yet ceaseless motion of the ocean, Kai unfolded his front legs just a bit so he could concentrate on the shark. For long moments, Kai hovered as motionless as he could in the water. He drew upon the mingled powers of his hoard and his own legacy as a water dragon to heal this creature that shared space with him in the ocean depths.

Deep concentration finally bore fruit. With an abrupt wrench, the shark jettisoned herself out of Kai's loose grasp. She swam away through the shimmering murk of the water, her body a large grayish-white blur. Completely healed.

Satisfied, Kai turned his attention back to his ship. A sudden shadow overhead flashed across him. Startled, he glanced upward. He expected a whale, or perhaps another pod of dolphins to be skimming their way through the water above.

His heart about catapulted out of its giant chest as the unmistakable shape of a boat barely fifty feet above shivered on the surface of the water. Kai snapped his head back around to look at the ship again, a shocking dread sending massive amounts of adrenaline streaming through his system.

A tiny figure bobbed in front of him, scuba fins descending from two legs gently swimming at the bottom of the black clad body. The force of his approach sent a slight wave through the water, and the figure turned toward him.

A woman. A human woman, a diver. Right beside the long-lost shipwreck that kept his gold hoard captive. Staring right at him, camera in one hand, a piece of his own gold held in her other hand, as he hovered not twenty feet from her in his dragon shape.

Clearly able to see him despite the fact that he should be utterly invisible to her human eyes.

A FLASH of movement to the right caught Gabi's eye. She quickly turned her head, camera coming with her. Grinning with delight, she watched as a colorful school of scythe butterflyfish waved and danced as if one, playing in the waving giant bladder kelp that grew off the ledges by the wreck. She filmed the fish for a few moments, enjoying the flashes of yellow and black as they darted around. Just as quickly, they were gone. Turning her attention back to the Santa Maria, she continued her official work.

She could hardly wait to tell Lacey about this. Her best friend, a museum curator who far preferred dry land yet still was always excited to hear about Gabi's adventures, was the only living soul outside the crew's university department that knew how close Gabi and the team had been to this discovery. Well, and her abuela. It would be about a week before Gabi even talked to Lacey, because when Gabi worked, she stayed really focused and didn't communicate much with anyone, except her family. But damn. She'd have an awful lot to share with both her confidantes when she was back on the mainland.

"Heading down the masts, checking out the hole on the northwest corner." Shane's voice murmured in her ear. Gabi responded so he knew she'd heard.

Gently, she let herself continue to drift along the side of

the ship. It was in amazingly good shape for something so long settled on the ocean floor. Part of the team's quest was to figure out why. Most ancient shipwrecks were in pretty bad condition. The Santa Maria looked like she had been sunk a mere decade ago, rather than the more than three hundred years she'd rested in her watery site.

Camera still steady in her hand, Gabi zoomed in a bit on the wood of the ship's side. The vessel had been traveling from the islands of Hawaii to the California coast bearing trade items. But since it originally had been made in New England, Gabi knew the wood used for it was most likely some type of oak. Oak was sturdy—but it was also prone to rotting in a long-term undersea situation, particularly if it had not been treated with one of the high quality, water-insoluble resins of the time. But even treated wood should show far more sign of rot and damage than did the Santa Maria after all her years here.

Then how, she mused yet again as she stared at the nearly perfect wreck before her in the water, *did it stay so—*

A sudden, enormous movement to her left yanked her attention away from the ship.

For the next thirty seconds, Gabi's life went into a slow-motion reel. As she swung her head toward the movement, expecting another large school of fish, the hand holding the camera dropped loosely to her side, her fingers releasing the camera in pure shock as she gaped at the giant sea creature staring at her from merely a few lengths away.

Shimmering aqua, green, and white all mixed together to create a luminous hide covering a creature Gabi could only describe as being a—a dragon.

There's a dragon. I'm looking at a dragon. A real dragon. The rational part of her mind thought the words quite calmly. Her heart, though, threatened to explode its way out of her body.

A long, sinuous neck ridged with spikes that glimmered faintly in the water ended in a large, wedge-shaped head. It frankly seemed just as surprised as she was. Gigantic green eyes that were about the size of her own face gazed at her with a multifaceted beauty that captured her even in her dreamlike shock.

Focused intelligence stared back at her from those eyes.

It's looking at me. It knows it's looking at me. The same conversational tone of her own mind echoed in Gabi's head as she stared at the stunning creature.

It almost shimmered in the water, powerfully resplendent and jaw-droppingly immense at the same time. She somehow instinctively sensed it was male. Gigantic wings, nearly translucent in the membrane-thin sections between the long, beautiful joints, suddenly unfurled to each side, sending waves toward her. Gabi startled backward through the shimmering green water until she smacked into the side of the Santa Maria.

As she stared, her body somewhat sliding down the ship because she'd stopped the gentle paddling with her feet, the creature abruptly turned and shot off like an arrow through the waters. The long tail and powerful hind legs propelled it away so quickly it vanished from sight almost immediately.

After a long, unblinking moment despite the fact that her vision was now obscured by the cloud of silt and bubbles left behind by the creature—which somewhere in her scientific mind she vaguely realized meant it also must be able to breathe air—Gabi experimented with her voice.

"Um, Shane?" She sounded surprisingly calm. "Did you see that?"

There was a pause before his voice sounded in her ear over the mic. "See what? You find some more artifacts?" Eagerness strengthened his voice.

"No." Damn, her voice sounded stupidly chipper. "But, I did see some sort of unidentified ocean life. You haven't seen anything?"

A longer pause, then a sudden movement to her right

badly jolted her. Shane swam around the side of the ship toward her.

Wow. Despite her calm voice, she definitely was a little freaked out. Not to mention quietly, immensely thrilled as the truth settled into her more and more with each passing second.

Shane's head swiveled as he looked around the area. "I don't see anything. Was it a shark, maybe?"

He didn't sound worried. Gabi wouldn't have been either, if it had just been a shark. The general human populace tended to well overestimate the dangers sharks posed to divers, even the feared great white shark. She actually loved sharks. They were cool creatures.

What she had seen most definitely had not been a Carcharodon carcharias, or any other type of Selachimorpha. She'd seen a—something like a Draco Volans?

Yeah. A dragon. But one that seemed to be able to fly through water rather than air. And it was a real one. A freaking gigantic one.

"Definitely not a shark," she answered Shane in what was still a calm voice. "But I sort of dropped my camera. Help me find it?"

Grumbling good-naturedly under his breath, the sound a bit staticky in Gabi's ears, Shane helped her look down along the bottom of where the ship rested partially on the ledge. Dammit. The camera had been dropped into the canyon below the ship. There was no way they'd be able to find it, not without a substantial search.

Gabi looked at Shane. "How's your camera? You having any better luck than I am today?" *Just stay calm,* she sternly advised herself. If she could just focus on mundane things like work, she could ignore the fact that she'd just seen a dragon.

The part of her that had been raised on the utterly serious stories her grandmother had always told her about spirits and ghosts and old legends was threatening to rise up and overwhelm the methodical side that she'd studied so hard for many years to learn to use overall.

The part of her which knew without a doubt that every old story her abuela had ever told her was actually real.

Later. Later, she could carefully assess what had just happened. She could confirm that she had just seen one of the legends come to life. For now, though, she had to be a scientist. A scientist who had stupidly just lost her camera.

And who had just seen a real live water dragon swimming in the Pacific Ocean.

3

"**C**ome here often, sailor?"

Throaty, somewhat drunk little giggles followed the words. Kai couldn't help but smile at the girl who had just uttered that terrible pick up line. She was attractive enough. Compact, busty, blonde hair down to her ass, clearly looking for some playtime below decks, so to speak. Normally, he would have had no problem saying yes to her. Agreeing to dance and booze for a little bit before enjoying a night of pleasure.

But tonight he was on a mission. Tonight, he was only looking for one woman.

Too bad he had no idea what the hell she looked like. He just knew she wasn't this girl.

"Sorry, sweetheart," he said, giving her a lazy grin as he checked her out, much to her delight. "Hate to say it, but I'm waiting for someone else tonight. Maybe another time?"

Another fit of giggles had the girl nodding. She scrawled her name and number down on a bar napkin before leaning forward to tuck it into the front pocket of his pants, her fingers lingering just a little too long as she planted a kiss on his cheek.

She breathed into his ear, "Anytime, sailor. I'm on the island all week."

Kai waggled his fingers at her as she drunkenly wobbled back to her friends, tossing him another look over her shoulder that almost sent her plummeting as she stumbled over her heels. He chuckled a bit, but it was in pure understanding. That was his type of girl. Stumbles like that were how he ended some nights himself, half the time.

Okay, more than half the time.

With a quick frown, he banished the thoughts to that blank place he'd found as his dragon earlier today, diving and swimming in his beloved ocean. His only allowable focus at the moment was to find the woman who'd seen him underwater. The woman who had seen him in his dragon shape. That should not have happened. He'd automatically been cloaking himself, as all dragon shifters did in their wild forms. They were invisible to the human eye. Yet it had been extremely obvious that she realized what she was looking at in the long moment before he finally came to his senses, turned tail, and swam faster than hell away from the strange woman.

The woman who'd not only seen him, but had been poking around *his* treasure. And also actually holding a piece of it.

Kai still was shocked and fascinated on multiple levels. He hadn't been able to touch his treasure himself for the past five years. Not since the spell. He'd also been under the distinct impression that no one else would be able to touch it either. Every member of the Long family had come with him to the hoard, each one trying to get to it and pull it out themselves to see if there was a simple way to break the spell. No luck.

They then brought down beneath the waves some of the human members of the fealty family that had willingly and lovingly served the Longs for millennia to see if they could touch the treasure themselves. Fealty families were composed of humans that were blessed with longer, healthier, just a touch more magical lives than the usual human. Just as trusted as a dragon shifter, the human family members that ferociously and protectively served the Long family would never betray a dragon shifter. In fact, they would do anything, including give their own lives, to protect the Longs. Not that dragon shifters need that much protection. Usually.

Despite everyone's best efforts, no one was able to touch Kai's treasure hoard. It was as if some sort of invisible force field pulsed around it, repelling them when it only should have repelled any others who were not a part of his family. A force field that had somehow been set, they finally realized, by the last-minute death spell that had bound the hoard upon his mate's untimely demise as she tried to protect it from thieves five years ago.

Kai had not allowed any members of the Long's fealty family to serve him after the horrible incident. He'd traveled alone for so many years, aimlessly roaming the planet in his dragon form, that he'd had no real need of them. At least, that was his excuse. If he were ruthlessly truthful with himself, he knew it was simply because he could no longer endure stark reminders of his loss, in the form of people around him who had known and grieved her as well.

After his initial period of mingled shock, mourning, and numbness, Kai had finally reached the grim conclusion that even if he couldn't touch his own treasure, the very spell that repelled them all still would ensure its safety, as their own spells had for centuries. No one could ever find the shipwreck. The family had been very careful to alter historical documents to indicate that the shipwreck had occurred far from where everyone else thought it did. Everyone thought it had been sunk by a mighty storm, coming to rest at the very bottom of the deep ocean, hundreds of miles off the coast. In actuality, the shipwreck lay very close off the shore of Santa Catalina Island.

Despite the initial upset that the shipwreck had caused in Long family ancestors, it eventually was deemed perhaps one of the safest places to keep some of their treasure hoard. No better place could ever protect it, especially with each member of the Long family placing a tiny bit of personal power into the additional blocking spell that never let the shipwreck show up on any modern scanner or even to casual human eyes, should any diver ever come to the area. The wreck was visible only as shadows to the naked eye from either the air or surface of the water.

Except that now, it was no longer a secret. Kai wasn't sure yet exactly what that would mean, but it couldn't be good.

The babble of the bar and its smells made him both wince and wrinkle his nose a bit. He usually liked it here. Tonight, however, it felt like a necessary evil he had to endure in order to find the woman who had been able to get so close to his spelled hoard. Kai had no idea how she had not only found his shipwreck, been able to see him, and most importantly been able to handle part of his personal treasure hoard. But he certainly intended to find out.

An odd sensation had shivered through him when her fingers, even though encased in her dive gloves, softly caressed his gold. He'd felt as if she'd reached into his own heart and very gently touched it. As if she were touching the most amazing thing she'd ever encountered in her life. The shock upon shock of the moment had so disoriented him that he fled. His compass was off about that, too. Kai Long never ran from anything.

Wanna bet? The darkly angry tone of his older brother slid into his head, challenging his thoughts. Snarling to himself, Kai refocused on the bar.

Even though it was a Tuesday, it was also summertime on Catalina. Any night of the week this time of year, the place hopped with frenetic, sexy energy. He carefully looked at every party that tumbled through the doors as he sat at the bar, nursing his whiskey sour as he watched for the dive crew to come in and celebrate their find.

Being not just well-known with the island locals but well-connected had almost immediately led Kai to the California University's maritime archeology program and its exploratory dive team, which he'd known about for years. He always shook his head at the team's nickname: Ancients Quest. Sounded more like a reality TV show than an academic research group. While they weren't being public about what they were doing, there was no doubt it was them. They had a lab on the island and probably spent more time diving in these local waters than almost any others in the world. If anyone had a chance of ever stumbling on the wreck, it could be them.

Kai had a secret weapon that he used to check up on the details of the team. He didn't typically use his position at the Institute to nose around the potentially nefarious doings of dive teams, for the simple fact that they pretty much never were nefarious. But earlier today, he'd made a trip to the office he didn't spend much time in and went through certain records. His sleuthing uncovered a few things. The names of the dive team members, and their stated purpose for the dive.

Their stated purpose had nothing to do with where he'd inadvertently discovered them earlier today. Something nefarious was definitely afoot.

The only others in the world who might possibly have been able to find the Santa Maria, masking spell notwithstanding, would be other dragons, or commercial treasure hunters. Kai knew the strength of the Long family spells were too strong for other dragons to break, so he dismissed that thought. As for commercial treasure hunters, it would only have happened if they'd gotten exceptionally lucky and stumbled upon the ship's actual resting spot. He checked up on every commercial team on the planet, which numbered very few. Not a single one of them had a female diver at the moment. But the academic Ancients Quest team did. Two divers, one shipboard operations. From the names he'd dug out from all their signed paperwork, he wasn't quite sure which one might be the woman he'd seen. However, he was going to find out. Tonight.

Jason, the bar's owner who was also one of the evening's bartenders, had told Kai that varying members of the dive team often came in here when they were on the island. They were a good crew, he said. They seemed like really decent people.

Right.

Finishing his drink, Kai pushed his glass across the bar counter toward Jason, nodding his head to signal another one. To his credit, Jason didn't say a word or change expression as he whipped up another perfect whiskey sour with practiced ease and slid it down the bar toward Kai. For one thing, Kai held his liquor better than nearly any human could. His dragon shifter genes insured that, not that Jason knew anything about those. More importantly, he never caused trouble. On the most practical level, even though as a lifelong island homeowner he had a car he was allowed to drive here, he walked almost everywhere on the island like everyone else did, which Jason knew.

Sipping his drink, Kai let the energy of the day roll over him and calm the flurry of questions that had spun and danced in his mind since his encounter with the woman hours earlier. He really hoped she was attractive. Young would be nice, too. And not hitched to some other guy.

Kai knew how to open women's legs and lips. Jaw hardening, he thought of how he'd practiced that art form with relentless accuracy during the past three years. He was a charming bastard when he wanted to be. He could get women to drop secrets by using his own smooth sweet talk. It worked for him every time, no matter a woman's age or relationship status. Sliding through life with his remaining primary goal being to have ever increasing amounts of fun that involved enormous adrenaline rushes by bedding every woman he could find across the world was more than enough to encourage him to actually get up every day.

Even on the occasional day when the ice around his heart had constricted so hard that it threatened to never allow him to breathe again.

"Hey." Jason's voice, low from behind the bar. "Earth to Kai. That's them coming in right now."

Kai snapped his head around. A group of about seven or eight people had just come into the bar, their exuberant spirits instantly apparent. Quickly, Kai glanced through them, trying to pinpoint the right one. Three women were in the group.

A tall, slender blonde. Maybe. But he was pretty sure she was too tall to be the diver he'd seen.

The short, solid woman looked like she wasn't the type to take shit from anybody. Hmm. If it was her, Kai would have his work cut out for him.

The third woman in the group, who came in at the tail end, finally caught his eye. Waves of dark hair settled around her shoulders as she flipped around to laugh at something her companion said, the guy following her in. Every line of her body screamed self-assurance, independence, and an irrepressible delight for life that Kai could sense even from across the room.

Something about her seemed oddly familiar, too. Kai narrowed his eyes a bit and stared at her. They settled at one of the tables, clearly ready to enjoy their evening.

Despite himself, Kai felt the slow, tingling thrill of the chase come over him. This girl was gorgeous. If he hadn't had an ulterior motive, he would've gone for her anyway. She seemed like just the type to enjoy a night of romping fun with him, and then not worry too much about being set loose in the morning. In fact, she seem like the type just as happy to set *him* loose.

Even so, the challenge was still implicit. He sat casually on the barstool, taking another long, slow sip of his drink as he regarded the party as they excitedly laughed and chattered among themselves. He'd still have to tread carefully. But that didn't matter. Kai Long had enough tricks up his sleeve to make women willing to spill their deepest secrets to him.

Anything to help him forget.

With a quick tip of his hand, he slammed back the rest of the drink, then stood up. "Whatever that woman is drinking," he said to Jason, jerking his chin a little bit at the gorgeous girl he still didn't take his eyes off of, "I'm buying. Except make it the highest-end liquor you have, and put everything on my tab." Without looking back, he sauntered across the crowded room, heading straight for the woman who unknowingly held the key to his most important secret.

4

The excited energy of the group bounced over to Gabi, making her feel as fizzy as the bubbles of the champagne in the small glass she held. The Deep Blue Bar wasn't really used to people calling for bottles of champagne. It was just a casual beach bar. Even so, they did keep bottles of bubbly in stock. The bartender, also the owner and a nice guy, greeted Gabi and the crew when he brought over a bottle, opened it with a flourish, and poured them each a small glass.

"Whatever you guys are celebrating, thanks for coming in here to do it."

The table burst into laughter again, their high mood absolutely uproarious and willing to get silly for almost any reason. Gabi raised her glass toward the team, everyone following suit. "To us!" Before she sipped her drink she added, "And to the pieces of history that thank us for finding them."

"Here, here," echoed around their small table as everyone else tipped back their glasses.

Gabi had managed to keep her analytical academic side and her wildly questioning old world side carefully balanced ever since her incredible encounter with the dragon beneath the water earlier. Thoughts tossed around her mind in an unrelenting whirl before she finally managed to put the kibosh on them and focus strictly on the rest of the day they'd spent meticulously documenting their stupendous find. The bumpy press of the small gold nugget against her finger was an uncomfortable reminder of her hidden purpose there.

Frankly, she could hardly wait to use the little bit of the shipwreck's treasure for her means, then return it to the ship so it could end up being documented along with everything else. She really was just—borrowing it for a short time.

That fabricated misrepresentation of the truth creeped and crawled up and down her spine the entire day, until she was finally able to get back to her little room at the lab's housing unit and carefully deposit it in her desk drawer. She'd deal with it first thing in the morning.

She'd also finally broken down and called her family's home just before leaving for the bar, eager to share the spill of her thoughts with someone who would understand: her grandmother. But her brother Mateo had answered and said that abuela was sleeping. Gabi was loath to have her disturbed and simply said to give abuela a kiss from her when she woke and that she'd call back later in the week.

There wasn't anyone else in her family she could really talk to about this. Even though her dad had been raised with some of the same stories, he didn't embrace them nearly as passionately as Gabi's abuela did. He'd been so proud of Gabi when she'd gone to college, then grad school, attaining degree after degree and accolade after accolade. He was very proud of her for being a scientist with a very logical mind. She knew there was no way he would appreciate hearing anything about freaking *dragons* swimming beneath the sea.

Besides her grandmother, her best friend Lacey was the only other person Gabi could think of to talk to. Feeling edgy and restless, she broke her own usual vow to focus on work and her own playtime when on the island and left a message for

Lacey earlier that day. She hadn't heard anything back yet. Hopefully it meant Lacey was getting down and dirty with that sexy billionaire Gabi just knew was meant for her bestie.

In the meantime, all Gabi could do was drink champagne, celebrate discovering the shipwreck with the rest the team, and just quietly let the back of her mind spin as it tried to figure out what the hell was really going on. The one thing she knew for a fact was that she wasn't crazy. She'd seen a dragon. And at some point, she'd figure out what it meant.

"Whatever it is you're celebrating, I'd be more than happy to pay for another bottle of champagne for you and the table, gorgeous." The low, bone-rattling, sensual voice came from Gabi's left. She swung her head around and up to look at the man speaking.

Wow. Abruptly, all thoughts of shipwrecks, scientists, fantastical beasts, and pretty much everything else in the world disappeared from Gabi's head. Staring at her with a slow, teasing grin was the sexiest guy she'd ever laid eyes on in her entire life. Tall, fit, just brawny enough that she knew he could go all night and then some, the guy was pretty much a wet dream walking. Mocha brown eyes that seemed to have glints of ocean-green sparks in them were set in a face so ridiculously gorgeous that Gabi pretty much wanted to lick the man.

She swallowed hard. The entire crew had stopped talking. She felt Shane kick her under the table, and without looking at him—even if she could have dragged her gaze away from Mr. Sexy staring back at her—she knew Shane would be wearing his "you'd better jump on that right now, girl" expression.

Gabi's usual sense of game seem to be slow on the uptake today. She blinked at the guy and half opened her mouth to respond. Except her mind felt ridiculously blank. Oh, come on. She knew how this worked. Guy, bar, come-on, bam. Easy.

Then why couldn't she think of a single remotely intelligent thing to say?

"Better yet, maybe you'd like to join me alone for a drink?" His deep, rolling voice whispered over her nerve endings, setting every single one she had to tingling. "I'll still buy another bottle for your table. But I'd like to get to know you a little better." Mr. Sexy's expression was an open invitation.

With a forceful jolt, Gabi managed to lurch herself back into the world. *Buck up, Gabriela,* she muttered in her head. *You've got this.* Arching one eyebrow at him, letting her best devilish grin spread across her own face, she answered in what sounded like her usual steady, flirtatious voice, "Sure. It depends on which bottle of champagne you order, though. Are you gonna go all cheap on my team's asses? Or are you gonna throw down with the good stuff? Because they're awesome. And so am I. We deserve the best."

Whoa. Well, yeah. She was usually pretty sassy with guys. But this was a little over the top even for her.

Mr. Sexy's grin just unfolded into a low, rippling laugh that traced itself over Gabi's skin, tickling at her already aroused nerve endings with the promise of something incredible. Oh, yeah. She knew what that meant. She and this guy had chemistry. She could tell that right now.

Tonight, she'd be celebrating in more ways than one.

"Seems like the lady knows what she wants, and knows very well what she's worth. I'm Kai."

He reached out a hand to her. Gabi smiled even more at hearing his name. Kai. It meant ocean in Hawaiian, which this guy looked like he was. That had to be a good sign. She was down for anything that had to do with the ocean. Especially a very sexy, very interested guy.

"Gabriela," she said, reaching her own hand out toward him. "My friends call me Gabi."

"Gabi." Sultry and rich, his voice wrapped around her name as if it were an exotic taste dancing over his tongue and lips. Gabi's hands trembled just the tiniest bit. Holy crow. She'd never heard anyone say her name like that before.

Not in a way that was pretty much beginning to make her squirm in her seat with delicious anticipation.

"I have a feeling it's going to be very nice to make your acquaintance, Gabriela." This time, he virtually savored every syllable of her entire name.

Gabi had to swallow the gasp as the force of just his voice rocked her. Wow. Yes, it was definitely going to be more than just a good night. It was going to be a mind-blowing experience to remember. She could already tell. From the way the other two women on the team looked at Kai, she could tell they definitely agreed with her, and most likely definitely wished they were in her place instead.

"Same," she managed to say back.

And then their hands touched. Despite her response to merely his voice, Gabi wasn't at all prepared for the physical contact. Sensuous, cool electricity rolled between them, shattering through her body. She suddenly felt as if she were encased in the slow, rolling waves of the ocean itself, their slide and throbbing power sending what felt like a liquid caress over her suddenly boneless body.

So pleasurably shocked by it that she could no longer speak, Gabi simply sat there, holding Kai's hand in what looked like a simple handshake. Something deep inside her, though, was loosening.

Shivering with desire.

Thundering with the sweet, booming echo of pure certainty that whoever this man was, he was a lot more than a simple night's tumble.

As the self-assured, wildly sexy Gabriela took his hand with hers, a seismic shudder wrenched its way through Kai's body. The sensation itself was so unexpected, so unfamiliar, that pure shock kept his face expressionless, his body outwardly unmoving.

But inside, everything shifted at once.

The dark, welcoming oblivion, the unfeeling blankness he'd sought to maintain for so long now, jolted sideways. Something deep inside him stirred beneath the dull, faceless and nameless darkness he preferred over all else. Kai had no idea what this new sensation was.

All he knew was that it terrified him.

Taking a deep, silent inhale to steady himself, he made himself picture the void of the deepest part of the ocean as he swam through it in his dragon shape. Regaining the soundless, empty, pure oblivion he craved. After another long moment, the bizarre tumult within him subsided. Reflexively squeezing his fingers once around Gabi's hand, he relinquished it with a teasing slide of his fingertips across her palm. As her eyes widened and she visibly swallowed, Kai let a smile cover his face again.

This sort of casual interaction, he could handle.

"So. I see you all had a bottle of Vilmart here." His tone was breezy. In control. "I'll have Jason bring you a bottle of Cristal next. He keeps them here just for me."

Several gasps rose from the table at that. Cristal wasn't exactly the kind of fancy, outrageously expensive drink people expected when they walked into this beach bar. And certainly not offered up by a total stranger.

If only they knew.

Kai gave them all a courteous nod, adding, "The lady here said you're all worth it. My immediate goal," he looked back at Gabriela, enjoying the rosy flush in her cheeks, "is to make her happy. Shall we?"

She nodded, that saucy little grin coming back to her face as she apparently regained her own composure a little bit. As she stood up, the slightly older man at the table, the one Kai had instinctively assessed as being the group's leader, and who had not taken his watchful gaze off Kai the entire time, quietly said, "Have fun, Gabi. I expect you bright and early at 7a.m. tomorrow. I'll be looking for you if you don't show."

A direct, clearly fatherly threat.

Without missing a beat, Kai smiled and bent back over the table to stretch his hand toward the man. "The name is Kai Long, sir. You can check with the owner here. He knows me very well. He'll even give you my home phone number and address if you feel like you might need to send out a search party in the morning. But you won't have to. She'll be wherever it is she needs to be."

A slightly expectant hush still blanketed the table as the older man gave Kai another long, piercing look. Although his expression didn't change, Kai sensed the man was coming to silent conclusions about him and the situation. Then he curtly extended his own hand. "Everson Booth. Good to meet you, Kai Long." Suddenly snorting, he added, "Frankly, I'm not that worried. I'd bet you another bottle of champagne that she could kick your ass. Gabi is pretty tough."

At the lighter tone, everyone at the table erupted into somewhat relieved laughter. Kai laughed with them as he shook the guy's hand, then stepped back to Gabi's side. "Duly noted. I definitely like the sound of you already, Gabriela," he added, looking down at her.

She was beautiful. She fit him perfectly, too. Her chin just reached the top of his shoulder, meaning she was an almost perfect height for him to kiss her when she stood right beside him. Smiling, the warmth of excitement over the night to come stealing over him, Kai held his hand to Gabi's back and gently steered them both away from the table.

Gabi surreptitiously studied Kai as they wove their way through the crush of bodies in the bar toward the patio door.

He apparently meant for them to sit out in the cool, fresh evening air. His hair, a black so deep it was shocking, so dark she knew that in full sunlight it would almost appear to be blue-black, was shaved close to his head. The warm golden tone of his skin was so smooth, and he smelled so damn good, that Gabi once again was nearly overwhelmed by the desire to lick him.

For cripe's sake. She was acting like some sort of horny teenager. As they reached the patio doors and he stepped forward to push them open for her, gesturing for her to go ahead of him, she caught a flash of what looked like leather encircling his neck. The leather cord held a small, bone-white piece of what looked like wood nestled right in the hollow of his throat. Her eyes wandered down to the V of his button-up shirt where his chest disappeared beneath it. She found herself wondering if his pecs would feel as good beneath her hands as they looked under his shirt. Stumbling a bit as she went through the door, she caught his amused expression.

Okay, fine. He just caught her checking him out. Well, that was what this was about, right? A one-night stand between two consenting adults who clearly had a lot of mutual attraction zinging between them. Sliding sexy Kai a wink, she threw a little sass into her hips as she stepped in front of him.

She almost swore she heard a little groan behind her as she went out onto the patio, pausing to look for a free table. Kai gently took her upper arm with his hand, once again sending that splash of deliciously icy awareness racing through her. "I've got a special spot for us. The owner and I go way back. We have VIP seating, for someone who's very definitely a VIP lady."

Normally, Gabi would've rolled her eyes so hard at such a cheesy line that she practically would have broken them. Right now, though, she heard purely sincere desire in his words. The tingle racing through her sizzled between her legs, setting off delicious little shocks.

Bizarre as it seemed, she wanted to follow the mouth-wateringly hot man wherever he decided to take her. Something about him called to her. As if she already knew him.

Tossing him a grin over her shoulder, she replied, "Lead the way, then. Let's get this evening started."

5

K ai watched as Gabi seated herself at the patio table reserved for VIP parties. That basically meant for Kai and whatever woman he was wooing at the moment to spend the night in his company. He had actually been the one to loan the money to Jason so he could open the bar in the first place. Although Kai was a completely silent partner in terms of how the bar was run, it did afford him small perks, such as being able to claim the VIP table any time he was here. Set on a slightly raised dais behind a closed gate on the patio, commanding a riveting view of the lights that circled Avalon Harbor as they were illuminated against the darkness of the ocean beyond, it was the perfect place to charm any particular girl who was proving to be a little more challenging than usual to get to spend some quality time with him.

This girl—rather, this very sensual woman—wasn't actually a challenge. She clearly was all in for whatever fun they decided to get up to this evening. But he wanted to impress the hell out of her anyway. Her legs, long and sexy beneath the flirty little dark pink and brown skirt she wore, caught his eye again as she stepped up onto the dais. Kai felt his balls tightening in anticipation as she glanced back toward him. That lively, sexy smile was making him so hard he was beginning to ache.

She placed her phone in a prominent place on the table. "Sorry," she said, shrugging a little. "My grandmother's not well. I like to be available as much I can when I'm away from the city."

Despite her obvious interest in him, Kai had also instantly sensed that Gabi wasn't just a good time girl, someone to play with for a single evening, then never really think of again. He could tell she had no fear of her own sexuality, and would certainly have no problems being willing and open with him. Yet he could also sense that she was a little different than the others. The care in her voice as she mentioned her grandmother oddly tugged at him. It made her seem more intriguing than most women. More genuine.

Kai gave himself an internal head shake. It was probably just because he really needed to find out what was going on with her knowledge of *his* shipwreck and *his* treasure. Nothing else.

An odd rumble echoed deep inside him, low but there. Kai felt the side of his eye twitch in reflexive reaction, but he managed to keep smiling at Gabi while shoving it down. His dragon. Rumbling at him in—dissent.

Interesting.

"So this is the special table you take all the girls to that you really want to show off for, isn't it?" Gabi's tone was pure flirtation, just like the invitation in her pretty cinnamon-brown eyes.

Kai had to laugh as he stepped up behind her, closed the gate again, and pulled out her chair for her. "Okay, you figured that out. Just because I wanted to treat you like the lady you clearly are." He moved around the table to his own seat as Gabi burst out laughing. Damn, he really liked her laugh. Low, rich, and totally open, it told him she was filled with a vibrant enthusiasm for life. Something in her eyes seemed a little hidden, but he chalked that up to what should be a natural semi-guardedness when meeting a strange guy.

His dragon rumbled again. Kai felt the slightest jolt of—recognition?—as he kept gazing at Gabi, letting her laughter wash through him. Breathing evenly, he pushed his dragon down with even more force. Whatever that was about, he wanted no part of it.

"I get called a lot of things, but lady isn't usually one of them." Gabi idly played with the menu on the table in front of her, her gaze not leaving his.

"And what sort of things do people normally call you?" He grinned at her, enjoying the wildly comforting scent of the ocean sprinkled on the light breeze around them as well as the most maddeningly sexy scent arising from the beautiful woman seated across from him. "Let me take a few guesses. Adventurer, first of all. Definitely."

Gabi raised one eyebrow, still smiling at him. "Go on," she encouraged as he waited. "So far, you're on a good track."

Kai laughed again. She was really easy to be around. He liked that. It also would make his goal of getting information from her simpler. "Badass." That was a bit of a guess, but he'd definitely gotten that impression from her mere presence. The way she held herself, the way she talked. "You're a badass who takes life by the throat and doesn't let go until it gives you what you want. Sounds like you can defend yourself pretty well, so that makes you even tougher and hotter."

"Hot, huh?" The very tip of her tongue slipped out for just a second to graze her upper lip as she said that.

Kai felt another wave of desire splash through him at the sight. He swallowed hard to keep his expression from getting too hungry at the moment. This little verbal repartee was fun. He wanted to keep it going. "Definitely hot. A woman who can defend herself and enjoy life is a real turn on."

The rosy flush, making Gabi's gorgeous golden-brown skin an even more beautiful shade on her cheeks, told him that she liked that. Emboldened, he took another step, urging her closer to the direction he wanted the conversation to go. "You must like the ocean to be here on the island. So tell me. You're on vacation? Snorkeling, diving?"

He paused, carefully watching to assess her reaction. A teasing grin flared to life on her face again, framing it in such intense beauty that his mind stuttered for an instant. Muted but definite, his dragon roared inside him. Kai barely contained the shudder that wracked him with the effort to control his stirred-up dragon. This woman interested his dragon. Fascinated it, even. Kai damn well agreed, even though the level of intensity his wild draconic side felt was still somewhat disturbing. At the same time, though, it made him anticipate the night ahead with her more and more.

Gabi dipped her head and gave him an almost shy grin. "I do like the ocean, actually. My favorite place in the world to be is in the water out there." She waved a hand in the general direction of the low, throbbing hum of the waves gently crashing upon the shore. Her voice was so quietly fierce, he understood that her passion for the sea ran very deep. "What about you? You seem like the kind of guy who loves it out there, too."

She tossed the question back at him so quickly, so lightly, that for the barest hair of a split-second Kai froze. She couldn't possibly—no. That was ridiculous. There was no way she really understood what she'd seen earlier that day. Even less of a way she could associate it with him. She was simply being flirty.

Just like him.

Jason suddenly appeared at their side, coming in from the special hallway that led only to this little area. He brought out a bottle of the same champagne Kai had ordered for Gabi's whole table inside the bar. Gabi raised her eyebrows at it, glancing from Jason to Kai to the bottle then back to Kai again.

"Wow. You sure do go to some serious lengths to impress a woman when you want to, don't you?"

Jason chuckled as he expertly popped the cork and poured them each a glass. "I can tell you this much," he said. "Kai doesn't usually go quite this big for a woman. You must have something he really wants. I suspect it's your smile, beautiful." He grinned easily at Gabi as he neatly flicked his wrist to twist the bottle so that not a drop spilled when he ended the pour. Then he nestled the bottle into its ice bucket on the table. "Enjoy your night, you two." Flipping a grin at Kai, Jason left them alone again.

Kai raised his glass toward hers. She lifted hers back, letting them clink together. "Well, he's got that right. I have every intention of enjoying my night with you," she said, eyeing him over the rim of her glass as she tipped it toward the full lips that kept snagging his attention.

The vibrant yet sultry tone of her voice nearly made Kai choke on his sip. Watching her pull a bit of the champagne into her mouth, her delicate throat muscles working as she swallowed, nearly sent him over the edge. Hmm. Whatever sexy magic this woman was wielding, it seemed to be working on him pretty damned well. Almost well enough for him to forget the real reason for his need to seduce her.

Almost.

GABI COULDN'T HELP her smile as she kept looking at him. Kai. Picking up a guy, or being picked up by one, was par for the course in her experience. This felt totally normal. Yet at the same time, a tingle of extra excitement seemed to make the very air around them shimmer. The salty tang from the ocean mingled with the sounds of low chatter and laughter from the patio, above which they sat as if in their own private box.

She had to admit she felt like royalty right now. She appreciated that he was going the extra mile to impress her. He didn't know he didn't have to do that. The second he'd materialized by her side, she'd had that low, slow wash of craving that spread from deep inside her womb throughout every inch of her body. The one that she knew meant there was a serious spark of attraction between them, and she would be acting on it. Of course, she shouldn't have to tell him that. He wanted to toss out $300 bottles of champagne as if they were cans of cheap Budweiser beer, well, no problem. She was just going to enjoy this ride. Besides. Something about him just made her feel—comfortable. Familiar. And strangely protective.

"So. Want to tell me what it is we're toasting to?" The gorgeous depths of Kai's eyes, which now that she was close enough to him she could see were deep chocolatey brown that seemed to have the oddest little flecks of jade green in them, held her in a shiver of anticipation as he regarded her over the glass of champagne. "What you all were celebrating in there?"

Gabi wiggled her eyebrows up and down and flashed him a mischievous grin. She was feeling more relaxed around him by the second. "I'd tell you, but then I'd have to—I don't know. Do something nefarious to you."

A startled laugh pealed out of him. She really liked how it relaxed his face. "Nefarious, hmm?" he said, the green in his eyes seeming to brighten. "I didn't peg you for the nefarious type. So. You're a searing enigma, wrapped in a riddle, bound up in an incredibly sexy package. Is that what you're trying to tell me?"

Kai took another sip, regarding her over his glass with those astonishing eyes as his smile still crinkled his skin. Something dark and delicious in his gaze had Gabi shifting in her seat again. She sipped her own champagne, which was incredibly, ridiculously good, and felt her head whirl. "I'm trying to tell you that I think I like where this evening is headed." Gabi kept her voice light as she spoke. But she also kept her gaze directly on his.

He inhaled sharply, moving his glass away from his gorgeous face and putting it back down on the table. The sheer hunger abruptly visible in his expression rippled over Gabi like the tides, creating an answering sensation in her own body. Going on blind instinct, instinct that told her not only would she have an incredible time with this man tonight, but that she simply felt utterly comfortable with him, which was odder than hell but true, she blurted out the thought at the top of her head. "I had no idea when I came in here that I'd meet a guy who I'd want to be part of my private celebration tonight. I think," she said in a low voice as the tingles throughout her body jittered and jived, "that's exactly what I'm saying."

Those flashes of green in his otherwise velvet brown eyes sparked more brightly at her words. Gabi saw his pulse thump in his throat. Again without thinking, she let her hand reach across the table. She lightly touched her fingers to the side of his throat, feeling the jump of his pulse as she slowly ran her hand down over his collarbones.

She wasn't sure who was more surprised by her bold action.

Kai drew breath to speak, but before he could, her phone vibrated on the table by her arm. Gabi's heart skipped a beat when she saw the demanding name on the screen. *UTEI.*

Underwater Treasure Exploration, Inc. A commercial treasure hunting company.

The company she secretly had been working with.

Her breath suddenly stolen by agitated nerves rather than aroused anticipation, Gabi flicked her eyes up to Kai, then back down the phone. Shit. There was no way they would be calling her, on today of all days, unless—

"Kai, I'm so sorry." The words dragged out of her. "I have to take this. It might be an emergency." She stood, grabbing up her insistent phone at the same time and not letting herself look back at him. She might not be able to walk away from the man with intense eyes and an electric reaction to her otherwise. "I'll be right back." She hurried away from the table, opening the little gate that led down to the main patio.

Only when she was away from him did she swipe her thumb to answer as she headed straight toward the far end of the patio. Away from Kai and any other prying ears as she took the phone call that might possibly end her career—but also save her grandmother's life.

———

KAI WATCHED Gabi's beautiful ass move at a smart pace away from him to take her mysterious phone call. Genuine concern had flashed across her face when she looked at the caller ID. Kai sipped at his drink, savoring the exquisite taste as his mind and body roared around one another in a bizarre, mildly upsetting confusion.

She was stunning, she was funny, they clearly had enormous chemistry, and she still knew something that he had to learn from her. Those things were all true things. Yet something else flared beneath it all as well. Something deep inside him, in a place that felt caught between his stomach and his chest. The dark, usually welcoming pit of his shadowed inner sanctuary was suddenly shifting. Threatening to toss him off balance.

He wasn't sure what to make of it. He definitely knew he still didn't like it.

After only a few moments, Gabi came back across the patio to their table. Her expression had changed, and she didn't sit down. Damn it. Kai stood up, already knowing his potential evening with this gorgeous woman was over before it barely started.

Her eyes darted uneasily, but her voice sounded genuine. "I am so sorry. I—have to go."

Concerned, he asked, "Is everything okay? Is it your grandmother?"

Gabi's face clouded briefly. She shook her head. "No. Something else in my world of crazy."

By her nervous, clipped tone, Kai sensed he wouldn't get far if he pushed her.

"I promise you," she added with sudden fervor, those cinnamon-brown eyes abruptly locking on his, "this isn't some kind of weird thing where I asked a girlfriend to call so I could get out of this. I would so much rather stay here with you."

Despite his concern for her obvious trepidation, Kai couldn't help a smile. He could easily tell she was telling the truth. Beautiful Gabriela wanted to stay with him as much as he wanted her to. "I know that," he told her. "I believe you."

He said the words very casually, honestly meaning them as a reassurance. But they came out with such unintentional conviction that both he and Gabi were drawn up short. Surprised at his own emphasis. Gabi looked at him, the beautiful golden brown of her eyes studying him with blatant curiosity and a touch of regret.

A long, odd moment held them. It was one of those moments in which the background mutter of the people in the bar faded away. One of those moments in which all Kai could sense was the wild, exquisite scent of this beautiful woman. Like an intoxicating mix of sweet jasmine, the bright snap of ginger, a fresh ocean breeze, which, along with the low, comforting throb of the ocean in the distance, gently pulsed around them both.

As if in an acceptance of the two of them.

Together.

With an abrupt, fierce shake of his head, Kai said in a deliberately lighter tone, "Another night, then."

Gabi looked at him for another long second before she suddenly whipped up her phone again. "Give me your phone number." Her voice was firm.

Damn. She was something, all right. He rattled off his digits, watching her long, pretty fingers move as she tapped his number into her phone. She kept going for a moment, then looked back up at him with a quick smile despite her slightly worried eyes. He felt his phone buzzing in his pocket and grinned back at her. "That's you?"

She nodded. "Yes. Call me, Kai. Tomorrow. I'm on the island for the rest of the week."

She unknowingly echoed the words of the tipsy blonde barfly from earlier. But this time, they meant a hell of a lot more to him.

With that, Gabi turned as if to walk away. Then, with the mercurial yet decisive flash that he was beginning to sense was part of her exuberant nature, she suddenly turned back to him, stepped forward, and reached her hands up to pull his face down to hers. Startled, he let it happen. Her lips touched his in a light kiss, quick and gentle. Even so, there was a definite zing. A sweet yet wild connection between them. One that stirred his dragon yet again into thrumming with something aroused.

Something possessive.

He knew she felt the connection too, because she jumped. But when she pulled back, she was smiling.

"Tomorrow." Her eyes were suddenly serious again, but this time it was a seriousness born of desire. Then she turned and walked away, her beautifully sassy hips swaying beneath that skirt, her dark brown hair tumbling loosely over her bare shoulders as she left the bar.

Kai allowed a slow, pleased smile to slip over his face. He'd do more than call her tomorrow. She didn't know it, but she carried a slight residue of his gold with her. He'd felt it ever since she walked into the bar. She didn't have the gold piece that she picked up from the shipwreck with her, but it was somewhere nearby. When he was this close to his gold, it called to him like a beacon. So attuned to it he was, as well as definitely to her, he knew that if she was either on the island or in the ocean tomorrow, he would be able to find her.

Much more intrigued than he normally would have been

at the thought of seeing a woman in the daylight, after an evening unfortunately not spent tangled in her luscious, beautiful limbs, he caught up the bottle of champagne and headed back inside the bar to drop it off at the party of academics who still unknowingly held all his own secrets in their own hands.

6

The gold nugget weighed heavily in Gabi's left hand as she nervously twisted her phone around in her right hand. Stopping short in front of the window on the east end of the room, she looked toward the lightening sky over the California coastline. Normally, she enjoyed the quiet and stillness of early mornings before the bustle of the day began. Considering that she had had about three hours of sleep the night before and that she was about to take another step in the terrible scheme she had agreed to, it was a wonder she was even standing.

In addition, there was the fact that she'd seen a freaking water dragon swimming under the sea less than twenty-four hours earlier.

And then there was Kai.

Images of wickedly sexy brown eyes teased and danced in Gabi's head as she pivoted on one foot and began pacing back the length of her room. She'd spent maybe half an hour with Kai last night, yet she hadn't been able to stop thinking about him, to the point that she'd had trouble getting to sleep.

Despite *I look forward to seeing a lot more of you very soon* being all he'd said in a text he'd shot her not ten minutes after she'd left the bar last night, she'd been left hot and bothered as she tossed and turned later in her bed, imagining his sexy mouth doing all sorts of things to her body before she finally fell asleep.

Wicked, nefarious, oh so delicious things.

There was also the other thing. The thing looming in her head even more strongly than sexy, intriguing, strangely compelling Kai. The one thing worrying her stomach so sick that she hadn't been able to continue her evening with him after the very brief yet quite unsettling phone call.

Shaking her head, turning on her heel to once more pace in the opposite direction, she flipped her phone around her hand and glanced down at the screen again.

Let's see it. Otherwise the deal is off.

The message seemed to glare up at her.

A car door slammed somewhere outside, causing Gabi to jump a little bit. Her nerves were tight.

The phone call last night from the head of UTEI, the commercial treasure hunting organization, had been chilling. Despite the casual greeting, she'd sensed instantly from the man's voice that he knew. Somehow, he knew that she'd found the ship and thus its treasure. He had asked point-blank where she was in the process. When she'd started to fumble out an answer, caught so off guard by his phone call as well as Kai's unexpected attentions, he made the tsk-ing noise that often caused her blood to run cold the other times they'd talked. Calmly, he'd said, "Ms. Santos. We know you found it. What I need to see is proof that the gold is there. First, a photo of it. Then the coordinates, as we agreed. Or don't you remember our conversation?"

Gabi had shivered slightly despite the relative warmth of the evening. She'd said that she wasn't near the gold right then but that she would send him a photo of the nugget later that evening. In fact, she'd put off sending them the evidence of the find, even though she could have done so as soon as she'd gotten back to her little living quarters yesterday afternoon. She was half afraid they'd start moving on retrieval before the crew had time to properly document the site. As much as she needed what she would be getting in exchange for revealing the wreck's coordinates to UTEI, she still dreaded the actual steps she needed to take to get to that outcome.

She dreaded looking at the truth of the fact that she was doing something awful, no matter how critically important her reasons.

"See that you do. And I suggest you ensure that happens very soon, Ms. Santos," he'd said in that same eerie, calm voice before disconnecting the call. She'd had to take a minute to compose herself before going back to the table and Kai, but it didn't matter. Her potential evening with the sexiest, most interesting guy she'd met in a long while had been shot all to hell.

She was crazy to ever have taken up with UTEI. But it was too late now. She had no choice but to go through with it. Looking at the sparkling little gold piece in her palm, she carefully closed her fist around it. Removing it from the shipwreck had been necessary. Taking a photo of it with the expedition camera had been out of the question. All photos were logged. Instead, last night she'd texted the treasure hunting outfit a photo of it taken with her phone, adding that she didn't have the exact coordinates for the wreck yet. That would have to wait.

A day's grace before she took the next step to disturbing the biggest archeological find in a century—and the next step to saving her grandmother's life. Clenching her fist to help steel her resolve, she nodded decisively to herself. No. She didn't have another choice. And she wasn't going to back down just because the guy she talked to was kind of creepy.

Today, she was going back down to the wreck. Down into the gorgeous, glorious, mysterious ocean. Thinking of that, she deliberately allowed her thoughts to shift from the ugly yet necessary scheme she'd gotten herself into over to the other elephant in the room.

Or rather, the dragon in the room.

Casting a quick glance at the time, she turned on her laptop and fired it up. Stepping back across the room to its little kitchenette, she poured herself a mug of coffee before returning to her laptop and curling up on the small easy chair that she'd dragged over to the east-facing windows so she could watch the sunrise each morning. The beautiful pinks and pale oranges banding the horizon weren't quite enough to make her smile as they usually did. Small lines furrowing her brow, she took a sip of the coffee before putting it down and skimming her fingers over the computer keys to find the site she was looking for.

"Gotcha," she murmured to herself as she found it just where she'd left it in her bookmarks.

She'd been in grad school, getting the importance of source citation pounded into her head as a necessary step along the path of legitimate research, when on a lark one day she had searched the global hive mind for local ancient legends. While the Los Angeles area wasn't exactly ancient, it had history that went far beyond the hundred-odd years of Anglo settlement. Along with her best friend Lacey, who'd already decided that she was fascinated by old California history, she'd begun the habit of doing informal research. It was something just for fun between the two of them, in which they would each try to find some of the more obscure or sometimes even ridiculous aspects of local history.

Including the wild legends and tall tales brought into the general melting pot of the area by the many different cultures that ended up settling here.

Spurred by her grandmother's unwavering belief in the old ways, the particulars of which she'd never really shared with Lacey, Gabi had found herself drifting toward searching for legends about otherworldly types of things. Things like magic, witches, even silly things like vampires and werewolves. Even people who could shift into animals.

Such as dragons.

From the time she was a tiny girl, Gabi's abuela had entertained her with highly detailed stories of dragons that swam in the oceans, bathed in the mountain lakes, flew in the skies overhead, and sunbathed on the heated sands of the deserts that sprawled out past the city. She'd told her that these creatures had fantastical, magical powers that made them invisible to human eyes. Only very special humans could see them on occasion. She'd told her granddaughter that she herself had been one of those special people, a long time ago. But something had happened to end it, and she'd stop seeing dragons. Even so, she'd never forgotten them.

"There are mysteries no one understands or believes even exist, *cariño,*" her grandmother would tell her while Gabi listened and popped yummy *conchitas* or some other favorite treat into her mouth, feet dangling from the kitchen chair as she watched her abuela make dinner. "But that doesn't mean they aren't real."

Abuela had never stopped believing. She never wanted Gabi to stop believing either.

Gabi's father, who'd also grown up with same stories, always dismissed them. He humored his mother, and didn't mind her clinging to her silly old beliefs, as he sometimes called them. But he didn't really like that Gabi enjoyed those stories.

That deep in her heart of hearts, trained scientist or no, she believed them.

"Well, you were right. It's all true, abuela," she whispered to herself as she brought up the site she had found several years ago and started looking for a particular article. "Dragons exist. And I can see dragons, too." The scientist in Gabi was mocking her right now, demanding she go through the appropriate stages of scientific inquiry. To not simply believe in what she'd seen with her eyes. But the little girl in her refused to *not* believe it. And here, on the web page in front of her, she found the words she'd been looking for.

Another person's tale of seeing water dragons in the ocean. Of the shimmering blues and greens and whites on hides that matched what Gabi had seen yesterday. A story about a dragon that could turn into a man, or a man who could turn into a dragon. A story about an entire class system of them, along with other creatures, that existed side by side with humans. Blissfully unaware of such things in their world, people rubbed shoulders with dragon shifters, as the article called them, every day and never knew it.

An entire amazing world that supposedly existed alongside the one Gabi knew to be real and normal. A world filled with such myths like the ones her grandmother had been telling her all her life.

Staring at the very sensible, not remotely crazy-sounding words of the article, ignoring the painting of a dragon on the side of the page that clearly had been lifted from some art history book somewhere, Gabi took another thoughtful sip of her rich dark brew. When she first began showing Lacey these things, her best friend had laughed and dismissed cultural legends like those, saying while they were important to the storytelling tradition, obviously they weren't actually real. Gabi had shrugged and not mentioned them again. Her best friend in the world was even more logically minded than she was, having been raised in a fairly no-nonsense family. No, aside from people like whoever was behind this website—which of course none of the WHOIS information would tell her—the only person in the world right now who would believe what she had seen was her grandmother. She would have to wait until she got back to the mainland and she could speak to her abuela herself. Perhaps by then she would have more time for her thoughts to settle, as well as her emotions.

And by then, she should also be in a much better position to help her grandmother with the biggest battle of her life.

As she closed her laptop and rose to carry her coffee mug to the sink, Gabi's phone began ringing to the tune of her latest favorite song. Her heart stuttered for a second, caught between concern that it was the UTEI contact again and the silly hope that sexy Kai was on the other end of it. When she looked at the caller ID, however, her heart skipped a beat in genuine fear. She frantically swiped the phone on.

"Mateo? What's wrong?"

Her younger brother's voice instantly replied, "Nothing, sis, relax. Sorry." He sounded genuinely contrite. "I didn't mean to scare you by calling so early. Abuelita's fine." Mateo sighed. "But hey, mama wants to make sure you'll be here Sunday night for dinner. She's inviting someone she wants you to meet."

Relief sweeping her body that abuela was okay, Gabi's next feeling was irritation. Her mother, old-fashioned to a fault, was determined to save her daughter's soul by finding her a much more suitable husband than the first jackass Gabi had foolishly hitched herself to when she was 19. She knew it was only because her mother loved her, but it still drove her crazier than anything. Because all the adult Santos children still lived in the greater Los Angeles area, the whole family tried to get together for dinner twice a month. Over the years since Gabi's divorce, her mother had proved herself meddlesome, always inviting the sons, nephews, cousins, grandsons, third cousins fifteen times removed, whatever it took, of her friends from church and work to be there when Gabi was present as well. As long as they were Catholic, single, and seemed relatively sane, she did her best to shove them in her youngest daughter's path.

The only positive memory Gabi had about her short-lived marriage was that during it, her mother had stopped badgering her about finding a husband.

"For crying out loud," she muttered to Mateo, grabbing her notes and a bottle of water to stuff into her bag before she left the room to go meet Shane at the other end of the building so they could walk down to the dock together. "Will this ever stop?" Carefully, she tucked the gold nugget into the tiny little pocket that was part of the design of the swim tank she'd donned today to wear under her wetsuit. Its job for her done, she meant to return it to the shipwreck today.

Her brother's answering groan came down the line. Being two years younger than Gabi and the baby of the family, he was still, in his mid-20s, more than old enough to be married in their mother's eyes. She also pushed any remotely eligible girls in his face every chance she could. He hadn't quite gotten around to telling their parents that he was gay, and had known so since he was seven years old. Gabi knew that one day his dodging the matter would finally blow up in his face, but for now she and the rest of their siblings covered for him as best they could.

Their old-fashioned Catholic mama and her acquiescent husband were forces to be reckoned with. Terrifying, hurricane-like forces when they were crossed. Gabi had been able to play the enraged, temporarily man-hating ex-wife card for some time now, even though that hadn't really worked in her favor as far as her mother was concerned anyway. In her devout mother's eyes, you never got divorced. Not even when the asshole you'd married turned out to be the biggest cheating jerk in the world.

"Nah, she'll never stop till hell freezes over," Mateo said, sounding resigned. Gabi could practically see his shrugging shoulders. "But anyway, she wanted to make sure I checked in with you about it. I'll be out of town the next couple of days, and I know you leave to dive early. How's it going, by the way? Find anything good yet?"

As Gabi left the room and started walking down the hallway of the small bungalow unit the university maintained as employee housing for the lab personnel, she felt the slight twinge of guilt. Damn. Lately, she felt like she was fudging the truth to everyone she knew and cared about. But the crew couldn't tell a single soul about the shipwreck discovery just yet. Not yet. No one could know about it.

Which didn't at all explain how UTEI somehow already knew. The whole thing was getting messy. She didn't like it a bit.

"No," she said, superstitiously crossing her fingers behind her back as the guilt flogged her a little harder. She was definitely still Catholic in that way at least. "Yeah, tell mama I'll be there on Sunday. But I swear, Matty, if he's an ugly old guy like the last one, I'm gonna disown mama's matchmaking ass this time."

Mateo's laughter spilled into her ears as she left the building. "I'll tell her she'd better find you a stud who will be faithful all the rest of his days if she ever wants to see her dreams for you come true again."

"Guys like that don't exist," she replied with some acidity. The memories still hurt, despite having happened long ago. Catching sight of Shane, she waved to him. "I have to go. See you Sunday. Give abuelita a kiss from me, okay?"

"Of course," her brother answered seriously. All the grandkids in the family loved their grandmother with fierce, protective adoration. "Don't worry about her, Gabs. We'll figure out something." His voice sounded certain, though an undercurrent of fear wavered beneath it.

Gabi said good-bye and ended the call, doing her best to ignore the thudding of her own guilty unease. She was doing something. She could only hope it was the right thing.

7

Kai stood at the very edge of the long balcony that extended from his house over the ocean. The dawn was already stunning and clear, promising to remain so throughout the day. The ocean called to him, its pull as strong and undeniable as ever. The watery expanse covering nearly three quarters of the globe had been a more sheltering place to him than anything else his entire life. Despite that, as he prepared to dive in he felt mingled curiosity, hope, and a disturbing thread of confusion that irritated him to no end.

Last evening's unfortunately interrupted encounter with Gabi had left him restless and aching most of the night. He still longed to taste her sweet lips, even as he longed to figure out what the hell she was up to.

At this very moment, however, he also longed to hold the sparkling treasures of his hoard in his dragon claws. To feel their power course throughout him. Re-energizing and strengthening him. It was a revitalization he should be able to feel naturally. But the death spell that kept him from literally holding his gold was slowly yet surely eroding his vitality.

With images of Gabi's sexy, smiling face and the alluring sparkle of his gold and jewels trapped beneath the sea dancing together in a weird mingling throughout his mind, Kai dove off the balcony, entering the water in a clean slice. He kicked out and downward for a few strokes before allowing his dragon shape to flow over him. Reveling as always in the freedom of this form, he did a couple of whirling spins in the water just for fun before shooting off with unerring accuracy straight toward the shipwreck.

Sunlight sparkled off the surface of the water, sending its beams down to light his way as he swam faster than any ship could go on the surface. While he didn't need the sun's light to guide him, he enjoyed it anyway.

When the Santa Maria finally loomed up before him, the comfort of her listing bulk and the sure sense that his gold was there both eased and encouraged him. Maybe, just maybe, he could finally scoop up his hoard, luxuriate in the feel of his full power, and take it all to another safe location. One that he could finally access.

One that the death spell could no longer touch.

Emboldened by absurd hope, Kai dove straight toward the ship, his large silvery claws extending as he aimed for the large hole in her side, through which some of his hoard was easily accessible.

Twenty feet.

Ten feet.

Five feet.

Slam.

Pain cracked through Kai's enormous body as he seemed to crash into an unyielding invisible wall. He catapulted off of it, bubbles and silt exploding everywhere, obscuring his vision as he somersaulted helplessly through the water.

Away from his gold. Still unable to touch it.

He loosed a raging bellow that thundered and echoed beneath the sea, one that mimicked both the physical pain from crashing against the shields of the death spell as well as the renewed rage and loss that accompanied him every time he realized yet again that he could not touch his gold.

His mate, the one to whom he had pledged devotion and knew he had it in return, had in her last agonizing moments set a spell upon their mingled hoard that now prevented him from accessing the very thing he needed in order to live the long, full life of a dragon shifter.

The devastating sense of betrayal and confusion that always arose when he thought about it loomed over him. What felt like spikes of angry, blazing hot fire stabbed into his chest. He unleashed another bellow, this one tinged by something sharp and ugly that threatened his very being. His very soul.

His heart.

No. That veered far too close to the place he had no desire to explore. Kai let the rage sweep over him instead, finally finding his balance again and streaking away from the ship. He raced into the deep, sunless depths of the ocean to find the buoyancy he craved. The silence, the blankness that was far more desirable than the heated agony that seemed ready to shatter him every time he contemplated the horrible history of the death spell.

He had to be able to touch his gold again. He had to be able to feel like himself again.

The only answer was to go to the tantalizing mystery that was Gabi Santos, and figure out how it was that while she had managed to breach the walls of the death spell, he himself still could not.

A slow smile spread his mouth open, showing his huge, sharp teeth to any small creatures who dared to swim near a water dragon. He knew exactly how to get the raven-haired spitfire to himself today. If he played his cards right, he'd also be able to kiss the gorgeous woman again as well. Satisfied by both those appealing thoughts, he swam hard back toward shore.

"YOU DON'T SEEM VERY TIRED this morning, sunshine." Shane elbowed Gabi as they walked through the quiet early light toward the boat dock. "I thought for sure you'd be draggin' ass after a night with Mr. Gorgeous-and-Loaded."

Gabi rolled her eyes and tried to keep things light. "Hey, I'm like the Energizer Bunny. I just keep going and going."

Her words had the desired effect of making Shane laugh and steer the conversation to his own conquest from the night before. She just didn't feel like telling him she hadn't actually gotten down with Kai. For some reason, the practically chaste but still incredibly promising kiss they had shared in the bar seemed too precious a thing to talk about with anyone else.

What on earth was wrong with her? Gabi always liked to be the life of the party. Land a guy, reel him in, and release him after having some fun. But last night—last night, as promising as it had seemed, and as much as she had genuinely enjoyed her brief time in Kai's company, was nothing like her usual modus operandi. Yes, she'd wanted to play with him. Yet she also really wanted to see him again, and not just because he'd been a missed opportunity.

When they arrived at the dock, the rest of the crew was already aboard the research vessel, readying it to go out. Everson, however, waited on the dock for Shane and Gabi. "Hey, kiddo," he greeted her, his strange tone immediately telling her something was going on. "Sorry, but you're going to have to stay on shore today. Word from above."

Gabi stared at him. "What? Whose word?"

Shane glanced from Gabi to Everson before quietly slipping off to the ship with a sympathetic half wave at Gabi. Everson shook his dark, shiny bald head, spreading his hands out in front of him in a "who the hell knows" gesture. "Remember the environmental task force? The ones from the Marine Institute here on the island? Apparently they have some questions about our standards practices. What we filled out on our compliance forms." His tone turned more irritated. "They want to meet with someone on our team today to go over what we've been doing so far. You were requested by name, Gabs."

The sunny brightness of the day was like an extra slap in the face as Gabi contemplated spending it indoors instead of beneath the waves. Not to mention, she thought with an additional lurch of alarm, as her hand automatically went to the front of her swimsuit top beneath her light wrap, her plan to return the gold nugget.

And get the coordinates for the UTEI group.

Feeling sick, she frowned as she contemplated any potential standards her own team might have missed. The Ancients Quest team followed all the environmental requirements with stringent accuracy. She knew as well as Everson that there was nothing to question. "I don't get it," she said, shaking her head. Her dander started to rise. "First of all, we got checked off on all of that before we were even allowed to *think* about searching for 'ancient indigenous remnants' off the coast of the island." Her tone turned a little sarcastic as she mentioned the team's cover story. The cover story wasn't precisely a lie. It was in fact something the team had researched. But that specific project had ended six months ago. At least they could all speak intelligently about it to anyone who might come across them out here and idly question what they were doing.

They just hadn't specifically mentioned on their compliance forms that they also sought the Santa Maria.

"Why would someone ask for me?" Gabi restlessly moved from foot to foot, agitated at not being able to get on the boat with the others. "You're the team leader. Shouldn't they want to talk to you?"

Everson shrugged as he touched her shoulder in an apologetic gesture. "That's what one would think. I tried to argue that point, but I was shot down. Apparently the chairman of the board at the Institute somehow knows you, and wants to speak to you directly." His lips twisted downward as he gave her a sympathetic look. "Gabi, I'm sorry. But you know how important this is. We can't raise anyone's suspicions. You're land bound for the day. I promise we'll try not to make any more big discoveries without you, kiddo."

Gabi sighed as she longingly looked at the research vessel with the bustle of the rest of the crew on it. She knew perfectly well that they would make more discoveries today. Considering it would be only the second day down at the wreck, it was almost assured they would. "You know I want you guys to find all the cool stuff," she said somewhat grudgingly. Even to her own ears, her voice sounded a bit whiny. Shaking her head, she added, "Sorry. I sound like a spoiled little kid. All right, I'm heading back in. But," she added, frowning again, "isn't it kind of weird that they got ahold of you so early in the morning? Who's even awake over there yet? Maybe we did miss something." Her voice jigged slightly as her thoughts turned more edgy. If they really had messed up their environmental standards somehow, it could affect the rest of the dive.

Everson shook his head, already jogging toward the research vessel as Liesl waved to him that they were ready to go. "I don't know, Gabs. The department assistant called me about ten minutes ago. She said the chairman is there now. So you need to get over there and spend the day going over the environmental regulations with him. Sorry," he called again over his shoulder as he boarded the boat.

Gabi stood on the dock, thoughts in turmoil as she watched the research vessel head out into the bright sunny day, toward the century's most amazing discovery that she wasn't able to be part of today. Pushing down the desire to curse like an uncivilized little brat, she took a deep breath, turned around, and slowly started walking to the island's Coastal Marine Institute.

Whoever the hell its board chairman was, she would kill him with kindness.

Gabi felt obstinate enough to go straight to the Institute dressed as she was—basically, in her swimsuit ready for her dive—but of course she first went back to her room at the housing unit to change into something more appropriate for an office day. And for meeting with someone who potentially could throw a massive kink into their wreck salvage.

When she walked though the glass doors of the Marine Institute, she couldn't help a slight smile. She really loved this place. She'd been coming here since she was a little girl, fascinated by the occasional tours offered to the public that showed how the Institute rescued and cared for injured marine mammals, and released back into the ocean the ones that they could. Her grandmother had been the one to introduce her to the Institute she was very young, taking Gabi and her siblings across on the ferry for a day trip. That trip had sealed her fate of eventually becoming an underwater archaeologist. No one in her family had believed her at the time when she'd said she knew what she wanted to be when she grew up. Except, of course, abuela.

Gabi still remembered staring at the Institute's display that showed a diver, a guy of course, surrounded by beautiful and happy underwater ocean life as he explained what he did. Of course, it was a voice recording in the display, because the diver was just a mannequin in a dive suit. But it was a real-life underwater diver who was speaking on the recorded tape. The one tiny display among many in the museum that mentioned how archaeologists sometimes found remnants of ancient human life on the ocean floor, such as shipwrecks, fascinated Gabi more than anything else in the world. She was one of the very few who actually lived out her childhood dream.

As she crossed the floor toward the reception desk, she smiled at the sleepy-looking young woman sitting there. "I've never been here this early, either," Gabi said as the woman stifled a yawn. "But apparently the chairman of the board is here and wants to speak to me to make sure that we're upholding our permit agreements for our dive? I'm with California University."

The woman nodded, apologetically covering her mouth. "Oh, excuse me. It is a little early," she said, managing to smile. "He's waiting for you in the boardroom upstairs. Elevator's down the hallway, second floor. You'll see it. It's kind of hard to miss."

With those cryptic words, the woman waved Gabi toward the sole elevator down the hall. Feeling suddenly bemused, Gabi followed her directions. The elevator stopped on the second floor. When she stepped out, she couldn't help her gasp.

Floor-to-ceiling windows lined what was basically a giant open room. An enormous mural on the north wall depicted a scene of underwater life painted by the hand of the man she instantly recognized as the world's most popular marine life artist. The windows looked out on the ocean, which beckoned with tiny breeze-tossed whitecaps in the early sunlight that illuminated everything.

A dark-haired man stood at the far end, dressed in a short-sleeved top, casual pants, and trendy black water sandals of the sort that surfers and lifeguards wore. His hands were clasped behind his back as he stared out over the ocean. Without turning around, he said, "Amazing, isn't it? My parents designed it themselves when the Institute was started. They felt that no one would want to work here if they were trapped in stuffy offices. So they brought the outside in, to remind anyone who ever met in this room that part of their duty was to help protect the fragile, incredible life out there in that ocean."

From his very first words, Gabi's mouth had been opening even as the blood suddenly seemed to thump in her head and race throughout her body. Everything in her tingled as the dark, liquid tones of his incredibly deep voice caressed her every nerve ending.

When Kai Long turned around to look at her, that panty-melting, slightly cocky smile on his gorgeous face as he beckoned her toward him, Gabi snapped out the first thing that popped into her mind. Even though just the sight of him was nearly enough to weaken her knees and slick with wet heat that suddenly tingling place between her legs. Even though his tall, dark, and insanely sexy self was not at all what she'd expected to see this morning.

"You? You're the one who just cost me a day in the ocean?" Fire shot out from her voice. "If this is your idea of foreplay, buddy, you have a few things to learn about women."

She slapped her hands on her hips and glared at him for all she was worth. But the smile on his face just grew wider. Tamping down the ridiculous excitement rising in her chest from the simple reality that she was in his presence again, she lifted her eyebrows at him. In the most imperious tones she could manage, she said, "Well? I'm waiting to find out who you think you are that you can boss me around this way."

8

Kai had to sharply rein himself in, as well as his suddenly roused dragon, as Gabi stood there like the sexiest, most ravishing little spitfire he had ever seen in his life. Her tone and expression told him that she might prefer his head on a platter right now. Yet the slight increase in her heartbeat, which his dragon senses easily picked up from across the room, as well as the enticing sharp rise in her pheromones, told him she was very intrigued.

Good. It would help him keep the upper hand.

His dragon rumbled inside of him, seeming irate at that high-handed attitude. Kai managed to keep a smile on his face even as he internally frowned. He didn't know what was going on there, but he didn't like it. Not one bit.

Still unmoving, he gently tipped his head and beckoned her toward him again. "Please, Gabi, come here. I'd like to show you something." Confident in her response, he waited.

She crossed her arms over her ample chest and narrowed those flashing eyes at him. Fighting back his body's reaction to how her sweet curves filled out the fitted pants and sensible blouse she wore, Kai waited. In his experience, the longer he held out, the more pliable women were when they finally gave up and came to him.

Gabi, though, seemed determined to keep surprising him. "Oh," she said, underscoring her words with another snappy little head shake. "I don't think so. First of all, I'm supposed to be meeting with the the Institute's chairman of the board. What you're doing here, I have no id—"

Kai held up a finger and slowly wagged it at her. She stared at him as he said in a deliberately low, sensual tone, "Gabriela." By the way she slightly flushed at the way he said her name, he knew it was working.

He certainly didn't have to let her know that something about her luscious presence was working on him, as well.

"I *am* the chairman." He stayed planted where he was, looking at her with a grin still on his mouth. "And yes, I know all about your team's exploration. I looked up the environmental compliance forms that your team filled out. Everything appears to be in order. However." He paused, giving the silence a heavy weight. "I do have some questions."

Gabi swallowed, sudden nervousness visibly stealing over her. Aha. She was worried that he knew the true nature of their expedition. He had to admit he certainly had not known. The University was always doing some sort of research trip or other, often submitting environmental compliance forms to the Marine Institute as they trawled the waters off Catalina. Yet while Kai loved the Institute, he was its board chairman, not the day-to-day director. Someone else went over all compliance forms submitted by research groups to make sure they were in order.

After he'd seen the Ancients Quest team vessel in the water above the Santa Maria, however, he'd gone to the Institute and checked all their forms, which had been filed months ago. Everything appeared to be in order—excepting the fact that they most definitely had not put down the coordinates of the shipwreck's general area on the application form. That was one thing Kai had done to ensure that no searchers ever got close enough to the actual wreck, just in case the masking spells on it failed to keep it from detection, which was always a possibility when a cloaked item was specifically sought. If those coordinates ever appeared on a permit application, it would be triggered in the Institute's internal system, alerting him immediately via text.

No such trigger had been alarmed in recent years. Definitely not from this crew's form.

Apparently, the team was a lot sneakier than he'd ever suspected. Looking at Gabriela's growing flush as she sucked the corner of her sweet bottom lip into her mouth, even though the fiery expression on her face never wavered, he started to get the distinct impression that she might have been the one behind the actual nature of the quest.

She had taken a specific interest in it from the start.

Several long beats passed as they stared at each other. Kai knew he wasn't imagining the tension in the room. Yet despite the suspicious direction of his thoughts, it was the good kind of tension. The sort that reassured him that a woman was definitely interested in him. The kind of tension, he noted a little sharply, that meant he had to watch his step. He definitely still intended to feast upon Gabrielle's every luscious inch. But he also desperately needed to find out as soon as possible how she'd gotten to the gold.

The gold of his hoard. Some of which he knew without a doubt that she had with her at this very moment. It called to him, faint but clear. This woman held some of his gold right now. He ached to reach for her and find it, hold it in his own hands.

He ached to hold *her*.

Kai swore inside, keeping his features calm. Damn. His dragon was more alert, more unsettled than had happened in years. It was disturbing on many levels. Forcefully, Kai refocused on the situation. Get the girl, get the gold, get the answers. It should be simple.

After another long beat of mutual assessment, during which Gabi seem to come to some sort of internal decision, she finally just shrugged. "Fine," she said, walking across the floor toward him. "I'll bite. What is it you want to show me, Kai? Or is this just some sort of excuse to see me again?"

This time, Kai let his chuckle escape him. She was funny, and thought quickly on her feet. It made her even more intriguing. His dragon rumbled in appreciation, making Kai tighten his jaw for a moment. Taking another silent inhale, he looked at Gabi. "No, definitely not. I don't need an excuse to see you again." The register of his voice dropped even lower, allowing the deep, aching thrill he'd felt the second she'd stepped into the room to wash through his voice.

She had stopped again, several feet from him. They stared at each other, the mood stretching into a languorous hush. He sensed the whisper of her purely female attention running beneath her professional veneer. Yet she didn't say anything. She merely waited for him to continue.

After a long moment, during which his attraction to her buzzed through him, Kai went on. "I wanted to talk to you about the environmental compliance, Gabi, because I know how much historical research means to you. I looked you up last night," he added. He was rewarded by her sudden inhale, which caused her breasts to swell beneath her shirt. More fire spiked in her eyes again. He liked that. "Gabriela Santos," he went on, as if reciting from a stats sheet. "You graduated with your masters degree, with honors, two years ago, joining the Ancients Quest team during your first year of grad school. This is your fifth season with them. You pay attention to detail, protocol. But perhaps most importantly, you have," here he paused and slowly drew out the word, "passion."

He paused for another long moment, examining her with genuine curiosity. She fidgeted just a bit under his gaze, although he sensed her pulse beating even more strongly. Then he zoomed in, searching for a breach in her guards. Testing her.

Testing, if he was being honest, himself and his own trust levels. "However, you don't have true passion for what your team's application said you're looking for, Gabi."

She looked back at him, wariness suddenly visible on her strong, beautiful face.

Steeling his resolve, he went on in a more stern tone. "What you specifically have passion for is the ancient ship-wrecks that had to do with the old trade lines operating throughout the known world many centuries ago. You don't want to find out about the simple history of the ancient indigenous cultures that lived here. What interests you," he took a step closer to her, suddenly letting his voice drop into the danger zone, "is gold. Your resume may say you're an underwater archaeologist, Gabi. But tell me the truth. In reality, you're a treasure hunter, aren't you?"

GABI FELT about fifteen different emotions roil around inside as Kai's words slivered their way through her. From the tone of his voice, he didn't have a very high estimation of treasure hunters.

Then again, neither did she. The sick, slightly shameful feeling lurched in her stomach again. Forcing it down, she forced herself to tip her chin up and look at him with all the bravado she could muster. "Excuse me? Last night I was adventuresome, enjoyed life, and you wanted to see more of me. Then today you accuse me of being a common thief? I don't like where this conversation is going."

She expected him to contest her words. Instead, he burst

out laughing. His face instantly changed from grim and somewhat haunted to open. Vibrant, even. Caught by the change, she stared at him. He turned and stepped back toward the windows.

"I was just checking," he said in a casual tone. "We had problems before with teams not telling us the truth." He looked back over at her, beckoning her forward again. "I'm pretty good at reading people. You don't seem like the type to keep secrets, Gabi."

He turned his head away from her again as he said those words, looking back out the windows, so he didn't catch her flush of embarrassment. Giving herself an internal shake, she stepped up to the window beside him.

"No, I get it," she said, also gazing out toward the ocean. "I believe in preservation and conservation. I really do." Her voice was soft with her own conviction. "I don't believe in individuals hanging on to the literal treasures of the past for themselves. History should be on display for everyone to know about."

She truly did believe that. It was the only reason she had made her deal with UTEI. Knowing that they would put the treasure on public display, and be able to do so with far more panache than the University, was what kept her going in spite of all her trepidations about the whole thing. But she wasn't about to tell Kai about that. Not yet, at least.

She looked at him and lightly touched him on his forearm, knowing there would be a spark. There was one, racing up her arm as she felt his muscles lightly tense beneath her fingers. Pulling her hand away before she did something really stupid, like run it over his amazing pecs, she added, "Sometimes, people make decisions out of desperation. I can see how you might be suspicious. You're right. I definitely have an interest in old shipwrecks with holds full of treasure. Hey," she added with a hint of laughter, "I loved the Pirates of the Caribbean ride at Disneyland when I was a kid."

He snorted softly at that, still looking at the view of the beckoning, endless ocean. She was intensely aware of his spicy masculine scent only inches away from her, his broad chest encased in the casual black button-down top she found herself wishing she could unbutton right then and there. She hurried on so she could keep a grip on herself. "When I went to school and started finding out the truth, about the antiquities black market, and how much of the world's history has been lost or deliberately destroyed, it just slayed me."

She paused. Taking a deep breath, she shared one of those small things that made her vulnerable. The sort of thing she didn't usually tell people. But that strange sensation she had in his presence, the knowledge that simply being around him made her feel so comfortable, told her she could tell him anything.

Well. Almost anything. This bit of her family history, though, she could share.

"Look," she slowly went on. "I get it, I really do. Branches of my own family were wiped out, their history erased, a long time ago."

Kai turned to look at her, empathy flashing across his smooth, gorgeous features. She shrugged. "Part of my own legacy. There wasn't very much there for me to study. Besides, it was kind of too painful. My family hangs onto stuff like that. So I studied the big, glamorous things instead. Most people can't help but be fascinated by treasure." She tried for a lighter note. "All that sparkles, right?"

As if to himself, Kai nodded. "Indeed," he murmured.

Another beat held them before he gestured at the ocean. "Look out there, Gabi. What do you see?"

Puzzled, she looked out at the seemingly endless flat expanse of water. "The ocean?" she ventured cautiously, wondering if it was a trick question.

He nodded. "Exactly. The big, beautiful, mysterious ocean. She holds a lot of secrets, as you know."

"Mm-hmm." Gabi studied him out of the corner of her eye as he spoke. He seemed so intent all of a sudden. As if he were about to share the key to life with her.

"Secrets," Kai said more slowly, turning his head to look at her, "that sometimes get found."

Gabi looked up at Kai as he said that. His rich dark gaze held hers with more seriousness. Those fascinating green sparkles in the depths of his eyes held her in rapt attention. The firm line of his lips was testament to his suddenly grave mood.

Those lips were also so damned kissable, only a few inches from her own mouth, that Gabi had to stop herself from moving toward him. She bit the inside of her cheek instead, forcing herself to breathe normally. But Kai seemed aware of the same tension between them. His mouth slowly softened even as the funny lights in his eyes brightened. Their gazes locked as silence draped them with an enthralled current that seemed to leap from him to her.

Everything inside Gabi felt loose, pliant. Desirous liquidity rolled through her, making her limbs feel deliciously heavy. The tiny hairs on her arms, the back of her neck, tickled with awareness as they stood up with the ripple of sweet goosebumps.

She sensed it coming.

Slowly, Kai leaned toward her. As if she were magnetized to him, she tilted her own head up, angling it toward him. He kept his eyes open as their lips met in a long kiss. The tremendous intimacy of that made Gabi's knees shake even as she trembled all over from the sensation of his mouth on hers. First light, then more confident, Kai's lips played over hers as his hands gently stroked her shoulders and arms.

Gabi couldn't hold in a little moan. Sweet, deep desire washed over her, rolling through her in waves of anticipation. She put her hands on his chest, allowing herself to feel the muscles that rippled beneath her fingers. She pressed herself against him as their mouths tasted and touched with increasing urgency. A hardness pressed against her thigh, further shortening her breath as that wild buzz of attraction shivered around them both.

"You taste better than anything I've ever tasted before." His low, urgent voice tickled against her lips as one of his hands stole around her waist, stroking and pulling her even closer.

She huffed out a shaky whisper of a laugh. It felt as if her head was about to whirl off her shoulders. She was still fully aware of the fact that she stood in the man's boardroom—casual and pleasant a boardroom though it was, it was still a place of business, for crying out loud—at about seven in the morning. That she'd been imperiously summoned and yanked from her planned day under the waves, exploring the find of a lifetime. That being around Kai, a stranger to her, felt so normal and comfortable she'd literally wondered if she actually had known him from childhood or something.

All those things mattered yet didn't matter. Not when he was kissing her breathless and senseless, churning the storm of passion between them to what had to be, she thought in a daze, at least hurricane force levels. Her body wasn't lying to her. She wanted him, he wanted her, and the gravitational pull they had toward one another was undeniable. There was a raw, real need there that transcended the merely physical sparks dancing between them.

This was crazy. It was mind-blowing. It was fun. It was damned sexy, most of all.

Gabi let herself be pulled back into Kai's embrace as his lips and tongue again tangled with hers. Wetness slicked between her legs. Her nipples felt like super-sensitive, hard little pebbles against him. His hands pressed against her ass, drawing another moan out of her that he swallowed with his increasingly ardent kiss. Gabi felt like everything was swirling around her, through her. Feeling Kai touch her, kiss her, shoved away everything else in the world.

She willingly let it.

But after a long, head-spinning time of being solely in the moment while she was pressed against every delectable inch of the incredible man, Kai ended the kiss and gently stepped back. He was breathing faster, and his eyes were so dark, except those funny bright specks of green light in them. His face looked wild, close to feral. Confusion flickered across it as well. She sensed that pulling away from her wasn't easy. Yet he had. He took a long breath, holding eye contact. Then he shook his head a bit, as if shaking off a thought.

"So, Gabriela." His voice was so deep it reverberated through her body. "Although that was an unexpected pleasure, I did call you in here on business. We need to go over that."

He turned away from her, walking over to the large desk by the window. Rustling through some papers on it, he plucked out a few and held them up toward her. "Let's go over the forms your team filled out. Step by step."

When he looked back over at her, his face was more controlled. She stared back at him for a long moment, still breathing heavily herself.

Okay. Play time would have to come later. Which really was fine, since passionately kissing him this early in the morning while in a public building was a little crazy, even for Gabi Santos, daredevil extraordinaire.

Swallowing hard, she walked to the desk on steady legs. "Let's see, then," she said in cool tones, reaching for the papers.

As he handed them over to her, though, Kai did let one corner of his unbearably sexy mouth quirk upward in a half grin. His eyes studied her, slightly challenging, still cocky, and definitely still telling her he had desire for her. He didn't say anything, but Gabi knew one thing for sure. She was still going to kiss the hell out of this man, sooner than later, and let him

rather

touch her all over. All damn over, and it was going to be really, really good.

Simultaneously soothed and aroused by that bone-deep knowledge, she just smiled back and settled in for a day of paperwork, doing her best to keep herself in check around the man who seemed to melt her brain cells each time she saw him.

9

Sunlight sparkled on the water as the research vessel charged across the ocean. Gabi stood at the prow of the boat, looking out across the endless expanse of water as they neared the location of the shipwreck. The tang of the ocean was especially crisp today, whipped up by the healthy breeze. *Finally.* Gabi's exuberance at getting back to the wreck was hard to contain. Even though she had been kissed into a tingling paroxysm of delight yesterday, and couldn't forget about it, she was also still a little mad at Kai for having kept her away from the Santa Maria.

No matter how crazy attractive he was, and how much anticipation she had about seeing a lot more of him very soon, and how much she just bizarrely felt safe in his presence, she wasn't about to let any man come between her and her career passion. She nodded her head decisively as the vessel gradually slowed as they reached the dive site. Nope, she was going to get some of the glory again today.

Though she had to admit yesterday had been frustrating in more ways than one. After that amazing kiss early in the morning, the rest of the day had been strictly businesslike. She and

Kai had gone over the team's compliance paperwork line by line. He'd focused on certain parts of their answers, such as their planned exploration coordinates. After a brief moment of wondering if he somehow knew about the wreck site, she managed to say that they might have to widen their search area depending on what the search equipment read as they went along.

That, she'd told herself as she slightly squirmed, was true enough.

He'd pinned her with a long look, his gaze slipping down to the pocket of her pants into which she'd slipped the gold nugget after she'd quickly re-dressed for her meeting with him. She hadn't been sure why she brought it with her. Obviously she had no intention of showing it to Kai, or anyone else. Sending the one photo of it to her contact with UTEI had been enough. But being separated from it had somehow made her feel weirdly agitated. She felt a strong need to keep it close to her. When Kai's gaze went there, staying longer than a casual glance warranted, her heart had hammered. But he finally shrugged and let the moment pass.

Then, in apology for pulling her off the ocean for the day, he'd taken her on a private tour of the Institute, letting her see some of the behind-the-scenes work. It was fascinating. She was pretty sure he'd enjoyed it just as much as she had. She discovered he had just as tremendous a love for the ocean and its denizens as she did, not to mention he, too, was an aficionado of nautical history. That was a pretty cool surprise, really. But at the end of the day, he'd simply very politely said, "It's been a pleasure being in your company today, Gabi. I'll see you tomorrow."

With those cryptic words, he'd left. She didn't see or hear from him again the rest of the day.

No wonder her marriage hadn't worked out, she muttered in her head. Men were a mystery.

Seriously, Kai was the most interesting, challenging man she'd ever met. Despite her aversion to anything serious with any guy ever again, she was intrigued by him. Like, really intrigued. Another night of restless, sexy dreams left her still aroused and a little pissed off in the morning. Fine, she totally lusted for the man, as well as found him to be a great conversationalist and just fascinating overall. But really. She had work to do. Resolute, she'd focused on the day at hand and the joy of heading back into the ocean.

Yesterday, the team definitely had seen some more fascinating artifacts at the site, though they had not made any major new discoveries. Yet. Gabi was bound and determined that today, she would find more deeply intriguing parts of the wreck's secrets, diligently catalogue them all, and—perhaps most importantly—return the gold nugget to where it belonged. It nestled again in the little space at the front of her swimsuit top, pressing in a hard little reminder against her chest. With a twinge of shame, she began suiting up alongside Shane, ready to head back into the deep blue and regain her equilibrium.

Just before she reached to remove her phone, strapped to her arm in its waterproof case where she usually carried it when she was onboard any type of boat, sudden shouts startled them both. It was Liesl. "Someone's heading right for us!" the tall blonde called out, shading her eyes against the bright morning sunlight. "A sailboat."

The research vessel fell silent as everyone turned to look in the direction Liesl pointed. Sure enough, the bright white of a sailboat billowing in the breeze skimmed toward them.

Directly toward them.

"Dammit." Everson looked around at the crew. "Remember our cover story, folks."

Everyone nodded. Gabi's stomach knotted. Liesl, who had hoisted a pair of binoculars to train them on the sailboat, suddenly put them down. She looked at Gabi. "No way. I think it's your guy from the other night."

Gabi's insides lurched in a thrilling combination of excitement, nerves, and pure shock. "What? Give me those." She grabbed the binoculars, fiddled with the focus, then nearly gasped as the image sharpened directly on the fancy boat and the man steering it. He cheerfully raised an arm and waved, looking right at her.

It definitely was Kai.

How the hell had he found them out in the middle of the water? Practically in the middle of the Pacific Ocean? Okay, they weren't exactly a thousand miles off the coast of Catalina. But still, they were far off course for anyone to simply run into them. As Gabi watched, he maneuvered the very nice sailboat until he was as close to them as he could get. Despite her surprise and growing, narrow-eyed suspicion, she couldn't help but admire the masterful way he handled his sexy little craft. It sure didn't hurt that all he was wearing was a pair of black swim trunks. His chest muscles rippled in the sunlight, his strong abs flexing as he easily balanced on his boat as it gently rocked in the slight ripples of the water.

Damn. The man was sexier than hell. Torn between a desire to demand how he'd found her in the middle of the ocean and an equally strong desire to just throw herself overboard, swim over to him, and tackle him to the floor of his own boat in a shameless display of lust, Gabi only managed a semi-sputtering speechlessness.

Everson, wary and protective as always, came to the rescue. "Sweet ride you've got there, Kai Long." The crew's boss walked closer to the railing to examine Kai's boat. He let out a low, admiring whistle. "Fancy champagne and fancy boats, huh? No half measures for you. We had a Bristol when I was a kid. Almost ruined me for anything else." Everson shrugged. His tone and stance appeared casual, but Gabi knew he was being extremely watchful. "But then I discovered science and research, and it was all over. This baby is my only boat at the moment." Everson lovingly patted the railing of the bulky research vessel.

Kai laughed, his voice echoing across the water to them. "Looks like it's really well rigged out with some good equipment, though. Every scientist needs that when they're exploring the ocean blue. Even though," he added, the mildly confrontational tone in his voice carrying low and clear across the water, "she's a bit clunky compared to my racehorse here." He stroked the railing of his own fancy, powerful boat.

The possessive way he touched his boat, how his fingers glided over her, slammed through Gabi as if he'd been touching her. Despite her indignation at his untimely presence, and the ridiculous notion that he'd managed to track them out here like he was some sort of super-spy, she felt suddenly, wildly caught by her sharp interest in the man standing so casually on his sailboat. Sunglasses shoved back on his head, muscles flexing in the sunlight as he easily kept his balance on his lightly rocking boat, he was pretty much the image of an insanely sexy Poseidon. Her heart hammered inside, pummeling her ribcage with her arousal and yearning.

Yearning? When on earth did she ever yearn for a guy? Especially one she barely knew? Hotter than hell kisses notwithstanding. Swallowing hard, she kept herself still, training her eyes on Kai as she forced herself to focus on the historical scientific mission at hand. "You're not making fun of our boat, are you?"

Kai laughed. "I'm just saying she's a different breed than mine here. This baby," he gently slapped the side of his sailboat, "is sensitive as well as strong. She handles a lot differently than your research vessel. Probably," and now his voice took on a challenging tone as he grinned, looking straight at Gabi as he threw down a stinging gauntlet, "too much for you to handle, I'd say. What do you think, Gabi Santos?" His eyes traveled openly along her body, the appreciation clear in his gaze even as his words confronted her. "Can you handle a sleek beauty like this, or are you out of your element here?"

Liesl gasped and Shane laughed in disbelief. Despite her best intentions to remain coolly collected, in two seconds flat, all Gabi saw was red.

———

KAI COULD SEE the outraged tilt of Gabi's head from where he stood. He also had a damn fine view of her stunning, luscious body encased in a sensible yet flattering ruby red two-piece swimsuit. Just like that, his cock stirred to very firm attention. He could sense her hesitation over the situation, although it seemed she was leaning toward verbally duking it out with him. She gave a single glance toward her crew leader, Everson, who watched with a vigilance Kai would have missed had he not known the exact reason they were here.

They were nervous he was about to find out their true purpose.

Much as he wanted to watch, from a safe distance, as they descended to the shipwreck and saucy, sexy Gabriela touched his gold again, yesterday's second instance of interruption in tasting her sweet decadence had made up Kai's mind. Oh, he'd been the fool who had interrupted it himself. His dragon had gotten almost out of control while Kai was kissing Gabi, to the point he abruptly felt his usual hold over his wild side slip a bit. He told himself it was because of the small piece of his treasure, which he felt calling to him from the pocket she'd tucked it into for whatever reason.

Yeah. That had to be it.

Even so, shocked and confused by his intense reaction to her, he'd steered the day back to a more professional space, then deliberately left without making any plans to see her that night. She made his head spin in a way he didn't understand.

Frankly, it made him wary and suspicious.

But then he'd had explosively sexual dreams about her all night long, somehow tangled up with his gold and jewels as they tantalized him from an unreachable distance. When he'd awoken after the restless night, he'd vowed that today he would finally taste her to his full leisure, hear her breathy voice as he made her come again and again.

Then he would winnow out the truth from her about how it was that she could handle his own treasure.

Kai waited for the sexy spitfire to respond to his deliberately challenging words. He'd already figured out that Gabi was quick to rise to bait. He only hoped his was attractive enough.

After a barely perceptible shrug from Everson, Gabi looked back at Kai. A mix of annoyance, frustration, intrigue, and unmistakable desire played over her strong, gorgeous face. Planting her hands on her her hips, she didn't disappoint him. "Oh, yeah? Let's see about that." Her impassioned voice carried quite clearly across the water.

She turned to the crew member standing beside her, handed over the binoculars and camera she'd been holding, and with agile ease climbed to the top of the low railing of the research vessel. Kai raised his eyebrows, half shocked and half pleased at her boldness. She nodded her head once, as if making a decision. In the next breath, she launched into the water, diving in with clean simplicity, then breaking the surface while already stroking toward his sailboat. Gabi reached the side of it in moments, her head poking up out of the water like that of a beautiful seal.

"You didn't tell me you were also a mermaid," he said. He couldn't keep laughter from rumbling out of him as he bent down to extend a hand to her. She grasped it, then he easily swung her up onto the deck of his boat.

"You just hauled me up like I was a feather." Despite what he could tell was still indignation framing her words, she apparently couldn't help the little laugh that slipped out of her as well. As she shook her head, water droplets sprayed across them both. As they sprinkled over his skin, small chills of anticipation whispered over him along with Gabi's sleek, clean scent.

His balls tightened so painfully hard at Gabi's teasing reply they almost hurt. She was so sexy, so beautiful, and so willing to just have fun that it was about to drive him beyond crazy. The soothing blankness he craved was with him, cocooning him in the shelter of a familiar sensation.

The sensation that he was about to have his world rocked by this gorgeous woman.

A roaring deep inside him started so quietly, so faintly, Kai didn't notice it at first. It grew in intensity, forcing itself up through him.

Desire.

Want.

Need.

His dragon. Wrestling with his human side for control.

Kai shoved the creature back down so hard he almost stumbled from the effort.

Gabi turned and waved back at the research boat. "I'll play double duty with paperwork this afternoon, Everson," she called out. Reluctance edged her voice. "Dante can go down with Shane today, is that cool?"

"No problem, Gabs." Everson eyed Kai again, but all he did was give him an accommodating wave. "We've got it over here. Call if you need anything." He nodded toward the phone strapped to Gabi's upper arm, which Kai had noted and thought was an incredibly smart way to wear it if one was on and in the water a lot. "Have fun," Everson added in a deliberately casual tone. With that, the crew leader turned back to the others on the research boat and started talking about early native inhabitants of the island and something about ancient fishing vessels and underwater caves.

Keeping his face expressionless at their attempt to throw him off the scent, Kai simply waved at the rest of the crew, then looked back at Gabi.

She once again had her hands cocked on her sweetly generous hips. "So. You really think I don't know how to sail this thing?" She pushed past him, deliberately letting her shoulder rub against his chest as she strode over to the wheel. Kai sucked in a quick breath at the sensation of her skin touching his, even so briefly. It was as if he were a teenage boy who couldn't control anything. Turning his back on the research ship, he watched Gabi grab the wheel with expert hands to tack away in the breeze from the research ship, setting the course back toward the general direction of Catalina. "Let me show you how it's done, sailor." Her voice was a long, luscious tease over him as a delighted grin spread across her face.

Damn. Even if he didn't have to find out how she'd been able to get to his gold, and what they planned to do with it, he wouldn't have been able to keep himself away from her anyway. She was a stunner.

Today, there would be no stopping him. He was going to taste her lusciousness again, continuing what they'd both wanted the other night before being interrupted. Stepping up behind her at the wheel, he let his breath whisper over her shoulder, enjoying her slight shiver as he did so. She leaned almost imperceptibly back toward him. His entire body tightly attuned to her, like the electric sizzle from lightning as it flung itself from sky to ground.

"So," he began, allowing his voice to roll over her. "As I recall from the other night at the bar, our conversation was just starting to get interesting. For instance," and he let his grin come out in his voice, "your world of crazy seems like it has a hell of a lot of fun adventures in it. Scuba diving, research. Meeting strange, dangerous men at bars on small islands."

Gabi's laughter whipped over him in the breeze as the sail caught the wind and they picked up speed. "You might be a stranger to me, but you're not dangerous." She seemed almost surprised by her own conviction.

Kai stepped behind her completely, putting a hand on either side of the railings around the wheel. He could tell that Gabi sensed his presence directly behind her by the sudden inhale his heightened dragon senses could pick up. A spike in her beautiful scent wafted to him. He groaned softly, fully aware that she could hear it.

"You think I'm not dangerous?" His voice was low in her ear. Despite his efforts to push it back, he felt his dragon roughening his tone. Guiding his daring words. "I'm definitely dangerous, Gabi. Because I have every intention of dangerously violating every inch of your body that you want me to. I also have the dangerous intention of the two of us putting on a shameless, voyeuristic display right here on the sailboat, out in the middle of the water where anyone might come upon us. Or is that too adventuresome even for you?"

GABI'S MOUTH DROPPED OPEN, although she managed to keep the sailboat on a steady course. Kai's deep voice and provocative words wrapped around her body, swirling into her with a flash of the liquid desire that had begun when she first laid eyes on him and had yet to completely dissipate. She also still felt strangely comfortable in his presence. Her sixth sense was never wrong. Kai was a good, decent guy.

Even though he was also a bad boy who'd just outrageously propositioned her.

"Definitely not," she said in a smooth voice, though she had to swallow first to make sure it would work. "I like the sound of that. It's the kind of dangerous adventure that's right up my alley."

Gabi glanced to the side and slightly behind them. The research vessel was disappearing in the distance. She definitely felt the very sharp tug of regret that she would not be diving down to the wreck today. That she was indeed letting a guy come between her and the work she loved. Yet she was protecting both it and the research crew. Even so, she couldn't help but feel insanely turned on that she was about to get down and dirty with a super sexy guy on his sailboat in the middle of the Pacific. With Kai. Surprising, controlling, guarded, intense, yet also relaxed, laughter-filled, multi-layered, and just fascinating Kai.

"I have to admit I've never done anything risqué on a sail-boat in full daylight before," she added, hearing the breathless quality in her own voice. "But you present a compelling case."

There was a short pause, then Kai stepped so close to her that his body pressed against hers from behind. Gabi almost yanked the wheel sharply to the side as the contact with his body sent thrilling chills through hers.

"Steady on there, sailor lass," he rumbled into her ear. She would have laughed at that cheesy nickname, but his hands gently moved onto her arms, lightly stroking her from shoulders down to elbows and back again. The sensation intensified the tingles zipping and singing throughout her body and sucked her laughter back up into a quiet little gasp. "Where you taking us, anyway?"

At the moment, Gabi wasn't quite sure where the hell they were going. "Hadn't really thought that far ahead." She gasped more loudly as his hand left her arm and gently dropped down to her waist. His fingers, broad and strong, very gently stroked the bare skin there just above her hip.

"Then I have just the place in mind." He murmured the directions into her ear, his fingers swirling small strokes on the skin above her hip bone and somewhat scrambling her brain as she adjusted course.

"Yes. Dead ahead now. There's a small reef where we can drop anchor and just..." His voice dropped even more, into a sensual weave of desire. "Relax for a while."

Legs shaking a bit, Gabi turned her head slightly so that his chin pressed into her cheek. "This wasn't how I envisioned my day. But I think I can definitely get into this."

10

er entire body humming with delight, Gabi expertly steered Kai's fancy sailboat to the spot he directed her. His long, lean body worked with a graceful yet very powerful strength as he set the anchor for the boat. They lazily bobbed on the water, nothing in sight for miles but the endless expanse of blue-green ocean and the dark hillside rolls of Catalina Island to their east. The way the boat bobbed down between the slight swells of the water, they couldn't see the glittering Los Angeles shoreline behind the island. It was as if nothing in the world existed but ocean water, the distant hills of the island, the bobbing sailboat, and the two of them.

Every inch of Gabi's skin felt more attuned, more alive than usual. The typical excitement of being just on the edge of hooking up with a new guy, especially one as alluring and attractive as Kai, swept through her. But aside from that, she felt an extra little flip of something fluttering deep inside her. An intensity, a certain knowledge that everything that was about to happen between them was choreographed yet primal. Familiar, yet unknown. Utterly amazing in its newness, yet also so strangely familiar it was as if she would know what his body would feel like beneath her fingers before she even touched him.

But that was crazy. She'd never laid eyes on the man before the night before last.

Feet slightly spread on the deck of the boat in the casual manner of someone long familiar with even the slight roll of watercraft anchored in ocean, Kai looked like some sort of ancient oceanic god. His muscles rippled and slightly gleamed in the morning sun, the muscles in his legs gently flexing as he almost unconsciously kept his balance on the subtle yet constant movement of the deck.

She watched him, her pulse beating more rapidly in her throat, as he slowly strolled toward her, slipping his sunglasses off his face and casually dropping them onto the rail seat. Not ridiculously brawny like a body builder, rather he had more the physique of a lean, incredibly strong fighting machine. Gabi could practically feel the power rolling off of him as he came toward her. Cool, delicious waves of desire flowed deep inside her, sending tingling flashes of longing along her limbs. She was already damp between her legs, just from the expression on his face. He gazed at hers if she were something he wanted so badly he would do anything for her. As if she were his possession.

As if she were already his.

Kai stopped a few inches away from her, close enough that she could see those funny little bright green flecks swirling in the dark brown of his eyes. *Trick of the light,* she thought somewhere in the back of her mind. The desire washing through her was quickly tiding over her rational thoughts and gently drowning them in the expanding pool of desire that was spreading out from between her legs to every little spot on her body.

"I can see your sexy nipples through the top of your suit, Gabi," he said, his voice dark and deep. "I want to see your eyes, too," he added. His voice dropped down to a baritone so low it almost vibrated through her head.

The double whammy of this incredibly sexy man not only admiring her body but wanting the intimacy of looking into her eyes was like a laser bolt of ravenous delight straight to her clit. Gabi opened her mouth slightly, inhaling sharply against the roof of her mouth. She felt more than heard herself begin to breathe quickly. A satisfied smile of anticipation unfurled across the slash of Kai's mouth. He reached out to very gently pull her sunglasses off her face. They were already dried from her impromptu swim, though her hair was still wet and salty. He set them down on the rail seat as Gabi blinked against the bright sunlight. In the back of her head, she noted it was strange that he hadn't seemed affected by the full sunlight the way she was, but that thought almost immediately dissipated into the soft wash of desire pulsing through her limbs.

Kai reached out his other hand and gently stroked the backs of his fingers over her cheek, along her chin, slowly down her throat, and onto the bare collarbones between her breasts.

She definitely could tell that her nipples were tenting out. It wasn't just from her dip in the ocean. No, this was pure, naked desire racing through her body and engulfing every nerve ending in anticipation.

"You're so incredibly beautiful." Kai's voice was a murmur that swirled into the breeze, mingling with it in a way that made it seem as if the ocean itself was sighing into her ear.

She let a half smile tug up her lips as she replied. "Thank you, dangerous man." She let a teasing note color her words, half trying to mask her slight breathlessness as well as the sense she had of beginning to lose control.

But she couldn't fool him. His own lips quirked up as he responded in a murmur, "It's only the truth. And you like hearing it."

Gabi half choked on her own breath as it caught in her

throat when he turned his hand around to let his palm and then his fingers caress downward over her breast. She couldn't stop the little moan that escaped her when he deliberately began playing with her hardened nipple. "Oh," was all she could say as the wild sensation of his touch robbed her of speech even as it brought roaring to life the very turned on state of her body. Her restless dreams and ceaseless thoughts of him exploded in a miasma of want that was so fierce, so sudden, that it took her even more by surprise. Gazing straight back at him, she caught the same look of naked, abrupt startlement on his face.

For a long moment, as the sunlight poured over them and his hand clasped her entire breast, something wild, deep, and more true than anything Gabi had never before felt in her life held them both.

Together.

After another long, silent beat, during which Gabi felt some sort of confusing knowledge whipping through her, the moment broke when Kai gave a tiny shake of his head. He reached out his other hand, curving it up behind her neck and threading his fingers into the damp strands of her hair. He found the small band that held it in a ponytail, gently worked it loose, let it drop to the ground so that her hair wetly tumbled against her shoulders and back. Gently pulling her phone in its protective little case off her arm, he pulled apart the case's velcro strap with a small ripping sound, then carefully attached it to the rail above the seat.

"In case your family needs to reach you," he said, shrugging at her with what was almost diffidence.

The knowledge that he remembered that, that he took the time to be sure her phone was secure on the sailboat and nearby in case it rang, did something funny to her heart. Swallowing hard, she forced herself

"Damn, Gabi." The lingering sense of that strange, wild something tumbled beneath his voice as he stared into her eyes. The jade flecks in the onyx depths of his irises held her mesmerized. "I need to taste you right now."

His voice was so rough with pure need that she swayed where she stood. Gabi's answer was to reach her own hands up around his broad shoulders and strong neck, pulling his face toward hers.

The second their lips met, Gabi knew she was done for. Sharp, aching thrills jetted out along all her nerve endings, coursing along her limbs and seeming to make her entire body buzz. Kai's mouth crashed down on hers as his hands pressed her close into him. His hard chest anchored her soft curves as she willingly molded herself to his every inch. Her tongue sought entrance into his mouth, which he allowed with an appreciative moan letting her know how much he liked her eagerness.

She felt his hands busy on her back, trying to figure out how to take her bathing suit top off. Puffing out a light giggle into his mouth, Gabi stepped away for a moment, giving him a teasing glance as she simply lifted her arms over her head. "You have to pull it off of me," she whispered, enjoying how his impossibly dark eyes seemed to darken even more at her directive, while the jade lights in them sparkled in the sunlight. "And hurry," she added, her voice breathless despite her bossy order.

Groaning, Kai reached forward and roughly yet carefully pulled off her swim tank, releasing her full breasts into the bright sunlight of the day. "Oh, damn," he whispered with such reverence that her nipples perked up even more. He reached forward to skim his thumbs along the taut little peaks, making her gasp. "That's right," he said, his eyes looking up to hers as he lazily circled his thumbs around her nipples. "It's been killing me, waiting to hear you make sounds like this."

Feeling abruptly inarticulate, Gabi could only nod, still snared by the intensity of his gaze. She didn't even spare a thought for looking around to see if there were any boats remotely nearby. She couldn't care less if someone had been spying on them with high-power binoculars at the moment. In fact, the naughty kick of being somewhat exposed turned her on even more. The jolting deep within her rapid heartbeat was odd, though. She didn't usually feel this comfortably intimate around a man. Not real intimacy. Not the kind that counted in the deeper sense.

But something about Kai Long, something aside from the sexy, hard planes of his body, the abruptly sensual tilt of his mouth, the promise of deeply fulfilled desire in his expression each time he looked at her, tugged at her. Something more intense than mere physical attraction thumped in her chest as well.

Something that was both appealing and terrifying.

Pushing it aside, she gave way to the moment and the sensations flooding her breasts from the small yet arousing pressure of his thumbs on each ultra-sensitive nipple.

"Looks like you dried off from your little dip earlier," he murmured, the depth of his voice throbbing through her. "Let me fix that for you."

As Gabi watched, her breath stuttering in her chest, Kai took his hands from her breasts, licked first one of his thumbs, then the other, and returned them to her aching nipples to swirl around them in long, wet strokes.

She jerked her face up as she gasped, pressing her breasts forward into his hands with the greediness of all the pent-up, restless desire she'd had since she first laid eyes on him in the bar. A self-satisfied smile claimed his face as he spread the rest of his fingers over the fullness of each of her breasts, kneading and stroking and pressing while his thumbs still worked over the super sensitized buds. Shivers of delight raced along her entire body as Kai touched her in the streams of sunlight scattering off the lapping ripples of the Pacific Ocean spread about them in every direction.

Still looking at her, Kai's voice dropped into the air in a

deep, unyielding command. "Take those off, too," he said, dipping his chin at her swimsuit bottoms. "Because if I have to wait another second, Gabi, I'm going to rip them off you with my bare teeth."

KAI's HEART slammed in his chest just as his cock swelled at nearly full attention as he waited to see what Gabi would do. The cinnamon of her eyes darkening to rich mocha was his answer.

She was definitely just as turned on as he was. Just as eager, just as impatient. He had the distinct impression that if he slipped his hand into those sweet swimsuit bottoms right now and dipped a finger inside her, it would come out covered in her sweet, creamy juices as testament to just how damned excited she was right now.

It took every ounce of his strength to merely stand there, thumbs still turning lazy circles on her gorgeous nipples, and wait for her to take the bottoms off herself. Inside, his dragon roared and strained against his control. Urging Kai on. Urging him to take this woman with all his strength and desire, to show her how much he wanted to pleasure her. To see her eyes turn nearly black with need, to watch her mouth pant open just as her legs would part for him in wet, wild longing.

Claim her, the thought swelled and boomed deep inside him. *Claim her.*

Kai forced his breath to exhale and inhale out of him evenly despite his jolt at that crazy thought. No. There would be no claiming. That was far more than anything he had planned, ever. It had to stem from the fact that he'd been practically useless with desire for her since he'd seen her, but had yet to fulfill that need. Plenty of late night fantasies about her had played out when he was alone in his shower at home both the previous nights, but wickedly hot as they'd been, they hadn't been enough to sate his need.

He was just horny, dammit. That was all. Swallowing hard and pushing back on his dragon's bizarre desire with all his might, Kai watched as Gabi gave him a seductive smile.

She took one step back from him, then another. His hands ached with loss as her gorgeous breasts left them, but he hardened even more, if that were possible, as she gently slipped her hands down to her swimsuit bottoms, hooked her thumbs on the sides of them at her hips, and slowly, provocatively, began shimmying them down her stunningly luscious body.

Kai was pretty sure he was about to swallow his own damn tongue as he watched her. Everything else in the world faded away at the sound of the lapping water, the far-off call of seagulls carrying through the air from where they circled near the island, and the blissful eroticism of watching this stunning, opulent woman so willingly and ardently strip for him on the deck of his sailboat.

"Like this, sailor?" Gabi's voice was low and sultry, dragging like softened coral over his sensitized nerve endings. Crazy tingles raced their way across every inch of Kai's skin, making him feel abruptly lightheaded from sheer desire for her.

As he watched, she did a slow little dance with her legs and her hands, moving the swimsuit bottoms down over the sweet curves of her thighs, past her knees, to land in a small scrap of red cloth by her feet. With a long, teasing smile, she stepped one foot out and kicked them away with her other foot. Then she spread her arms to her sides, cocked one leg up on the toes of her foot with her knee slightly bent in front of her, and with all of her gorgeous nakedness displayed before him, murmured, "So. What do you think?"

11

W hat Kai thought was that all his thinking was completely paralyzed. His brain simply stalled out as he stared at her exquisiteness before him. All smooth golden skin, except for the paler parts from the swimsuit that she obviously wore often, Gabi was a breath-taking sight to behold. The stunning bounty of her breasts, the soft curve of her belly, the beautiful span of her hips, the strength of her thighs and calves. Her toned arms, waving around as she did a little shimmy for him, slightly rolling her eyes at her little exhibition even though she still gave him a seductive smile, urged him forward. He went right to her and ran his hands down the length of her arms, then back up to capture her hands and gently bring them behind her back, causing her chest to arch out toward him. "I think I like it a hell of a lot," he said, his voice so serious that her teasing smile was abruptly, literally swallowed as she stared back at him. He could see the pulse speeding in her neck, smell her natural scent of jasmine as it spread into his senses with its sweet allure.

He wanted to bury himself inside the succulence of Gabi's body as soon as possible. "You are insanely beautiful." He leaned down to touch one of her still hardened nipples with his tongue. A babble of inarticulate, blissful sound rolled out of her. Chuckling against her sweet breast, he moved his head to her other one, stroking and swirling his tongue around the peaked nipple. Drawing back for a moment, looking up at her, he said, "This is what my tongue will be doing to another part of you in just a few moments." She gasped, arching her back even more to thrust her breast into his mouth again.

Kneeling on the deck, ignoring the hardness of it against his knees, Kai placed his hands around the gorgeous swell of her hips as he gently bit at her nipple. Gabi hissed slightly, but then she thrust herself toward him even harder, moving her hands down to the back of his neck and his shoulders, which she seemed to be holding onto for dear life. He smiled against her skin, tasting the tang of saltwater mixed with her own sweetness and savoring it.

Then slowly, carefully, he traced a line with his tongue down between her breasts, toward her belly button, over the sweet roundness of her belly.

Gabi moaned above him, spreading her feet firmly on the deck. He glanced up at her. Her head was tossed back, her eyes shut, her face illuminated in the sunlight. She was utterly in the moment, and seemed thoroughly uninhibited.

Kai felt his balls tighten in even more anticipation of exploring every inch of her body and having her in turn explore every inch of his. Never before had he been so eager to make a woman come. To taste a particular woman. To hear her voice when she moaned in pleasure at what he was doing to her. To feel the sweet luxury of her body moving in perfect rhythm, in total cadence with his.

Tightening his hold on her hips, Kai ran his tongue down into the heavenly crease between her legs where she kept her sweetest treasure.

GABI BUCKED and pulsed beneath his tongue, a cry ripping from her mouth at the divine sensations shooting out from where he nestled his dark head between her legs. Spinning tidal waves of feeling roared through her, swirling and churning right at the point where his tongue stroked her nub, lapped at her folds, and drank of her like he'd never tasted anything more luscious. Like she was some sort of delicious, precious nectar he wanted to lose himself in.

"Kai." Her voice was a throaty gasp. "Don't stop. Don't you dare stop."

"Like hell I'll stop," he growled into her. His vibrating lips and tongue as he spoke sent more quivers into her right there, causing her to keen like she was some sort of wild animal. Utterly lost to the feeling of sheer bliss about to crash over her.

Damn. She'd known it would be good with him. Yet just his first lick told her exactly how spectacular it was about to be.

His fingers drifting down to her bare ass, which he stroked and kneaded even as he pulled her hips closer to him, Kai swirled his tongue around inside her, then gently began nodding his head up and down, making his tongue stroke her up, then down, then up, then down.

Gabi was pretty sure her head was about to blow right off of her body. She knew her short fingernails were digging into his shoulders as she pressed down on him, but she didn't give a damn. Hell, she was stark naked on the guy's sailboat, had her hips shamelessly thrust in his face, and her mouth was making sounds she hadn't even realized she was capable of. Clearly, she was past the point about caring if she left her mark on him.

Just like he was leaving his mark on her.

"Taste so good," he murmured at the end of an upward stroke, just before starting a new downward stroke.

Gabi's only response was to gasp, spread her legs even more, and hold on as she rode his amazingly strong, thoroughly talented tongue.

"Kai," she warned, the feelings of the past few days' and

nights' worth of constant arousal coalescing so quickly in her she knew an orgasm was about to surge over her. "I'm going to—"

He tightened his fingers on her ass even more, his thumbs clutching the fronts of her hip bones as he pressed his face closer in between her legs and swirled his tongue faster and harder, circling her clit. Rhythmically diving deep into her wet folds before stroking upward to play with it again. The rhythm of all his movements was steady and even, but so strong, so wild, excitingly unknown and unpredictable, that she blew over the edge before she could even finish her sentence.

Screaming into the sunlight of the day, the dancing ocean breeze playing through her hair, Kai's intoxicating scent of wild bamboo and deep marine swells washing over her, Gabi came so strong and hard she literally collapsed onto him even in the middle of it, her shaking legs unable to hold her up.

Her voice chanted his name again and again through the stunning climax that shattered her body.

Slipping one hand behind her, his mouth and tongue still not leaving her beautifully spasming core, Kai gently took her to the deck as he drank up the last of the trembles that flowed out from beneath his tongue's slowly easing strokes.

Boneless, spent yet still aroused and ready for more, Gabi flopped back onto the deck, sucking in lungful after lungful of air as Kai easily pulled his body up to cover hers. "Look at me," he said, his voice ragged with some sort of dark, primal need that had her snapping her eyes open. The flashes of pine-green lights in his eyes startled her even as she let herself fall into their depths.

"Yes," he breathed, slowly lowering himself so she could feel his silken hardness pressing onto her thighs. "That's what I dreamed your face would look like. But I missed the actual moment when you were coming and screaming as you fell apart under my touch."

Even though she had just done exactly that, and was no

stranger to sexy talk from guys, Gabi still felt the delicious flash of renewed craving tumble through her like mini waves.

"This time," and he ran his hand up her leg, over her hip, tickling along her ribs and breast and neck before gently fisting in her hair, "this time, I want to see your face right under mine when you come again while I'm inside you. I've been waiting for that from the moment I met you, Gabi," he groaned, before lowering his mouth to hers and feasting on her mouth as ravenously as he just had between her legs.

Gabi tasted her own spices intermingled with Kai's deliciously salty tang and the purely masculine scent of him that was driving her more wild by the second. Her greedy lower lips, which apparently hadn't been fully satisfied, sharply tingled with another spasm of desire. She arched her hips up against him even as she pulled his head down onto hers, claiming his mouth back with just as much fierceness as he claimed hers. His slight chuckle at her bold display of passion was met by a light swat to his ass as she gave him a naughty little spank.

Jumping slightly, pulling back his head just enough to look at her with an even more intense curiosity and rush of desire, Kai said, "Oh, really? Who's on top right now, hmm?"

In response, Gabi caught his lower lip between her teeth, giving an experimental little nibble as she kept her eyes open and looking straight at him. Gently releasing his lip, she murmured against his mouth, "You may be on top, my sexy dangerous stranger, but that just means I've got you exactly where I want you. So I guess I'm in control, after all."

Smiling in satisfaction as the shadows of desire made his eyes even darker and those funny little green flecks even brighter, Gabi ran her hands down his back, along his hips, and slid one underneath him to gently grasp his enormous, hard length in her hand. This time, Kai was the one who sucked in his breath, making a half strangled sound as his eyes half lidded from his arousal.

GABI GAVE a light squeeze with her hand. Kai sharply inhaled as his cock became even harder beneath her fingertips. Gabi's eyes, now practically the color of espresso, looked up at him with mingled desire, curiosity, and such trust that he felt something hard in his chest squeezing in response. His dragon, pushing against his mind and beginning to guide Kai's movements into a more primal beat, crowed with a firm acceptance of her trust.

For some reason, his dragon side seemed more attuned to and interested in this woman than anyone Kai had been with since—

He shook the thoughts out of his head and focused on the pure pleasure of this moment. Gabi's soft, lush body beneath his, the aching swell rolling over him which longed to slam into her, taking possession of her, the certainty of the mingled physical sensations he knew would sweep over them soon, all encouraged Kai to do nothing more than focus on this moment.

He pushed himself back slightly on one forearm and onto his knees, reaching with his other hand to first gently drag his thumb across her lips. Pressing into the corner of her mouth, he watched the pulse beat more strongly in her neck. She licked his thumb, then lightly bit down on it. Groaning, he gently brushed his hand over her cheek and down her body. His questing fingers traveled between her legs and dipped into the soft, hot, soaked folds and crevices that had exploded like the most succulent ambrosia on his lips and tongue moments earlier.

Gabi gasped again, her hand convulsively tightening on his rock-hard cock. Holding himself back, fearing he would move too hard, too fast for her, he said, "Put your hands over your head, beautiful." His voice was so deep from his need to get inside her that it rumbled between them. Eyes locked on his, hips unabashedly straining toward him, Gabi obeyed. The upward tip to her mouth as well as the sweet, fierce fire in her eyes, however, told him she was only obeying because she wanted to. Because she knew she was strong enough to not only say no to anything he asked, but also to ask him for anything she herself wanted.

He knew without a doubt that anything she asked him right now, he would do for her. First, though, he needed to sink into her rich depths and feel himself actually encased by her softness and wetness. As her hands stretched out above her head, he shifted more of his weight onto his knees so he could reach out with his other hand to gently grasp both her hands in his and lightly hold them up there. Her breath snagged in her throat and she stared up at him, but the widening smile of thrilled anticipation spreading across her face told him she loved it.

"You ready for me, beautiful?" The deep timbre of his dragon sounded in his voice.

Gabi nodded, the drying strands of her hair still sticking to one side of her face and cheek as she spread her legs beneath him and tilted upward so he could have easier access. Her sheer responsiveness to him almost blew his control right then. He managed to rein it in with a mighty struggle, another small groan building in his throat as he reached down with his other hand to guide himself to the deliciously welcoming center he craved so desperately.

Positioning the nearly throbbing head of his cock at her entrance, he made sure he was nestled in just the right spot. Gabi's knees spread wider as she angled herself to receive him, her breath coming so quickly that she was panting now. Despite the early hour, beads of perspiration dotted her hairline and cheek in shining little dots, which only added to her beauty.

"Oh, damn, Gabi," Kai muttered in a savage whisper before gently easing himself inside her. She was so slick, so ready, that he slid in all the way to the base of his cock without effort, although the tightness of her inner walls held him in snug embrace. They both gasped simultaneously, Kai's hand tightening on her wrists as his other hand clutched her shoulder. Not taking his eyes from hers, he pulled back, and gently thrust forward again. Gabi's neck arched to the sky as she flung her head back, revealing her smooth golden neck to him. He reached down and tongued her fast-beating pulse, pulling out of her again only to drive back in more quickly this time.

"Kai," she said. Her voice was surprisingly steady and clear. "This is exactly how I was imagining it would feel with you for the last several days." This sentence, though, trailed off into another gasp as he plunged into her again, faster.

Harder.

With more intent.

Sinking into her depths, losing himself to her sweetness.

Claiming her. His dragon roared in approval, taking control. Kai couldn't remember why he should not claim her. Why he should not claim her lusciousness, her openness, her unfettered abandon that met him stroke for stroke and cry for cry.

Why he should not claim this amazing woman to be his, and his alone.

Knowing that the next time he opened his mouth his voice might be totally lost to the deep register of his dragon's tone, Kai began slamming in and out of her with earnest urgency. She felt so good. She fit him perfectly. The sweet spiral upward of his impending explosion spread throughout his entire body. Every limb was rigid with purpose and intention as he gently held her down, wildly, ever faster pumped into her, tensing himself in aching anticipation.

Even so, he just barely managed to hold himself back. To wait for her to come with him. He wanted to see her face the moment she shattered around him. If he came before her, he would be so lost in the sensations he was certain he wouldn't be able to keep his eyes open and watch her.

Holding himself back for another long moment was sheer agony, yet at the same time sheer bliss. Fascinated, he watched the procession of expressions rippling across Gabi's face as she neared her own release. Right now, she was the most beautiful woman he'd ever laid eyes on in his life. The joyous intensity on her face, the opening of her mouth and hoarseness of her breath only served to excite and urge him on.

He was about to erupt. Teeth slightly gritted, he forced out a word that he knew would be guttural and wild when he said it. "Now. Now!"

As if his voice had flipped a beautiful switch within her, Gabi let go. She convulsed around his cock even as she screamed out his name. Roaring out loud, hearing his dragon's rough rasp in his voice, Kai let go with her. Her face tightened and loosened at once as she came, her eyes nearly rolling back in her head as her inner walls convulsed around his cock. The view was so sweet it intensified Kai's own sharp, furious release, causing sparks to explode across his own vision.

Bending his head down to hers, laying his mouth on her neck, he cried out his joyous release into her neck, at the same time sending the rolling tidal wave of his breath into her and throughout her. Shooting the whisper of his name into her, leaving it incised into her skin, her heart, her very soul.

His dragon bugled with fierce, possessive joy as Kai claimed Gabi for his.

THEY LAY TOGETHER, entwined in a wet, sprawled heat, just heaving muscles and limbs coated with sweat. Gabi felt the languor that followed the most amazing orgasms of her life spread throughout her as she nestled into her dangerous, sexy stranger's arms. Her sexy, gorgeous, familiar *Kai*. His breath tickled over her skin and gently played in her hair as they basked in the sunshine on the boat's deck.

When everything finally quieted, Kai slowly pushed
himself up on his elbows, staring at her for a long time. He
reached his hand out to her face, gently stroking the delicate
skin by her eyes and lips. She admired his muscular thighs as
they rested on either side of her body, his gorgeous cock still
heavy as it nestled on top of her stomach. Grinning with
delight, she stretched her arms up behind her back and arched
herself toward the sun for a long, luxurious moment. Letting
her arms come back down, she looked at him again, still
smiling.

As his breath settled back into a regular rhythm, something
else slowly settled back onto his face as well. Something moved
in his eyes, something so deep that it momentarily stole her
breath again. Possessiveness. Pride. And then, something
darker. Something a little colder, a little more distant. Some
sort of internal battle surged across his face. His jaw muscles
worked, as if he wanted to say something but instead bit back
the words. He closed his eyes for a long moment, breathing
carefully in controlled measure. When he opened his eyes
again, the green sparks were gone. Unfathomable black pools
remained, as cold and impenetrable as a winter ice sheet. The
beautiful relaxation that had spread over his face long
moments earlier disappeared. Leaving behind a hard mask as
he stared at her.

Feeling abruptly chilled, Gabi froze. He pushed himself all
the way back and sat up, reaching over to grab her discarded
swimsuit. Then his voice dropped into the warmth with a
starkness that shocked her into struggling to sit up. "So. I need
to hear the truth from you now. Finally."

Gabi shook her head in confusion. She felt vulnerable all
of a sudden. As if the intimacy that had just happened
between them was a hazy dream. He backed away from her,
slowly standing as he grasped her swimsuit top. Not taking his
eyes off hers, he slowly brought the red fabric up in between
them, stretching it taut so she could see where his fingers

pressed onto the little decorative lump just at the vee of the top.

The little lump that was the gold nugget she'd tucked in there that morning, determined to put it back where it belonged at the wreck. She'd forgotten all about it during the bliss of enjoying Kai. A tight ball of anxiety thunked into her stomach as her eyes darted from it back up to his where he loomed over her.

"So." The cool seeping from his voice iced over the space between them, making Gabi protectively cross her arms in front of her. "Would you like to tell me, Gabriela Santos, assistant academic director of the underwater archeology program at California University, crew member for the Ancients Quest dive team, what you were doing stealing gold from a shipwreck that isn't even any of your damn business?"

1 2

Kai knew he towered above Gabi as she still sat on the deck, vulnerable below him. He knew he was looming, which frankly pissed him off really badly. He hadn't meant to do it this way. This not only wasn't his style, he actually really felt like an ass right now as he saw Gabi's paling face. But the terror that had lurched into him, after the effects of the most intense orgasm of his life had worn off and he realized with stark clarity what he'd just done—that he'd just *claimed* a woman as his—was horrific in its grip. Desperately, he instead sought the emptiness that had protected him for years now.

His dragon protesting the entire time, Kai managed to put up a wall between him and this stunning woman. Gabi, whom he had just claimed as his own. As being *his* woman.

No. He had to focus. His gold, his treasure, was all that mattered right now. He had a purpose here. It was to reclaim his gold, find out how she was able to touch it, break the spell on it, and leave. Alone, the way he preferred it. That was all. He'd seduced her and had fun.Claiming meant nothing, damn it all to hell. That was simply a slip in judgment. Now was the time for answers.

Even so, the knowledge that he was scaring her sent a pang of regret and distaste through him. His dragon blasted him with internal fire, equally disgusted. Yet before he could feel too bad for being an intimidating, coldhearted ass, bold-hearted Gabriela set her jaw and narrowed her eyes at him. As she abruptly scrambled to her feet, her own sudden fire flashed out of her beautiful cinnamon brown eyes.

"No," she said, advancing on him with a finger pointing into his chest. It shook a bit, but she seemed to regain her steadiness with every step she took toward him. "I think what really has to happen here is that *you,* Kai Long, island guy and amazing lover and secret chairman of the board and, and, whatever else you are," she sputtered, "*you* need to tell *me* how the hell *you* know about the shipwreck."

Charged silence held them both still in a tense tableau on the deck of the boat, both naked as jaybirds and, he knew, still smelling erotically and deliciously of one another's sweat and scent and the dizzying pheromones that could still do him in if he wasn't damned careful.

He held Gabi's swimsuit top up in front of him as if it were a prize. For just a second, he thought as he looked at the determined set of her chin, her furiously questioning raised eyebrows, and the pure fire sparking out of her eyes, maybe he was just waving a red flag front of a lady bull who was about ready to charge him.

He had to admit the thought kind of intrigued him. As did everything else about the gorgeous, mysterious spitfire he had just *claimed.*

Damn it all to hell.

After another moment, during which it was clear she wasn't about to budge, he redirected. "For starters, you just gave away your own proof."

Indignantly, she snapped, "I did not! How dare you try to trap me into telling you the truth about the wreck," she added, voice huffing.

Despite himself, Kai started to chuckle as he shook his head at her. It took Gabi a split second to realize she'd done it again. With a rosy flush of anger rising in her cheeks, she marched toward him. He couldn't help but admire the gorgeous bounce of her breasts, the soft curve of her belly, the beautiful swell of her hips as she charged directly up to him, glaring. "Damn it. You'd better tell me the truth yourself, and right now," she demanded, drawing up just short of him. "You already knew who we were when you saw us in the bar, didn't you?" Her mouth suddenly dropped open even as her eyes narrowed at him. "Wait a minute. Did you seduce me to find out about the shipwreck?" Her voice sputtered again. "You tried to trap me with sex! With amazing, mind-blowing sex!"

Despite his own churning upset inside, Kai couldn't help the swell of satisfaction that she'd admitted it had been great sex. Seemed like Gabi wasn't remotely a wilting little flower. No, she was like a beautiful, thorny, fully blooming rose. Proud, gorgeous, and more than capable of both defending herself and protecting her feelings.

He knew exactly what that felt like.

"Look," he started, raising his own eyebrows at her, still holding her swim top in the air above them, out of her reach despite her one swipe at it. "You certainly don't understand the story here. In fact, you wouldn't even believe a quarter of it so—"

"Oh, really?" she snapped. Damn, she was pretty when she was mad. "Try me. You might be surprised. I believe in a lot of things most people don't."

Kai paused for a long time, regarding her carefully. She appeared to be listening closely. Inside, he waged another brief battle. Somehow, though, it felt utterly natural to tell her. Perhaps it would shock her into admitting how it was possible she had touched his treasure. Narrowing his eyes a bit, he regarded her closely. She had to know about dragon shifters.

She simply had to. How else could she possibly have been able to break an unbreakable spell?

Fine, then. In for a penny, or a gold nugget, in for a pound. Or for an entire treasure.

Looking straight at her, he said, "Yes, that was me you saw down there. At the Santa Maria." Gabi's mouth dropped open at his stark honesty. He went on, keeping his voice steady. "That was me. That dragon you saw? That was me, Gabi."

Gabi stared at him with as much slack-jawed stupefaction almost as if he'd shifted into his dragon form right then and there.

"I was there because I was there checking on my treasure. In the spot it's been kept for centuries now. Untouched, undisturbed, and safe. Safe until you and your team came along, that is."

She had the grace to flush. Opening her mouth to respond, she never had the chance. An enormous splashing sound behind them yanked Gabi's gaze away from him to the waters off the bow of the boat.

"What was that?" she asked, even as she leaned her head around him to look at the water. Kai automatically turned as well.

Just in time to catch a glimpse of an enormous dark shape slicing through the ocean water beneath the boat.

"Holy shit," Gabi breathed. If he'd been looking at her, he was pretty damn sure her eyes would be bigger than her face. "That's much too large to be a shark, but it's moving way too fast to be a whale."

Abrupt fear smashed through Kai as he suddenly realized what was about to happen. "Hang on!" he yelled, throwing himself sideways to tackle Gabi and bring her shrieking to the deck of the boat.

"What the h—" she started to yell, just as Kai braced himself over her while he reached out to grab onto the railing.

Something enormous smashed into the side of the boat,

rocking it violently. The assault would've sent them both tumbling along the deck if Kai weren't tightly holding onto Gabi and grabbing the railing with his free hand. She screamed in shock, her luscious body rigid with terror beneath his.

"Brace yourself," was all he managed to get out before another gigantic crash smashed against the boat. The impact shoved the hull straight out of the water, bringing up the prow nearly straight into the air as if they were being hauled up on a pulley. Gabi gave another strangled scream, although he heard a backbone of strength beneath it that oddly pleased him even as he tightly held onto her.

Protecting her from the other dragon that was attacking them.

For an impossible eternity that was only a split second, the boat seemed to hang in midair, the prow still tipped toward the sky and the stern sinking beneath the water. Then it slammed back down, entering the water with an enormous shudder and splash. Kai's chin cracked against the deck of the boat and slammed Gabi's head into his hand where he safely cradled it.

He hissed with rage as he felt his fingers break from the force of keeping her head from slamming against the deck as well. Adrenaline shot through him in a panicked bolt as he wondered if she'd also broken something. She was human, and therefore far more fragile than he. He could heal himself as long as he could shift within an hour.

A female yell that was more scared and outraged than pained sent a wave of relief over his body despite the throbbing in his hand. "Are you okay?" he still asked, urgency as well as a cold splash of water smacking into his face as waves slammed over the deck from the force of the impact making his voice more warbled than usual.

Warbled. No. *No.*

With the sudden, sickening sensation, he realized what

was happening. "No!" His voice shouted in futile protest even as the deep warbling sounded stronger in his voice.

Gabi tensed from startlement beneath him, but she was about to do worse than that.

His dragon, fully aroused and abruptly raging out of his control, was rising within him. The shift was about to come over him, and for one of the very few times in his life, he knew he couldn't control it.

His dragon knew that not only were they being attacked, but that he had to protect Gabi. No matter what the cost, he had to protect the woman he had just claimed as being his.

GABI'S BODY was probably going to hurt later on, but right now she felt little more than a sort of numbed shock. Mostly because she didn't know what the hell was going on.

And because Kai, who was looking at her, had the strangest expression on his face. His eyes seemed to be getting lighter—no, the green flecks had returned, and they were getting brighter. He pushed away from her, his expression slipping from his own shock to something darker.

Something primal.

"Kai?" she whispered, hearing the tremble of fear in her own voice and hating it. "What's happening?"

Being on his sleek sailboat, out in the calm, sunny day, still stark naked after some of the best sex of her life—okay, undeniably the best sex of her life—and still in shock from both the really brief conversation about the shipwreck as well as the fact that *something* had just violently bumped the boat, like a monster out of *Jaws* or something, was all so incongruous that she couldn't quite wrap her mind around it. The bizarre clarity of what she knew had to be shock was making everything around her crystal clear.

Including the fact that Kai's eyes were—changing. She was

still close enough, sprawled on the deck of the boat. Her hair tangled over her eyes before she frantically shoved it away so she could see him more clearly. Chest heaving, she stumbled up onto her feet to stand. The pupils in his eyes were—getting longer. Elongating. The green was overtaking the black velvet of his irises, until all she could see were emerald green eyes that seemed to whirl around a long dark pupil.

Like the pupil of a cat. Or of a—

Gabi's breath heaved out of her as Kai took a step back from her, abruptly crouching down as he spread his arms out to his sides at the same time. He looked like he was about to take flight.

So fast that she was almost certain her eyes deceived her, a shimmer rippled along Kai's frame. A shimmer of indigo, sapphire, streaks of alabaster flitting through and making the entire thing seem like a dream.

Or like the shimmer and ripple of water over the hide of a dragon.

"Oh, my god." The words barely slid out of her, more breath than sound. Her thoughts slid out of her as well, leaving only a babbling, senseless chatter in her head.

And a slow, almost reverent feeling of beautiful vindication as Kai's form abruptly grew up and out, merging so quickly from that of a man to that of a dragon that Gabi's eyes couldn't catch the exact moment of transition.

Impossibly huge, the dragon—Kai—hovered just above the deck of the sailboat. Iridescent blue-black shimmered down along his ridged spine, while his underbelly shone a pearly-white and cerulean. His wings flared open, the thin membrane between the joints a pale blue that seemed to match the ocean behind him. She recognized him from the other day, far down beneath the sea by the Santa Maria.

Kai had been the one there that day. He had seen her by the shipwreck. The still-working part of her mind filed that away for the moment. The rest of her simply stared at him now.

Green eyes split by vertically-shaped pupils stared at Gabi, brimming with full human intelligence.

He was the most majestic, glorious thing she'd ever seen in her life.

"It's true," she whispered as she stood there, tiny and naked and defenseless against the enormous winged dragon in front of her. "Abuela was right. The stories are real, and you're part of them."

Her voice sighed through the quiet air as she just stared, utterly captivated by his magnificence.

Then all hell broke loose.

Kai regarded the beautiful tiny human as his wings slowly, quietly kept him hovering above the deck of the boat. She was perfect, she was amazing, she was his.

His.

The knowledge roared through his entire being, dragging up memories and sensations. He braced himself for remembered pain. There was only the merest whisper of it. Satisfied that he was right, that she was indeed his, he opened his mouth and roared his exultation.

Gabi opened her mouth right along with him and screamed bloody murder as she stumbled backward, tripped, and fell back down on the deck.

Idiot, Kai cursed himself, snapping shut what he knew was his fearsome jaw and huge, sharp teeth. Then he looked at her more closely. She was staring, screaming his name, and pointing.

But she wasn't pointing at him. She was pointing behind him.

Whirling in midair, his wings pinioning with a snap as he turned, he was unprepared for the lunge by the iron-grey dragon that shoved them both over the boat from the force of impact. He caught sight of Gabi's open mouth and her fierce eyes. She was already scrambling up, lunging after them, yelling words he couldn't catch, although he heard their courageous vehemence.

As if she thought she could help. Like a fierce warrior dragon queen of old, fearless and daring. His tiny, bold human.

Both enlivened by that thought and enraged by the unprecedented attack, Kai whirled again on the other dragon, making them both tumble from the sky toward the ocean below. With an enormous splash, they entered the water, immediately sinking beneath the surface as they locked in battle.

As a water dragon, Kai immediately had the upper hand. The ocean was his element. The grey dragon was a classic dragon, better suited for battle in the skies. Even so, their struggle was stupendous. Water churned and frothed as they slashed at one another, spinning and whirling beneath the waves, snapping with opened jaws and roaring bellows that echoed under the sea.

He was sure all nearby life fled in terror as two epic monsters of the sea fought. Hoping they weren't creating tidal waves that sloshed the sailboat anew, he slowly but steadily led the other dragon away from it, tumbling through bubbles and once or twice arcing straight up into the air above the water to then perform a death drop down on the other dragon. Briny ocean water filled his nostrils and mouth again and again, adding to his deadly joy in the suddenness of being able to fight.

To expend even more of the tightly-bottled energy that had leashed him for too long, no matter what his more pragmatic human side might think. *Foolish*, he huffed, eyes narrowed on his target.

The fight was short-lived. Classic dragons could hold their breath underwater for a long time—but they couldn't actually breathe underwater as Kai could. With a sudden wrench, the grey jerked himself out of Kai's slashing grasp and shot up to the surface. Kai followed faster than thought, but when he broke into the air, lunging out with his wings spread and angrily flapping sheets of salt water everywhere, the other dragon was already a length away. He turned his head back toward Kai, hissing. "This isn't over, Long. Your treasure has weakened now beyond safekeeping."

Bellowing with rage, Kai made as if to pursue. The grey gave a deliberately insulting whap of his tail in the air, creating a sharp crackling sound like a bolt of lightning. Then he bolted northward, his wings pistoning hard as he attained full flight speed. His mocking huff, the equivalent of dragon laughter, floated back in the stillness of the day, leaving an ugly film on it.

For a long moment, Kai hovered in the air, his own wings beating the air with lingering adrenaline and fury. The grey had vanished into a speck on the day's bright horizon, but it didn't matter. Kai knew who the other dragon was and what his unanticipated attack meant.

Because Gabi somehow had broken the spell on Kai's gold hoard, the wards had partially crumbled. The dark dragons of the world, those noxious ones who preferred stealing established hoards over either creating or legitimately inheriting their own, had sniffed it out and were beginning to move in.

From a day that had started so well, it was spiraling into one far less than stellar.

Kai looked back down at the sailboat. Gabi, his tiny, fearless human, stood at the prow, hand shielding her eyes as she stared up at him. He noted she was still naked. Smiling to himself, he glided back over to the ship, dropping down to hover over it as he shifted back to his human shape.

Gabi sucked in a quick, audible gasp as he thumped back onto the deck on two human legs and strode over to her. Her strong, gorgeous face, still half-shocked yet also filled with vitality, and deliciously naked body filled all his senses.

"So," he said as he stopped about an inch away, soaking in her heady scent while his fight endorphins still ran high. He shrugged. There was nothing more he could conceal, as far as the truth about his kind was concerned. "Now you know the truth. The next move, Gabriela," and he bent his face toward hers to more deeply inhale her sweetness, "is yours."

GABI'S entire body still zinged with the aftereffects of tremendous physical joy, followed by horrific shock, followed by a ferocious sense of passion. Passion to save him. To cheer him on. To support him in whatever way she could.

The only thing she really couldn't do was help him fight a dragon. Seeing as how he himself was a dragon, and she was just a human. A human who'd just realized how incredibly tiny and vulnerable she was in comparison to him as she'd witnessed his amazing other self in all its gigantic, amazing presence.

Wild excitement shot through her again as the reality of the situation threatened to explode inside her. The legends and stories were real. Really real.

Kai was really a dragon. In the flesh. Witnessed by her own eyes, which meant—

Wait a minute. She snapped her gaze out over the water, then toward Catalina Island rising in the distance.

"Hold on," she said before she even knew what would tumble out of her mouth. "There's no way other people didn't see what just happened. You're huge! And so was that other —dragon."

She whipped back around to look at him again. He kept his gaze on hers, silent and watchful. Still so sexy it about made her wet again, even after all the insanity of the past few moments. "The stories my grandmother always told me are true," she said. Part of her tingled with enormous delight at that fact. "How is it that no one has ever seen you before? Or any of your, uh, kind?" She tripped over that part, suddenly uncertain. Who and what he was, who and what his kind were —all those were things her abuela had always told her about. All the stories Gabi had heard from her since she'd been in the cradle.

They were all real.

Kai's face was still watchful as he answered, although she saw the slight tug upward of the corner of his lip. "We cloak. It's a shifter thing. No human can see us in our dragon forms."

"But I saw you," she immediately replied. "Both of you. I'm pretty sure I'm human." She raised an eyebrow at him. "And what the hell do you mean, 'cloak'?"

Kai's stance remained easy and open. She suddenly realized he was giving her ample space to come to terms with everything she'd just seen and experienced in the space of what felt like about thirty seconds yet also felt like a lifetime's worth of sudden, deep knowledge.

She hardly knew him. On the surface, she wasn't foolish enough to trust him. Yet on some more authentic, deeper level, she did. She sensed without a doubt that he would never hurt her.

The real question however, was if he'd ever lie to her. The guilty flush rose through her as she realized she'd been the one lying to him. Well, not precisely lying. Keeping secrets.

Secrets.

The gold nugget.

Feeling another shock of cold wash through her, she looked wild-eyed around the drenched deck of the sailboat. The red top piece of her swimsuit was caught tightly on the railing. Lunging for it, she almost sagged with relief as she felt the hard chunk of gold still in it. The bottoms were gone, but she hadn't lost the piece of the Santa Maria's treasure that she had removed in order to prove to the UTEI treasure hunters that she could hold up her end of their bargain.

Clutching the swimsuit top in her hand, she looked at Kai. He stared at her swimsuit with the strangest expression on his face. Longing. Anger. Amazement. A deep, aching loss that seemed old yet fresh at the same time. Dragging his gaze up to hers, he snagged her eyes with the harsh intensity of his own.

Gabi suddenly felt very strange. Lightheaded.

In two long strides, Kai was back at her side, his expression melting into one of more concern. "Easy. You just had about five different shocks. Come here. Sit down." He guided her to one of the rail seats, letting her sink into it. Gently pushing on her back so she had to lean her head forward, he said, "Sit like that for a minute. Hang on. Going to get you some water."

As he turned away to slip below decks, she couldn't help her typical slightly saucy, slightly sarcastic reply. "Water, water everywhere."

She didn't mistake his poorly concealed snort of laughter as he thumped down the stairs. Well, she could still make him laugh. That was more than she could do for herself at the moment.

Kai reemerged moments later, a large tee shirt and shorts grasped in one hand, water bottle in the other. He unscrewed the plastic top and handed it to her. "Drink."

Gabi straightened up slightly so she could sip the water, swallowing faster as she realized she was indeed actually thirsty. The cool, filtered liquid somehow served to soothe her and bring her back to feeling more like herself. She waited a couple of moments for the little dizzy spell to pass before she murmured a quiet thank you.

He sat beside her, close enough to touch but not quite. She sensed he was still giving her space.

"I saw you by the wreck of the Santa Maria, didn't I? And at the bar that night. You somehow recognized me, and sought me out. Didn't you?" Even as she spoke, she realized it was true. Combined with her distress over not only having taken but now lost the gold nugget, but understanding that he'd found her attractive only because he wanted something from her, sensitive information or she didn't even know what, shredded at her chest with sharp, unexpected pain.

Come on. Buck up, she whispered to herself. She'd just met the guy. He didn't mean anything more to her than a fun tumble.

Then why did it suddenly feel like someone was stabbing her heart with a bunch of small, hot pokers?

KAI STAYED motionless in the seat beside her as casually as if they'd simply been enjoying a day of sailing together. Yet he was completely tensed as he waited for her reaction to her realization of the truth. Now, she really knew his biggest secret. Which—

Wait a damned minute. Apparently his brain was so addled by insanely fantastic sex and the tremendous surge of adrenaline from the attack that he had clicked pieces together. Losing his casualness, he snapped his head around to look directly at her. "You're right. How could you have seen me? And also the other dragon? Yes, we do cloak," he went on a musing tone, sorting out the pieces out loud as Gabi's head slowly came up to look at him with puzzlement evident on her own face. "We have the ability to hide our dragon shapes from human eyes. No humans can see us, except—"

He narrowed his eyes slightly at her. "Gabi, are you from a dragon fealty family?"

The utter, genuine bewilderment on her face as she shook her head immediately told him she wasn't.

"I don't understand," he said, frowning. Damn, she was so beautiful he longed to simply reach over and just engulf her with another kiss. He sensed for both their sakes, this wasn't the time.

"I don't know what to—" Gabi began, before being abruptly interrupted by music.

Her face changed from confused to worried in nanoseconds. "My phone!" She jumped to her feet, looking around.

Kai stood up as well and looked down at the rail seat. The velcro had held fast. The phone in its waterproof case was still securely attached to the railing.

Gabi fumbled with the case and got her phone out, answering quickly. Just as quickly, fear filled her voice. She began babbling in Spanish to whomever was on the other end. Looking at Kai, her features frozen in distress, she switched back to English. "Mateo, slow down. What do you mean, she collapsed?"

Without waiting for her to ask, Kai sprang over to the boat's anchor, muttering a quick oath as he realized it had been broken in the attack. Taking a cursory glance around the boat, he finally felt a bit of relief that she appeared still seaworthy. Striding to the sails to quickly adjust the rigging and ready them to go, he then grabbed the wheel and set her on course.

With a terrified dread that squeezed his heart because he knew himself how it felt only all too well, Gabi said, "Hurry. As fast as you can." Her words were clipped with fear. "It's my abuela. My grandmother. She collapsed. They're taking her to the emergency room right now."

It seemed like all her kickass strength and certainty had drained from her in a split second, leaving her merely an anxious family member worried beyond belief about someone she loved.

Setting his jaw as he allowed the cool, blank numbness so familiar to rise in him in response to her pain, Kai sailed them as quickly as possible back to the island, leaving all their unanswered questions and unease behind.

For now.

G abi shifted in the chair again, trying to get comfortable. Her inclination was to pace, but she was afraid to move around too much or make noise in case she jolted her grandmother out of sleep. Instead, she simply sat there in a corner of the sterile room, staring at the tiny, frail body of her grandmother curled up in the hospital bed, lines running out from her arms to machines.

Just the sight made Gabi feel hollow and terrified inside.

Her abuela had collapsed in the kitchen yesterday, right in the middle of making a sandwich for herself and a snack for one of Gabi's nephews. Gabi barely remembered getting from the island back to the mainland. She kept calling Lacey, but her best friend wasn't picking up. Kai's worried yet also oddly distant eyes also haunted her, as did the crazed, scattered images of everything that had happened in the past several hours.

She could hardly believe so much had happened in such a short time span. She'd lived what felt like three lifetimes in about seventy-two hours. Now she understood how people her age could get gray hairs.

Putting her feet up onto the chair so that her knees were

bent in front of her, Gabi dropped her head onto her knees and closed her eyes. Wrapping her arms around her legs, she took several deep breaths to settle herself. By the time she'd arrived at the hospital, her grandmother was stable. A flurry of family members had met her in the waiting room, including Mateo and her mother. The hospital was limiting visitors, so the family was taking shifts to go in and see her. Gabi had finally gotten in. Seeing her father's worried, haggard face, she'd urged him to go with her aunt down to the hospital cafeteria to get some coffee. She promised to not step a single foot out of the room until he returned.

As she'd watched her aunt drag her father out of the room, Gabi had felt a new pain inside her. Pain born of the terror that she could lose someone she loved very much. The doctor said the cancer was pressing on abuela's lungs. It had caused her to get short of breath earlier today, enough that she'd actually passed out. The main reason she was actually in the hospital was because she'd hit her head when she fell onto the kitchen floor in front of Gabi's nephew's horrified eyes.

Gabi tightly hugged her legs as she pressed her face into her knees. Nothing in the world mattered but that her abuela, the glue that held her family together, would be okay. Unfortunately, insurance sucked. Although many members of her family had good jobs and contributed to the medical care beyond what abuela's insurance covered, no one had enough to get her the best treatment. The only treatments that had a real shot of saving her life.

Except for Gabi. Because she was doing something that went against her entire moral code. But when it was family, she would do anything. Anything at all.

"Gabriela, *corazon*. You're supposed to be on the island. What are you doing here?"

The scratchy but steady voice had Gabi's head off her knees even as she swung her feet to the floor. "Abuela! I thought you were sleeping." Gabi went to her grandmother's side, gingerly taking one frail-seeming hand above the bedcovers in her own. To her surprise, though, her grandmother squeezed back with some firmness.

A smile teased at her abuela's voice as she went on in Spanish. "Now, now, my lovely girl. I just slipped and got a little bump on my head. Nothing to worry about. I am still strong."

Gabi looked at her grandmother's soft, beautiful face. A patchwork of wrinkles and lines across her skin told the story of her long lifetime. Gabi was her grandmother's youngest child's next youngest child. Her grandmother had been fifty-five by the time Gabi was born. She'd always been incredibly healthy and spry, until the cancer had been diagnosed late last fall. Even so, she kept up her spirits as well as most of her health. Even though chemo and radiation had been challenging, Gabi's grandmother was one of the strongest women Gabi had ever known. Despite that, she couldn't help the tears that welled up in her eyes as the sweet, light brown ones of her grandmother looked back at her with some concern.

"*Corazon,* don't you do that. You tell me instead what's been going on with you. Tell me about your research. My Gabriela, the brave and daring woman who dives under the sea." Her voice grew dreamy, as it always did when she spoke of the ocean.

Gabriela knew she got her love of the sea from her grandmother, who also always had loved the ocean. Gabi had tons of childhood memories of picnicking at the beach almost every weekend, body surfing in the waves, making sand castles, listening quietly to her grandmother's tales when they sat alone as her brothers played in the sea under the watchful eyes of Gabi's mother and father.

"So. Tell me about the last time you went diving down beneath the waves." Abuela smiled. "I want to hear all about the underwater creatures you saw. Any sharks this time?"

Gabi laughed at her grandmother's avid tone. Like Gabi, her grandmother never had the massive, irrational fear of sharks like most of the world's population did. In fact, when Gabi was little, her grandmother had often told her stories about the animals that lived under the sea. She said they were just like people in that they too had families, loved ones, and things they wanted to do in their lifetime. Gabi had always eaten it all up, despite her father's mutters that she was going to grow up to be a dreamer with silly old notions crammed into her head.

Instead, she'd ended up a respected scientist on a good career path. One who also happened to half-believe a lot of the stories her grandmother had always told her. So much so that seeing a dragon beneath the sea hadn't shocked her nearly as much as it should have.

"Okay," Gabi said, blinking back the wetness in her eyes as she carefully settled on the edge of the bed, still holding her grandmother's hand. "So." She lowered her voice a little bit, glancing at the door. Her grandmother was the only person in the world who knew what Gabi and the team were actually looking for, although Gabi hadn't told her about the deal she'd made with UTEI. Deep inside she knew she felt too ashamed to admit it to anyone. But her grandmother could keep a secret better than anyone else Gabi knew. She was the one who'd encouraged Gabi's love of ancient ships and treasures. "We actually found it a few days ago," she whispered.

"You did!" Great interest flared in her grandmother's eyes, even though she kept her own voice quiet. It warmed Gabi's heart to see that. She was half convinced that her stories about the hunt for the Santa Maria had kept her grandmother's health good for the last couple of months. "Tell me all about it. Is it intact?"

Gabi nodded, quietly telling her grandmother everything about the discovery. She told her about the way the sunlight slanted through the seaweed and across the yawning underwater caverns and canyons. The way the huge masts of the ship were unbelievably still intact. About the hole in the side of the ship, which indicated that it had been attacked rather than lost in a storm as everyone had always supposed.

Looking up at the door one more time, Gabi lowered her voice even more and leaned toward her grandmother. Her own eyes darting furtively to the door and then back to her granddaughter's, abuela leaned close as well.

"But—that's not even the most amazing thing that happened that day. I—abuela." Gabi closed her eyes for second, the thrill of everything suddenly jolting through her again as all the images of the past couple of days flashed through her mind in rapid-fire succession.

Opening her eyes again, she looked at her grandmother and whispered in very quiet Spanish, "They're real. I saw one. Actually, I saw two." She took a deep breath. "Dragons. You were always right." In a fierce whisper, she said it again. "Dragons are real." She paused, wondering how much she should share. Looking at her grandmother's face, what she saw was a blaze of fascination oddly mingled with what seemed like sadness. Also joy, along with the unwavering belief in Gabi that she'd always had. She knew her grandmother could never find shame in her, no matter what.

Taking a deep breath, she carefully went on. Telling her grandmother the entire story. Well, she didn't exactly give her details about Kai, she pretty much blushed and skimmed over the sailboat part, though she was pretty sure her grandmother probably had a good idea what had happened. Abuela simply listened quietly the entire time, her expression never changing. Once or twice, though, Gabi could have sworn she caught the glint of tears in her grandmother's eyes.

It was only when Gabi admitted that she still had a piece of Kai's gold that her grandmother struggled to sit up in the bed, her eyes suddenly flashing with the same inner fire Gabi knew she had inherited from her. "Gabriela." Her grandmother's voice was serious, even stern. She clutched Gabi's hands hard between her own, fixing her granddaughter with a firm

stare. "You have to return his gold to him. It is the most important thing. You cannot even understand how important it is. It
is more important than anything else that you do that."

"But—" Gabi started, but her grandmother shook her head.

"No. Gabriela, you know I never tell you what to do.
Mostly because I know if I did, you would never listen to me."

Gabi barely managed to stifle a snort. She gave a self-
deprecating shrug of her shoulders. Her grandmother knew
her very well. "But this one time, Gabriela, I'm telling you to
listen to me. You cannot separate the dragon from his gold."

Gabi's eyes returned to her grandmother's again. Such
intensity, such seriousness emanated from her grandmother's
expression that Gabi's breath caught in her throat.

"Separating a dragon from his gold hoard is extremely
dangerous. And I think perhaps it might be dangerous for your
own future, Gabriela. You must return it immediately. Now."

"But I—" Gabi began. Her grandmother clutched her
hands hard, shaking her head fiercely.

"Promise me you will do this, Gabriela. Now."

"Okay, okay." Gabi retreated. "I promise."

Her grandmother sighed and closed her eyes. She was
quiet for such a long time Gabi thought she had fallen back
asleep. But then one of her sweetly gnarled hands moved on
the sheet and her lips curved up in small smile. "You know,
Gabriela, I too could see the dragons when I was much
younger."

Gabi nodded. She'd grown up on her grandmother's tales
like these. She realized now, with a jolt, that while she'd always
half believed them, her encounter with the truth this morning
—was it really only this morning? It felt like a year ago—now
made her understand that those had been the hopeful wishes
of a child. She had never actually believed before.

Now, she did. Softly, she asked, "Tell me more."

With a dreamy sigh, her grandmother continued. "His
name was Maleko. I met him before your own father was even

a spark in my eyes. It was before I knew your grandfather." Her voice softened with memory. "I was younger than you are now. I still believed in magic, and wishes coming true. He came out of the ocean one night like some sort of undersea god."

Stunned, Gabi blinked. Her grandmother went on in a quiet, almost pensive voice. "Maleko was the most stunning man I had ever seen in my life. He said he had been watching me. As it turned out," she laughed a little bit, "I knew him already. He worked at the Marine Institute on Catalina. The one you love so much, Gabi."

Beyond startled by the parallels of her encounters with Kai, Gabi cautiously nodded.

"By the time he told me his secret," her grandmother went on, the smile still playing on her lips, "I was already completely in love with him."

"Abuela! You never told me about this." Gabi's startled words didn't stop the flow of her grandmother's story, who went on as if she hadn't been interrupted.

"He didn't want to scare me, but he said he could never withhold the truth from me. He changed his form right in front of me, and he was the most magnificent creature I had ever seen in my life. He shimmered like the ocean. Green and white, with spikes on the back of his neck, and some along his tail that flattened when he swam fast. But he could still fly." Her grandmother's eyes opened. She looked at Gabi with a glorious smile that lit up her entire face. "He could fly. He used to take me flying. At night, because even though he could shield himself so that no others could see him, there is less air traffic at night." Her grandmother's laughter bubbled out, so girlish and merry that Gabi stared at her. "Air traffic. He was less likely to bump into an airplane while flying at night, you understand."

Her grandmother laughed harder, as if at a joke. But a single tear slipped out of one eye.

Concerned, Gabi said, "No, don't tell me the stories if they're upsetting. You need to be resting and relaxing right now."

But her grandmother, still strong and sassy despite her age as everyone in the family knew, shook her head. She didn't bother wiping away the tear as she looked directly at Gabi. "Maleko, my dragon man, the one who had my heart, and whose heart was mine, had treasure. Gold. They all do, you know. Dragon shifters. That's what they call themselves."

Her piercing eyes looked at Gabi with such clarity that she suddenly felt as if her grandmother could see into her very soul. Nearly holding her breath, she waited.

"My dragon man, he had treasure indeed. He showed me once. The biggest amount of riches I have ever seen in my life." Her voice still held the soft amazement of an experience that she must have had, Gabi realized, well over sixty years ago. "Listen to me carefully, Gabriela. I don't know exactly what's going on, but I can see in your eyes that your dragon shifter man, your Kai, means a lot to you. Without his treasure, Gabriela, eventually, he will die. This is what happens. Whatever has been taken from him, must be returned. Do you understand?"

Voice suddenly ringing with the authority Gabi remembered from her childhood, abuela firmly said, "He needs you. He needs you, the same as he needs his treasure. I know this. You need to go back there, Gabi. Now. I will be fine," she said, shaking away Gabi's protest before it could leave her lips. "Bah. This," she waved her hand in the air, indicating herself in the hospital bed, "is just a little thing. All of the family is hovering around me like gnats on a hot summer day. I need to send one of them away, so it might as well be you."

Despite herself, Gabi managed to whisper out a small laugh.

"Gabriela." Her grandmother's voice held a soft warning.

"Do not lose this kind of love. Hold onto it for the treasure that it is by itself. Believe me."

A slap of pain harder than anything Gabi had ever heard before sounded in her grandmother's voice. Gabi's heart constricted.

"What happened?" she asked, searching her grandmother's wistful eyes. "What happened to your dragon man?"

Her grandmother sighed. "They often fight, these dragons. Just like people, there are good dragons, and there are bad dragons." She shrugged, a soft, sad smile around her lips. "Someone tried to steal my dragon man's gold. Another dragon. They fought. And he was killed."

Her voice was simply accepting of what was a very old wound. Even so, Gabi couldn't help her gasp. Her grandmother made a shooing motion with her hands. "Things happen for a reason, my love. I was meant to meet my Maleko for the short time that I did, and to know what it's like to love a man like that. A dragon shifter man like that." A shadow of joy edged her words even now. "After he died, many years later, I met your grandfather. If I hadn't, you would not be here at this moment." She shrugged again. "But my story is not your story." Her tone brooking no disagreement, she pointed at the door with a surprisingly steady hand. "Go to him, Gabriela. He needs you."

As Gabi gathered her things to leave, giving her grandmother's soft if slightly papery cheek a kiss, when she left she thought she heard her grandmother quietly add, "Just as you need him."

15

Kai ended the phone call as it once again went straight to Gabi's cheerful voicemail. Swearing beneath his breath, he tossed the phone onto his kitchen table. Striding through his house, he burst out onto the deck that led outside. His insides were a boiling, roiling mess. Something was wrong. Very wrong. He didn't know what, but the knowledge that something terrible had happened wouldn't release him from the constricting sense of dread he'd been feeling since the very early hours of the morning. Leaping into his sailboat, he steered her directly toward the shipwreck, pulse pounding the entire way in a sick, jagged rhythm of nameless fear.

Barely pausing to anchor the boat when he reached the site, he dove off the side toward the water below, shifting into his dragon just barely as he entered the waves. Propelled by the dire unease that was so intense he vaguely wondered if this was what people prone to panic attacks felt, he shot through the water, heading directly for the Santa Maria.

A water dragon swimming at full speed was the fastest creature in the entire ocean.

An uneasy dragon was both fast and utterly terrifying as

he swam with single-minded purpose. Ocean life of all types scattered as he raced by them, heedless in his need for one thing.

His gold. He had to get to his gold.

The closer he got to the shipwreck, the more the ugly sense of foreboding alarm increased. Something was not right. Something was so wrong, on so many levels, that it spurred him to streak though the water ever faster.

Yet as soon as he got close to the wreck that housed his gold hoard, the heart of all dragon shifters that kept their powers intact, he immediately knew what was wrong.

As the dark bulk of the Santa Maria rose before him, agony ripped through Kai's massive frame. He flung open his wings, dragging himself to a churning stop above the ocean floor. Opening his mouth, he howled a raging bellow of draconic pain. Of shattering, unspeakable loss.

He could not feel it. None of it. His gold, the mingled treasure hoard that had belonged to him and his dead mate, was gone. Everything was missing.

Taken.

Stolen.

Gone.

As the stunning truth settled over him, one thought surged forth, over his dragon's repeated agonized calls beneath the water.

Gabi. Somehow, some way, she was responsible for this. Yesterday, rushing her back to shore to go to her grandmother's side, Kai had completely forgotten about the small piece of his treasure that she still had. He'd been so stupidly concerned for her own well-being that he'd ignored the fact that not only did she have it, she hadn't offered up the real reason why she had taken it in the first place.

The real reason how the gray dragon had found them out there. The real reason behind all the trickery, all the hidden secrets he kept seeing concealed in her eyes. Somehow, she was mixed up with the dark, thieving dragon from yesterday.

Jaw clenching, teeth gnashing together in rage, Kai turned and shot toward the shore of the island

Somehow, Gabriela Santos had stolen Kai's gold.

GABI'S PHONE warbled at her yet again. Shane gave her the side-eye as she glanced down at it, but he didn't say anything. He hadn't asked why she wanted him to dive down to the site with her today, on what was supposed to be a dry research day at the lab, going over the photos and notes they'd taken so far at the wreck. He hadn't asked why they were going alone. Why she hadn't asked Everson for permission. Technically, since she was an associate director, she didn't have to ask. Yet this was still seriously against protocol.

But even though Shane had paused for a long time when she'd called him last night to ask for his help, he'd finally said yes without asking more questions. She'd assured him it was really important. Since she'd never yet lied to him, he saw no reason to question her, she guessed. Biting the inside of her own lip to keep her mouth from trembling, she looked down at her phone. Kai's name pulsed on the screen. It was the third time he'd called her that morning. The day after the wildness of sex with him, her discovery that he was a dragon, his fight with the other dragon. The other dragon who must be one of the bad ones her abuela had mentioned.

Clutching Kai's gold tightly in her left hand while she stared down at the screen, Gabi firmly turned the volume off and then flipped over the phone so she couldn't see his name flashing on it in seeming accusation. She had to return his gold first. Then, and only then, could she face him.

The only sound was that of the boat traveling through the water, waves lapping off its sides as they skimmed over the surface of the ocean toward the wreck of the Santa Maria. Gabi firmed her jaw as she looked over the sparkling blue-green waters that dazzled and beckoned the further out to sea they headed. She'd slept poorly at her small apartment in L.A. the night before after leaving the hospital, haunted by dreams that seemed to mock her. Images of gold buried in its watery grave, the no-nonsense face of her boss, Everson, her grandmother's urgent plea and firm command as she directed Gabi to save both Kai and her own future, the increasingly annoyed voice of her UTEI contact as he, too, had called her multiple times yesterday and even this morning as she took the earliest ferry she could over to Catalina, leaving more and more chilling messages each time.

And Kai. The obsidian eyes, the flash of sunlight across his rippling muscles as he'd hovered above her on the deck of the sailboat, nothing in his expression but pure longing and enjoyment as they melded their bodies together. The stunning beauty of his dragon form as he'd flown in the sky and then dove into the depths of the ocean, battling the other strange dragon.

The surety that if she didn't return his gold piece to him that she would somehow injure him beyond repair.

The devastating knowledge that she was betraying her team in order to save her grandmother's life.

Everything whirled around inside her like a merry-go-round she couldn't disembark, one making her dizzier and more distraught by every second.

Shane finally spoke, very carefully. "We're almost there."

Gabi waited for more, but when she looked at him, he simply shrugged one shoulder toward their destination, his hands still firmly clutching the wheel. Gratitude flooded her as she reached over to gently squeeze his upper arm in thanks. She, Shane, and Lacey had all been good friends in grad school. They both had her back, and she had theirs.

Yet when Shane found out the truth, she had a feeling he

might never talk to her again. Swallowing at the sick feeling inside her, Gabi nodded. Within moments, Shane slowed the boat to an idle, then killed the engine as they drifted over the spot where the wreck lay. As they readied themselves to go overboard, checking and double checking one another's equipment as they went through the usual safety routine, Gabi made certain to tuck the gold nugget securely into the glove of her suit. It pressed painfully against her palm when she flexed her hand, causing her to grimace and shake it open. This time, though, no matter what, she would return it to its rightful place. To its place in Kai's treasure hoard.

She felt strangely disquieted, even nervous. Glancing around at the bright, beautiful day, she took a deep breath and attempted to center herself. Come on. She was Gabi Santos, thrill seeker and bad ass extraordinaire. Wasn't she? She was doing the one right thing she could right now. It had to be enough.

Doing her best to pull on her innate sense of adventure and love of the adrenaline rush to get her through this, she took a deep breath, gave two thumbs up to Shane, and rolled over the railing of the boat to splash into the water alongside him

As they descended through the waters to the wreck site, Gabi felt increasingly uneasy. She struggled to find her usual sense of elation and comfort of being in the ocean, the one place that felt like her most real home. Yet the pit of her stomach felt heavy and her nerves frazzled. She carefully looked around as they began swimming toward the wreck, wondering if something dangerous cruised in the area. But everything looked as it always did. The bright green fronds of kelp swayed and danced in their underwater forests, punctuated by the occasional colorful flashes of schools of fish that darted in and out. The seafloor was undisturbed. As they approached the wreck, Gabi loosened the tight ball of fear that had seemed trapped in her throat. The Santa Maria was fine. Everything looked the same.

Everything looked the same—except it didn't. Dread suddenly gut-punched her again. Gabi's stomach seemed to drop out as unimaginable horror filled her.

Shane, who had been swimming a few yards away from her, backpedaled suddenly. Gabi paddled in place, staring at the ship as Shane swam to her and grabbed her arm. She turned to look at him, knowing her own expression would be the same as the one on his.

Shock, and genuine anguish.

Gabi looked back at the Santa Maria. The old ship listed far more to the left than she had before. The original hole in her side, the one the team had speculated had been caused by 18th-century pirates, was now an enormous ugly gash that clearly had been created by modern implements.

Even as she made herself start moving forward again, Gabi knew in her heart of hearts what they would find when they got there.

Carefully, glancing around again to see if anyone else was there with them, Gabi swam through the gentle, unending motion of the water to the edge of the hole in the ship, very gently grasping the jagged side of the broken boards. Shane swam past her through the giant hole. The two of them paused, still gently paddling in place, as they looked down at where the amazing treasures of the ship had lain just yesterday.

She was empty. Looted.

Kai's treasure was *gone*. His dragon hoard, as well as her team's stupendous find, and the only way Gabi had of paying for the treatments her grandmother so desperately needed, was gone.

Somebody had stolen all of it.

Shocked despair kept her limbs heavy when they finally headed back up to the surface.

This time, it was Gabi who didn't say a single word the entire ride back to shore. Shane glanced at her several times, once or twice reaching out to gently touch her arm. He finally stopped asking her what was going on when she simply didn't answer his repeated questions. Instead, he vaguely talked about his planned date for the evening. His voice sounded so strange the entire time that Gabi knew he was just barely managing to stop himself from freaking out. He was rambling in order to fill the dreadful shared knowledge.

The shipwreck had been ransacked. Professionally ransacked. The insides of it, the things that had nothing to do with gold and jewels and treasure, had been left intact. Logically, in some corner of her mind that was coolly ticking along, assessing the scientific ramifications of the situation, Gabi knew there was still a wealth of startling information to be found in the Santa Maria. It was still a fantastic discovery. The California University Ancients Quest team would still go down in history as being the ones who found her.

But when the truth finally got out, Gabi Santos' name would also go down in history as belonging to someone who had been nothing more than a lying, selfishly driven scientist who turned her back on everything she held dear so she could sell out to the other side. Correction. She would be known as a *former* scientist, one discredited and disgraced beyond repair, who had opened the floodgates to the ugly underworld of antiquities looting and trafficking. It didn't matter that she'd done it to save her grandmother. That part, nobody would care about or remember.

Once she and Shane had gotten back on the boat, she immediately went for her phone and called the UTEI number of her contact. Straight to voicemail. Then she called their office in the Bay Area, but that too went unanswered. Not leaving messages because Shane stood there, able to hear every word she said, she ended both calls with a hideous feeling of horror and dread pitting her stomach.

A cacophony of thoughts hammered her brain at completely random moments, one thought not seeming to follow another in any logical order. She would never get paid by UTEI for her part in what had turned out to be a disaster. She would never be able to afford to get her grandmother the necessary treatments. She would be fired. Abandoned by her friends. Her family probably would never talk to her again, more deeply ashamed of her behavior than by her failed marriage.

And then there was Kai.

He would never talk to her again. Kai would... What? What would happen to a dragon permanently separated from his gold hoard? Would he just fade away into nothingness? She had no real idea of what the loss of his gold meant. She simply knew from what her abuela had said that it was a horrible, terrible thing. That eventually, its loss would kill him.

And it was all her own damn stupid, idiotic, careless fault.

As they approached the island, Shane abruptly stopped his vague babble about his date. "Hey. Someone's at the dock." He shot her a quick look. "I though you said you didn't tell anyone we were going out this morning."

Still feeling numb, Gabi shook her head as she shaded her eyes and looked at the figure standing on the dock. Frowning slightly, she said, "You're the only one. I have no idea who that is."

"Gabs." From the seriousness of Shane's tone, she knew he was about to try again. "What's going on? You can tell me. I'm your friend."

Gabi kept her eyes trained on the figure as it became larger the closer they got to the deck. "Oh, Shane." Her throat felt tight. "I will tell you. But let's find out who that is first."

Total silence enveloped them as they reached the dock. Gabi felt shaky when she finally recognized who stood there waiting for them. She'd only once met in person the guy who was in charge of UTEI, or at least the guy who'd been her contact there. She met with him six months ago so, as he'd said, he could assess what kind of person she really was. Apparently she passed muster, though she'd never seen him again. He continued the rest of their business arrangement over the phone. She'd committed his face to memory after that first nerve-racking, sickeningly hopeful meeting. Something about him had felt slightly off from the beginning, very slightly ominous. But she'd ignored the sixth sense she usually knew served her well. She'd ignored it because she had no choice.

That might have been a huge mistake.

Disembarking as Shane tied the boat in, Gabi stepped onto the dock. She forced herself to walk over to the man, Shane protectively shadowing her heels. Slowing as she got close to the UTEI contact, she stared. There was a very satisfied smile on the man's arrogant face. Smug, almost.

"We meet again, Gabriela." He smirked at them. "Such a pleasant surprise. Just came back in from a run out to see the Santa Maria, did you now?"

"What the hell—" Shane began, beginning to push past Gabi. She grabbed onto his arm, hauling him back while also shushing him.

"Shane, I've got this." Glaring at the man, she drew on her shaky courage and mustered her best bravado. "Like my friend said. What the hell is going on?"

The man, clad in an expensive-looking linen suit, wore mirrored aviator glasses through which it was impossible to see his eyes. Steel gray hair arranged in artful waves on his head and an aquiline nose betrayed a certain class level. He merely broadened his smile for a long moment before replying. "I had come down here to check on your end of the bargain, Gabriela. But events the other day changed everything for us."

Now Shane's gaze shifted to Gabi, confusion blooming across his face. "What's going on here? Who is this guy, and what is he talking about?"

The sense of shame that had niggled at her for months now draped Gabi from head to toe. She couldn't look at Shane. Instead, she tried to refocus her shame into anger. Voice somewhat heated, she said to the man, who frankly was beginning to make her skin crawl a bit, "I don't understand what's going on. But...it's gone." Her voice cracked. "The treasure is gone from the Santa Maria. Someone else got to it before we could. I'm sorry," she ended on a whisper. She didn't need to be looking at Shane to know that the silence holding him was filled now with utter shock.

The UTEI man tutted and shook his head. His voice sounded positively oily when he spoke. "On the contrary, Ms. Santos. You did just as you should have, and you led us right to it." He smiled broadly. "My actual employer is the one who now possesses the treasure. As we had planned all along. You simply hurried along the process in a way we never anticipated."

This time, Shane gasped out loud.

"I don't understand," Gabi said, voice still a whisper. She suddenly shivered in spite of the heat of the day already starting to seep over the island. "Who—what are you talking about? Your actual employer? You mean UTEI?"

"UTEI!" Shane's voice yelped in alarm. "Jesus, Gabi. Are you mixed up with them? What the hell have you done?" The disgust and growing rage in his tone felt like a physical punch to Gabi. Yet she deserved no less.

"Oh, I do work for UTEI, yes, indeed." Another smirk. "However, UTEI works for someone else. The bigwig in a certain gold trade, shall we say." He chuckled to himself, as if at a private joke.

"I don't understand." Gabi felt utterly impotent and help-less each time she thought or said those words. It was pissing her off, but it was true.

"In due time, you will." The oily voice was almost enough to make her literally gag. "I simply wanted to extend our deepest thanks for your help in retrieving the gold, Ms. Santos." He executed a smarmy bow at her, doffing an imagi-nary hat with a derisive flourish. Shane gaped at him just as she did. "Your—special meaning to its owner was the key we needed to its recovery."

The odd hesitation as he said that just confused her more. She felt ever more lost, as well as anxious and distressed. "I—then you did take it. All of it."

"Naturally. We have been after that particular hoard for many years now. It was well worth the wait." His brilliant white teeth gleamed at her as he bared them in a nasty smile.

Hoard. Gabi's stomach lurched in renewed horror. She took a step back from him. Oh, god.

"So dreadfully sorry we'll have to renege on our part of the bargain and not pay you after all," he went on. "You fell into that trap too easily. Humans." He contemptuously shook his head as Gabi's stomach plummeted. "Always so greedy. And so foolishly led."

With a bark of laughter, the man lifted a hand in mocking farewell as he started to turn away. Almost as if an afterthought, though, he paused and swung his head back around. "Oh, and Gabriela?" He lowered his glasses from his eyes and looked straight at her.

Gabi was close enough to him still to see the odd, bright green glints glittering out from his eyes. More jolts of shock ripped through her at the familiar sight.

"Do give our regards to Kai, and tell him we thank him greatly for his contribution. He will know who we are." A positively sinister smile then crept over the man's face. "Such a terribly sad thing, when he lost his mate. She fought valiantly, that one. Too bad," he sneered right in Gabi's face, "he wasn't man enough to save her in time."

With that, he turned and walked down the dock, whistling a jaunty tune. He disappeared around the corner as Shane and Gabi stared after him.

The world around Gabi seemed to lurch, although she knew perfectly well she was still standing on solid ground. Mate? Kai had lost a—mate? She wasn't quite sure what that meant. Somewhere in her heart, though, she knew it must be a terrible thing to have lost. Something that must have scarred him deeply.

Because a mate sounded an awful lot like the sort of partner for life a dragon might have.

"What a freaky weird guy. And you." Bitterness coated Shane's voice as he took a step away from her. "Gabi, what the hell? You had a hand in this? UTEI? You got mixed up with them? Treasure hunters." He spat out the words in disgust. "They have no reverence for real historical work. I can't believe you did this. What was possibly worth getting mixed up with a bunch of low-down, scummy treasure hunters? They're nothing more than thieves. How could you not have told me?" He shook his head, as if trying to clear cobwebs from it.

Gabi's voice came out a hoarse croak. "My grandmother, Shane. I had to do it. For her. I had no choice."

Staring at her sadly, but also like she was the most foul thing he'd ever encountered in his life, Shane shook his head again as he backed off another step. "You betrayed us and all of history. Nothing is worth that. *Nothing.*"

Her breath going ragged as the shock began to turn into angry, helpless tears, Gabi clenched her fingers. Feeling more sick than she ever had in her life, completely drained of willpower and energy, she stared, unseeing, toward the laboratory building that had housed her dreams for the last several years.

Shane flicked his glance over Gabi's shoulder. "Sailboat coming in. If I'm not mistaken, it looks an awful lot like the one your boyfriend had the other day." His tone was cold. Stricken.

Faintly, Gabi protested, "He's not my boyfriend."

"Whatever." Shane's muttered voice ground into her heart. "I'm out of here." Turning on his heel, her friend strode away down the dock as well, tremendous hurt and rage pouring off of him with every step he took away from her.

With another shaky breath, Gabi turned to look back out

over the ocean. Yes. It was Kai, coming in on his sailboat. Wondering whether some sort of strange, magical dragon shifter abilities allowed him to somehow sense wherever she was—which really wasn't that far-fetched, considering the fact that he could turn into a dragon in the first place—she stared at his beautiful, sleek boat as he quickly and easily slid it into a slip on the other side of the dock. Her heart stuttered, mimicking the uneven rhythm of her thoughts and emotions.

He was here. That had to be a good thing, right? Because it didn't look as if he'd disappeared into a pile of gold-less nothing, like he was about to fade into oblivion. He was here, solid and real and alive.

He also looked utterly hollow. From rage.

Kai stepped out of the boat in a fluid motion, landing on the dock with a heavy thump. He strode directly over to her. As he drew near, Gabi saw something else in his expression as well. Pain. Grief. But most of all, his features resembled that of a granite mass.

Unyielding.

Unforgiving.

"Where is it?" The strange, booming sort of snarl beneath Kai's words made Gabi's heart lodge in her throat. His dragon. His dragon boomed beneath his voice. Clearly very close to the surface.

Well, damn. Apparently the loss of his gold did have an effect on him. It made him terrifying. Wondering wildly if Kai would dare shift into a dragon right there on the dock that was publicly visible to many despite the early hour, she tripped herself up by then immediately wondering if he would be visible to anyone else but her.

Completely stymied by the confusion of her own thoughts, Gabi stared at Kai with her mouth slightly parted as she tried to get out words that would make sense.

"I—it's gone. You went down there?" Gabi knew she was

hedging even as she spoke. To her own ears, her voice sounded guiltier than hell.

Kai, clad in board shorts and a dark gray T-shirt that left none of his delicious musculature to the imagination, close-cropped hair still wet from what must have been his swim down to the ship, loomed over her. He actually loomed. Despite her instinctive trepidation, Gabi felt the flare of her usual fire surge to life.

Narrowing her eyes behind her sunglasses, she forced herself to straighten her own spine. "Don't come swooping in here all scary like that. It won't help anything." Despite herself, her voice wobbled a bit.

He didn't budge, lips pressed into a thin, hard line. Then he snapped out, "This is no longer a game, Gabriela."

His voice bit off her name as if it was something distasteful. Gabi recoiled as the painful shock of it slapped at her. "My treasure is gone." Kai's voice was flat. "And somehow, I know you had something to do with it."

When she didn't reply, completely uncertain as to how she could possibly respond with anything that would help, Kai savagely ripped the sunglasses from his face. Gabi sucked in her breath. She'd recognized pain in his expression. Yet that was nothing compared to what she could see in his eyes. The usual bright green flecks dancing in them seemed dull.

The loss of his gold did hurt him. Literally, physically hurt him.

She hadn't completely understood the importance of a dragon's treasure to his well-being.

She had been more than a fool. She had been callous and selfish.

Stumbling over her words, completely lost as to how to handle this, she stuttered when she spoke. "Kai, I never, ever meant for this to happen. You have to believe that. They didn't tell me they were going to take everything. They were supposed to take just some of it to sell. Not everything. And when I first agreed to it, I had no idea about"—she waved one hand around, trying to encompass everything she was having difficulty articulating—"you."

She squeezed her other hand tightly. Something in her palm cut into her skin. Uncurling her hand, she looked down. The tiny gold nugget glittered up at her. She'd forgotten she'd been holding it again during the entire boat ride back into shore. As she looked back up at Kai, she saw his eyes had fixed on it as well. His pulse beat in his forehead, neck cording as he clenched his jaw.

Shaking, Gabi held it out to him. "I was returning it to your hoard," she whispered. "That's why Shane and I went down there this morning. My—my grandmother told me I had to return it to you as soon as possible. She knows about your kind. She knew you needed it." Gabi's voice trailed off into silence as he just stood there, staring at the tiny piece of gold in her hand with an expression that shared nothing of anything he might be feeling or thinking.

Then, after a long moment, a ghastly smile spread over Kai's face. He shook his head. Absolute deadness settled over his features, although she could still see pain clawing its way out of his eyes. "It doesn't really matter anymore," he said, his voice flat. Frozen. "It is too small and will do me no good. You betrayed not only me, but also apparently the team of people you considered friends. Unforgivable," he whispered. "Everything you've done is unforgivable."

Gabi almost forgot to breathe, trapped by the horrible deadness of his voice. It felt as if an abyss yawned beneath her feet, threatening to suck her down. Her horrendous shame and fear whirled around inside of her, blending together in a sickening concoction. Kai's expression didn't change.

"It wasn't on purpose." Gabi's voice sounded hoarse to her own ears. Ragged. But even as she spoke, the truth of his words settled into her very bones. "But you're right. I betrayed everyone." She felt light-headed. "Especially," she forced out against the bile rising in her throat, "you."

Kai stared at her for another long beat before he gave a single, curt nod. "Yes." The simple word echoed with the hideous truth. Voice grating, he went on. "Let me explain something. In the dragon shifter world, we don't usually marry, the way humans do. We mate." His voice snapped out the word, quickly. As if it hurt to say it. "We discover our mates. Our destined mates, with whom we are meant to spend the rest of our lives."

Gabi felt cold chills shudder all over her despite the warmth of the sun. She stared at Kai in shock.

"My true mate," and suddenly he thrust his face toward hers, speaking the words with savage enunciation, "the only mate I will ever have, died five years ago trying to protect our mingled treasure hoard. She gave her life to save us. You?" He barked out a cutting laugh that sliced into Gabi so deeply she literally wondered if she was bleeding. He hissed out the next words, his face hollow. "I don't know what you are, aside from someone I never again wish to see."

Gabi's mouth was so dry that she couldn't get any words out. Not that she had the slightest idea what to say.

Without another word, Kai turned and walked away from her, his stride stiff and jerky. Leaving her standing on the dock, alone.

Before she could even try to find her voice to call out to him, her phone angrily buzzed. Looking down, she saw a curt text from Everson. *Just had a chat with Shane. You'd better call me right this second, Gabriela. If anything he said is true, you're done with the team as well as the university.*

Closing her eyes, Gabi sank down onto the slowly sun-warming surface of the dock, curling her hand back around the cold, useless lump of gold. She had just lost everything in life that she cared about. Including, she knew with a soul-rending jagged whip of pain, the one person—the sexy, amazing, heartbreaking dragon shifter man—she'd just realized she wanted more than anyone else in the world.

The one she knew without a shadow of a doubt she had fallen in love with.

The one she had just lost forever.

16

Kai charged forward, his right arm cocked back, then released the full power of a rage-filled punch.

The speed bag exploded in a shower of its innards, the red faux leather that had contained it seconds before, and the twisted metal from where it had been attached to the anchor holding it to the platform. Rotating around from the force of his own forward momentum, Kai was spun into his older brother. Eli didn't bother to steady Kai, opting instead to simply step backward so that Kai stumbled to a graceless halt. Letting out a string of inventive words, Kai glared first at his brother, then at the punching bag.

Eli lifted a sardonic eyebrow. "Well. I can see that the immediate removal of your hoard has not quite yet affected all of your power." Narrowing his eyes a bit as he studied Kai, his brother then said more slowly, "Or is there something else going on?"

No. Not even bothering to glare at his older brother, Kai stalked over to the full-body punching bag in the corner of his home gym and began pummeling it with enraged grunts.

Eli, as well as Kai's parents along with two of his other siblings, had arrived in Los Angeles several nights after Kai's world had thoroughly imploded yet again. It had pained him to call them, particularly because of his angry pride at not having had to rely on his family's strength for the last several years, but even he knew this loss was a family matter. Somehow, everything had gone to hell, and he was in no shape to even begin figuring out how to fix it.

The dangers of a death-spelled hoard being filched by another dragon were far greater than that of a regular hoard being stolen. Oh, that sort of theft was still a crime of the greatest moral reprehensibleness, as well as one punishable by death according to every dragon council codex worldwide. Truthfully, Kai had never truly worried about such things for his own hoard. Lazy, criminally-minded dragons often spent an entire lifetime stealing bits and pieces of other dragons' gold hoards in order to enhance their own power and lengthen their own lives. The Long family, however, was a very old lineage that was strong in numbers as well as power. Other dragons never bothered to try taking their gold, knowing it would be a fruitless endeavor.

Kai grunted again as he thumped the punching bag even harder. It was clear he had been too complacent in his belief that both the death spell and the additional concealing spells he and his family had placed on his treasure hoard at the wreck of the Santa Maria would keep it forever hidden from sight. They forgot to count upon one unforeseen factor: the presence of humans who were just as greedy as dragons, even if they didn't understand the true nature of the treasure.

They'd also never counted on the presence of Gabi, who had betrayed Kai beyond all repair. Even if it hurt so much he thought he might die from the pain of being without her. That sense of pain, of feeling anything, infuriated him even more than the theft of his hoard.

Kai slammed his left fist into the bag this time. Its seam popped in the back from the force of it. The faint scent of sawdust drifted through the air in this corner of his gym. Jaw clenched, he attacked the bag again. And again.

"That hasn't been helping for the last twenty minutes. You really think it's going to start helping now?" Eli's voice, practical and annoyed at Kai as ever, served nothing more than to fuel Kai's anger.

With a roar, he attacked the bag with the same fury and rage with which he had assaulted the smaller speed bag. Slowly but surely, the seams on the back and sides ripped more and more with each fiercely aggressive punch.

In between each slamming punch he threw, Gabi's stricken face rose before him, the way she had looked when he had seen her on the dock and realized the truth of what she had done.

Slam.

No matter how hard he punched the slowly tearing bag, he couldn't erase her sweet, gorgeous, thoroughly despairing face from his mind. Or her voice, imploring him to listen to her.

Slam.

Her devastating lies that had destroyed so much more than she was capable of understanding.

Slam.

His final punch ended the bag's stability. Ignoring the judgment and disappointment he could feel boring into his back from where he knew his brother stood glaring at him, Kai savagely finished the job until the punching bag was nothing more than an empty sack hanging from its anchor, the contents of its insides littering the floor of the gym.

For several moments, only the sound of Kai's gasps as he slowly cooled down and the far-off steady thump of waves meeting shoreline down below the house filled the room. Finally, once Kai's breathing had returned to normal, his brother spoke again. "What was her name?"

Kai's head snapped around to glare. Eli stood there, arms crossed across his chest, regarding Kai with a great deal more compassion than he would have thought. Wary, Kai didn't answer.

Eli blew out a less patient huff. "Kai. The long reach of the Long family," and here his slightly mocking expression as he uttered the inside family joke made even Kai wryly twist his lips for a second, "found out what happened. Sort of." He eyed Kai for another moment. When he spoke again, his voice was more hesitant. "Look. There's a theory about how everything fits together. Before I tell you that, though, I want to know her name."

Despite his inner anguish and rage, exacerbated by the sense of his thoroughly demoralized dragon lurking somewhere in the shadowed corners of his mind, Kai couldn't prevent an instinctive flare of protectiveness. "Why do you need to know her name?"

To his surprise, the sympathy in his brother's eyes intensified. "Because," Eli said in a softer voice, "the way you just answered my question tells me that the theory was right."

Annoyed now, Kai snapped, "What theory? And her name," he ground out, "is Gabi. Gabriela. Now tell me what in the hell you're talking about."

Stalking over to the open windows that led to the balcony outside the gym that overlooked the ocean, Kai stood in front of them to let the ocean breeze caress his face. Even just saying her name was painful.

"Because," his brother said, stepping beside him to also regard the ocean, "there's a very good reason that she was the one who somehow managed to break the death spell."

"I know that!" Kai roared, clenching his fists at his sides. Apparently, destroying two punching bags still wasn't enough to soothe the turmoil he so desperately wished he could replace again with the numbness that had been his friend for the last several years. Inside, his dragon stirred in the shadows, rumbling. "That's what I was trying to figure out. Why she could break it. How." He slammed one hand into the palm of his other, still gripped by frustration. "Obviously, she was working with whichever dragons wanted to steal the gold. They somehow figured it out, got her close to it, and had her break the spell. It's the only explanation, even if I don't fully understand it yet."

More firmly, his brother said, "No. That's not the only explanation. We think," and by that, Kai knew he meant the entire family, "she wasn't a willing partner in this. I think it was at least partially a coincidence. Also, that she was used. Your Gabi."

Kai barked out a laugh as he watched the waves roll onto the beach, draw back, then roll back in. A seagull made a hoarse call as it flew several hundred yards down the beach. "You're talking in circles. Spit it out."

With a thoroughly exasperated sound, Eli grabbed Kai's shoulder closest to him and half spun, half pushed his brother around so that Kai was looking at him. Automatically, his fists clenched again. To his surprise, though, his brother didn't rise to it as he normally would have. Instead, though his expression was still annoyed, something in his eyes stirred with so much sympathy that Kai's mind stumbled over itself. Inside, his dragon quietly roared again. But not in confusion, like Kai.

In despair, frustration, longing.

Longing for the woman he had claimed as his own.

"That," his brother said, gently jabbing a finger at Kai's chest, "is exactly what I'm talking about. I can see your dragon right now. He's close to the surface. Our esteemed mother, who is right in all things," the corner of his mouth lifted in a long-suffering grin, which Kai couldn't help but answer with a snort of agreement, as they both along with their other siblings bore the brunt of their mother's unerring rightness about the world and each of their paths in it during their entire lifetimes, "had a hunch. Apparently the information they discovered while they're up in San Francisco has confirmed that."

Their parents had traveled to the Bay Area, checking leads

as to who had taken Kai's treasure, while his other brothers were spread out in Southern California following similar leads. Kai had been too enraged, despairing, and, he angrily admitted, feeling bitterly wounded by the machination of the theft of all his gold and Gabi's role in that to want to help. He'd refused to do anything but stay here in his home, beating the hell out of his gym as he tried to find that numb center. He knew perfectly well that Eli had been assigned to keep an eye on him.

After another long stretch of silence, he wrenched away from Eli and threw up his hands. "Tell me, dammit. What was her hunch?"

Eli kept his gaze steadily on Kai's as he responded in a quiet voice. "As it turns out, Kai, she is your mate. Gabi. That's how she was able to break the death spell. It was designed to break automatically when you once again found a mate." Though the words were direct, the tone was still filled with bottomless understanding and compassion. Very gently, he added, "Or when your mate happened to find your hoard."

Kai forced himself to stand still as a thousand things suddenly seemed to swirl around at once. His dragon roared again, and again, each time more strongly and with conviction. Thoughts crashed around in his mind as he tried to put all the pieces together. Hope, that damned stupid little emotion, flung itself wildly at the fortress he'd built with relentless intensity.

His *mate*. Gabi was his mate. Logically, it made complete sense. Yet...

"Impossible," he said in the most dismissive tone he could muster to mask everything whirling around inside of him that threatened to break free and shatter all that had been holding him together for the last several years. "I would have known. Dragons always know when they meet their mates. I knew when I met mine. She died. That was all." He bit out the words.

His brother nodded, never looking away from Kai. "That's

true. Except, however, in cases where a dragon has convinced himself that he can never again have a mate. Except in cases where a dragon has convinced himself that the potential pain of losing another mate is not worth it. Except," Eli's eyes bored into Kai's, "in your case. That woman is your mate. Looking at you right now, I can tell she is. You're not angry just about the gold, Kai. You're angry because you think she betrayed you."

"She did betray me!" The words exploded out of Kai with such force that they ended on the bellow of his dragon strongly trying to come out of him in his human form. The green of his dragon's eyes were probably overtaking his. He saw his brother's eyes respond in kind in automatic reaction to the threat of another dragon bursting out from the human side's control. But his brother, the steadfast, responsible, always-in-control older brother of the family, held his ground. "Kai, she's your mate."

Kai's dragon boomed and roared inside him, demanding to be let out. Kai could actually feel his wilder form pushing at him below the surface, as if the sharp ridges of his spine were about to come pushing out of his human skin. He struggled to control it, shocked by the tumult within him. Desperate, he jumped on the only thing that would keep him focused. Anger. "She is not my mate! That's impossible."

Not backing down an inch, his brother countered, "Of course it's possible. Why couldn't it be possible?"

Half blind from the struggle to keep everything in check, Kai shouted, "Because my mate died! My mate died, and I cannot have another."

The heartrending truth of those words ricocheted around the room. Oddly, though, their impact didn't shred Kai as he'd feared they would.

Stepping closer to Kai, the green flecks of his own dragon's eyes brightening, Eli shot back, "Then why are you so angry at this Gabriela? Why did you care so much about what you perceived as her part in the theft of your gold?"

"Because I love her!"

Kai's bellow rang around the room, seeming to shatter the very air as he stared with shock into the pleased, nodding face of his brother. Eli at least had the grace to not say anything more as he watched Kai grapple with the truth of what he'd just said.

He loved her. He loved Gabi.

Because she was his mate.

Even if she weren't, he knew with every molecule rushing and zipping inside his body that he would love her anyway.

Love. Just the word itself sent a bizarrely calming effect through him. His dragon still rumbled beneath the surface, but it was now based more in satisfaction and acceptance. He loved her. That was why it hurt so badly to know that she had betrayed him.

Dazed, he said it again. "I love her. Oh." The truth of that statement smacked him like a thunder clap.

Then the other implications stemming from that realization flashed through his mind just as quickly.

"They used her. The dragons who stole the hoard used her to get close to it." His voice went flat. Dangerously quiet. Turning his head, he looked out at the deep, wild blue of the ocean, which beckoned to him as she always did. He listened for the faint call of his gold, but there was still no answer. All the truths washed over him, leaving him with a clear vision that he abruptly realized he'd been lacking for years now. For all the years since his mate had died.

His first mate.

Yes. This made sense. As he stood there, letting his mind tick over everything in this new, cool reflection of all the recent events, it made every bit of sense. His first mate, Leilani—even as he consciously thought her name to himself, he realized with a slight jolt that it was not accompanied by the jagged snap of pain to which he had simply responded by freezing it out—her last thought had been of him. Her very last, utterly selfless act had been for *him.*

Death spells were not always consciously set. The death spell happened when a dragon died very close to his or her gold hoard. The last thoughts of the dying dragon became inextricably bound up into the spell that protected the gold.

In her last moments, protecting their mingled gold hoard against the very same sort of evil, lazy dragons who tried to steal treasure from other dragons, her thoughts had been of Kai. She must have known she was dying, and had known what that would do to him. Her last thoughts had been that he would once again find true love. That he would once again find a mate.

Kai swallowed hard, staring out over the ocean. Yes, Gabi had been searching for his treasure for her own ends. Yet her coming across it had broken the death spell unbeknownst to both her and him. The dragon treasure hunters she already had been mixed up with could not possibly have known anything about the specifics of the death spell. No one could possibly have known.

No, his brother was right. Different characters and ambitions had all clattered up against one another upon the discovery of the Santa Maria and the ancient treasures she held, setting into motion a chain of events that ended up here. Now.

A chain of events that had brought Kai a gift such as one he never believed he would again have.

A new mate.

Gabi. The true mate, he realized in the incredible bubble of clarity that still surrounded him, of his heart and soul.

The mate from which he had walked away, convinced she was only out to hurt him for her own gain. To raise her own star on her career path, to elevate her cachet in the eyes of her peers, and, most importantly, to save her grandmother. But even the short time he had spent with Gabi told him she was honest and forthright. She was utterly passionate about her work.

She had only betrayed her own personal values in a desperate, last-ditch attempt to save someone she loved. It was not her fault that through her actions she had unwittingly stumbled into the vile schemes already in place by others far more devious, and deadly, than she. Kai would have made the same desperate sort of choices if his back had been up against the wall. Anything to save those he loved.

He could understand that.

Kai had been a fool. An utterly blind fool. He had allowed the years of freezing out the world to shield himself against the massive pain of the loss of his first mate to also freeze out his ability to comprehend anything beyond that self-absorbed pain.

He turned back to look at his brother, who still gazed at him silently with that mix of compassionate yet knowing understanding on his face. "You've been pissed at me all these years because I wouldn't get my head out of my own ass and start living again, haven't you." Kai made it a flat statement rather than a question. "It wasn't that you really wanted to have a bigger hand in the business again. It was that you saw me floundering, and nothing you did, nothing any of you tried to do, helped."

His brother nodded. "I'm your all-knowing older brother," Eli said, deadpan. "Why on earth would you ever have listened to me?"

Despite himself, Kai snorted a bit.

"So," Eli said, rocking back a bit on his heels as he gave Kai a questioning look. "Now that you figured all that out, what's your next move?"

Kai's thoughts still clicked along with a clarity as deep and wide as the ocean.

"I need to go find my mate and abjectly apologize to her," he said simply, shrugging with total acceptance of the truth.

"Then just hope she forgives me." His voice hardened. "Before I can do that, though, I need to go find those thieving dragons and kick some ass to get my treasure back. Get my full power back. You in?"

Eli's smile turned into something dangerous. "Absolutely, brother of mine. That was the other thing I wanted to tell you," he said, his voice tipping toward the lower registers as his own dragon surfaced, making the jade lights in his eyes brighten even more. "We wanted to make sure you first understood what Gabi was to you. Then, we wanted to tell you some more good news. We know exactly who took your gold, and exactly where it is. So." He jerked his head towards the open doors leading outside. "You ready to go get it back?"

Kai was already heading for the door. "Hell, yeah. Kick their ass, get my gold, then go find my mate. That last part, though," he added over his shoulder as he took the stairs from his balcony down to the beach two at time, his brother at his heels, "I can handle on my own."

"I should hope so," Eli muttered.

Kai just laughed as they burst out into the sunlight, heading straight for the water to streak hard north in their dragon forms and kick some major ass.

17

The fan blew with desultory effort in the middle of the living room, doing little more than to stir around the oppressively hot air. Southern California was gripped by a heat wave the likes of which hadn't been seen in well over a decade.

"It's fine, *corazon*. Leave it. The heat's not that bad."

Gabi aimed a vicious glare at the broken air conditioner set in one window of the room. It had fizzled to a stop shortly after dinner last night, leaving the house hot and uncomfortable until the unspecified time this morning the cheapest repair guy she'd been able to find would be able to get here. She glanced at the clock on the wall as she pulled her hair away from her sweat-sticky neck. Already past 11am. She'd called twice this morning, but the guy said he was running around town fixing other broken units. They would just have to wait their turn.

Pasting on a smile as she glanced at her grandmother, trying to conceal her concern, Gabi tried cajoling her yet again. "Mateo's place has air-conditioning, so does mine. You know it won't take long to get—"

Her grandmother, stubborn as anyone in the family, held her slightly trembling hand up toward Gabi. "The repair company said they will be here soon. They will. We just have to wait. Stop worrying about me."

Gabi turned away and headed toward the kitchen to pour them each another glass of iced lemonade, shoving a sweaty hank of hair off her face as she went. She also needed to hide what she knew was her troubled expression.

Abuela was dying. Gabi knew it, her grandmother knew it, everyone in the family knew it. Oh, it wasn't going to happen tomorrow, or the next day, or likely even the next month. But they had exhausted their options for treatment, and all she was getting now was what her insurance still covered. Which, frankly, just wasn't enough.

Gabi had nothing left to offer but hope in an attempt to keep her own spirits up as much as she could for her grandmother.

She only broke down when she was alone. She couldn't afford to show anyone the complete failure she felt like.

Everson had fired her the same morning she and Shane had realized that the Santa Maria had been ransacked of her treasure. Gabi may have made a horrifically stupid bargain with the devil that was UTEI, and she may not have mentioned it to anyone, but never in her life had she been an outright liar and she wasn't about to start then. She'd called Everson and told him everything straight up, trying her hardest to keep her voice from shaking as the memory of Kai's flat, dead eyes still haunted her.

She knew Everson had been almost overwhelmed by his disappointment in her. He told her he would still write her a good recommendation when she started looking for another job, but he would also tell the truth about why she had been let go from the most prestigious university in the state, not to mention what was by far the most prestigious underwater archaeological team in the country.

Gabi knew that her chances of being hired in a reputable academic setting ever again were zero to nil. Her only options would be community colleges, the thought of which made her cringe since that would be boring classroom-only time. Or, of course, finding work with a commercial treasure hunting operation like UTEI. Places like that tended not to care about someone's tarnished academic history. They just cared about getting employees who could deliver on the job.

The funny thing was, no one seemed able to get ahold of UTEI. She'd been certain that the news would be trumpeted around the world about UTEI's "discovery" of the century. Despite checking every news outlet possible for the next several weeks, she heard not a single whisper. Nothing. And each time she tried to called UTEI, no one ever answered.

Slowly, she realized they had not been the treasure hunting corporation she had believed. They had no intention of ever putting any of the gold on public display. Clearly, they had acquired the Santa Maria's treasure—Kai's treasure—for a wealthy private collector with no intention of letting anyone in the world ever see the gold again. They'd apparently delivered on that end, and seemed to have deliberately fallen off the radar.

That realization had sunk her more soundly than the ship itself.

Worse, she strongly suspected they had some sort of tie with the so-called "bad" dragons of the world. Her UTEI contact was a dragon shifter, she was certain. Her reaction to his presence had told her he was not a nice one, either. The whole situation, she'd realized over the weeks since everything had happened and she'd had plenty of time to think about it from every possible angle, had been some sort of elaborate set-up.

She'd somehow played right into their greedy hands.

Gabi poured the lemonades for herself and abuela, brought them back out to the living room, then returned to the quiet, dull motions of her morning. The repairman arrived. He fixed the air conditioning, charmingly flirted in Spanish with her grandmother, who seemed to love it, and cut them a deal because, as he said, her grandmother was the prettiest lady he'd seen all year, which caused more blushing. Gabi couldn't help but smile at that, even as she had her worry spike again when after the man left her grandmother went to an enormous coughing fit that she clearly had been holding in the whole time he was there. Hiding her fear, Gabi simply brought some water and re-fluffed the pillows behind abuela's back rather than saying anything more.

She knew her grandmother didn't want to focus on inevitabilities. She was far too practical a woman for that sort of nonsense.

The remainder of the morning droned on like a horrible, yawning space that flattened Gabi more and more each minute. This was going to be the rest of her life.

Her precious grandmother was going to die because they lived in a poorly-managed healthcare system and no one in the family had enough money to help save her.

Gabi was going to be unemployable unless she completely changed fields, which would only further break her heart.

And of course there was one more thing. She was going to die an old, unloved maid because she'd betrayed the only man in the world she realized she truly wanted: Kai Long. The man of her dreams she'd never known she needed, who was etched so deeply on her heart she knew without a doubt that all the stories of love at first sight were undeniably true.

Gabi's cell buzzed, and with it her stupid heart leapt into her throat. Every single time her phone made the slightest noise, a tiny piece of her heart pounded with the foolish hope that it was Kai.

It wasn't him. Despite her usual wave of disappointment at that, she still felt a small bit of gratitude as instead she saw the name of her one remaining best friend flash across the screen. *You hanging in there?* Lacey asked.

Gabi managed a smile. She'd finally gotten ahold of Lacey

a few days after her final disgrace. Her bestie had indeed hooked up with her hottie billionaire boss, as Gabi had long suspected she would. Gabi was overjoyed for her and almost didn't tell her everything of her own stupid, sorry tale, but they always talked about everything. So she did—except, of course, the part about Kai being a dragon shifter. She'd have to ease into that. She'd simply told Lacey that the gold on the ship belonged to Kai's family, which was why he felt so betrayed by her. That part was quite true.

Lacey trusted Gabi and believed in her. It was a simple blessing that she had at least one friend who still championed her. Shane—well, Shane was pissed off, no doubt there. But he was maybe not quite as ready to string her up anymore over Goldgate, which he had eventually taken to calling the whole sordid affair in his multiple texts and phone calls to her. Each of his contacts ran the gamut from still being incredibly furious at her, to worrying about her after she was fired, to finally telling her what was going on with the team and the wreck. He hadn't forgiven her yet, but he finally, grudgingly, acknowledged that he understood the reasons behind what she had done, even if he didn't agree that she had been right to do it. He thought that eventually, Everson and the rest of the team wouldn't be quite so stunned and hurt, either. But it was going to be a long, hard road to get to that point. Like Lacey, who had oddly seemed to understand and forgive right from the start, Shane would come around eventually. Their friendship was too strong to permanently break. Even if he would perhaps never quite trust her implicitly again.

Unlike Kai. Who would neither come around, nor trust her even one whit. Who was one day, sooner than he should, going to die due to her part in the loss of his essential gold hoard.

Ruthlessly smashing down the hot flash of agony in her chest, she texted Lacey back.

Doing okay. With abuela now.

Lacey's answering text shot right back. *Got some good news for you!*

Gabi sighed to herself. *I need good news. Hit me.*

Lacey's next words had Gabi's eyes widening.

Sebastian said you have a job at the Center if you want. I told him everything. Vouched for you. He says he's always wanted to fund some underwater research. He vetted you, thinks you'd be the perfect person to get it going. Tell you more details later, but you in?

Gabi stared at the screen in disbelief—and wild hope. The Bernal Center, the brainchild of billionaire—and Lacey's new fiance, apparently—Sebastian Bernal, was a world-class museum and research center here in Los Angeles, famed for its devotion to proper antiquities care and display. Lacey worked there. Gabi had always thought it would be cool to work there, too, except that there was no underwater archaeology department.

She belonged in the sea. Maybe she had ruined her chances everywhere else, but if this was a shot at the life she loved, she wasn't about to say no.

What?!?!?! Details schmetails, she confused her phone into trying to autocorrect. *You must be magic in the sack for him to have agreed to this, bestie. I owe you bigtime!!!*

Lacey sent a smilie emoticon, then said, *Gabs, you are a good person. You deserve another chance. Just want to see you happy.*

There was a long pause as Gabi chewed on her lower lip. Slowly, she typed back. *Thanks. Don't think I'll be really happy ever again, but this will help me feel a lot better. I really fell for him.*

Lacey answered immediately, again stealing Gabi's breath.

Gabs. Kai will forgive you. I promise he will. Sebastian knows him, they talked earlier today. Can't tell you more right now but trust me. Kai will forgive you. He didn't know everything.

This time, Gabi's heart threatened to bolt out of her chest. Sebastian knew Kai? And Lacey had some intel about Kai that Gabi didn't know? She quickly shot back a *???* in response, but Lacey didn't answer. After several long, quiet moments passed, she knew that was all Lacey would share for right now. Despite her burning curiosity and thumping heart just at seeing Kai's name on the screen, she finally tossed the phone back down on the table in mild frustration.

At least there was one piece of crazy good news she could share with her grandmother right now.

"Abuela," she said, looking up from where she sat at the table in the living room, her tablet still open to the document page where she kept tweaking cover letters for job applications. Allowing cautious excitement to bubble up in her, she firmly turned the tablet face down. "Abuela, you'll never guess what just happened!"

The next five minutes were filled with commotion, joy, and speculation, her grandmother laughing in delight with Gabi. Then the main house phone rang. Abuela's eyes lit up even more at that, since it most likely was one of her many friends calling as usual to check up on her and chat for a time. But abuela's startled voice brought Gabi up short, causing her to sharply look over.

"Yes, this is she. Who is this, please?" Her grandmother glanced at Gabi with an odd expression as she spoke on the phone, then looked away. "I see. Yes. Tell me more."

The annoyingly one-sided phone conversation included a series of yeses, noes, one *I understand,* and long pauses during which she intently listened to whatever was being said on the other line. Then she finally said a quietly dignified, "Thank you. We will see you shortly," before hanging up.

Gabi raised her eyebrows. Still very calm, abuela looked back at her. "We need to get ready," her grandmother said. She sat up and swung her feet to the floor beside the couch. Pausing for a second, going slightly pale, she shook her head even as Gabi jumped up to go to her. "No, I can certainly make it to my room to put on going-out clothes. I only need your help down to the car."

Bewildered, Gabi repeated, "To the car? Where are we going?"

With a deep breath, her abuela stood up, smiling as she managed to stand without swaying. With a decisive nod, she fixed her granddaughter with a firm, almost regal look. "We are going to see your dragon man. Right now. Oh," she added. "Bring that gold piece with you."

———

KAI'S HEART thumped so hard as he paced along the huge ferry dock that he wondered if it would stomp its way right out of his chest. He glanced back down at his phone. There had been a brief flurry of *What's going on?* and *How did you get my grandmother's phone number?* texts from Gabi after he'd called her grandmother. And finally, a heartbreakingly simple, *I'm so sorry, Kai.* The messages finally stopped when he didn't answer, presumably because she was driving herself and her grandmother to the ferry.

He would also bet, he thought with a slight grin, her grandmother had noticed what she was doing and probably had told her granddaughter to stop questioning and get going. He'd never met the woman, but from what Gabi had said about her and from his own conversation on the phone with Valentina Santos earlier, he got the sense that sick or not, she was still very much in charge of the Santos family.

When the ferry appeared in the distance, he finally managed to stop pacing and simply stand waiting for it. As Gabi and her grandmother finally appeared, his dragon roared inside him, mightily beating his wings against Kai's mind. Desperate to see Gabi. To be close to her.

To be with his mate.

Kai took several deep breaths. First things first. When the car rolled off the ferry, he stepped forward, silently handed Gabi his residence pass to put on her rearview mirror, and simply opened the door so he could slide into the backseat. "It's very nice to meet you, Mrs. Santos," he said, nodding at Gabi's grandmother as she half turned from her seat in the front to stare at him for a long moment. He saw some tears pooling in her eyes as she gazed at him, but didn't embarrass her by mentioning it.

Instead, he merely observed, "I can see where Gabi gets her fire."

Gabi's grandmother managed to smile broadly at that, then turned around to face front again. Despite all her texts earlier, Gabi now sat frozen in the front seat, not looking at him. Struggling to keep himself calm and controlled for the moment, Kai merely gave her directions to his house on the island, which she followed without a word. The only noise she made was when they turned up the driveway to what even he knew was a mansion. "Wow," was all she said, jaw dropped as she stared out the windshield. Her grandmother, however, merely smiled and nodded, as if she expected it. The look on her face was wistful.

When Gabi cut the engine in the circular driveway by the large front doors, she finally looked at Kai. He almost cracked right then from the expression on her face. The luminous cinnamon-brown eyes studied him with a mixture of enormous regret, longing, and confusion. What hurt him most of all, though, was the slightly beaten-down expression she wore. Again silently swearing at himself for being a blind fool ten times over, Kai just got out of the car and walked around to the passenger door to let her grandmother out.

As Gabi exited the vehicle and walked around to join Kai and her grandmother, he couldn't help but notice her miles of long, strong legs extending out from the ends of her white shorts. A pretty blue tank top, fitted and hugging her curves closely, outlined the beautiful breasts he longed to touch. Sternly reminding himself to be dignified, because for crying out loud her grandmother was standing here too, Kai tore his gaze away in time to notice Gabi noticing him noticing her. Yet her expression didn't change from the cautiously curious one she'd been wearing ever since the ferry pulled up. Instead, she took a deep breath and finally spoke.

"Will one of you tell me what's going on, please? Why are we here? Is this your house, Kai?" Gabi looked up again at the sprawling white building nestled into the edge of the hillside.

Kai nodded as he extended his arm to Valentina and slowly began walking with her up the winding ramp that paralleled the stairs. She seemed to be doing pretty well, but this close to her, he could sense the illness deep inside her. Hoping against hope he hadn't waited too long, Kai answered Gabi. "Yes. It's been in my family for a few generations now. It actually belonged to a relative I never met. No one else in the family wanted it after he died, so it sat empty for a long time." He shrugged. "I traveled back and forth between Hawaii and here so often for the family business, though, that I took on this place. Seemed fitting. I've always loved this island."

Taking a chance, he casually added, "I have to admit Hawaii is pretty awesome too, though. You should see it one day, Gabi. I think you would like it there."

She looked at him but didn't say anything. They went through the grand front doors, which Kai had always thought were a little over-the-top but they came with the house, so he'd simply left them as is. As they entered, Gabi stopped dead, looking around.

"Holy—wow," she said again.

Kai wasn't sure from her tone if she was impressed, over-whelmed, or simply avoiding the real topic of conversation.

As Gabi stood still, her grandmother very gently extricated herself from Kai's grasp.

"It is still very beautiful here," she murmured as she moved into the center of the huge great room. He could sense the flood of emotions from her as she looked around. He turned and looked back at Gabi, who still stood motionless in the doorway. She'd definitely caught what her grandmother said, however.

"Still very beautiful?" Gabi's voice finally had some of the sass he longed to hear. Just the sound of her voice made him ridiculously happy. He had missed this beautiful woman so much over the last few weeks, once his misplaced rage at the loss of his gold had been redirected to the truth.

He and Eli, along with other family members and the help of an old family acquaintance, the very powerful dragon shifter Sebastian Bernal, had found Kai's stolen gold hoard in northern California. Sebastian, who had been called for any help possible by one of Kai's other siblings on the hunt to find it, had known instantly who had taken it. There was a large network of evil dragons up there who specialized in large-scale thievery, antiquities theft, and outright mafia-type tactics to get what they wanted without working for it themselves. While their leader had recently been killed, the network still existed, unfortunately enough. Yet the current disarray in their organization had allowed the Long family to successfully battle to retrieve Kai's treasure.

Being finally reunited with his gold had been a powerful moment for Kai, as he felt its full strength flow through him with a delirious force once he was able to actually handle it again. But even that thrilling experience had paled in the face of his one true desire: to go to his mate, shuck his idiotic pride, apologize to her—and then keep her by his side forever.

If, that is, she wanted that, too.

Before he could say anything, though, Gabi planted her hands on her hips, shoved her sunglasses up on top of her head to reveal her narrowed eyes, and demanded in a fiery tone, "You'd better tell me right now what's going on. Why are we here? Did you just call me out of the blue for—for what?" Her vexation apparently back in spades, she threw her arms out to the sides. "Tell me. Right now," she warned, her voice dropping a notch as she glared at him.

Kai couldn't help the slow grin that broke out on his face at that. His beautiful, fiery spitfire was back. There still was a chance for the both of them.

18

Gabi stood in the doorway of one of the most palatial homes she'd ever stepped foot into, staring from Kai's insufferably gorgeous presence to her grandmother, who was slowly walking around the huge room as if she wandered an art gallery filled with fabulous paintings.

Whatever was going on here, Gabi was confused as hell. She didn't like being in the dark. Kai didn't seem to be outraged at her. Her grandmother had told her that he was the one who called, and he wanted them to come to the island, and yes, yes, she was absolutely fine and could make it, but Gabi of course had to drive. Gabi had seesawed from wild elation to terrible guilt to utter confusion back to wild elation the entire time it took for them to get here. Then, finally catching sight of his tall, strong shape waiting for them when they pulled up on the ferry had shaken her heart. Kai. Just seeing him again after the weeks of emptiness had enormously brightened her day, although it had also suddenly made her so ridiculously nervous that she couldn't even look at him during the brief drive to his crazy huge house.

To her surprise, her abuela answered her demands.

"Gabriela, this young man has something he wants to show you. He is going to help me at the same time."

Her grandmother turned in the middle of the room to look back at Gabi. Her eyes gleamed with tears. All of Gabi's ire abruptly vanished. Rushing past Kai, she went straight to abuela. "What's wrong?"

Her grandmother gently shook her head, waving Gabi off. With a peaceful smile, she turned to Kai. "You have kept the house much the way he had it when he lived here," she whispered. "With just a few modern touches now, of course."

Completely floundering, Gabi stared from her grandmother to Kai and back again. "When who lived here?"

In answer, Kai strode by her, his spicy male scent enveloping her and threatening to render her slightly dizzy. He went to her grandmother, smiled at her, and gestured down a hallway. "This way, ladies. It's here now. Back home with me. Truly safe forever."

With that, he moved down the hallway. To her surprise, her grandmother followed him without question. Gabi started to protest, but abuela flapped a shushing hand behind her and kept walking.

Despite how huge the house was, it wasn't ostentatious. It didn't scream an exaggeration of wealth. Instead, it was open, airy, comfortable. Floor-to-ceiling windows seemed to be in nearly every room they passed as they went down the hallway. Bright sunlight poured into each room. The ocean-side rooms had gorgeous vistas of the sea. The hallway gently curved, and suddenly widened into an enormous, round room that was filled with light.

Momentarily dazzled, Gabi shielded her eyes and peered upward. It seemed as if the entire ceiling was one enormous skylight, through which the sun came in to wash the room in as much brightness as if it were outside, although thankfully the heat didn't come in with it. "It's gorgeous, Kai," Gabi breathed, her gaze sweeping over the tall white columns around the edges of the open room.

Her grandmother said in a reverent voice, "Ah. Your beautiful treasure hoard."

Gabi's head snapped around. In the center of the room, on a small dais, lay the sparkling treasures of the Santa Maria. Even though Gabi had seen them before, even though she had seen them in situ at their original place on the ship, she still couldn't help her own small gasp of appreciation. The very air seemed to shimmer, as if motes of gold and jewel dust floated in the air, sending out tiny brilliant little sparkles of light as well.

Despite the enormous beauty, she felt a sense of sharp disappointment. "Kai," she said with some hesitation, looking at him. "Is it all here? All yours?"

He seemed to understand exactly what she meant. "What's mine is here, yes." His voice was soft as he looked back at her. "But I know what you're asking. About letting the world be able to experience the history of the treasure that the Santa Maria carried. That's why the portion of the gold that did not belong solely to me has been donated to an outstanding museum that will keep it on display for the world, forever."

The portion of the gold that did not belong to him... Gabi started to shake her head. Then, clarity dawned. "Oh," she said in an even quieter tone. "You mean—the part that belonged to her. To your mate."

The smile on Kai's face spread into a soft joy that uplifted her. No pain remained in his expression.

"Yes. It was no longer mine to keep," he said simply. His smile was peaceful. "There are some pieces of history that should be visible to all people," he added. "So it's at the Bernal Center. Where, I believe," and now his smile broadened even more, "you have an excellent job offer waiting for you. In addition, the Center's owner would like you to set up that particular display. You and everyone on the Ancients Quest team will receive full credit for its discovery." His smile filled with something light and joyous and open, he added, "And you have my blessing to do the honors of handling it all, Gabi."

The kindness and forgiveness in those simple words staggered her. She couldn't say anything for a moment, feeling her throat clog up. She looked around, grasping for something else so she could regain some composure. Then her hand tightened on the heavy gold nugget in her pocket. Pulling it out, she held it toward Kai. "This is yours." Her voice cracked a bit. Nervous, almost shy, she waited for his reaction.

Kai's eyes never left hers. "Place it onto the rest of the treasure, Gabi." His voice was as strong as the sea, yet as gentle as a ripple in the water. "It's waiting for your touch."

The room felt breathless. As if everything waited for her to do this one thing. Slowly, Gabi walked to the sparkling gold and jewels of Kai's hoard. Reaching out, she felt her hand pass through something that felt warm and comforting, though with a tiny bit of a spark. Startling a little bit, since she saw nothing but air, she carefully nestled the gold nugget into the shining hoard.

Something deep and true settled over her as she did it. It felt inexplicably *right*. As if a missing puzzle piece had been snapped into place, and all was well in the world again.

As her eyes examined the dais, she faintly creased her brow. Everything on it was completely in the open. Exposed.

"Wait. Anyone can get to it," she started to say. But to her surprise, it was her grandmother who shook her head.

"Gabriela, can't you feel it? Your dragon man has a spell around his gold. A protective one. A safe one." Abuela looked at Kai with a pleased smile on her face. "A spell that he created himself. One that protects his treasures from anything and anyone that would try to take them away. A spell that allows *you* into it as well." She looked at Gabi, her face softening into a smile of such joy and satisfaction that Gabi stared. "Because it is attuned to you now, too."

Speaking to Kai though her eyes remained on Gabi's confused, blinking expression, abuela added, "She doesn't quite understand everything happening here. This is new to her."

"Yes. But you understand the truth of a dragon's treasure, don't you, Valentina? The power it opens up in me." And even though Kai spoke to her grandmother, his eyes were also trained on Gabi. Just as pleased, but also hopeful. She thought she even detected the slight hint of nervousness in them as well.

Looking from Kai's tall, broad body filled with health and vitality to her small, somewhat frail grandmother's form, Gabi shook her head at them both, trying to figure out what on earth was going on. "It's really time the two of you stop speaking in riddles." She gave them each a stern look.

Her grandmother simply smiled at her, then looked at Kai. "Your dragon man is going to start healing me. It is one of his gifts. Being near his treasure—all of his treasure," she added with a soft, elated look at Gabi, which again totally flummoxed her, "allows his gift to shine. So. Shall we begin?"

Gabi watched as Kai nodded and turned to her grandmother. Reaching his hands out, he said in a soft voice, "Hold my hands. Simply be. It will feel a little strange, as if the ocean water is rushing through you and washing you clean."

Abuela nodded. Somehow, Gabi knew not to speak.

Long, quiet moments passed. Even Gabi could sense something enormous stirring in the room. Something huge, powerful, and filled with such gentleness and blessing that she literally felt a tear tracking down her cheek. Kai and her grandmother stood there, near the rich sparkle of his treasure, Kai's head slightly bowed and eyes closed as he concentrated on—whatever it was he was concentrating on. They remained like that for just a few moments. Then it was over. Gabi's grandmother blinked open her eyes, smiling. She gently squeezed Kai's hands before releasing them.

Looking at her carefully, Kai said, "How do you feel?"

Gabi stared at the two of them, still puzzled but also touched by a soft, gentle feeling of peace. Whatever just happened between them, it made her feel soothed. She looked at her grandmother. Her eyes seemed to sparkle, her cheeks were rosy with a slight flush of health, and something about her seemed more firm. More solid.

Her grandmother smiled at Kai. In a delighted voice, she whispered, "I feel a little younger." She looked at Gabi and laughed, the sound itself seeming more vibrant than Gabi had heard in years. "I do feel younger. Better."

Kai nodded, a smile of relief and gratification on his face. "There's a ways to go," he warned. "Full healing doesn't happen overnight. I'm not a magician. But I am stronger, thanks to your granddaughter, and thus able to use my natural healing ability to its full potential." Softly, he added, "Valentina, your cancer will be gone. It will take a little while, but it will be completely gone."

Abuela nodded. "Yes," she said simply. "Your strength is good. Just like his was." The wistful smile was back. "You will heal me. I feel it working already."

Gabi clapped a hand to her mouth, eyes suddenly over-flowing. Kai looked over at her, the green flecks of his dragon's eyes whirling in his dark brown irises. Despite her confusion, she simply laughed with joy through the tears. Taking her hand away from her mouth, she quietly said, "Okay. Finally, will you tell me?"

Her grandmother answered, smiling at Gabi before she looked back at Kai again. "Your dragon man, *corazon,* is a heal-er." She said it simply. As if it were the most natural thing in the world. "Like his great uncle before him. Maleko. Another dragon man whom I loved very much and lost far too young." Her voice softened. "But enough of that." She appeared to brush any lingering sadness off of her. "The two of you have much to talk about. I wouldn't mind taking myself on a tour of this house again, and enjoy how my body feels a little better now than it has in a long time. Would that be okay with you, Kai Long, master of this lovely mansion?"

Kai smiled and gave a small but very courtly bow to Valentina, who giggled and blushed. Just for a split second, she looked like she must have when she was a young woman. Touched, eyes still watery, Gabi just smiled.

"Of course you may. And she will be perfectly safe here," he added to Gabi as she started to open her mouth to ask just that. "There is, of course, a great deal of security on the entire house." Then, a question apparent in both his voice and on his face, he said, "Let's give your grandmother some space. I want to take you up onto the roof, anyway. It has the most amazing view."

HEART BOOMING IN HIS CHEST, Kai led Gabi up to the roof of the house. On the occasions he chose to fly rather than swim in the ocean, he launched himself from this spot. The roof was really a giant deck, surrounded by astounding three hundred and sixty degree views. Most dragon shifter homes had such places, which served as takeoff and landing zones for occupants when in their dragon shapes.

Between starting the healing process on her grandmother and the simple joy of being here with Gabi, his entire body was in a state of nervous anticipation. Inside, his dragon rumbled with equal excitement, ready to greet his new mate with the respect and love she deserved. First, though, Kai had to be utterly certain that she wanted this, too.

Gabi stepped out onto the deck and looked into the lowering sun as it slanted its gorgeous light across the ocean. "'This is stunning, Kai." She turned to look at him as he moved up beside her. "Why didn't you show me your house before?"

Kai looked at the magnificent woman standing beside him

as she gazed at him with honest curiosity. But before he could even open his mouth, she figured it out.

"Oh. Because—because this was your home with her. Your first mate." Her voice was very quiet.

But he was already smiling, easing the moment and assuaging her fears. "Yes," he admitted with thorough ease. "Yes. Leilani was her name." It felt good to share that with Gabi. As if he was sharing a piece of his painful past in a way that put it into the light, and made it once again beautiful. Open, free, and no longer hurting. A memory to be treasured, rather than hidden away.

Like he had done with his actual treasure hoard for so many years, carrying on a family tradition that didn't need to be. His gold deserved to be in the light as well.

Sighing, he went on. "I feared bringing you here would hurt too much. But as it turns out, she gave me an enormous gift when she died."

Inside, his dragon quietly roared in approval. "She gave me the gift of loving me enough that she knew she wanted me to be able to love again, to allow myself to be loved in return again. She was right," he said in a low voice, closing the distance between himself and Gabi. He gently stroked her cheek. "She was right. I froze my heart against the pain, but then you came along and cracked it wide open again."

He closed his eyes, took a deep breath, then opened them to look directly at her. "I thought you had betrayed me because I was too scared to want to allow that sort of love back into my life again. It was far, far easier to simply push you away by making you the bad guy." He paused to clear his throat, knowing his voice was about to crack a bit. "I am so terribly, abjectly sorry for how I treated you, Gabriela." His voice whispered into the air, trembling with the intensity he felt. "I was a fool, and I was cruel to you by walking away, instead of listening to your side. I'm sorry, Gabi. Please forgive me for being blind and stupid."

He gently slid his hand through her gorgeous, thick hair to cup the back of her head, groaning slightly as her full lips parted a little bit as she looked at him. "Gabi, I am more than ready to open my heart to you. I want you in my heart and with me forevermore. You're my mate." The sheer power of that truth rocketed through his words as he spoke them. "Will you allow me to be yours?"

The golden beams of sunlight lit Gabi's skin and her stunning eyes as her mouth trembled open into a smile. "Yes, Kai. Yes, of course I forgive you!" Tears made her eyes shine. "Forgive me too for just not understanding. For also being stupid."

"You are forever forgiven, my beautiful Gabriela." He whispered a kiss across her cheek, enjoying the softness of her body so close to his.

She giggled suddenly. "What a pair we are, huh?"

He simply stroked her cheek in answer, smiling.

Firmly, she went on. "And yes, I am ready. I want to be your mate, and I want you to be my mate as well." She laughed again, shaking her head as she reached her hands out to wind them together behind his neck. "I don't even know exactly what that means. I just know that I am yours, and you are mine. Forever." She said the word with such fierce possessiveness that Kai's dragon roared within him in sheer joy.

Kai let his happiness blaze through his entire body, spilling out through his smile and his words. "Then, woman," he growled, "Kiss me. Mate."

In answer, Gabi allowed him to pull her toward him and meet his hungry lips with hers, playing and teasing and loving and shortening his breath at the pure pleasure of holding his gorgeous mate in his arms while he kissed her senseless.

But there was one more thing he wanted to do for her. One amazing thing he knew her thrill-seeking heart would adore. After allowing a long, luxurious moment of kissing and touching to happen in the beautiful sunset light, he said, "Gabi. Do you trust me to keep you safe?"

She nodded, her eyes dark with her desire even as she smiled at him with an intensity he suspected reflected in his own face. "Good. Because I want to take you somewhere."

With that, Kai stepped back almost the full length of the deck on top of the house. Then, still smiling at her in what he figured was probably fairly idiotic joy but he didn't care, he allowed the change to come over him, shifting into his dragon shape.

19

Gabi's breath caught in her throat as her gorgeous, sexy Kai—her *mate*—turned into an equally gorgeous, incredible and stunning dragon before her very eyes. Huge, long, the aqua blues and greens and pearly whites of his hide seeming to ripple over his body as the last of the sunlight sparkled on it, he was so magnificent she felt her heart beat even harder.

He stood for a long moment on his four strong legs, each one ending in wickedly curled silver claws that she knew without a doubt would never hurt her. Then, he inclined his head at her, bent his left front leg down onto the knee, and tipped his shoulder at her.

No way.

"No way," she breathed out loud. "Really? Can I?" Another thought struck her as she stared at him. "Will I—I won't fall off, will I?"

Immediately and fiercely, he shook his head at her. She instinctively knew he wouldn't let it happen. Ever. Her entire body quivering with the insane joy of multiple lifelong dreams coming true all at once, she carefully walked over to her magnificent dragon shifter mate. Reaching out a tentative hand, she touched his hide.

"Oh!" she couldn't help saying again. She'd half expected him to be cold, but he was warm and soft beneath her hand. She gently ran her fingers down his front leg, mesmerized as the color of his hide literally rippled when her fingers gently pressed down against it. "It's amazing," she whispered.

He made a deep, strange sound from his mouth. She snapped her head up to look at his giant wedge-shaped face.

"Are you laughing at me?" she demanded, although she couldn't help the fact that her own lips were tipping up into a grin.

He made the noise again. Yes, it definitely sounded like laughter. Then he uttered a more impatient sound, nodding his shoulder toward her again.

Wow. Okay, then.

She was about to ride a dragon. Her dragon. Her Kai.

Taking a deep breath and thinking of all the other halfway crazy things she'd done in her life, Gabi scrambled up his front leg and clambered onto the spot just below his neck that seemed perfectly made for her to sit. The sharp ridges there extended up the base of his neck to his head, and down his back to his tail, but the space where she sat was free and clear. It seemed perfectly made for her.

The ridge directly in front of her also seemed to be made for a human hand to hold onto. She reached out and found it sturdy but not sharp. It was warm and firm. She realized with renewed amazement that it was still part of him. A part of Kai.

Holding on tight, clamping her bare legs to his sides and taking several deep breaths, she said, "Okay, big guy. Don't you dare drop me." A touch of nervousness laced her voice. "I think that would definitely make abuela kind of sad. Me, too."

With what clearly was the rumbling dragon version of a snort, Kai turned his head back on its long, sinuous neck to look at her. His huge, gorgeous jade green eyes, which now were the reverse of his human ones in that they had deep brown flecks glittering within the green depths, regarded her calmly. She couldn't hear him or anything like that, it wasn't like he was talking to her. His expression, however, clearly conveyed the message that never in his life would he let her fall. It utterly erased the tiny snap of fear she felt.

Kai turned his head forward again, spread his mighty wings, and gently vaulted into the air with Gabi on his back.

"Holy shit!" Gabi's yell spiraled through the air as the deck of his house, then the whole house, then the hillside, then the tip of the ocean lapping up onto the land just below his house all fell away below them as they launched into the sky.

They were flying.

She was flying on the back of a dragon. On the back of her dragon mate. Her Kai.

The Pacific Ocean rolled out long, flat, and blue to the western horizon where the golden ball of the sun sank behind it. The shoreline of the mainland rose and tumbled to their left as Kai gently banked and flew south, his wings flapping with tireless energy. Gabi held on to the strong green-blue spike on his neck, feeling the warmth and strength of his body emanating through her legs where she tightly gripped him.

She was flying on the back of a dragon. An amazing, indescribably perfect dragon shifter who was her mate. This was incredible. It felt as natural as if she had been doing it her whole life. Laughter escaped her in warbling bubbles of joy.

Still holding onto his spike with one hand, she stretched her other hand down the side of his neck and leaned her chest and face against him. Squeezing hard against him, she shouted, "I love you, Kai Long. I love you!"

Kai flung his head back as he flew, loosing a bellow that shivered from his head along his body, down to his tail and through every inch of Gabi's body as well.

They flew for long minutes, Gabi in a delirium of joy. Eventually, Kai gently turned his head back to her, putting the tip of his nose against her leg. She could only see one of his huge green eyes, but she sensed he was trying to tell her something. She had no idea what, but he had asked her to trust him. She did, implicitly.

So she nodded at him, her face still almost split in two by the enormous smile she'd been wearing since the second he lifted off into the air. He nodded back, turned his head, and flew down until they gently skimmed just above the waves of the ocean, his wings dipping in and out.

Then, his only warning another gentle shudder that went through his entire frame, Kai dove both of them down beneath the waves and into the ocean.

Gabi couldn't help opening her mouth in what started as a gasping scream, and simply turned into gasping joy as they dove into the beautiful ocean she had loved her entire life.

It was as if she had a bubble around her. A bubble that wasn't keeping her dry, no, she was definitely soaked from her hair down to her toes, but she somehow was breathing air. She was still on Kai, holding onto him.

And she could see clearly. She could see the underwater forests of kelp, schools of colored fish, canyons and hills and cliffs and clefts, and the occasional dark lump that they sped by too quickly but she wondered if was perhaps another ancient shipwreck beneath the sea.

Kai had taken her into his element so she could experience it just like he did.

Gabi laughed and yelled into her crazy air bubble, "This is the most amazing thing ever!"

Another slight shiver went through Kai. She sensed he was about to do something else. Still wildly grinning, she gripped harder onto his spike just before he sent them into a spinning, whirling torpedo motion through the ocean.

Kai boomed out another dragon roar that echoed through

the water as they spun through it. Gabi's stunned laughter joined his call. She'd never before felt so alive. They swam under the ocean for what she was sure were miles before he surfaced into the air again. He spun straight up out of the water, skimmed over the top, dove back in, came up again. They raced and bobbed over and beneath the waves in this fashion for several more miles, Gabi's heart pounding with exhilaration as she clutched her mate close.

Finally, Kai stopped. Bobbing in the waves, he reached back to gently nuzzle her again with his head. Then, with a slipping splash, she was off of him as his enormous form disappeared and the gorgeous human man was there instead. Treading water, Gabi flung her arms around her wet, salty mate. She kissed him thoroughly as their legs tangled together, gently churning beneath the waves.

"What do you say to all this so far, mate?" Kai growled playfully, every inch of his hard length pressed against hers in the water.

Gabi grinned as the incredible beauty of a marvelous future with this man spread before her. "I think, mate," she said, a giggle tickling beneath her words as the gentle waves lightly splashed around them, "that you'd better get me back to dry land and a soft, nice bed where you can have your wicked way with me." She grinned at her incredible dragon shifter man.

As the rising moon's silvery light spilled all around them, Kai kissed her again, long and deep and wild and all hers. Her dragon shifter man.

"Anything you say, Gabi. My mate," he whispered against her lips, the rumble of his dragon still ringing in his voice. "The most treasured mate of my heart, now and forever."

The End

Thank you for reading *Thrilled!* I had so much fun writing about Gabi & Kai. It made me want to meet a water dragon shifter!

What's next for the **Dragon Mates**? Ash & Teagan's story in ***BURNED.*** Turn the page to read it.

BURNED

Beauty and the beast...with dragons!

To find the key to a dragon's treasure
From the fiery mouth of the clouded mountain
The scorched carmine dragon must emerge
To battle in fearless resolution for his stolen gold
And to claim the heart of his eternal true mate

-Ancient Connolly Clan Oracle

1

Narrowing one eye at her opponent, Teagan Lambert gripped her sword more tightly, then let out a banshee yell as she lunged forward with a killing strike.

Too bad her adversary was way better at this sword fighting thing than she was. With a neat sidestep at the last possible moment, he got out of her path just as her momentum carried her too far forward. Of course she tripped over her own feet, her heavy longsword helpfully unbalancing her as well. She went down hard in a scramble of limbs, emitting a yelp of pain that sounded more like that of a pocket mouse than of a wild banshee.

Smoothly twisting around, her sparring partner and class instructor leaped over her like the freaking ninja he and pretty much everyone else in the class was, sword tip pushed into the soft, exposed part of her neck. "Bam. You're dead." His voice seemed to carry to all corners of the training room.

Ears burning as she felt every eye in the place staring at her, Teagan very carefully nodded against the poke of the practice sword on her tender flesh. "I surrender," she said, her voice coming out pretty much like, well, a mouse's squeak.

Great. The joke of the class was providing entertainment once more. A sharp ding of old pain kicked her as past and present seemed to meld for a wobbly second. It kind of sucked.

The class instructor stepped back, pushing up his face shield and reaching down his free hand to help her up. She took it and lurched to her feet. Automatically slumping a little bit as her height brought her almost to eye level with him, she also pushed back her face shield. Shoving sweaty hair out of her eyes, she still gasped for breath.

"Fall of the giant," she thought she heard someone in the class whisper. But when she flicked a quick, pained glance at the other students, everyone's attention was trained on their instructor as he discussed everything she had done wrong. Yeah, her down-talking inner voice was making things up again. *Buck up, Teags,* she muttered in her mind. *You, too, can be a ninja. One day many, many decades from now.*

Sighing, she turned her attention back to the instructor. He was close enough that she could see his irises. They were always a little funny-looking up close, though she'd never been able to pinpoint what it was about them. Well, this was Los Angeles. In her brief time here, she'd discovered that some of the residents did funky body-morphing stuff just because they could. For all she knew, he'd had some crazy surgery to make him more like a sword-wielding warrior of ancient times, complete with special eyesight or something. Or maybe his girlfriend liked it. Who knew, in this crazy town?

"So what happened here," he said to the class at large, "was that Teagan forgot to allow for the fact that her opponent might use her own body space against her. You," he jabbed a finger at them all, "need to be prepared when facing an attacker. Lose your concentration against someone who knows what he's doing, and you'll lose the fight. Remember that you hold the power when you face down your opponent, so long as you remember the first unsuspecting strike is always yours. If you don't forget that, you will always have the upper hand.

Now," he said briskly. "Let's go through it again, step-by-step and in slow motion. Everyone pair up."

As he motioned her to step back into her opening stance, then proceeded to take them through the sequence step by incremental step, Teagan made herself pay close attention despite the remaining faint burn of embarrassment. Well, overcoming her fear of being put on the spot had been one of several goals she'd had when signing up for this class. That, plus the fact that *hello,* she was learning how to fight using a sword. How freaking cool was that?

Pretty darned cool for an oversized academic nerd who'd never had a boyfriend. She might not be date material, but she could at least learn how to swing an ancient weapon, courtesy of the Institute of Ancient Battle Arts.

After a few more practice runs with everyone paired off, Teagan felt somewhat more confident about her ability to perfect this particular move without giving her power over to an opponent. Okay, maybe not quite yet. Eventually, she would master this move. But at least with each new practice, and new resulting face plant, she was getting somewhat better at understanding what she was doing wrong. That had to count for something.

When the class was over, it dissolved into small knots of chattering people. Teagan went to put her practice sword away, carefully placing it into its carrying case. She'd use it at home to drill in the moves they'd worked on during this session before class next week.

As she slipped her bag over her shoulder, zipping up her hoodie in anticipation of the cool air that would greet her in the late evening outside, she gave a single wistful glance back at her classmates. Maybe someday she'd get close to them. After all, she'd only been coming here for a few months now. Many of the students had attended classes at the Institute for years.

Swallowing her sigh, she headed out the side door to the

dimly lit parking lot at the back of the building. As she walked to her car, pushing aside the familiar, oddly comforting sensation of aloneness that pretty much had been a part of her entire life, her thoughts moved ahead to what she still had to do before she could go to sleep tonight.

Feed Mouser as soon as she got home. She'd be doing that under her cat's baleful golden-eyed stare and indignant meows at her lateness.

Take a quick shower to get rid of the sweat and stink she'd accumulated during class, then grab dinner for herself.

Finally, sit down to her computer to answer some work emails. The nights she had sword class were the only ones during the work week that she didn't head back to her actual workplace to keep pushing through to the wee hours. Teagan not only really loved her job, she'd immediately realized the day she started it how competitive it was. She had to work extra hard just to keep up. Anyway, tonight at home she'd have to answer the five emails that had come through on her phone just before class had started, all of them from her bossy, occasionally mean coworker about their current joint project. Teagan wrinkled her nose at that thought, pulling her sweatshirt a little more tightly around her as a breeze sashayed through the parking lot. Her coworker was an unfortunate drawback to what was otherwise her dream job. Oh, well. At least the woman wasn't Teagan's boss.

Then, of course, she would have to check back on the work she had sent to said bossy coworker earlier that day. Oh, yeah, and then she'd have to remember to—

A door angrily slammed. The sound of heavy, menacing footsteps echoed in the otherwise empty parking lot.

Teagan stopped short, her gaze shooting toward the sound as she abruptly cut off her thoughts. The Institute was in a reasonably safe area of town, but this was still L.A. Teagan had just moved here over the summer, straight out of her internship back at the museum in the placid Midwestern town where she'd gotten her master's degree. While it was exciting to live in L.A., she'd been pretty darn scared by all the big city horror stories with which her somewhat nervous family and friends had regaled her prior to her move here. Granted, their stories came only from watching TV shows, since none of them had much experience living in a really big city either. But still.

Abruptly, she saw a dark shadow moving through the parking lot.

Teagan almost stopped breathing.

The tall, broad figure of a man wearing a hoodie pulled over his face strode through the quiet, empty lot.

Directly toward her lonesome self.

Crap. Double crap. Holy freaking crap. She was about to be murdered.

Teagan tried to swallow, but her throat was so dry and tight she couldn't manage it. Her hand gripped convulsively around her practice sword, which not only wouldn't be really useful in the event of an actual attack, but also was securely tucked into its soft-sided carrying case. It wouldn't pack much of a wallop.

Oh, god. He was getting closer. Walking with purpose straight for her.

She'd be spirited away to some creepy basement where he would perform deviant experiments and other horrible things upon her helpless body. She'd never see her family again. Mouser would never forgive her for leaving him alone, foodless and with a dirty litter box.

The figure drew even closer, the man's steps cracking loudly as he pounded along over the pavement. Almost as if he was massively enraged and just itching to shed someone's blood.

Barely twenty feet away now and still heading toward her like a wall of hideous doom.

Teagan felt a tiny, alarmed noise work its way out of her

throat even as she stood still frozen. Then the words of her instructor drifted through her head. *Remember that you hold the power when you face down your opponent, so long as you remember the first unsuspecting strike is always yours. Remember that, and you will have the upper hand.*

Still shaking, she blindly raised her sword, still in its case, and briefly positioned herself into an attack stance. Then she abruptly plunged forward, a shaky yet audible banshee cry tumbling out of her mouth at her parking lot assailant.

ASH CONNOLLY GRIPPED the steering wheel of his car so tightly he was half afraid he might crack it. Well, the left side of it at least. His stupidly useless right hand could barely hold onto the wheel, let alone break it. Inside his mind, fairly close to the surface because of how annoyed he currently was, his dragon loosed a softly echoing bellow of irritation and frustration, batting his good left wing against Ash's mind while his right wing sort of fluttered and trembled in a pale imitation of its former glory.

At the weak beating of his damaged wing, Ash felt incensed, which was amplified by the fact that he generally was an easygoing guy. But right now, he was annoyed simply by the fact that he was annoyed. Grinding his teeth, as turned the car into the parking lot behind the Institute of Ancient Battle Arts, slipped into a parking space, and killed the engine.

The second he stepped out, the late evening's chill hit his bare head with a brief ripple of the breeze. Slamming the door shut, he pulled his hood up around his face, then stalked across the parking lot toward the private back door to Nick's office.

The hood wasn't against the cold, however. Feeling a glare stretch and pull against the scar tissue on the right side of his face, Ash scowled even more as he headed toward the building. If only he hadn't given Eamon an extra day of vacation because the man apparently had gotten more serious about the woman he was on vacation with. He had called a few days ago to tell Ash he was staying in the Caribbean a few days longer—yes, *tell*, not request, because that's what an employee, father figure, and lifetime fealty man wrapped into one did with his young charge, even a charge who was now in his thirties and perfectly capable of taking care of himself. If only the new sword that Ash had been very impatiently waiting to get his hands on hadn't finally been repaired, and Nick claimed he was too busy to deliver it, Ash wouldn't be here himself tonight.

In public. Forced out of the sanctuary of his home that he virtually never left anymore. Except, he allowed himself to grudgingly snort in some self-deprecating amusement, for the fact that he had an admitted obsession with the Irish history that had been an interest of his since childhood. Yes, conspiring events as well as the emergence of an ancient sword that had once belonged to a centuries-old dragon king of Ireland, one in Ash's family lineage, onto the antiquities market had propelled him out. Still, he was currently being pushed past his comfort level, and both his old friends were the ones doing the pushing. His dragon warbled irritated agreement inside his mind.

Eamon's highly reasonable voice echoed in his head from their brief conversation the other day. *You're more than capable of driving over there on your own,* he'd said calmly. *It will be dark anyway, Ash. No one will see you. You can do this,* his longtime fealty man, childhood protector, and beyond loyal employee had quietly added, a depth of understanding welling in his voice. He didn't offer any sympathy, though. He knew well enough that Ash wouldn't accept that. Not from anyone.

Ash had more than enough sympathy, even the occasional bout of pointless self-pity, for himself.

He straightened his shoulders, irate at the usual twitching as the irked muscles of the right one were stretched. His steps fell even more heavily as he marched toward the back office, annoyance still propelling him along. In fact, he probably—

In the space of a single heartbeat and a wild cacophony of noise, Ash became aware of two things.

One, he'd been so engrossed in his own thoughts he hadn't paid attention to his surroundings, which meant that he was about to walk right into someone else.

Two, a nervous yet determined scream abruptly battered his eardrums as the figure charged at him, waving some sort of long object around as she dove toward him.

She? His dragon rumbled an equally bemused agreement at the certainty that it was a woman. Then she was almost on top of him. She landed a blow across his left arm, one delivered with surprising strength, if not quite enough accuracy to bowl him over.

Startled, instinctively defensive, Ash stumbled to the side. "Hey!" He threw up his hand before him, warding off another blow. "What the hell are you doing?"

The woman also stumbled back a step, the stick thing still raised threateningly in her hands. The image unfortunately was ruined by the fact that her hands were shaking so violently she was probably about to drop her weapon at any second. Even so, she stammered out in a surprisingly firm voice, "I h-have pepper spray in my purse, and I'm n-not afraid to use it! And I'll s-scream, and everyone inside will come running to c-cut your head off with their swords!"

Ash blinked. He couldn't help a startled burst of laughter. The lights in the parking lot were dim enough that he could just make out the bottom half of her features beneath the shadow of her own hood. Full lips, strong chin, and a wash of creamy skin that seemed to sport a constellation of beautiful, small golden splotches, like a sunburst.

"W-why are you laughing at me?" Her voice wobbled, but she kept on, a thread of pique running through it. "I mean it. Don't you come another step closer to me."

The object, which Ash finally realized had to be a sword and a carrying case since, naturally, she was coming from the Institute, still shook violently in her hands. He restrained his temper, as it had nothing to do with her.

Using his dragon reflexes, which were so fast he knew she would hardly be able to follow the movement, he whipped out his hand to grab the object, instantly recognizing by the feel of it in its case that it was only a practice sword. Easily, he flipped it out of her hands. She gasped in absolute horror, another small scream bursting out of those amazing lips.

Really, he was noticing her shapely lips right while she was apparently trying to attack him for no good reason? His dragon softly bugled an agreement, a curious fascination with the woman keeping him otherwise silent in Ash's head.

Now, that was interesting. Pushing it aside for now, Ash narrowed his eyes as he regarded the frozen woman.

"First," he said, balancing her sword in his left hand, which had become a great deal stronger than his right hand, "I applaud your bravery. That was a nice first strike. But you seem so scared that I think you weren't going to be able to defend yourself very well."

She swallowed, the movement against her throat instantly drawing his eyes to the smooth skin there. Yanking his gaze away, he went on. "Second, if I had wanted to do something nefarious to you, don't you think I would've been paying attention to where I was going and would have already seen you?"

She just stared at him in continued horror. Well, since he couldn't see all of her face, he wasn't quite sure of her expression. Actually, maybe she wasn't quite all that terrified now. Wouldn't she have either fainted or bolted if she were?

More casually, testing the waters, he went on. "You have to admit that your reaction to a non-event was a little over the top, don't you think?"

At that, she straightened, that strong chin of hers jutting out somewhat. Aha. It seemed there might be a little fire in her after all. Of course, the woman clearly was taking sword fighting lessons at the Institute. She couldn't be a wilting flower.

Voice less shaky now, she flung back, "I don't think it was over the top at all. And," her hand suddenly scrabbled in the purse she had slung over her shoulder, coming out still trembling yet triumphantly holding a small bottle of what he assumed was pepper spray, "I can still defend myself against you."

She rather defiantly shook the bottle in his direction, pushing her hood back away from her face so that it fell down just barely behind the back of her head.

Ash suddenly lost his ability to speak. Utterly taken aback by the sight of her, he could only stare for a long moment as a brief gust of wind kicked a few dry leaves around the pavement of the parking lot. Coppery red hair spilled out from under her hood, pulled back from her face but with several tendrils curling out and around. Big eyes, which Ash thought might be brown but couldn't quite tell in the low light, looked at him with an expression that danced the line between nervous, then defiant, then nervous again. Luscious lips were set in features unadorned of makeup, still showing a telltale sheen of exercise sweat on her brow, yet so uniquely, stunningly beautiful that Ash stared transfixed at her. The gorgeous explosion of freckles all over her face and chin, still bringing to mind a beautiful constellation, extended down her neck and then beneath where the material of her sweatshirt covered it up.

His dragon also stared in a fascinated silence that filled space in Ash's mind. The woman was like a warrior queen of old. A tall, gorgeous, strong warrior woman standing before him, despite the fact that her hand still trembled and her eyes were huge with nervous trepidation.

"Well? I—I've got the upper hand here. Um..." She bit her

lip, again pulling his eyes to her generous mouth for a brief second. "Can you give me my sword back, please?"

Her voice jostled Ash loose from his bizarre fascination with her. He nodded, manners and sense returning to him. "Of course. Look, I'm just coming in here to see Nick. The owner? I'm guessing you know who he is. I'm a client of his just like you are. So really," abruptly, despite himself, Ash suddenly felt his mouth ticking up into a smile, "you have nothing to worry about from me. I have no particular desire to attack you. Or anyone else."

She studied him, eyes still wide but seeming a touch more relaxed. Gently, he extended her case-covered sword back to her, handle first. Her gaze dropped to it for a second before skimming back up to his. Damn. She was gorgeous, and obviously did not know it at all. She was so unlike the types of self-absorbed women Ash had been surrounded by his entire life that he felt slightly flummoxed. Even so, he owed her an apology. She'd been genuinely scared of him.

"I'm really sorry," he said as she tentatively took her practice sword back. "You saw a big figure of some strange guy walking through a dark parking lot right at you. And my thoughts were—somewhere else, so I wasn't paying attention to anything." He shook his head, once more irritated with himself. "I must have terrified you," he said with genuine remorse.

A tentative smile flashed across her face, lifting up those beautiful lips for a brief moment. Ash's dragon rumbled, the sound equal parts confusion, captivation, and approval. Approval? Huh. Ash didn't have time to parse that, though. The women took a breath, released it, and nodded.

"Yeah, you kind of did freak me out. Sorry I jumped you with my sword. Um, it's just a practice sword." She sounded almost contrite. Almost. "It wouldn't have done much damage inside its case anyway. I have to admit that ever since I moved to

L.A., I've been a little on edge." She smiled as she relaxed more. "It's such a big city, always so much going on everywhere. I'm not used to that," she added somewhat shyly. The rich sound of her voice, like velvet wrapped around a pillow, stroked the air.

Ash let himself rock back on his heels slightly, trying to make himself seem a little less imposing. Yet this gorgeous pretend warrior woman was close to his own height. She had to be at least six feet tall. He wondered why he'd sensed any nervousness from her. She was an imposing figure on her own.

"In fact," her voice now relaxed too as she even lowered the arm that held her spray, "just the other day, this woman at work I'm friends with said—"

The breeze suddenly snapped into high gear, flipping back the other direction across the parking lot. It whisked Ash's light hood back off his head, exposing his face completely beneath the parking lot light.

The beautiful warrior woman's eyes widened at the full sight of him. She gasped in shock. Her hand flew to her mouth as she stared at the ravaged right side of his face.

It was as if ice cold water had been dumped on Ash, sending a chill through him.

Right. He was a monster. A dreadful, ugly beast of a man.

This sort of situation was exactly why he never went out in public anymore.

Inside, his dragon keened, a ragged, aching sound that slashed across his mind. Ash let everything painful and ugly and enraging slam back down over him, the brief moment of tenuous connection with a beautiful woman shoved away.

This sort of horrified response, he was all too accustomed to.

"I beg your pardon," he said in chilly tones. His hands went up to pull the hood back over his face even as he turned to start walking toward the far side of the building and the private entrance to Nick's office. "I didn't mean to frighten you. Have a good evening."

He brushed past her, her tantalizing scent of spiced cinnamon wafting to him and drawing another bizarre, hollow-sounding keen from his dragon. Straightening his shoulders, Ash picked up the pace, ignoring the slight drag of his right leg with gritted teeth and a renewed surge of massive annoyance.

And another emotion he didn't feel like naming. One that hurt too much to acknowledge.

Behind him, she cried out, "Wait! Oh, my god, that wasn't what I—that was so rude of me—I'm sorry! Wait! Please, I'm so sorry!"

But Ash ignored her, as well as the sudden, sharp pinch somewhere in his chest as he walked away from her.

He was nothing more than a monster, and no one who saw him would ever let him forget it.

2

Teagan stared at the priceless old book in front of her, gloved hand raised slightly above it in preparation to turn the page. All she saw, though, was the expression on that amazing guy's face the other night when his hood had fallen back and she'd seen the terrible scars.

She was the most horrible, awful, cruel bitch in the world to react that way. She still felt completely terrible. He had been smiling at her, she'd just been able to see it in the shadowy lights of the parking lot. Then his hood had fallen back, and she'd gasped, dramatically covering her mouth in horror like a stupid twit. Right that second, his face had frozen into something she had instantly recognized.

A practiced mask to cover up his pain. She knew exactly what that looked like. It was the same sort of mask she herself had adopted throughout much of her own life.

She'd hurt him, a total stranger who had started to sound like a really nice person as they talked. Even after she'd attacked him with her training sword for no good reason at all except that she had a highly overactive imagination. He'd talked to her, he was nice, and—okay, fine. He was kind of really fascinating, even in their interaction that had lasted bare minutes. He also had a really gorgeous face, at least the part of it that wasn't so terribly scarred. His eyes were a dark forest green, at least in the dim light of the lot. Something had sort of shivered through her with interest in his presence, after she became convinced he wasn't planning to ax murder her.

Then she'd gone and overreacted to the scars on his face, which probably every single person who ever saw him did. Of everyone in the world, Teagan should have known better than to react that way. She knew exactly how awful it felt to have someone look at your face in disgust.

Seriously. She should be committed. She also should be chastised for the rest of her life. She didn't know who he was, she would never see him again, but she knew without a doubt *he* wouldn't forget how cruel she had been.

It was enough to make a girl just want to go back to bed and pull the covers over her head. Unfortunately, being a responsible employee didn't really allow that.

"Really, Teagan, I can't imagine this is that difficult of a task for you." A grating, snippy voice jolted her back to the present moment. "But if it is, I can handle it. I knew you weren't ready to work on projects like this one yet."

The woman the voice belonged to, who happened to be on the short side and, among many other reasons, apparently hated Teagan for her height, started to push Teagan out of the way.

On the other side of the work table, another voice tolerantly said, "Celia, let her continue. You're supposed to be helping to train her, remember?"

Teagan inhaled a very quiet breath as Celia muttered something ungracious under her own breath but stepped aside. Their direct supervisor, Walter Ainsworth, was a really decent guy. He was so laid back he insisted his team call him Walter rather than Mr. Ainsworth, even though using first names for department heads was generally discouraged at the Center. Even so, Teagan paused for longer than was necessary, suddenly frozen in a brittle tangle of nerves over what she was about to do. "I'm sorry, Walter," she said, nervous habit overtaking her. "I actually wasn't paying close enough attention. It's okay if Celia does this one."

Walter shook his head, silvering strands of his hair catching light in the room. "Absolutely not," he said, smiling kindly at Teagan. "Your internship years are behind you. You need to keep working on this one today. I have faith in you. Go on," he said, nodding at the ancient manuscript whose unfortunate damages Teagan had been working on cataloguing for a few days now. "*The Book of the Near Hills* is ready and waiting for your healing touch."

Teagan didn't have to look at Celia to know the woman was shooting daggers at Teagan from her eyes, though she wouldn't do it openly in front of Walter. Taking a deep breath, Teagan pushed aside the image of the scarred man she'd been so cruel to and focused every last bit of her attention on the text before her.

The Book of the Near Hills hailed from one of the areas of history that fascinated Teagan the most. The Irish and Scots ancestry on her mother's side had hooked Teagan ever since they'd taken a trip to Ireland when she was just a kid to reconnect with her maternal family roots. They'd done a trip to Jamaica that same year, to explore her father's Jamaican roots, but it was her sister who had become taken with that culture. Teagan herself had simply fallen in love with the romance and mystery of ancient Irish kings and queens, and the myths and legends she'd at first read for fun and then later studied with academic earnestness all the way through her master's degree. She loved it so much, in fact, that she was pretty much killing herself by working somewhere in the vicinity of twelve to fifteen hours a day here in her dream job at the renowned Bernal Center, driven purely by love of her work.

Leaning closer to the text, she carefully examined the small tears in the page, not to mention the greatly loosened binding, that had prompted the book's owner, a wealthy collector, to send it to the Center in hopes it could be repaired properly. As she looked closely at the tears, Teagan abruptly brightened. Yes, she definitely knew how to fix this type of damage. She'd done something exactly like it during her internship just this past summer.

Buoyed by the wave of confidence, she nodded. "Yes, you're right. I do know how to repair this one." Talking quickly, making sure she didn't look at Celia, Teagan listed each step she would take to restore the precious old book to a state much more like its original.

"Excellent," Walter said in an approving voice after she'd finished her explanation. "You've got this, Teagan. Celia," Walter turned his attention to the smaller woman, "I've got something else for you to work on today. Let's go to the archive room and I'll show you."

With a saccharine smile that Teagan caught out of the corner of her eye, Celia nodded with fake excitement. "Of course. Actually, can I meet you there in just a few minutes? I need to add a note to my log before I forget."

Although Teagan wasn't looking directly at the woman, she had a strong suspicion that Celia might have actually batted her eyes. Walter, who had worked in the archival and restoration profession for thirty years and had been here at the Bernal Center for the past ten, was a nice guy who was generally aware of everything that was going on in his department. He was also, Teagan thought with a slight internal eye roll, a man. Which meant he wasn't impervious to female charms, no matter how deliberately charming they were.

"Of course, no problem," he said in a genial tone, turning to leave the room. "I'll check back with you in an hour to see how your progress is going, Teagan," he added over his shoulder as he left.

Celia waited until the sound of his footsteps in the hallway faded before she leaned down over the book, getting in

Teagan's way. "I can't really see when you—" Teagan began in a tentative voice.

Celia cut her off by shaking her head and standing up again to her full height, which meant that the top of her head really only came to about Teagan's elbow, and looked at Teagan's face. "Oh," she said in overly earnest tones, "Don't let me get in your way here. I am completely sure you're going to do an excellent job restoring this book." While they weren't exactly beady little eyes, when she narrowed them they sure were awfully small. "But I was wondering. Have you really been using that spot removal cream I told you about? Because I don't see any change in your skin. Your face is still all splotchy."

Teagan swallowed hard as the familiar old rush of embarrassment and self-consciousness snaked its way up through her. Thanks to the same Irish genes she loved so much, she had the unfortunate tendency of flushing pretty hard when she was uncomfortable. Which, naturally, made the freckle explosion across her body only intensify.

Celia's eyes widened as she shook her head in mock consternation. "Oh, no. I didn't mean to put you on the spot. Oh, just look at you." She pointed right at Teagan's face. "They really stand out when you get all red like that, don't they?"

Teagan swallowed again and returned her attention to the book in front of her. She had to blink a few times against the familiar sharp prickle in her eyelids. But no way, dang it all. She would not let this woman get under her skin. Celia was just a coworker. Not a boss.

Except that she definitely knew how to get under Teagan's skin. Almost literally.

"It's okay," Teagan mumbled, hunching down more over the manuscript. "I'd like to get started on this before Walter comes back."

If she looked at Celia right now, she was certain she would

see a triumphant smile on the mean little woman's face. She'd seen it enough times before that she knew exactly what it looked like.

"No problem!" Celia's voice chirped with false positivity now. "Enjoy working on the manuscript. I hope you manage to do okay at it. Don't make any awful first-timer mistakes, now!" On that note, Celia turned on her heel and marched out of the room.

Teagan bit the inside of her lip, blinking again a few times again before the manuscript came back into focus in front of her. Interestingly, Celia hadn't actually put any log notes into her daily work log. Teagan sighed. She knew mean girls like Celia really, really well. She'd grown up surrounded by them in her public high school. Little drama queens and captains of the cheerleading squad and prom queens and all that junk that she'd never had any time for.

Not, of course, that anyone would've ever asked her to do any of those things. Go to prom, be on the cheerleading squad, be part of the popular girls' group. Teagan had been way too busy reading books about ancient Ireland and dreaming about kings charging into battle on their fierce steeds, fighting dragons, rescuing maidens from towers. Or, more likely and definitely more her favorite type of story, fighting right alongside their fierce warrior queens.

Closing her eyes for a brief moment, taking a deep breath to center herself once again, Teagan visualized one of her favorite historical persons. Queen Boudica, who had spurred her imagination ever since she was a little girl and her mother first told her stories about the flame-haired queen of ancient times who easily vanquished her enemies and was as strong as any man. The fierce queen's history also had prompted Teagan's interest in swords.

"You love studying all this ancient stuff." Her best work friend, Savannah, worked in another wing at the Center but had happened to meet Teagan during her first day on the job.

She'd instantly created a friendship just because that was the kind of person Savannah was. "Why don't you take some sword fighting classes? They're totally a thing. My cousin's boyfriend has been taking lessons at this place for a while now. He says there are a fair number of women doing it, too. Here, check it out." She'd done a quick search on her phone, then texted Teagan the website for the Institute.

Teagan smiled now as she opened her eyes to look down at her project again. Okay. Between Queen Boudica and Savannah, she would be able to survive her snippy little coworker as well as her first year working in one of the most prestigious museums in the country.

Even if she was a mean girl herself who gaped at strange guys' scars and made them feel awful.

Sighing deeply, Teagan got back to work.

An hour passed in blissful quiet as she worked on the manuscript, carefully applying the glue in infinitesimal amounts while using the minuscule tools that very gently repaired these irreplaceable pieces of history. This was basically her happy place. Did that mean she was a total geek? Pretty much. Coming from a family of academics, it was pretty normal. It had also taught her that the life of the mind could be pretty brutal. Especially in the workplace. Colleagues like Celia used anything at their disposal to claw their way up to the top of a fairly rarefied food chain.

Teagan grimaced slightly as she kept working. Fine by her. She didn't really want to get to the top of any food chain. She was happy enough just working in this world-famous museum. It had been the culmination of a lifetime of dreams to land a position here. She didn't need to get to the top of any heap at the renowned Bernal Center. Just having a job here, with as little interaction as possible with other human beings, aside from someone awesomely nice like Savannah of course, suited her fine. She just wanted to do her job well, work hard enough to get noticed for doing a good job so she could start to get bigger projects, really cool ones, and be able to keep said job for as long as possible. Her whole life, for example. Was that too much to ask?

Just as Teagan leaned back to stretch out her tight muscles, the scatter of a woman's happy laughter followed by the deeper rolling voice of a man snagged her attention. More laughter followed from other people, all of it sounding just ridiculously, well, happy. She reflexively glanced out in the hallway through the door Celia had of course left open. A tall, dark-haired, undeniably gorgeous man strolled down the hallway, his arm possessively wrapped around the shoulders of a curvy, beautiful blonde woman. The two of them looked at each other with adoring gazes. Walking alongside them was another couple, also featuring a stunningly handsome man with a deep tan and a vivacious woman with sparkling brown eyes, both of whom also looked at one another with such pure bliss it would almost be sappy, if not for the fact that it was indubitably genuine.

Teagan smiled somewhat wistfully. Sebastian Bernal, the owner of the Bernal Center, a multi-gazillionaire, and former dedicated playboy, had recently fallen head over heels in love with Lacey Whitman, one of the curators here. Teagan recently had done some work for Lacey, helping one of the senior conservators to restore a book from Lacey's area of expertise in old California history. She'd enjoyed their time chatting. She hadn't dared, of course, ask much about Lacey's upcoming fairytale wedding of the century to Mr. Bernal. Pretty much every woman working at the museum who had crushed on the charismatic owner of the place was quietly abuzz with speculation about the ceremony details, which were sure to be epic. Teagan didn't really like gossip. She also definitely didn't know Lacey well enough to ask for any insider scoop. They'd spent most of their brief interactions together discussing their love of history and their own particular era interests, but that had been it. Regardless, Teagan had found

Lacey to be a really nice person. Maybe she'd become a friend someday, too.

The other couple was Gabi Santos, a recent hire who had set the museum to talking about some industry tumult of which she'd been a part. But she'd apparently brought such a fresh, energetic take to the underwater archeology department that she was the new darling of the Center. Teagan had interacted with her only a few times as well, but she'd immediately liked the high-spirited woman. The man next to her, Kai Long, who basically looked like a surf god wrapped up with a drop-dead sexy Poseidon of the deep, was a committed defender of marine life as well as Gabi's fiancé. Teagan had only seen him once before, since he didn't work here. He seemed just as besotted with Gabi as Mr. Bernal did with Lacey.

Teagan sighed again as she watched the lovebug pairs continue down the hall, still deeply wrapped up in one another. Then she got back to work. But even as she focused intently on the current page needing repair, she let her thoughts drift. Deep inside, Teagan had always wondered if her own storybook prince charming was out there somewhere, ready to sweep in and shower her with declarations of undying love, pretty baubles, millions of dollars, and a faithful promise that he'd adore her and only her for all the rest of time.

Well, truthfully she didn't really care about the millions. Or pretty baubles. Declarations of undying love might be nice, but she wasn't holding her breath. She was a nerdy scholar, and she knew it. She liked old books. She liked old things. Her idea of a good time was discussing ancient history, for crying out loud. Of course, she didn't really mind going out on a date, not that those had ever led anywhere. Nor that she'd had that many dates in her entire life. In fact, the last time she'd been on one had been—

Wow. Had it really been that long? Her cheeks flamed slightly as she realized that yes, yes it had. She'd last been on an actual date during the first year of her internship back in

Illinois. So that was...about two years ago. Like all of them, it had been a terrible date, but still. Two years ago was pretty pathetic, even for an avowed nerdy girl. She was still in the prime of her life and all that.

"Good thing I have you to fill my days and nights," she murmured at the ancient text spread out before her on the worktable.

"What was that?" The voice sounded behind her from about two feet away.

Yelping, Teagan about jumped out of her own skin as she whirled around, heart pounding. "Holy cr—uh, whoops," she ended, eyes widening.

Walter and none other than Mr. Bernal, freaking powerful gazillionaire owner of the freaking Bernal Center, stood directly behind her. They must have crept in on soundless cat feet. Or, more likely, she'd just been so focused on the book she hadn't heard them approach. Teagan sucked in a breath, the adrenaline spiking through her. Really, this was the second time in less than twenty-four hours that she'd had the life just about scared out of her. Maybe she should stop listening to her sister's weekly phone calls detailing the latest news of murders and stranglings and such in the greater Los Angeles area, and just stick to reading ancient manuscripts filled with bloodshed resulting from battle with swords and crossbows instead. She was a lot less likely to get offed by a sword, and it sounded like a more interesting way to go anyway.

Smiling apologetically from behind Mr. Bernal, Walter said, "Oh, I'm so sorry. I really didn't mean to frighten you. I'm glad to see you're so engrossed in your work," he added, that approving look on his face again.

Teagan glanced from one man to the other, knowing her face was starting to flame simply from being on the spot. Though neither one of them seemed to be staring at her freckles. If someone wasn't being cruel about it, like Celia, it didn't bother her all that much anymore—except when it was people who actually mattered. Like her very important employers. Both of them standing there staring at her like she was a particularly intriguing specimen.

"Ah, okay. I—I'm sorry, did I miss a meeting or something?" She hardly dared to look at the owner of the entire Center, who was like a rather terrifying hurricane force. She fixed her gaze on Walter, who had been like a sweet, protective uncle to her ever since she started working here.

"No, no, nothing like that." Walter waved away her concerns. "We're actually here because I wanted Mr. Bernal to see your work personally. What do you think, sir?" Walter grandly gestured at the book Teagan had been working on.

Teagan gaped at them, still completely flummoxed.

"If I may, Ms. Lambert," Sebastian Bernal said, stepping toward the manuscript, a severe look on his face. "Teagan, isn't it? An Irish name."

Startled, Teagan stepped aside, just barely managing to murmur, "Yes, it's Irish." As Mr. Bernal leaned down to study the book she'd been working on for the past three hours, she cast an anxious look at Walter. But he just shook his head, smile broadening, and stepped forward to join the big boss in examining her painstaking repairs to the ancient tome.

Well, apparently she wasn't about to get fired. So... This had to be a good thing, then?

The two men looked at her work for some time, quietly commenting on this repair, that new problem to fix, the overall quality of the binding, the high caliber of the vellum pages despite its signs of deterioration, the precision of Teagan's glue work, and so on. It was somewhat torturous to stand there and listen to them discuss the quality of her work. Teagan forced herself not to fidget. But she couldn't control the color she knew flared in her face and neck, making her freckles stand out even more prominently in a clear signal to anyone who had known her for even an hour that she was highly uncomfortable.

After another long moment filled with murmurs, they looked up at her. Mr. Bernal raised his eyebrows, glancing over at Walter. "You're right, just like you always are. She's good." He nodded his head, suddenly assessing Teagan in a way that made her even more nervous. "Your work is impeccable, Ms. Lambert. You were a first-rate hire, as both Walter and my lovely fiancée attest." A dazzling, devoted expression briefly illuminated his face as he said that. Even as she felt a tinge of startled warmth that Lacey must have mentioned her with praise, Teagan also wondered, for the ten millionth time, if any guy would ever have an openly worshipful expression like that when thinking about her. "I do believe you will be a credit to the Center," Mr. Bernal went on in more objective tones, "for the project we have in mind for you."

Teagan was more confused than before. "This project?" she tentatively asked, gesturing at *The Book of the Near Hills*.

"Yes and no." Mr. Bernal offered a cryptic smile. "Your background in ancient Irish history has been well documented. I also read your master's thesis." He gave another short nod at Teagan's dropped open mouth. "Excellent work. It demonstrated very strong knowledge as well as an obvious passion for the era. Now then, the book in question." He pivoted so neatly that Teagan's head swam. "It was recently acquired by a client who collects items from that era, mainly due to a family history." Gesturing at *The Book of the Near Hills,* he added, "The same client who owns this book."

Something odd flashed across Mr. Bernal's face when he said that. Teagan was still too busy grappling with the fact that the owner of the entire Center had actually read her master's thesis that she couldn't even begin to try to figure out what else might be going on. Still lost, she bobbed her own head, a faint smile pasted onto her face.

"The books were actually purchased together," he went on, "but the other one is the more valuable and not quite as badly damaged as this one. But it does still need some repairs."

He gave her a stern look. "While Walter will, of course, continue to oversee your work, you will go to the client's estate later this week to show him in person images of the repairs to this book you have made so far. He will approve them or not."

The tang of the glue surrounded Teagan like a comforting cloak as she stared at Mr. Bernal, pulse quickening and mind tumbling. Wait, what? She was being given a project of her own?

"Really?" she breathed, glancing from him to Walter. They had to be pulling her leg. She was too new to be given this responsibility. Wasn't she? Besides which, it was highly unusual. "Don't clients usually come here if they're local, to see the work in person?"

Mr. Bernal's face tightened for an instant, with something Teagan almost thought was regret. His eyes, she suddenly noticed, reminded her of her sword master's. They had just the faintest bit of odd similarity to them. Almost as if the pupils were slightly contracted.

Or maybe elongated a bit? Teagan stared hard at his eyes for a moment, magnetized by curiosity.

Mr. Bernal narrowed them at her, then raised an elegant eyebrow.

Oh, crap. Rude, rude, rude. Would she ever learn? Swallowing hard, she glanced back down at the book as her flush rose more.

Smoothly, Mr. Bernal continued. "This is a special client. He is a close personal friend of mine, and he prefers to do business at his estate. As you've been working on the book since its arrival here, you will be the one to make the repair progress presentation to him." His voice held the brusque tone of someone used to being obeyed. "You will bring a work tablet with you, on which you will show him close up photos of your repairs. If he approves, you will then be tasked to work on the other book, which is currently located at his estate. I expect you to do an excellent job of," a brief hesitation made

Teagan frown in puzzlement again, "persuading him, Ms. Lambert."

Um, okay. That made no real sense, but sure. Nodding again, still not daring to look back up at the man in case she turned into a staring fool once more, Teagan murmured an appropriately affirmative response.

Walter chuckled with delight, drawing her gaze. He grinned at her, practically vibrating in his childlike enthusiasm. He was an absolutely brilliant man, definitely a bigger geek than even Teagan. "Oh, yes indeed! I knew when I hired you that you would do very well here, Teagan." He gave her a fond look, like a proud father would. Teagan flushed enough that she was almost tempted to fan her face. "You're definitely ready to move up a notch. I have no doubts you will handle the remainder of this project quite well."

Teagan listened, quietly thrilled and a little dazed still, as they discussed the details of the project. Walter added that he would send her an email later in the day that would have all the information she would need.

Whoa. So maybe she really was ready to take on bigger projects here. This could mean she wasn't nothing more than a geek who also was unnecessarily mean to total strangers—that zap of guilt shot through her again. Just maybe, this meant that things were about to start happening to her. Big, cool things.

Sudden movement behind Walter and Mr. Bernal as they were still talking snagged Teagan's attention. Celia, silently hovering in the doorway. From the nakedly murderous expression on her face, she had caught the tail end of the conversation. The conversation that said Teagan was moving on up.

Catching Teagan's eye from behind the oblivious men, Celia's mouth twisted into a mocking smile as she slowly shook her head, eyes narrowed. Holding her fingers together around her face then flicking them apart to indicate a smattering of freckles, she leveled another dismissively snotty look at Teagan before abruptly turning and stalking away.

Teagan's stomach clenched unpleasantly as the self-doubt roared back in. It slapped at her, making her cringe as all her old mistakes and missteps filled her head.

Somehow, she'd screw up this amazing new opportunity. She was nothing more than a tactless geek who couldn't get a date or excel. There would always be a Celia, or a gorgeous man to whom she went above and beyond to be thoughtlessly idiotic and cruel, to make sure she couldn't forget it.

3

Sweat poured off of Ash as he dropped to the floor of his home training gym after a flat bladed blow landed hard across his forearm. He stayed down there longer than he intended to. It was beyond maddening, but apparently he could only perform at about seventy percent of his former rate of strength. Also of lung power. After a year of slowly building himself back up again after the accident, his body seemed to have hit a plateau from which it couldn't go higher.

"Get up." Eamon's calm yet uncompromising voice brooked no protest. "At this point, I would have already cut your head off. You're not fast enough."

Ash half gasped, half roared back. "I can't get up! This is as good as I'll get after an hour's workout." Disgust roiled in him, setting his dragon roaring inside him as well. "Without my gold, half useless as I am, I'm never going to get any better than this." He punched his good fist into the mat beneath him. "This is it, damn it to seventeen hells."

He truly despised the bitter rage that clung to his voice, but he couldn't seem to stop it. The morning's workout had been tough, for Eamon had pushed him harder than he had the previous week. He'd been doing so every week since Ash had been able to start trying to heal as much as was possible.

Then, of course, there was the stinging memory of the stunning warrior woman who had gasped in horror at the sight of his ravaged face. It still deeply rankled him for some unknown reason. His dragon rumbled back at him, this time sounding almost a little peevish.

Eamon wasn't about to let him get away with this pity party. "You are no longer an invalid, Ash." His voice sliced sharper than his blade. "Get up and fight back. Now."

Somewhat surprised, Ash dragged his gaze up to his fealty man. Eamon awarded him a dark look, the challenge obvious by his suddenly mulish expression.

Very well then. Eamon wanted to push him even more, was that it? Fine. No way in hell would Ash let this test go that easily.

Without warning, he sprang to his feet, even though his muscles felt heavier than ballast. His lungs shrieked at him. Drawing on his dragon, who now thundered in support in his mind, Ash leaped forward. Arcing his arm overhead, he whirled a half step to the side, then slammed his own practice blade at Eamon in what might have been a killing blow had they been battling with actual swords.

At over a century old yet looking like a very fit man in his early fifties, Eamon had learned a lot from dragon shifters in his years of serving them. He'd also picked up the extra layers of protection that all fealty family members gained during their many years of service and loyalty to dragon shifters. That meant that right now, he actually was faster than Ash. He flipped out of the way at the last second, though Ash's blade did catch him on the elbow.

Eamon's arm shook from the contact. He snarled out an oath.

Struggling to get enough air to speak, Ash managed, "You

didn't get enough exercise on your vacation, Eamon. You're getting sloppy."

Abruptly, Eamon laughed. He relaxed back into a casual stance as he rubbed his elbow with his free hand. "I didn't have much time for exercise." A small, private smile crept onto his face.

The tone of his voice was so full of a quiet yet distinct joy that Ash felt equal parts pleased for his old friend as well as faintly jealous. Pushing aside the unbecoming emotion that only revealed his shortcomings, he opted for teasing instead. "Oh, is that why you needed the next day off, too? Because you didn't have time for exercise. I see how you are." He gave his fealty man a pointed waggle of his eyebrows.

He was rewarded by the sight of Eamon turning bashful as he studiously examined his elbow.

Ash's eyes widened suddenly as a genuine grin slipped across his face. "Oh, I do see. You really like her. I'm glad for you, Eamon," he added seriously. A smile of faint remembered pain flitted across Eamon's face, although genuine contentment mostly shone through. Eamon's wife, a woman who had been like a second mother to Ash, had died in a plane crash many years ago. Ash had long thought Eamon might never love again, but a member of another fealty family had caught his eye at a large gathering of dragon shifters last year. It seemed she might indeed be the one to bring some joy back to Eamon's life.

"Yes. It's a good thing." Eamon's smile still playing around his lips. Then he leveled a keen gaze at Ash. "It would be for you, too."

Hmm. Ash's dragon softly bugled in his mind. Turning, Ash headed to the small wooden stand that held the practice swords. Placing his down on it, he turned to the wooden chest beside it and worked open the lock. "I don't think so. Going to the Institute by myself was a mistake. I startled a woman there. A beautiful woman." Just the thought of her made him pause for a moment. Her gorgeous features danced through his memory. Despite himself, it brought the faintest of smiles to his lips. Eamon caught that, eyebrows raising. But Ash frowned as the next memory of her aghast gasp echoed through his mind again as well. "She about had a heart attack when she saw my face. "

Eamon tapped thoughtful fingers on the hilt of his sword. "Interesting. Would Nicholas have known who she was?" Eamon's expression was still gentle, but questioning and pointed.

Ash felt his face harden more. "That part of my life is over, Eamon. And I didn't need to bother Nick with asking. Why inquire about a woman who reacted to me as if I were more frightening than even the hunchback of Notre Dame?" The bitterness slid through his voice again.

Heavy silence was the only response. Firmly ignoring the vision in his head of burnished red hair atop the most devastatingly beautiful face he'd ever seen, and definitely ignoring his dragon's fiery huff, Ash shut that all away. Time to focus on what he could control. Hopefully, that is. Carefully, he opened the lid of the chest. Stepping back, he gave a satisfied nod at the sight inside it. A stunning ancient sword, recently restored to its shining glory, gleamed up at him.

Yes. That right there was what he had left to live for. It was enough. It had to be.

Eamon stepped up beside him. Making an admiring sound, he looked down at the shining gold symbols etched into the otherwise silver metal of the blade. One was a classic Celtic cross, with an added flare indicating that it had been made to be wielded only by dragon shifters. The others were ancient Ogham letters proclaiming the weapon's name, and finally an obscure dragon rune over which they still puzzled to decipher. "What a find, Ash. It will help you as soon as you begin using it."

Ash nodded. Pushing aside the unbidden thoughts of the

strange woman, ignoring his dragon's oddly plaintive whuffle of sound as he pictured her lush curves visible even beneath the baggy practice clothes she'd worn, Ash reached out to run light fingertips down the flat part of the blade. Edged with smaller runes that few eyes in the modern world would be able to understand, let alone grasp the significance of, the sword was a magnificent piece of personal history.

"Nicholas outdid himself," he murmured. "Again."

"He always does," Eamon said agreeably.

Nicholas Brenton was one of Ash's oldest friends, along with Sebastian Bernal. The two of them had been present during the darkest moments of Ash's life, but he honestly couldn't remember those moments since he'd lost consciousness then and for a few weeks following the incident that had scarred his body and turned him into a recluse. He knew they both felt faintly guilty for the event, despite the fact there was nothing either one of them could have done to prevent it, or to help him heal any more than he'd been able to.

It had been a dragon tournament, Ash had caught the bad end of a charring flame during a bout, he was now scarred for life. The end. Yes, they had been there for it, and yes, they'd been his literal wingmen. Yet it still wasn't their fault. It wasn't even the fault of the other competing dragon shifter whose flame had blasted along the exposed right side of Ash's body. These things happened on occasion. Risks were taken at tournaments, and everyone there was well aware of those risks, although they were not common. No one was to blame.

Even so, Seb and Nick both had done everything in their power to help Ash regain at least some items for his gold hoard in the hopes that it would one day allow him to restore both more physical strength as well as the full gamut of his dragon shifter powers.

Being a dragon severely injured was one thing. Dragon shifters could find a healer and recover fully. But being an injured dragon with a hoard lacking its full size and strength?

That was disaster. That meant a dragon shifter with injuries could never regain all he'd lost.

Ash was truly scarred for life. Luckily, the slow acquisition of a few choice items for his gold hoard would restore greater power to him and, hopefully, some of his own strength as well. Like all dragons, Ash had a gold hoard. It was the source of his power as a dragon. His was lacking, unfortunately. To add terrible insult to already traumatic injury, a few key pieces of Ash's hoard had been stolen before he was burned. Their loss ensured that Ash had not healed properly. Despite both Eamon's and Sebastian's quiet inquiries, no one knew what happened to those pieces. They'd almost certainly been sold by the thief on the underground black market to another equally unscrupulous dragon shifter looking to increase his own hoard's power.

It was part and parcel of being a dragon shifter. The power struggles and gold hoard thefts were a regular part of their world, just the same way tournaments were. It had been Ash's terrible luck that he'd been injured when his hoard was so badly diminished.

Ash had slowly collected new gold to add to his hoard, which helped to a small degree. But if he were ever to truly heal, he'd need the stolen pieces of his original hoard to be returned to him.

Or for this long-lost sword of his ancestors to unlock its magic for him.

Repairing the sword had been a part of Nick's attempt to help him if at all possible. This sword in particular was an astonishing find. It had belonged to the ancient line of Connolly shifters. Ash's illustrious ancestors. Just finding the sword had been a boost to his hoard. His being able to use it could only increase the unseen magical connection that shifted power to all dragons from their hoards. Most pieces of a gold hoard were carefully locked up, kept safe by a spell warding cast over them.

A sword, however, could actually be used. Some dragon shifters still used them in private organized duels, fought only when in human form. Using a sword the way it was intended helped transfer power to the dragon to whom it belonged. Especially if it hailed from that dragon's own family.

Thought lost centuries ago, this particular sword had somehow found its way to a human antiquities trader in England, who in turn had bought it from a local human family who'd apparently had the sword unknowingly stashed away in the attic of a great aunt who'd died not long ago. When they'd cleaned out her house to put it on the market, they'd discovered the sword tucked into the very wooden chest that held it now. They'd sold it to the local antique store, and the shifter trader who'd then discovered it in turn had received a princely sum for putting the sword onto the shifter-only market.

Ash had paid through the nose for it, which was irritating considering that it had belonged to his family originally, but that was simply how things worked in the constant maneuvering between shifters for power. Naturally, he'd bid privately, using a proxy at the actual auction. No one knew he now had it, aside from his closest friends. Although he had been forced to buy it as part of a lot, the additional cost had been well worth it.

The sword had come with two equally ancient books. One was currently at Seb's famed museum, The Bernal Center, being repaired by one of his junior conservators. That book was a mere adjunct to history, blandly titled *The Book of the Near Hills* and pretty much about just that: page after page of small, cramped writing that described in infinitesimal, excruciating detail the rocks, trees, hollows, peaks, ponds, lookout points, windswept crags, and even more merciless minutia of the hills nearest the town in which the learned Irish monks who had penned the thing lived. Since the town also happened to be the one from which Ash's ancestors had hailed, he'd decided it should be kept as part of his collection simply for posterity's sake. As it had little more to offer than being a very minor footnote to history, he hadn't minded it being repaired by a junior conservator rather than the head of the department, who would usually stabilize and restore any damaged books that came into Ash's possession.

The other precious book, however, rested in a magically warded case in Ash's personal library. That one was the true treasure.

In nearly pristine condition, though it did have some pages that needed repairing, *The Book of the Dragonborn* was written by and for dragon shifters, written almost entirely in runes undecipherable to most human eyes. It was bound to the sword and described the history of some adventuresome Connolly forebears. Most likely, it also held magically hidden pages that would be visible only to shifter eyes, as did many ancient books kept in dragon families. Ash felt extraordinarily lucky to have had both the sword and book fall back into Connolly hands. He had yet to crack the magical code that kept the book's secret history still hidden, but he studied it every day.

If those pages could be released to his shifter-enhanced view, he might gain some insight to recovering his damaged powers. It was a very long shot, but he had nothing but time to spend on it. In the meantime, the sword definitely held great power, being from his very own lineage. The more he used it, now that its loosened handle had been repaired by Nick, the more he would increase his strength and even some healing.

"All right then." Carefully yet firmly, Ash picked up the sword out of its case. He literally could feel the hum of its power as he held it in his hands.

His earlier fit of pointless anger now abruptly overtaken by a surge of hope as well as a renewed burst of energy, Ash walked back out into the middle of his training room. Tucked into a side wing of the new house he'd bought several months after the accident, since he realized that his old place held too many memories he didn't remotely want to deal with, the training gym had become a daily visited area. He gently closed his left hand around the handle of the sword.

The fact that he had to use his left hand had been no small part of the issues he'd run into during his long, painful journey toward recuperation from his injuries. Ash was right-handed. Since it had been the right side of his body that had caught the worst of the charring, he'd had no choice but to relearn everything from his left side. Aided by the strength and encouragement of his dragon, the process had gone far more quickly for him that it would have for most humans.

Even so, it sure as hell hadn't been easy. Still wasn't, in fact.

Eamon watched him with a quietly pleased smile. "Go on, then," he said in a casual voice. "Just a couple of practice jabs. Nothing too intense just yet."

Ash nodded, testing a light swing with the sword weighted in his left hand. His moves were still awkward enough that it felt faintly sacrilegious to hold this particular sword with his less accurate hand. Yet he was the only one who would be able to do so and release the true power of the sword. Eamon, although imbued with more powers than any average human would ever see in a lifetime, was still not a dragon shifter and never would be. More importantly, he wasn't a Connolly.

Swords like this one had been made to be held and used only by certain shifters. Although Nicholas had worked with the sword while he restored it, he hadn't actually used it the way a sword should be. He hadn't truly practiced with it, certainly hadn't fought with it. Its powers weren't meant for him, either. This amazing piece of craftsmanship had been made for a Connolly to wield.

It was all on Ash to prove himself truly worthy of its ownership.

With a sudden swing, he lofted the sword, then arced it downward. The sword sang as it sliced the air. Ash pivoted, lightly jabbed, then practiced a move he'd once been able to do in his sleep. He was less graceful at it now, with both his clumsier left hand as well as the tight muscles on the right side of his body trying to interfere. But he still managed it.

Murmuring a soft grunt of approval, Eamon gave a half smile in pleased acknowledgement. In response, Ash jabbed again, then engaged in a mock swing toward Eamon. His fealty man nodded but inclined his chin to the practice mat. "On your own," he said, watching Ash and the sword with assessing eyes. "Run through a practice sequence."

Quirking his lips, pleased himself with how *right* the sword felt in his grip, Ash moved onto the mat and easily launched into a familiar sequence of steps, thrusts, and parries, fighting the air around him while Eamon watched. During one such parry, he abruptly thought of a set of lush lips, wild red hair springing out around a face skimmed with a shimmering design that lent it a unique, stunning beauty. The thought brought a quick smile to his face. Then he saw again her sudden recoil from him, the horror on her face. His dragon whuffled deep within him, sounding part aggrieved, part sorrowful. Stumbling mid-move, Ash cursed beneath his breath. He purposely shoved aside the image of the unknown woman.

He could feel the power of the sword thrum, seeming to light the air with a crackle of energy. However, no corresponding surge of power rose within him. Creasing his brow, he skimmed through all his moves again, this time more carefully. Yes, the sword's power was there. It was a good addition to his gold hoard as well as his personal family legacy. Yet an important aspect of it was missing. The part when the power transferred to Ash, helping make him stronger.

Helping him heal.

Ash swore as he ran again through the entire sequence, this time with deadly focus and a grim set to his mouth.

Eamon, too, wore an austere look as Ash clearly woke the power of the sword, yet it did not fully reciprocate.

Something blocked it.

"Damn it!" Ash's snarl whipped through the room. He stopped, holding the sword in midair before him. It glittered and gleamed, the soft pulse of dragon magic coming from it in steady, undeniable waves of power. Yet the power simply did not extend farther from the sword than immediately around it.

Useless for Ash's needs.

He stood on the mat, breathing steadily. The weakness of the scarred side of his body suddenly felt more pronounced. His right leg seemed tight, heavy. His right arm ineffectual.

In a word, he felt broken. Impaired. Unable to heal, unable to move forward. Unable to release the power of his ancestors from the sword crafted by their hands. Certainly unable to draw the positive, interested attention of a woman like the beauty he'd come across in the parking lot the other night.

Jaw tensed, he regarded the blade, safely held in his hand yet still locked away from him. Long moments passed while Ash contemplated everything he lacked and everything that might be still possible. If only he could find the answer and unleash the power of the sword. His mind spun through the possibilities. Somehow, there had to be a way.

His fealty man must have been thinking the same thing. At the same moment, they both breathed, "The book." The book and the sword had been sold together. They must work together somehow.

Ash looked at Eamon, but Eamon had already headed on swift feet to the door.

Impatience and yet another stirring of hope warred inside Ash as he waited. He realized within thirty seconds that the impatience would likely kill him, so he moved again through the practice sequence. He was nearly through it by the time Eamon came back, carefully ferrying the heavy, dark red leather-bound *Book of the Dragonborn* with him. He took it straight to Ash, holding it out as if in offering.

Ash met him halfway across the mat, then paused with a startled chuckle. "I've no idea what to do," he admitted, letting a sardonic grin creep out. "Wave the sword about and mutter ancient incantations while you pass your hand over the book and declare 'abracadabra'?"

Eamon gave Ash an astounded look before allowing the rare guffaw to escape. "I am quite glad you haven't completely lost your sense of humor." He shook his dark head as laughter quivered at the edge of his voice. "It quite brightens my days."

"Stuff it," Ash tossed back easily. The levity felt good. Sighing, he looked at the book for a long, critical moment. Finally, he shook his head and simply held the sword out toward the book. "Abracadabra?" he offered in a doubtful tone.

Giving Ash a bemused look, Eamon shrugged as he held the book out so it touched the sword. He quickly murmured a few sentences in a dialect of Gaelic so old and obscure that Ash stared at him, lost. Looking back up and catching Ash's gaze, Eamon shrugged again. "I may have just invited the sword out to drinks and dancing with this old book, for all I know." His eyes suddenly twinkled with mirth. "It's something my ma used to say to my da. She never told us kids the exact meaning. Said it was words from the ancients and we weren't to concern ourselves with it."

"Probably wise," Ash agreed, smiling for a moment despite his disappointment.

They both looked at the ancient objects. Still, nothing happened. Ash's dragon huffed out smoke in his mind, murmured a quiet bellow. Impatience sounded in his tone. There was no surge of power, no sense of being strengthened. Not even a tickle of energy beyond the basic hum that indicated any change might occur slowly. It was simply—blank.

"I don't understand. The sword is of my ancestors, and I

acquired it to be a part of my hoard. There should be something here." Ash felt the grimness settle over him again.

"Perhaps something is merely missing." Eamon eyed the sword and the book again. "What that might be, though, I have no idea." He gave Ash a long, speculative look before finally shaking his head again in some frustration. "We will think of it. I am sure of that." He frowned, still eyeing both sword and book with a speculative glance. "One small thought I had was that perhaps this tome needs minor repairs as well. I know you're loath to allow it out of here, but the Center's security is some of the best in the world."

Ash had to agree with that. Sebastian spared no expense in defending some of both the human and dragon shifter worlds' most priceless art at the Bernal Center.

"So if the repairs to *The Book of the Near Hills* go well," Eamon went on, "we can consider letting this book go in, too. It can't hurt. And it might even help."

Closing his eyes for a brief moment, Ash finally just nodded once. "Fine." His tone was clipped as he lightly hefted the sword in his hand, willing its power to spill over into him. Still nothing. "Set it up. In the meantime—well." With exquisite care, he placed the stubbornly unlocked sword back into its case, letting his hand drift over the mysterious rune etched into it. "I don't know what, in the meantime. Perhaps nothing."

As he left the room, though, a flash of red-gold hair and a brief yet devastating smile shot through his mind again. Damn it, why could the memory of such a minor encounter with one unknown woman still prod at him? His dragon abruptly sat up and bugled in Ash's mind, clear and loud. Blasting Ash's mind with images of the woman, again and again. Stopping short, Ash swung around to look at Eamon. To hell with it. "Call Nick, if you would, please. I'd like him to stop by when he can. I have a question about one of his students."

4

Teagan scooted her chair little farther back into the sun as she listened to her friend Savannah talk. Ahh, that felt good. While October in Los Angeles was not remotely like Octobers back in Illinois, it had been cloudy all day, just bordering the edge of chilly. Then, just before lunch, the sun had come out, the temperatures had warmed, and Teagan now felt like a lizard happily sunning herself, listening to her work bestie describe her latest conquest.

"So," Savannah leaned closer, dropping her voice, eyes sparkling, "then he started to go lower."

Teagan raised her eyebrows. In the short amount of time she'd been friends with Savannah, she'd already learned that the other woman was not remotely shy about any of the details of her sexual escapades. Not that Teagan was about to tell her to stop, though.

It was fun to live vicariously. She sure wasn't having any sexual escapades of her own. She actually never had, not really, although she hadn't quite yet worked up the courage to admit that to her much more experienced new friend.

"First just his fingers, then he followed with his tongue. It was *divine.*" Savannah's voice seemed to drop an octave on the word, and her eyes rolled heavenward. "So this is my second time with him, right? I'm thinking to myself, wow, he really knows what he's doing. So I might have to go out with him again. But sex might be the only thing he's good at." Savannah sighed and sat back in her chair. "The conversation with him never really goes anywhere. I guess I just have to accept the fact that he's mere eye candy and not much more."

Teagan laughed, spearing the last tiny bit of their shared piece of chocolate truffle tart dessert on the plate between them. The Bernal Center had several little cafés scattered throughout the vast complex, but this one was by far her favorite. It was light, open, and featured spectacular views of the Center's gleaming white buildings that sprawled west toward the sparkle of the Pacific Ocean.

For the millionth time, Teagan sighed happily. Her life felt almost complete. She had a challenging job she loved, a coworker who had become a real friend, a sweet little rental that was all hers, her cat, Mouser, for companionship, and... Well, dang it. It didn't sound like very much to other people. But for her, it was more than enough. It had to be.

"What about you, Teags?" Savannah smiled as she abruptly flipped the subject. "Met any incredible hotties yet at your kickass sword fighting class?"

Teagan started to shake her head, opening her mouth to say *no,* then paused. "Well," she said instead, very slowly. She'd been awful to the man, but for some reason beyond that, she couldn't stop thinking about him.

Savannah's eyes widened as she sat up straight, attention riveted on Teagan. "Ooh, you've got dirt for me!" She grinned. "Spill. Did you meet a guy? One who wields a sword like the ancient kings of Ireland?"

Teagan smiled. Savannah was teasing her, but not at all maliciously. She knew Teagan well enough by now that she'd managed to discover Teagan's lifelong fascination with the history of her maternal ethnic roots. Beside that, while Teagan had always been intrigued by ancient sword skills, she'd never been brave enough to actually learn them until Savannah nudged her into it.

To be honest, at this point there was only one big secret she was keeping from Savannah. But only because it was mortifying to think about, let alone discuss with someone who, although a good friend, still didn't need to know every single last detail about her.

But even though Savannah didn't know all her secrets, Teagan felt comfortable enough to tell her about what had happened with the mysterious, and mysteriously intriguing, man the other night. Telling would make it feel like a confession, which her occasionally-practicing (as in, only on the major holidays did they attend services) Methodist family would say was a good way to cleanse the soul.

"Okay, yes," she admitted, feeling her cheeks heat. "There was a guy. But I was horrible to him. Seriously awful."

Savannah's fork clinked down on the not quite empty dessert plate as she cocked her head at Teagan. "Uh-oh. Tell me all."

Wincing, Teagan briefly summarized what had happened, ending in a low, mortified tone on the part where she'd gasped at the man's horrific scars. "It was so cruel of me," she said, shaking her head at herself as the memory of his frozen expression at her reaction blasted her mind again and again. "And," she went on even more pensively, "I know better than most people what it's like to be made fun of. How I could have done that to him..." She twisted her lips down.

Savannah made a sympathetic noise. When Teagan shot her glance up to her friend, all she saw was genuine sympathy and understanding. Savannah had been one of the few people here at the Center who hadn't done a double take or some other sort of obvious acknowledgment of Teagan's outrageously freckled face when Teagan first got here. For that alone, Teagan would be forever grateful to her.

Slowly, Teagan went on. "Obviously I don't know what happened to him. How he got scarred, I mean. But actually," she went on thoughtfully, "I don't think he was burned when he was young. I think his reaction to me would've been a little different. More like me. Very unhappy with all the extra attention, but a lot more used to it. Oh, no," she whispered in horror, suddenly feeling even worse. "He's probably even more sensitive about it if this happened to him as an adult." She stared at Savannah in renewed horror. "Oh, my gosh, I probably ruined his day. Even his week!" Teagan felt sick.

Savannah leaned forward, reaching out her hand to gently touch the back of Teagan's. "Hey now, you don't know any such thing. You don't know the guy, and you don't know what was going on with him that day already. Besides, he's a grown-up and can handle things on his own." She shook her head. "You have such a soft heart, Teags. One you could be using to turn all that kind attention onto yourself instead of total strangers. Even hot ones."

Savannah leaned back, crossing her arms across her chest, abruptly regarding Teagan with a speculative air. Teagan felt like a butterfly pinned to a board. Which was an outrageously cruel practice, but that was beside the point. Shaking her head, she stared down her friend as firmly as she could. "Whatever you're thinking, Savannah, stop thinking it right this second. I've gotten to know you well enough by now to know when you have that look in your eye, it's probably not going to mean anything good for me."

Savannah laughed, the trademark big peal that drew a couple of glances from fellow diners. "Oh, don't you be afraid. Like I said, you're so softhearted you worry about hurting the feelings of a complete stranger, but you don't take the time to turn that concern on yourself. Well," she said dramatically, making a little flourish with one hand, "that's what Auntie Savannah, also known as art appraiser extraordinaire, is here to do for you." She jabbed her finger at Teagan, who nervously drew back. "You are a piece of art, and completely unaware of your own worth. Of how gorgeous you are. It's time to change that."

Teagan sat as far back in her chair she could, arms clutched defensively around her middle. She didn't like the sound of this at all. "I don't like the look on your face right now."

Savannah seemed as satisfied as a cat with cream. "Ah, little grasshopper. Don't you worry, this isn't going to hurt one little bit. Auntie Savannah has been dying for a new project, and honey, you're it. It's time for a Teagan makeover!"

Sheer terror gripped Teagan. A new project? A *makeover?* Oh, no. That was the stuff of nightmares. "I'm not one of those TV shows about remodeling old houses and putting them on the market, you know," she warned, ruining it by gulping.

"Oh, yes, you are!" Savannah pounced, grinning. "Project Teagan Makeover is a go." She nodded her head in the decisive fashion Teagan knew meant her determined friend's mind was made up and there would be no changing it.

Trouble.

The only way of escape was to deflect. "Um... Okay? But first," she hastened as Savannah's face lit up, "Walter has a new project he wants me to tackle. Something I'm starting this afternoon. Let me see if my nerves can handle that before you go all out on," she shivered, "Project Teagan Makeover."

Savannah's eyes widened as she exclaimed, "That's perfect!"

Teagan frowned. "Um, perfect because why?"

Savannah's eyes sparkled. "Because it's going to give you so much more self-confidence to get your first solo project here under your belt. You're going to rock it, Teagan."

The ball of nerves in the pit of Teagan's stomach began to churn once more. She raised slightly panicked eyes to her friend. "I don't know about that. I'm not sure I'm ready for solo projects yet."

"Yes, you are." Savannah's voice was so firm that Teagan almost believed her. "This is what I'm talking about. You don't have enough confidence in yourself. Such as believing me when I tell you that you're stunning."

Teagan shook her head. Rolling her eyes, Savannah went on. "You also don't believe that you are incredibly good at what you do here at the Center."

Well. Yeah. "I do love what I do here," Teagan admitted softly. Savannah nodded encouragement. "But," she went on slowly, "I've barely been here long enough for anyone to be able to assess my work. Walter will see that Celia is right. I don't know what I'm doing."

Savannah made a dismissive harrumphing noise, muttering something under her breath about Celia being a royal beeyotch. Out loud, she said, "Teagan, Walter is no dummy. Heck, Mr. Bernal is no dummy. They don't hire slackers or idiots here." She leaned forward, grabbing Teagan's hands with both of hers and squeezing hard. "Teags, you are in excellent company here at the Center because you deserve it. You would not have been hired except that you're very good at what you do. Are you still young, recently out of school, still learning? Yes. But they hired you because they see enormous potential. Don't let that nasty little piece of work Celia tear you down. She's just jealous." Savannah waved one hand as if she was swatting away an annoying insect.

Teagan's eyebrows shot to her hairline. "Jealous? Of what?"

Taking a long-suffering sigh, Savannah closed her eyes and briefly muttered for the help of some deity above. Opening her eyes again, she just said, "Operation Teagan Makeover, aka Operation Teagan Confidence Boost, begins this afternoon when you start a new project, and proceed to kick book conservation ass from here to next Sunday by how well you do on it. After that, we'll work on project Make Teagan See How Incredible She Is." Savannah poked a no-nonsense finger at Teagan, accompanied by a stern frown.

Teagan began to protest, but Savannah shook her head. "Hey. I may have been the one to talk you into going to the Institute to take lessons, but who's the one actually there leaning how to fight with a sword?"

Well. That was true.

"A *sword*, Teagan." Savannah emphasized the word with a little fling of her hands. "Do you even know how hugely badass that is? I may talk a good game," she gave a self-deprecating snort, "but let us both be sure of the fact that I have no interest in ever picking up a sword and swinging it around. You're a lot more amazing than you give yourself credit for, Teags." Her face was solemn although her voice was gentle. "As your newest bestie, it's part of my job description to help you recognize that."

There was a brief beat of silence during which Teagan tried to digest everything. Yeah, she'd had a very supportive family growing up, but tooting her own horn wasn't something that came easily to her. At all.

Savannah rescued her by grinning slyly. "Okay, now then. Let me finish telling you about my date last night. I didn't even get to the part yet about where he flipped me over onto my stomach and had his wicked way with me from behind."

Teagan swallowed hard, for some reason suddenly picturing the gorgeous scarred man flipping her over onto her stomach and—doing something wild and amazing to her. Whoa. But that was just an impossible fantasy. She had proven by her reaction to his face that she wasn't dating material for any guy. Her best bet was to just focus on her job, as well as her flourishing skills as an uncoordinated swordswoman.

Pushing away her steamy thoughts of the man in a tangled smash of lingering fascination and flusteredness, she listened as Savannah continued to give her every single detail of experiences Teagan would never, ever have.

5

After lunch, Teagan double-checked all of her supplies were in her satchel before she drove to the house of the collector. Walter had warned her that the man was slightly eccentric and didn't particularly enjoy meeting the public. He was a personal friend of Mr. Bernal's, which was the only reason she was being allowed in the house. He had an assistant who would show her the book, although the collector would also be present to discuss it. The man would be there remotely, watching somehow. Since Teagan had worked with antiquities and priceless ancient manuscripts since her graduate school days, she was accustomed to the occasional oddities of the very wealthy people who tended to collect them. She wasn't really discomfited by the thought of an unusual procedure by which the manuscript's owner would somehow communicate with her.

No, the part that scared the snot out of her was knowing that this was her first solo project, and it was kind of a big deal since the guy was a personal friend of Mr. Bernal's. Although Walter had assured her that she was the right one for the job, she had done some self-soothing by forcing herself to recall that the book was set in her favorite time period. Just like the book she was repairing at the Center, the photos of which were securely downloaded onto the tablet also tucked into her satchel.

By the time she pulled up to the fancy security gate outside the stately old home about twenty minutes east of the center, Teagan was still nervous, but overall more calm than not. She wore what she thought of as her personal suit of armor. It wasn't actually metal, of course. It was a pair of fitted yet classy dark brown pants—the color of which the saleswoman had called espresso with hints of mocha, whatever that meant—a cream blouse, and a pretty pale olive cardigan that looked professional and academic without making her look like her grandmother. She loved her grandmother, of course, but she herself wasn't exactly ready to be addressed as Granny. Finished off with a pair of sensible shoes she could stand around in all day without her back aching, and the work satchel filled with a magnification loupe and other such important implements, Teagan was as ready as she felt she could be. No matter how eccentric this old guy would turn out to be, she would do the Bernal Center proud.

She hoped.

Just before she'd left work, she'd taken a long, fairly appraising glance at her face in a bathroom mirror. Teagan didn't often look at her reflection. Over the years, she'd tried every cream under the sun, every medicated wonder product that would supposedly dissolve freckles into a smooth complexion, and all sorts of pricey brands of makeup designed to even out her skin tone. She was in the habit of wearing a light foundation every day, but she'd learned in junior high not to layer it on too thickly. That had been a huge mistake that had haunted her right up until the day she graduated high school. These days, foundation was good enough that it didn't make her freckles totally pop, but light enough that it still looked natural and not like she'd applied pancake makeup.

None of it mattered anyway. In the end, her freckles still showed. Usually, people didn't stare too long. Heaving a sigh, calling on Queen Boudica for strength, she headed to the collector's house in the comfortable boonies of Pasadena, about twenty minutes east of the Center.

After she was examined silently by the elaborate security system at the front gate, and apparently found to pass muster because the gates opened, she traveled up the winding drive to a house that easily had to cost several million dollars based on the neighborhood. Sure, this sort of wealth she was used to seeing. Most collectors had a lot of money. However, she didn't usually get to go to their houses. Mansions. Estates.

Taking a deep breath, she grabbed her satchel, walked briskly to the front door, and gathered her nerves again before reaching up to the door to knock. She barely raised her hand to rap the ornate knocker, which was a beautiful bronze dragon head that was a replica of one she knew hung in the Museum of London from an original that had been popular with the elite back in the mid-nineteenth century, when the door swung inward. She jumped a bit as a muscled, attractive man with a very sharp gaze gave her smile and graceful nod.

"Welcome, Ms. Lambert. Thank you so much for your time in traveling out here to look at Mr. Connolly's newest acquisition. I am Eamon Gallagher, his assistant. Please, come in." He gestured her inside, closing the door behind them and leading her down the short hallway that opened into a spectacular foyer.

Teagan raised her eyebrows at the spectacular inside of the mansion but managed not to say anything out loud. Holy smokes, this place was drop dead amazing. Nervousness balled up in her again. Old Mr. Connolly had to be loaded. Beyond loaded. He might even be a freaking billionaire. Which meant the book had to be very authentic and therefore very precious. The tightness in her stomach was a combo of excited nerves and nervous excitement. Or something like that.

Be cool, Teagan, she thought to herself. *Don't be a complete geek in front of the collector.* Lightly clearing her throat, she asked, "I was told Mr. Connolly would be observing as well?"

Ahead of her, Eamon nodded, the light picking up a few silvery hairs in his otherwise dark head. Teagan realized with a start that he was older than she'd first assumed. He clearly kept himself in excellent shape. Then again, if this Mr. Connolly had half the eccentricities as many of the collectors she'd worked with in the past, being his assistant was probably a really demanding job that involved a lot of running around.

"He'll be in the room with us, yes." Eamon turned them down yet another long hallway. He didn't offer any more information than that.

As they passed a beautiful tapestry that depicted a man on a white horse facing off a fire-breathing dragon, Teagan almost tripped over herself, staring. It was from ancient Ireland, most likely the fourteenth century. Quite well-preserved, it certainly cost a fortune and was likely a key piece of its specific historical era, at least as far as any historian of the time period would be concerned. Such as herself.

Her nerves and excitement both rose again. Wow, maybe this Mr. Connolly would have other things in his collection that she could see. Not, of course, that she would presume to ask anything like that on her first day on the job for him. So far, she decided that whatever his eccentricities, she would put up with them without a word if it meant she could see anything else from her favorite area of history.

After two more turns through what was clearly a large, if seemingly empty estate as far as any occupants that she'd yet seen, they came to a set of huge, dark wood double doors that were inlaid with carved characters. She instantly recognized them as being a very old, primitive form of Gaelic known as Ogham. More romantically, it was referred to as the Celtic Tree Alphabet for the stick-like lines that made up the letters.

Whoa. This was really cool. She couldn't help her exclamation of surprise. Leaning forward, she began to read silently to herself.

Eamon took a step back, folding his arms over his chest. "Are you reading that, Ms. Lambert?"

Teagan started. Oh, shoot. She was letting her geeky side show. Swallowing, she shot him an apologetic look. "I'm sorry. This is just—well, certain portions of Irish history are among my interests, and Ogham is one of them. I love it. I'm Irish on my mother's side as well," she added a bit shyly. "The people, the language, the history—it's all fascinated me since I was little. Anyway," she forced herself to stop babbling, because, good grief, she wasn't here to share her life story, "I've never before seen Ogham letters etched into wooden doors. They're usually carved into stone. These doors didn't come with this house, did they?"

Eamon shook his head, still regarding her as if she were an interesting specimen of—something. "No, they did not. They were from Mr. Connolly's family's castle in Ireland."

Okay, then. The mysterious old Mr. Connolly apparently was from long-ago royalty. Hugely wealthy and titled. Probably a bit pompous, too. Check.

"The inscription," Eamon continued, still giving her a sharply assessing look, "is copied from some very old standing stones in Ireland, still located on ancestral Connolly property. It's said to be an old family oracle, a puzzle of sorts for family descendants. Would you care to read it out loud?" He sounded almost challenging.

Oh, crap. Teagan wondered if she'd really messed up, but he lifted his eyebrows up a fraction and gestured at the door. Nodding, Teagan turned back to it and started from the top, translating the words to English as she spoke. "To find the—"

Eamon abruptly cut her off. "In the original Irish, if you please." His words were clipped.

"Oh, I'm sorry. I—ah, okay. Do you understand ancient Irish?" she asked hesitantly.

He nodded, again without offering any further explanation. Well, of course he did. The man would hardly ask her to speak it if he didn't understand it. Swallowing again, wondering why the hell she had such serious foot-in-mouth disease right now, Teagan turned back to the door and began to read aloud. In very ancient Irish Gaelic, as directed.

"To find the key to a dragon's treasure / From the fiery mouth of the clouded mountain / The scorched carmine dragon must emerge / To battle in fearless resolution for his stolen gold / And to claim the heart of his eternal true mate." The words lilted as Teagan spoke them. "Oh, my gosh, that's very poetic," she added, gazing in even deeper admiration at the writing. "Who knew the ancient scribes of Ogham had it in them?"

There was a potent moment of silence as Eamon stared at her, his expression completely unreadable. Oh, crap. Teagan almost could have sworn the entire house was listening to her. Well, that wasn't impossible. The owner might have the whole place bugged. Which, being an eccentric collector type, he probably did.

Maybe this was some sort of test? One she had failed by being too flippant. Oh, freaking crap.

Before her thoughts could dither themselves into knots, Eamon smiled enigmatically, then reached for the doors. Pushing them wide open, he gestured her forward. Yet when Teagan stepped in, he didn't follow.

She turned back to look at him. He shook his head, a quietly amused, almost wondering smile now playing on his lips. "Ms. Lambert, I have a sneaking suspicion you can hold your own with Mr. Connolly." As he projected his voice, Eamon's gaze went somewhere behind her shoulder.

Teagan turned around to see a small yet stunning library. Filled with an elegantly sumptuous yet understated wealth, the library pretty much encapsulated Teagan's deepest fantasies. Naturally, she'd been that girl as a kid. The bookworm, the nerd, the one who found solace in the imaginary worlds of the stories she would read in the books in her own family's library. Not that it was a library like this one. It was shelves scattered throughout her childhood home, stuffed to the gills with books of all kinds. They'd been a very welcome escape for her from the realities of existing in a world in which she didn't look like everyone else around her.

Swallowing again from sheer nerves, the sound seeming exceedingly loud in what was still an expectant hush, she stared in what was practically lust at this magnificent library filled with what her assessing scholar's eye knew was a veritable treasure trove of books. Old, rare, probably priceless books. Bound in leather, wood, honeyed linen, it smelled like lavish history. Plush and weighty, the air was redolent with the vanilla bean and sweet grass odor of antique paper, woods such as juniper and hickory, mossy oak, varying leather scents that brought to mind cardamon and marjoram. They filled the room like a velvet overlay of comfort and delight. It was a cornucopia of intoxicating riches for book conservator like herself.

Basically, her fantasy come true. She hoped she didn't drool on anything.

In the center of the room stood a large dark oak desk, piled with scrolls and books and even an old-fashioned quill in an ink pot, although she suspected that was a decoration to go with the ancient ambiance of the place. No one would dare leave actual ink sitting around to be possibly knocked into and spilled on irreplaceable old tomes.

To the left, set behind the desk, was indeed a wood and mesh privacy screen, unfolded into four parts. Teagan almost immediately felt observed by an unseen *someone* behind it. Her skin seemed to crackle with a strange yet enjoyable heat that curled over her like a tendril of lazy smoke. A shiver of something she couldn't quite name raced up and down her spine, leaving her close to breathless for a sudden moment.

Still pitching his voice so that he could be heard beyond Teagan, Eamon said, "Mr. Connolly, the conservator from the Bernal Center is here. May I present Teagan Lambert." In an oddly bland tone, he continued, "She just read the inscription on the door to me. In the ancient Irish. Out loud." He turned to her and gestured toward the screen. "Ms. Lambert, Mr. Ash Connolly would like to discuss the progress you are making on his book at the Center."

Teagan looked back at the screen. Silence and no movement came from that direction. After a long moment, she cautiously ventured, "Um...hello."

Almost holding her breath, half afraid whoever the man was wouldn't step out and half afraid he would, she waited. Aside from her own slightly rapid breathing, there was no sound in the small library.

Before she could do more than take in those few immediate impressions, there was sudden movement from behind the screen. A man walked around it. No, he strode around it as if yanked by a cord, heading directly toward her. Eamon sucked in a quick breath, as if startled. Teagan, however, couldn't take her eyes off the approaching Mr. Connolly. Oh, holy freaking moly. He wasn't old. Maybe eccentric. But definitely not old.

Whoa.

His face. The left side of it was young, not much older than Teagan, and drop-dead gorgeous. Russety-brown hair shot through with darker streaks of molasses, strong, arresting features that begged to be on a billboard selling power and money and sex, thick eyebrows that were both expressive and strong at once. And his eyes. Vivid forest green, they were touched by odd flecks of brighter green that almost seemed to —glow? Brilliant, intense, his eyes fixed on her as he came toward her.

But then there was the right side of his face. A pitted land-scape of shiny burn scars was etched into it, twisting the flesh. Although his right eye shone through as clearly as his left, it peered out from beneath the scant remains of the thick, dark eyebrow that obviously had once matched his left one. The pain of whatever had burned him must have been awful, Teagan thought in some far-off, hazy corner of her mind as she stared at him. It must have been a horrible, terrible thing that occurred.

The closer he got, she realized he was taller than she. That was nice. So was—oh. Wow. *Wow*.

Her gaze, which for some reason had decided to travel down his body, had snagged on the collar of his button-down shirt. The top two buttons were open. They revealed a tanta-lizing glimpse of his hard chest beneath it. A chest that was just so...manly. So defined. So wildly sexy.

Teagan's lower lip very slightly parted from the upper one as a sudden, totally crazy image whipped through her mind.

The image of her licking him in that very spot. Tasting the dark, delicious salt of his sweat as she lightly touched her tongue to the hard planes of his body.

H-holy crap. What was wrong with her?

Making her jump because she'd forgotten he was there, Eamon said from the doorway, "I imagine you can both handle things from here. Call me if you need me, Mr. Connolly." Something in his voice sounded almost—amused.

Without another word, Eamon withdrew, shutting the doors behind him. Leaving Teagan alone with the man stalking toward her like she was dinner. She felt the color flooding into her features, making her freckles pop out like beacons, as she gaped at his mesmerizing face.

A face, she abruptly realized with a deeply shocked jolt of recognition, she knew.

The mystery man from the other night. The one she hadn't been able to get out of her mind ever since their encounter.

"You!" she gasped. Then she just stared at him with dropped jaw.

"Well," the definitely not-old Mr. Ash Connolly said in that rich baritone voice, a darkness edging it as his stunning green eyes fixed on her. "My sword-wielding attacker. Back to finish the job?"

6

Ash's slightly ragged breath shivered apart the stillness of his library. He didn't take his gaze away from the woman, who stared at him with her mouth open. Just as she had the other night, she looked utterly astonished.

The bizarre force that had propelled him out from behind his screen, almost charging forth to meet this woman, still pushed at him. It was insanity, pure and simple. It had to be. Why the hell else would he want a beautiful woman to see his ravaged face so clearly? Especially one who had already reacted to it so badly once before?

It was his dragon that pushed at him, snorting tendrils of smoke and flame into Ash's mind. Making him feel heated and deliriously on edge everywhere. Urging him to get closer to *her*. The woman. To get next to her, so close that the intoxicating scent of her skin could envelop him.

Gritting his teeth, Ash willed himself to focus. She was a beautiful woman, yes. That was all. He hadn't been near a beautiful woman in far too long. His hormones still existed. That was all this was. Just a purely hormonal response to a gorgeous, curvaceous, fascinating woman.

His dragon roared in his mind.

The woman—*Teagan,* he let her name whisper through his mind—still just stared at him with wide eyes. Her face was so white, the freckles so pronounced on it, he thought she might be about to pass out. A nervous swallow drew his gaze to her smooth throat, where her pulse beat with hard thumps.

He knew his scars were on clear display for her. Even so, she didn't run screaming or literally exclaim in horror the way she had the other night. He'd shocked himself by stepping out into the light of the library, clearly visible to her. Yet he'd also felt oddly compelled to do so. Beyond his opening comment, though, he wasn't sure what else to say. The woman's mere presence was making him speechless. Which was unheard of for him.

He'd clearly lost his touch with the ladies.

The silence lengthened into sharp awkwardness. After another excruciatingly stretched out moment, during which the woman's beautiful chocolate-brown eyes stared back at his, she finally inclined her head in a short, jerky nod. "Oh, my g-god. H-hello," she said, her voice just above a whisper, shaking like a leaf. "I'm, ah, from the Bernal Center? I'm the one working on your book? The damaged one? Y-yes. That's me. That's why I'm here. In your home." He could hear the sheer nerves directing her babbling voice. "I never meant to—I didn't mean to be so awful the other night. And of course I'm not going to attack you again, that would be—oh, my god. I'm shutting up now."

She cut off her blathering by visibly clamping her lips tightly down. Her face abruptly flamed red, making the unique scatter of freckles all over her skin burst into deeper color. Ash couldn't help staring back, utterly taken by their intricate, unique artistry all across her equally glorious face.

For some bizarre reason, he wanted to—to *lick* the woman. To trace those beautiful markings on her skin with his tongue so lightly that she would gasp and tremble from his touch. Trace them, and mark them as his.

Mark *her* as his.

The thought so rattled him that he instead opened his mouth and said in an almost icy tone, "I gathered that from when my assistant introduced you. As for the other night, it's already forgotten. Completely."

Almost immediately, he felt a correspondingly sharp snap of regret at the embarrassment and even trepidation he saw in the beauty's expression. Ah, damn him. It wasn't in his nature to be overbearing, sharp, or worse yet, intimidating. Generally speaking, Ash was a courteous man. Yet right now, he couldn't seem to help his barbed reaction. Seeing the bizarrely intriguing woman again brought such an incredible rush of conflicted feelings raging around inside him it seemed his only recourse was to channel them into a self-protective anger.

It sure was a hell of a lot better than displaying his painful inner weaknesses to her instead.

"Of course." Her voice wavered. "So, I have images of the repairs I've done on your other book. Um, let me get them out." She moved toward the table, fumbling inside her satchel. Carefully removing a tablet, she set it down with as much care as if it were a delicate baby bird. She fussed over it, turning it on with such focus he knew she was simply trying to gather her wits about her.

Then she turned toward him in a nervous haste, knocking the small, heavy wooden bookstand on the corner of the table to the ground. It thunked onto the carpet. She stopped dead in her tracks, so quickly that she stumbled over her own feet. Her simultaneously horror-stricken and embarrassed face went that stunning rosy red again. It accentuated her classic features, the high planes of her cheeks, the proud sweep of her nose, the sweet rich brown of her eyes.

Damn, she was incredibly beautiful, despite her clumsiness. In fact, that made her even more endearing. Ash frowned as he thought that. Endearing? Really? Why did he keep thinking such things?

She saw his expression and apparently thought it was meant for her graceless move.

"I'm s-so sorry about that!" she gasped, reaching down to grab up the bookstand and put it back on the table with a trembling hand. "It was a mistake, I didn't mean to—"

Ash chuckled, then laughed with sudden delight. He had it now. It felt *comfortable* to be around her. Her sheer lack of either horror at his features, or the sort of transparent seductive attitude most women had had when they were around him back before he got burned, was truly refreshing. His dragon bellowed inside of him in approval. Even in a sort of possessive gratification.

At his laughter, her face suddenly ticked down into a slight frown. "Wait, are you laughing at me? I thought—you mean, you're not angry at me?"

Ash paused, taking a few deep breaths. "No." The admission startled him as much as it apparently did her, because she stopped fiddling with the bookstand. "I'm not."

He gave her another long, searching look, which she returned with a teetering mix of equal captivation and that hesitant shyness he'd noticed the other night. Quiet settled about them again as they stared at one another, locked into some sort of silent communication Ash couldn't even begin to understand. His dragon bugled inside him, more alert and aware than Ash had felt in many months. It was as if a bubble held him and the woman, Teagan, wrapped together in a space wired with sizzling heat and tension.

Clearly, she felt it, too. After another long moment, she very carefully let her huge-eyed gaze travel over the hideous scars that marred the right side of his face and extended down his neck, disappearing beneath his shirt.

Just as deliberately, feeling only an irrational desire to show the truth of himself to this stunning, perplexing woman, he reached up his right hand to slightly pull the sharply pressed collar to the side. He knew she could see the charring and ropy burn scars extending over the back of his hand, ending in a jagged pattern just over the tops of his knuckles. When it had happened he'd been in his dragon shape with his claws curled inward, thus sparing his fingers when in his human shape.

Small mercy, that.

Teagan's lips parted a bit, a very small whisper of sound that was an unsteady yet not horrified gasp tumbling over her lips. Instead, it was a sound laced with pain. Pain for him. She swallowed, the sound audible in the room only because it was otherwise silent, looking back into his eyes.

Ash felt his breath quicken and surge as his heart banged in his chest. A nudge of unease, the slight whip of trepidation, yet mostly a powerful longing to have her *recognize* him, to *know* him—which was definite madness, since he'd never laid eyes on her in his life before the other night—and, mostly, to *want* him, all whirled together as he pinned her with his gaze, his head still turned so she had no choice but to look at his ugly scars.

What in the hell was wrong with him? This woman was making him feel—half crazed. She apparently also maddened his dragon, who was still surging and trumpeting inside his mind, straining to get out.

The most insane part of it all, Ash thought as he struggled valiantly against his primal side, was that his dragon wanted nothing more than to leap out in a protective stance simply because this woman was here. All his dragon wanted to do was —protect her. From what, Ash had no idea.

Teagan's luminous eyes widened even more the longer she looked into his. Ash realized his pupils must have elongated somewhat, indicating that his dragon hovered very close beneath the surface. This time, he did swear quietly under his breath. She would think *she* was the insane one if he couldn't get control of himself.

Closing his eyes, he took a long, deep inhale through his

nose. Well, that was a bad idea. All it did was flood him with Teagan's intoxicating scent, like decadent sweet cream with a kick of nutmeg. It certainly didn't do anything to calm his dragon.

Teagan looked again at the spot where Ash's hand pulled back his collar, her eyes darkening as her face seemed to settle into an indecipherable yet deep emotion. Ash stood there, right hand displaying the ugly history recorded upon his body, his left arm held rigid at his side, fingers slightly curled in defense. His entire body felt hard and tense. Ready for—something. He wasn't quite sure what. Inside, he felt his dragon as poised and tense as he was, left wing half unfurled, every molecule of his body focused directly on the woman before him.

Slowly, Teagan raised her eyes up to Ash's face again. Keeping her gaze on his, she did something he didn't expect. She reached her hand slowly forward and up till her fingers touched the back of his right hand. As if in a trance, she let her fingers slowly trace the scars on the back of his hand. "Let me see," she finally said, her voice quiet. There was a certainty there, a strength, that she hadn't displayed before.

Startled, he complied. As he moved his hand out of her way, Teagan let her fingers slip off to land softly on his neck. Lighter than a butterfly's touch, she traced the ruin of his skin. She slowly rippled her fingers down the side of his neck, if she were playing the keys of the piano. Traveling the ridges of his scars, she gently touched the shiny patches of his disfigured skin. The room was alive with what seemed like the electricity promised by a thunderstorm. Ash's dragon rumbled deep inside him, just as startled and awed by Teagan's touch.

She moved her fingers down his collarbone, into the soft, smooth, unblemished hollow at the base of his throat. Her fingers stayed there for several beats of his pulse as the blood roared in his ears. An old desire, one familiar yet also completely new, hot and aching and endless, whispered along the nerve endings he had left. It trembled through his entire body, slamming into him wild images of kissing the woman senseless. Of tasting every inch of her luscious body while she lay in his bed.

His dragon bugled with need. With a nearly overwhelming insistence, he flung himself at Ash's mind, demanding to be let out so he could safeguard this woman. So he could—claim her?

One useless wing feebly beat at the edges of Ash's remaining rational thought, abruptly crushing him with the pain of loss and the bitter rage of impotence. Claiming a woman was out of the question for a damaged, scarred man like himself.

Faster than thought, Ash's hand whipped up to clap over hers, seizing her wrist.

"Stop," he said, his still dragon-roughened voice so low it was barely audible, "touching me."

As she touched him, Teagan's entire body thrummed with alternating waves of cold and heat as shock and another confusing emotion flared over her. Then Ash grabbed her hand in a viselike grip, breaking the wild spell that seemed to have overcome her and turned her into a crazy woman. His fingers pressed hard into the underside of her wrist, although not hard enough to actually hurt, as he wrenched her hand back away from him.

But he still held her wrist.

Furthering her enormous confusion, Teagan felt a sizzling spark race up her arm where his fingers lightly grasped her. Holy crap, it felt like an actual sizzle. Totally freaked by her reaction to him—she'd just reached out and *touched the man's scars!* Like a completely insane person! He was a client, for crying out loud. What in the crazy heck was wrong with her?

—she finally yanked her trembling arm away. Standing there, whole body now shaking, she felt light-headed.

"How dare you?" Fierce astonishment vibrated in his voice. His eyes, though, were filled with an odd wonder. Almost a tenderness.

Gasping, she shook her head like a jerky marionette, breaking the spell of madness that had seemed to hold her. "Oh, my gosh! I am so, so sorry!" The words wheezed out of her constricted, dry throat. "I have no idea what I was think-ing. I—you must think I'm insane," she whispered, staring at him as a cold terror now seemed to freeze her. "*I* think I'm insane."

The words fell into the room like tiny pebbles lightly dropped into a deep pool. They looked at each other for another long moment. The mystery man—Ash, she thought, which was really such a freaking cool name, and holy crap was he the sexiest man she'd ever seen in her life, scars or no scars, but it didn't much matter because he was probably about to have her thrown out of his house—took a breath, visibly trying to compose himself. His eyes, their bright green color like emeralds almost more alluring than she could handle, still fixed on hers.

It was like he was trying to figure her out. Or...was he trying to figure himself out?

Almost as if he could hear her thoughts, his face started to close down. Fascinated despite her horror at her behavior, Teagan watched it happen. First his eyes got cold and dark, then his entire face went sort of blank.

Right. This sort of thing, she recognized without question. The mask. He was pulling on the mask again. Hiding behind it. Well, could she blame him? She'd just gone all *Basic Instinct* on him. He was probably, she thought in a semi-hysterical babble of brain panic, about to call the police. Holy crap. She'd be hauled away in handcuffs. She'd be charged with assault. She'd—

"Thank you, Ms. Lambert." His voice was chillier than the ice cascading through her veins. "Please leave the tablet here. I will look at your photos to assess the repairs you have made to my book, then return it to the Center. Eamon will see you out."

The doors to the library opened. Teagan was aware of Eamon standing there, waiting for her, but she still felt rooted to the spot. She felt physically unable to make herself walk away from this man. From Ash. She stared at him. His hard mask was firmly in place, covering up the world-tilting moment that had swept over them both. His hands were now at his sides, fists clenched so tightly his knuckles were white on his left hand. On his right hand, the scars burned an angry red, the skin pulling taut. His hand trembled just slightly, making her realize how difficult it was for him to clench it.

The pain it must be causing him jarred her, causing a sympathetic reflex she longed to share. She opened her mouth to say something, anything, but he beat her to it.

"Good day, Ms. Lambert." He nodded toward the ornate doors, although his eyes didn't leave hers. Small flashes of what seemed like mint green flecks scattered amidst the overall darker shade made her blink. It was like there were other little lights in his eyes, lighting up within the darker shade. She could have sworn they were much brighter just a few seconds ago.

Swallowing, trembling herself as the enormity of what she'd just done hit her in another sickening wave, Teagan jerkily nodded back before walking away on legs that felt numb. As she left the room, the anxious jumble of her thoughts coalesced into one rhythmic beat that chased all the way to her car: something huge and significant had just happened.

The only problem was, she had no idea what it was, other than maybe the end of her career.

7

Ash strode around the darkened corner of his estate's palatial gardens, hands clenched into useless fists at his sides. His left eye twitched with the sensation of helpless fury that gripped him every other moment. Blowing out a harsh snort, he tried instead to take deep, relaxing breaths as his feet clipped along the flagstone walkways that circled the gardens.

His fists clenched again as he rounded the corner and stalked past a bed of exquisite chocolate cosmos flowers, their burgundy silk color teasing beneath the gentle glow of the low garden lights. Their color reminded him of the woman's eyes. Teagan's eyes. His right hand clenched and he stalked along faster.

Of course, his right hand could clench neither as tightly or firmly as his left. The skin pulled painfully, and the slightly atrophied hand muscles protested. Almost unconsciously, he tightened it again as he strode through the gardens. Testing it. It no longer throbbed with searing agony, the way it had in the first weeks and months of his healing. Even so, the skin and muscles would never be what they had been. They were damaged beyond repair. This was probably as good as it would ever get. Swearing under his breath, he picked up his pace, forcing his equally somewhat blighted right leg to stretch and work, even at this easy clip in what was not a huge area.

Behind him, another's footsteps sounded. Ash eased to a stop, trying to center himself. There was no need for his confused, strangely aggressive mood to be taken out upon one of his best, oldest friends in the world. His dragon contested that with an irritated bugle that ended in a snort, restlessly bumping against Ash's mind in a mirror of the consternation that flooded him. Growling at himself, Ash forced himself to focus on the moment.

On anything but the gorgeous, confounding, simply trans-fixing woman who'd abruptly thrown his life into a very unex-pected upheaval.

Only when the footsteps behind him slowed and then stopped completely did he turn his head. "I thought I was going to die an old man out here waiting for you," Ash snapped. Damn it. He'd wanted to sound lighthearted. Unfor-tunately, the irritation of his earlier thoughts clung to his tone. He winced at himself. It was a wonder he had any friends left, given what an ass he'd been behaving like recently. Cold, as he'd been to Teagan Lambert yesterday.

She'd let him *feel*, for a moment. Feel hope. Much as it had fascinated him, it also scared the hell out of him.

A good-natured chuckle was the only response. Ash turned fully around to see Nick shaking his head at him. Dressed in a tailored, expensive suit that might surprise his students at the Institute who were much more accustomed to seeing their sword instructor dressed in casual practice clothes, right now Nicholas Brenton looked every inch the wealthy, powerful dragon shifter he was. He shrugged good-naturedly at Ash. "Sorry I'm late. I was held up at the Institute. Now. What was so important that you needed me to stop by in the midst of my extremely important, busy day?"

At his mock haughty tone and expression, Ash couldn't

help but snort out laughter. It dispelled some of the moodiness that had gripped him. "Oh, stuff it. You may have the rest of the world fooled, but I know you're nothing more than a troublemaker still ruled by his hormones like a teenage boy."

Nicholas laughed in turn. The scion of a very ancient, well-blooded lineage that still held considerable sway over the most powerful European dragon shifter families, Nick had been not only quite the ladies' man but also a daredevil hellion in his wayward youth. Ash should know, since he'd been present for most of said wayward moments that had often landed them in very hot water with their elders. Their partner in crime, Sebastian Bernal, had completed the trio as they got up to an extraordinary amount of hijinks. In adulthood, Ash was often surprised they'd ever survived.

The two men were still Ash's best friends, despite how their time spent together had changed after the accident. They'd weathered a painful yet thankfully brief rift as well during Ash's subsequent deliberate withdrawal into seclusion. He still saw them often enough, but it almost always was in the private sanctuary of either his home or one of theirs. On occasion, Ash went to the Bernal Center to examine this or that ancient artifact, but it always was after hours or via private entrances. He and his friends no longer went out publicly to paint the town red. Those days were over for Sebastian anyway, ever since he'd found his mate, Lacey. As for Nicholas... Ash highly doubted Nick would ever settle down. Nick was still the consummate ladies' man, his general attitude toward women being that they were enjoyable in the short-term yet far too much work in the long term.

"That was a bit of a dirty trick you pulled the other night, by the way." Ash abruptly changed the direction of the conversation. A vivid flash of Teagan's dark red hair and stunning face burst into his mind. His dragon bugled in that newly possessive tone, still restless inside of Ash.

Nick gave him a puzzled look as he fell into step with him and urged them to keep walking around the garden. "I haven't played any dirty tricks on you. Not lately."

Ash huffed out another chuckle. He curled and stretched his damaged hand as they walked, willfully ignoring the bite of shortened, twisted muscles as he did so. "Making me come to the Institute. For the sword."

"Ah, the sword. Do you like it, then?" Fully justified pride rang through Nick's voice. He knew damn well how good he was not just as a swordsman and an instructor, but as a craftsman. He could not only forge a sword out of his own dragon's fire, but repair even the most ancient, magical ones in existence, such as Ash's recent acquisition—well, repatriation was more like it—from the auction. Nick wasn't from one of the oldest, most powerful, most magically inclined dragon lineages out there for nothing.

Allowing himself an appreciative grin, Ash lengthened his stride somewhat as they turned down a longer end of the garden. "Like it? That sword is by far the most amazing one I've ever touched in my life. Thank you," he added, turning to look directly at his close friend for a sincere moment. "I can't be sure how much it'll help me, but it's a good start."

Huffing out a satisfied exhale of quick relief, Nick nodded. He waved at Eamon, who had appeared on the back terrace of the house to set up the light lunch Ash had requested. Looking at Eamon, Nicholas frowned in concern.

"You sure he doesn't need more help here?" Nick gave Ash a slightly accusatory glance. "There are a few younger members from my fealty family who would jump at the chance to align themselves with you. The Connolly name is a powerful draw, Ash. They would do well here. And they sure as hell would never judge you."

Ash focused on his walking, ignoring the concerned look he knew his friend tossed at him, too. "No, Eamon has his routine down. I'm hardly demanding anyway. I just gave the man a week off," he added, deliberately changing the direction of the conversation. "He went to the Bahamas. With his lady love."

"He has a lady love?" Amused, Nick threw a thumbs up at Eamon, who didn't catch it as his back was turned. "Well, damn. Go, Eamon."

Ash nodded, prepared for Nicholas to press him on the need to get more help around his estate so as to ease the workload on Eamon, but Nicholas dropped it. Instead, he said, "All right, the sword will work out. What about the book? Have you asked Sebastian to set one of his conservators on it yet?"

Ash's dragon bugled again, the golden-red sheen of his hide rippling through Ash's mind as he sat back on his haunches and bellowed with a fierceness Ash hadn't heard for some time. He thought again of Teagan. Hell, it wasn't *again* so much as that he hadn't *stopped* thinking about her ever since she'd threatened to have his head sliced off in the parking lot of the Institute. And, of course, since she'd touched his face and his scars with the lightest fingers he'd ever felt upon his skin. The unexpected fierceness to her lingered with him as well. Then there was her beauty, matched by her incredibly voluptuous, strong, tall body that should be held close to his chest—

Well, what the hell? He was doing it again. Feeling insanely attracted to a woman he didn't dare touch. Even though she had inexplicably, maddeningly, thrillingly touched him herself just yesterday. The first time he'd met the woman, she threatened to chop his head off. The second time, she threatened his very sense of self by giving him perhaps the most erotic touch he'd ever experienced—and it hadn't been dealt with specific erotic intention at all.

Ash feared he might not survive a third meeting with the unpredictable, utterly beguiling Teagan Lambert.

His dragon snorted in his mind, more plumes of flame and

smoke heating the inside of Ash's head. Beside him, Nick stopped dead. Ash still walked forward a couple of steps before he paused and turned back to look questioningly at his friend. Nick stared at him, the brighter green of his dragon suddenly tinting his own naturally dark eyes.

"What did I say? I didn't mean for that to be a loaded statement." Nicholas abruptly crossed his arms over his chest and tilted his head a bit as he closely studied his friend. "But your dragon is suddenly very present. In an almost challenging way, Ash."

Ash felt the flare of heat in his head spread through his body as the echo of Teagan's rich laughter tumbled through his memory. Her creamy dark gold skin, marked by the intricate burst of freckle markings all across her face and down her neck, filled his mind. His dragon outright roared, beating his one good wing with mighty flaps and struggling valiantly to unfurl his crippled wing. At that display, which would be clear for any other shifter to see even though Ash remained in human form, Nicholas rocked his head back a bit, but he didn't waver in his stance.

"Very interesting," he merely remarked, still carefully watching Ash. Something like delight might have rippled beneath his tone. His own eyes flared even more with the brightness that indicated his dragon was close to the surface as well.

Ash tried to wrestle his wild side into submission, but his dragon wasn't having it. With an exasperated groan, he snapped his eyes shut, shaking his head before opening them again. "This is insane," he muttered. "I can't—I just—I met her for a total of what? Thirty minutes? This is impossible," he added with a frown.

Nicholas's eyebrows raised. "She? Oh, really." He made an exaggerated face of shock.

The effect was rather comical on his stern warrior features, but only served to make Ash snap, "Don't look at me like that. It's nothing. Just hormones, like your own stupid teenage boy hormones." He threw up his hands before spinning and stalking away from his addled friend, heading toward the terrace. "This is a simple reaction to being around a pretty girl. That's all."

Behind him, Nicholas snorted. "That's not what it looks like to me. Looks to me like she must be a lot more interesting than being merely a pretty girl. Spill," he commanded, jogging up behind Ash to fall into step beside him again.

Ash gave him a slightly incredulous sideways look as he headed toward the house and the enticing smell of the food Eamon had set up for them. "You're the one who should spill to me, actually. She's one of your students. That's why I asked Eamon to call you here. To find out," he words dragged out of him somewhat reluctantly, "more about her."

Nicholas stopped again. Ash sighed and turned around again as well. His dragon pushed at his mind, irritated and inquisitive at once.

"One of my students? At the Institute?" Nick's astonished tone reached Eamon, who cast them a glance.

Gritting his teeth for a moment, rolling his eyes skyward, Ash drawled, "No, at the other school you own. Yes, of course at the Institute." He struggled against his dragon pushing even harder at him to *do* something. Defend something. "You didn't know she was the one who's repairing the book? That she's one of Sebastian's conservators?"

Surprise had etched Nicholas's face until this point. Sudden understanding draped over it now as he stared back at Ash. Slowly, he began to shake his head, a grin spreading across his features as Ash glared. "Ah. Yes, indeed. You mean Teagan. Tall girl?" He raised his hand to indicate a spot just about level with Ash's eyes.

Frowning more, Ash nodded.

"Strong. She could take off an Amazon warrior's head with

one lop of her sword." Nicholas tapped the muscles on his fore-arms, flexing them as he grinned.

Ash's dragon began snorting smoke and fire again as Ash slowly nodded, eyes still trained on his old friend.

"Except, of course, she's still so bad at her sword handling that she's more likely to cut off her own head than anyone else's," Nick added with a grin, though he still kept his gaze trained right back on Ash.

Ash gritted his teeth as he thought about the way Teagan had knocked the small bookstand off the table in his library.

"And curvy." Nicholas rounded his hands in front of him, seeming to outline the features of a woman's body. His grin was so big now that it seemed ready to slit through his skin.

Ash felt the heat within him turn dark red as his dragon roared and bellowed inside. His jaw clenched. He knew his own eyes were probably so flecked with bright green they appeared like pure jade, the pupils slitting vertically as his dragon shoved and pushed beneath his skin in some crazed desperation.

A desperation to defend and protect what was his, and his alone.

Nick leaned forward, a thoroughly devilish glint in his own eyes. "She's not only outrageously gorgeous, so beautiful it's unbearable, especially because she clearly doesn't know it herself, she's also brilliant. Utterly brilliant in a way that turns a man on even more than that drop-dead stunning body of hers, with its curves that are totally fuc— "

Ash's dragon plunged with nearly unstoppable strength against his mind, straining the limits of his control. A roar bellowing out of his own human mouth, Ash launched himself at Nicolas, hands reaching forward in a crazed, blind attempt to smash or strangle or pummel, or all three.

With a booming laugh that was edged by some sort of bizarre glee, Nicholas easily spun away from Ash's lunge, flicking out his foot at the last second to deliver a glancing blow against Ash's upper left thigh. As he windmilled his arms to prevent himself from going down, Ash sensed more than heard Eamon's surprised exclamation from behind them. He staggered a couple of running steps past Nick before he managed to turn, slightly crouched in both feet, arms spread out beside him in preparation for attack.

Nicholas, the cackling bastard, just stood there roaring with laughter in Ash's gardens. He flung his head back and laughed even more as Ash glared at him while he ripped the air with a couple of choice words about Nick's parentage and looks.

By the time Eamon reached them, his expression thoroughly perplexed, Nick was bent almost double, gasping for air as he still howled with whatever he seemed to think was so funny. Ash had completely recovered, although he was breathing fast from the effort of holding back his still outraged dragon as well as the confused maelstrom of thoughts that slammed around in his mind.

Eamon gazed from one to the other as he slowly shook his head in despair, much as he had when they were young boys getting up to no good. Mildly, he said, "Really, Nicholas, I thought I was setting out a civilized lunch for two gentlemen. Instead, I am presented with two ruffians about whom I've half a mind to yank by the ears."

Ash blew out a harsh breath as he tried to regain his equilibrium. "He's definitely still a ruffian. One I invited to my house, even. Feel free to yank away."

Nicholas, who finally managed to get his laughter somewhat under control, wiped tears from his eyes. "Hey, I had to protect this expensive suit of mine. It was a completely unprovoked attack I needed to defend myself against." His words were punctuated by a devious grin.

Ash sputtered, "Unprovoked? You just said she seems—"

He snapped off the words so tightly his teeth clattered

together. Then he felt his entire face loosen with the dawning realization.

Eamon and Nicholas both looked at him. A slow, understanding smile filled Nick's face. "I simply," Nick said softly, "was attempting to make a point about the depth of your response to her when I started describing her as if I noticed how attractive she is. She is indeed attractive, Ash." Nick shrugged, seriousness on his face as he quietly added, "But I am not the one attracted to her. *You* are. Very much so."

Ash's dragon rumbled in him again, responding to the presence of another male shifter who appeared to be interested in his—

Ash bit the thought off so quickly he thought this time his brain rattled as well.

Equally understanding comprehension on Eamon's face didn't help matters either. Still looking at Ash with that irritatingly compassionate grin, Nicholas said, "I haven't seen you this interested in a woman since—well, since ever, to be honest." Nick shrugged his massive shoulders.

A quiet beat held them as Ash visibly struggled with his dragon. He was fascinated by the strength of his dragon right now. Ever since the accident, his dragon had been as shocked and restrained as he was. But this—reaction. His intense reaction to—Teagan, he made himself think as he carefully pictured her face again, felt the tremor work through him as he remembered the touch of her fingers on him—this apparently was enough to bring his dragon to an acute awareness of which he'd actually never thought himself capable.

Not even before he'd been burned.

At the abrupt reminder of his burned, scarred status, a whip of resigned fury stung through him again. Even if the presence of the sword in his life could help him somewhat, it was fact that he would never heal back to his former self. Never. Oh, he might regain some more use of his affected limbs that would allow him to exist like a shadow of his former self. Yet he would never completely be like he'd been before.

Ash Connolly had nothing to offer an incredible woman like Teagan except the mystery of the books he'd entrusted to her capable hands.

Brusquely shouldering past the others, Ash headed toward the terrace. He casually tossed back, "Thank you for the trouble you went to putting out lunch for us, Eamon. Nick, let's eat. I'm interested in hearing more about the provenance of the sword."

There. A change of subject would help matters immensely. Forcibly, Ash pushed aside thoughts of the stunning beauty.

Then his dragon screamed in his mind, the sheer power of it bolting through Ash like fire. He staggered on the flagstones of the path toward the wide sweep of stairway. In a fury of emotion, his dragon beat his wings in Ash's mind, the ruined right one valiantly working to move, although it hardly did.

"You okay there?" Nick's voice, now somewhat concerned, yet sounding far away as the nearly desperate bugles of Ash's dragon rang through his mind.

His dragon roared, flapping his wings with all his might, despite the damaged one barely fluttering. Yet the intent was there. As was the fierce drive behind his dragon's vivid reaction to Ash's desire to ignore the woman.

To ignore her scent.

To ignore the feel of her hand upon his chest, her fingers light and tentative as they reached up to trace the scars on his face and neck. The rich brown of her eyes intensifying as she touched him, her unique, arresting features stilled with anticipation as that moment had surrounded them both in a bubble of timeless magnitude.

The strange feeling of familiarity washed over him again. The sensation that he *knew* her. Which was impossible. She was a stranger. One who did not know who he was. Nor what he was. And one who he could never hope to intrigue with his wrecked body.

"It's nothing," he muttered through the tumult in his mind in response to Nick's question. He moved another step to the terrace, pushing aside a vision of a waterfall of silken dark red hair covering a starburst of complexity and beauty on a face he knew would be forever etched into his mind.

His dragon would have none of it. This time, his dragon forced a partial shift, bellowing out of Ash's mouth in a wild call that was inhuman. Imagined pictures of Teagan, her hair flying behind her like a pennant in the wind, laughing with unfettered joy, snapped through his mind as his dragon pushed them at him. The scent of her, bold and shy at once like sweet milk stirred with spiced cinnamon and nutmeg. The rich, exquisite way she must taste if only he could touch his lips to hers.

Ash stood ramrod straight this time, still shocked by the force echoing through him. His dragon was worked up still.

Or was it—*woken* up?

A few long beats passed before Nick ventured, "Nothing, hmm? You're fighting your dragon for control right this second, but nothing's going on? I see."

Ash pivoted on his good leg with flashing deadly grace, rounding on his friend and his fealty man where they stood behind him. They both regarded him with nearly identical expressions of knowing amusement. Glaring, he just shook his head at them, afraid that if he opened his mouth again another half-dragon roar would bellow out of him, encouraging a frightened neighbor in this quiet residential area to call the police and report a wild animal on the loose.

Nick seemed on the verge of speaking, his devilish grin boding no good for the words he planned to say, but Eamon neatly rescued the situation as he often did.

"I believe, Ash," he said with a single raised eyebrow as his expression turned more serious, "part of why your dragon is pushing right now is because you've forgotten to attend to something in the manuscript."

At that, it was Nick's and Ash's turn to stare with questioning looks. Eamon grunted a bit beneath his breath, a sound well familiar to them both as indicating uneasiness. "The last rune on the sword," he said quietly, his tone abruptly heavy. "I thought about it more last night and this morning. I meant to discuss it with you over lunch."

The slow puzzlement in Eamon's voice sharpened Ash's focus. "Go on." He felt his dragon settle into focused stillness in his mind, waiting for the loyal fealty man to share his thoughts.

One side of Eamon's mouth tugged up, but not in a real smile. More like a grimace of understanding that had come too late. "It's the key to what we didn't realize about the connection between the sword and the book."

At his slight pause, Ash impatiently gestured for him to go on.

Rather grimly, Eamon said, "The book *is* the key, Ash. It most likely contains the meaning of the runes on the sword. But since they're both Connolly artifacts—"

"Oh, hell and damnation," Nick burst out, sounding utterly disgusted. But it was aimed at himself. "I should have known that. It makes sense as to why they were sold as an unbreakable lot. But the title. *The Book of the Near Hills.*" He gave his head a savage shake. "Meant to mislead, and it did. Dammit!" Nick swore more creatively, face darkening.

He shook his head, looking at Ash with a sobered expression. Ash spread his hands, still lost.

Nick spread his hands out as if in supplication, still huffing in self-irritation. "The other book is the ruse. The fancy, beautiful, interesting *Book of the Dragonborn.* It's the sham book." Nick's voice was clipped, irritated yet admiring at once. "And the book you sent to the Center? The deadly dull, not at all remarkable, plain little text?"

Ash stared at Nick as his mind abruptly made the connection. Chills of hot and cold shivered up and down his skin as the implications snapped through his mind.

Nick ground out, "That book is the real treasure. It holds the key. Hidden in plain sight. I should have known," he muttered again. Nick had a great deal of experience with the connection of magical objects. But even the best could miss a trick.

Ash stood there, his mind quickly ticking over the information that abruptly changed everything. "So," he finally said, very slowly. "We missed something in that book. Which makes sense, now that I think about it. I barely glanced at it except to note that it needed repairs. The first few pages were so boring that—" He cut himself off with an abrupt snort of admiring laughter. "That I just stopped reading," he finished simply. "As anyone looking at it was meant to do. Very clever ancestors I had, it seems. Smart enough to outwit their own descendants."

"Almost outwit them," Eamon corrected with a brief smile. "Now that we know, all you must do is take another, closer look at the book."

"Easy solution," Nick agreed, though a sly look began to spread over his face again.

Ash needed to see the book again. The book, which was at the Center.

With Teagan.

Ash knew all those thoughts flitted openly across his face by Eamon's thoughtful, pleased expression, and Nick's widening grin.

"Not a word," he said in severe tones to his prankster friend. "Not one more word."

"Who, me?" Nick looked as pious as an angel for a split-second before he about busted a gut laughing again.

Ash bit down his answer. Instead, he thought of the luscious redheaded woman he would have to see again in person. The extraordinarily sexy, unpredictable, oddly alluring Teagan Lambert.

The one who made his dragon bugle with adamant fervor. The one who made Ash feel bizarrely protective. The one, he thought as calmly as he could, he was tremendously excited to see and scent in person once again.

Why she made him feel that way, he wasn't yet sure. But he damn well was about to find out.

8

When Teagan's alarm went off at six, the shrill noise sent her sitting bolt upright in bed, heart hammering in her chest as if someone had just jumped out and yelled *Boo!* Reaching out her hand, she fumbled around on her phone until she managed to slide the pinging sounds off. With a gasping groan, she collapsed back against her pillows, flinging one arm over her eyes in hopes of just a few more beautiful minutes of sleep.

Just as quickly, she sat up again, eyes snapping back open as the events of yesterday afternoon abruptly flooded back. The gorgeous, amazing, fascinating man. Ash Connolly. His book, his library, the mysterious something about him that just made her stomach flip with excitement. With a wild flare of attraction. She'd felt an odd connection to him. As if she'd known him forever. As if she could trust everything about him without question.

As if he was an essential part of her life. One that would change her forever.

Then, naturally, she had gone psycho and reached up to *touch the man's face.* Like she'd had permission or something. Oh, god. She was a crazy stalker woman. What was wrong with her? Why couldn't she just be a normal person for once? Most of all, why, oh, why did the universe apparently hate her?

An indignant meow from her bedroom door drew her attention. Mouser stood there, gazing at her with accusation in his limpid golden eyes. Her little Bengal tiger, she liked to call him for his striking looks, rawed out another imperious meow to let her know about the empty state of his tummy. Despite her traumatized thoughts, she managed a small laugh at her best little buddy's demands.

"Okay, okay, I'm coming, your highness." She pushed the covers off and swung her feet to the floor. Mouser turned and trotted toward the kitchen, another encouraging meow trailing behind him. Teagan had to admit it was really nice having a friend to live with, even if that friend was furry and four-legged and had absolutely no interest in Irish history except to shed his hairs on her books and her practice sword.

It was also really nice to live in an adorable little back house for a rental price that didn't eat up her entire salary. Her landlady, a tenured, well-known professor at UCLA with a penchant for really creative non-swearing, had gotten the sprawling main front house and this cute little cottage in back from her recent ugly divorce. Friends with Teagan's parents, she had gleefully rented the back house to Teagan for an insanely low price unheard-of in the greater L.A. area. Knowing that she could afford to have a tenant pay practically nothing because she now owned this place outright after her mother-truckin' son-of-a-monkey cheating mongrel of an ex had lost it to her made her, she'd told Teagan, totally blissed out. That was fine by Teagan. She was just lucky to have gotten such a great little place she could afford so close to work.

As she blearily padded after Mouser into the kitchen and opened a can of food to stave off his increasingly demanding cries, images of Ash Connolly's incredible library flitted across her mind. Just the library, of course. It wasn't like images of the man's face also flitted across her mind's eye. She wasn't thinking about him because he was undeniably gorgeous, despite the heart-wrenching burn scars on the right side of his face. Definitely not because he was far younger than she'd thought he would be. Older than her by maybe five years, but definitely not the crotchety, eccentric old man she'd first imagined.

No, she definitely wasn't thinking about him because of those things. She was only thinking about him because she had to work on his book. At least she hoped she still got to work on his book. This was her first big opportunity at the Bernal Center. She couldn't screw it up. Except that she already had. Groaning, she dropped her face into her hands. Mouser rubbed hard against her legs, purring strongly to show how much he loved the lady who fed him. Teagan lifted her head out of her hands. "I still can't believe I did that," she said in a mortified whisper.

Mouser just meowed again. Her cat didn't care about anything but his stomach. He helpfully stood up on his hind legs to lean his front paws on the cupboards of the counter beside her, staring at her in an apparent attempt to Jedi mind trick her into giving him his food right this second.

"Sorry, Mouser. Here you go," she said, placing his bowl down in front of him. He shoved his face into it, then briefly turned his golden eyes on her, bits of food in his whiskers and a tiny dab on the end of his nose, with a little purring meow before diving face first back into the bowl.

Sighing, Teagan thought about the richness of Ash's eyes, and the funny little bright green flecks of light in them. The ones that seemed to sparkle ever brighter the more they'd talked. Then there were the skin-rippling tingles she'd gotten just from being in the same room with him. The sheer masculine presence of the man had filled the library with a surging vitality and something else. Something fiery yet mysterious, hidden away behind his scarred face and those fathomless eyes.

A sudden vision of her reckless hand reaching out to touch Ash's face, his chest, flooded through her yet again. With a sharp inhale, she felt the color rush intensely to her face and flame over her entire body. Wait. Had she really done that? It wasn't some weird dream? Yes, oh, holy freaking crap, yes, she had. She hadn't imagined it. She had reached out and touched the man. And kept touching him. Because it felt good. Because she'd swear she'd felt some sort of intense spark when she did so.

Then he'd asked her to stop touching him.

Which meant she was some sort of—assaulter. Assaultant? Something. She had assaulted the man.

Suddenly not hungry, Teagan instead blindly made her morning cup of black tea—the real stuff, loose leaves, none of that powdered crud they sold in teabags that tasted like water. No, this was imported straight from Ireland. It was dark, robust deliciousness she drank every morning with a generous addition of milk. Today, though, the taste didn't invigorate her as it usually did.

Before she'd fallen asleep last night, she'd been half expecting her phone to buzz with an angry call from the Center, with Walter's disappointed, horrified voice on the other end informing her that due to her unpardonable behavior at the house of the client, she was immediately let go of her position at the Center. Released to wander in the wilds of the academic world, with no references. Just a ton of derisive laughter, pointing fingers, and shame following her about.

Holy crap. What if she really was fired?

Robotically, she dressed, gave a distracted kiss goodbye to the top of Mouser's head, and headed out the door. The entire way to the Center, her thoughts alternated between visions of the heated invitation she had imagined seeing in Ash's face, those stunning eyes of his deepening in their swirl of green with those bizarre yet fascinating bright points of light deep within them almost mesmerizing her, and visions of arriving at the Center to find that her employee pass no longer worked and she was barred forever from her dream career.

But her pass worked as usual to let her into the employee parking area, she pulled into a spot without any fanfare, and walked to the doors of the building without sirens blaring or anyone leaping out to drag her away in shackles to the loony bin.

As she nervously started down the hall to hurry toward her office, Teagan didn't allow the usual comfort wash through her as she walked through the building that had already started to feel like another home even in the brief time she had been here.

Just as she rounded the final corner to the hallway in the conservators' wing that housed her office, daring to breathe a sigh of relief, she ran right into someone. She stumbled back, gasping out an apology, the words dying on her lips as she saw who it was.

None other than Sebastian Bernal himself, owner of the entire danged Center and probably half the world for all she knew. Also apparently a good friend of Ash Connolly's.

Mr. Bernal had to know what had happened yesterday. Of course he did. Oh, god. He knew about her lapse of dignity. He knew, so he was about to fire her in person himself. Feeling her face for once actually drain of color, Teagan just stared at the man with wide eyes as her heart hammered out of control with dread.

"Ah. Ms. Lambert." He gave her a dark, assessing look.

Was his voice always that cold? That terrifying? Geez, it was as icy as Ash's had gone yesterday. Some sort of boys' club-house thing? Oh, god. She was done.

His face didn't change from its grim lines as he went on. "There you are. Please follow me to my office now." At a sharp clip, he turned and strode off in the other direction, not bothering to see if she was following.

The room seemed to sway around Teagan for a horrible moment. The severe tone of his voice and the hard look he'd given her threatened to make every molecule of oxygen in her body disappear, sending her to the ground in a faint.

This was it. She was going to get canned. She'd be a disgrace. She'd never work in the rare book field again. She'd have to move home to Illinois, live in her parents' basement, and hope to scrounge a part-time job at the local Dairy Queen.

She'd never see the intriguing, mysterious, gorgeous, haunted, and totally panty-dropping Ash Connolly again.

The crazy pain of that thought socked her even as she forced her suddenly heavy feet to move down the hallway. She'd never again see a man she'd met only twice, and the very thought of that abruptly made her incredibly regretful. What in the actual heck did that mean?

Mr. Bernal reached his office, the doors to it imposing in their hugeness. Opening them, he gestured her in, barely looking at her as he did so. Feeling light-headed with terror, Teagan slowly entered, eyes on the ground as she mentally calculated how much money she had in her savings account and how much it would take her to move back home.

Behind her, the door shut. Turning, startled, she saw that Mr. Bernal had ushered her into his own office only to leave her alone in it. Wait, what? He hadn't come in with her. Well, that made no sense—

"Teagan. We need to discuss my book." The deep, knee-shaking voice from behind her startled her so badly she almost fell over her own feet as she spun around yet again, heart slamming in what felt like triple time.

Ash Connolly, the panty-dropper himself, stood there. In the middle of Mr. Bernal's office, arms folded across his chest as he looked at her with an expressionless face. He didn't even offer an apologetic smile for scaring the snot out of her.

"Tell me this, too." His eyes, their shade a mixture of turquoise and jade, fixed on her with a searing intent she couldn't parse. "Do you make it a habit of going to strange men's homes and touching them as intimately as you would a lover?"

9

Ash thought perhaps the bewitching woman was about to faint at his words. Her face was pale, so unlike the wild blushing she'd shown him so far. The whiteness of her skin accentuated her freckle starburst even more, making her features all the more mesmerizing.

Again, he wanted to lean forward and trace a path from freckle to freckle with his lips.

His dragon bellowed with approval while Ash barely caught his own shocked exclamation and kept it tightly shoved inside. This was insane. He was still insane, damn it all to hell. Farking Sebastian was insane, as was Nick, as was Eamon. Why the hell hadn't any of them stopped him from coming here to face her like this?

Like a—a—hell, he didn't know what the hell like. Like a fool? Damn it to all the ancient Irish curses. Book or no book, magic or no magic, healing or no healing, being in the same room again with Teagan Lambert was a wild, stunning, potentially brain-melting mistake.

His thinking definitely melted when she wet her full lips with her tongue, slowly drawing the bottom one into her mouth in a clearly nervous gesture. Her eyes, their velvety chocolate irises barely wider than her huge dark pupils, peered at him from the curtain of burnt sienna hair hanging in loose, shining waves on either side of her face.

"I," she finally stammered out, still staring at him. "I'm not sure I can—that is, I can't explain why I did that—"

She broke off her stumbling words as he slowly, deliberately smiled at her. Damn, the woman was sexier than anything he'd ever seen in his life. What in the hell? It had happened once again. She made him want to not only smile, but to laugh and exult and feel—*happy*. Trying hard to draw on a presence of mind that seemed abruptly tenuous, he attempted to take control of the situation.

"Ah, thank you. I did want to see you blush again," he admitted. "I'm sorry if I startled you. But you're absolutely stunning when you do that."

A moment of silence held them again. A rush of heat suffused him as he took in Teagan's shapely figure and wide eyes staring at him from where she stood by the door to Sebastian's office. His dragon keened with low delight at seeing her standing there, so close to him. Her blush covered her face, her neck, and extended down past the material of her blouse that so unfortunately covered her sweet figure. Ash almost groaned at the thought of what her body must look like, naked and flushed that deep pink all over.

Swallowing the groan of appreciation that threatened to spill out of his throat, Ash gave himself another long, lingering moment to enjoy the beautiful curves on the tall, stunning woman before him. Her hips flared even beneath the slightly too large and very sensible skirt she wore, the hem of which was halfway down her calves, which were encased in tall black boots. Her blouse, colored like the fluttering leaves on the fall trees outside, covered the perfect handfuls of her breasts, which were faintly outlined beneath the silky fabric.

Ash's gaze paused as he saw the pendant she wore around her neck, nestled into the sweet hollow of her throat. Urged by his dragon and his own sheer longing to get closer to the object of his bizarre fascination, Ash abruptly took two long strides across Sebastian's large office, drawing up short just in front of Teagan. Her eyes widened even more as she inhaled a startled breath. He barely kept himself from reaching his hand out to touch the pendant, which his dragon instinctively recognized as being dragon gold. It was not uncommon for such objects to end up in human hands, due to the endless trade or outright theft that was a constant part of dragon shifter life. Sometimes, things just got loosed into the wider world. "That's an Irish Celtic rune." He let his eyes move up to catch hers. "And do you know what it means, my sword-wielding scholar?"

She swallowed, her throat muscles working and nearly making him reach out for real. He forestalled himself with an effort. Damn. Why did everything about him lately seem to want to lose control rather than keep it tightly leashed, as he had ever since he'd been burned? Why did this woman make him want to lose control? Most importantly, why on earth did she seem so perfectly suited for him?

It was a bitter irony times a thousand that he no longer looked as he once had. That he finally met a woman who truly intrigued him, yet had nothing more to offer her than his scars and angry pain. Ruthlessly, he swallowed back the bolt of useless bleak feeling. That would get him nowhere.

Lifting her fingers up to gently handle the soft gold shine of the pendant, which hummed to his shifter-enhanced hearing when she touched it, she answered cautiously, "Yes, I do. Do you?"

She seemed just as startled as he by the way she had boldly flipped around his questioning. This time, Ash allowed the broad smile to sweep across his face, utterly taken by everything about her. He relaxed just a tick. "Indeed. It's an ancient rune meaning *protection.* That's the general gist of it. More specifically, it means protection against one's dedicated enemies." He didn't tell her it really meant, to protect against dragon shifter enemies. No need for her to think him insane. "What enemies could you, Teagan," his voice abruptly lowered into a dark, sensuous caress of her name, "possibly have?"

The air between them suddenly charged with bright electricity, just as it had the day before. Ash could see Teagan's pulse beating wildly in her neck as her breathing quickened. He tamped down his dragon, who alternately keened and bugled and roared in the back of his mind, utterly entranced by this fascinating woman. The spark racing between them felt alarmingly intense.

Alarmingly *connected*, in a way that shook Ash to his core.

Teagan gave a nervous little half laugh, shrugging one shoulder as her fingers twisted around the rune pendant. "No one, I guess. Well, maybe against strange guys in dark parking lots who terrify lone women at night." She gave him a shy smile as she said that, her beguiling eyes shifting back and forth on his, clearly trying to read his reaction to her light teasing.

Ash swallowed away the disturbing zip of intimacy between them. "Point well taken," he conceded.

Damn, why had he come up so close to her? Her presence was making hot chills flash all over his body. His dragon still bugled with possessive intent in Ash's mind. Ash snorted to himself. Of course. After all, it had been his dragon's insistence that had propelled him to leave his home and drive to the Bernal Center, daring a public sighting once again. Well, he had used Sebastian's private parking area and private entrance to the building to gain admittance. While he couldn't fly in his dragon form to Seb's private landing spot on the building, he'd still managed to get himself inside without anyone other than Sebastian, and now Teagan, the wiser.

Forcing himself to turn away from her, he walked over to Sebastian's enormous desk, the section of which closest to them was cleared except for *The Book of the Near Hills*. The book that was not nearly as dull as he'd suspected.

Teagan apparently noticed it as he began walking toward

it. Startled, she exclaimed, "My book! Um, I mean, your book," she immediately added, the nervous babble of her voice causing another sudden grin of delight to flip over Ash's face. He was glad his back was to her so she couldn't see his apparent madness. "What—how did it get in here? I left it locked up in the workroom yesterday before I went home."

This close to the book, Ash could feel the hum of its power lifting toward him. Odd. He hadn't felt it at all when the book had first come into his hands. His dragon's attention was abruptly torn between the sumptuous woman behind him and the literary artifact before him that called to the ancient Connolly blood in his veins. As the seesaw of distractions gripped Ash, he took a quick inhale to steady himself against it.

"Yes. I asked Sebastian to bring it here so that I could look at it. With you," he added, hearing invitation in his own voice. Damn it to hell. Get him around a beautiful woman, half lose his mind. Quickly, he went on. "I looked at the photos of the repairs you'd done on it so far. Very impressive. Well done."

She flushed but managed to smile in thank you.

"However, I needed to see the book again in person." He didn't say that seeing her again in person was also a very nice reward for once again venturing outside his home. "As it turns out, there may be a connection between the book and the sword that was sold with it. I didn't realize it originally."

"Oh?" Even in her flustered state, he could sense her inquisitive academic's mind latching onto that interesting tidbit.

"That, and my other book. The one you came to see the other day."

There was a pause as the events of that meeting clearly filled both his mind and hers. She pulled her bottom lip between her teeth, causing a wave of something alarmingly hot and jagged spill over Ash's senses. He wanted to—touch the woman. Everywhere. Tamping down the crazy desire, as well as his dragon's snorts of encouragement, Ash took a steadying breath. "Your work was impeccable, so I've had the other book already delivered to your office. It will be waiting there for you."

In a faint voice, she said, "Oh. Thank you."

Another pause, during which Ash assessed his own ability to stay both gentlemanly and professional. Deciding he could, he said, "Come stand next to me, Teagan." *So my dragon doesn't make me crazy between whatever it is in you, and whatever it is in the book that's causing whatever madness is in me,* he added silently to himself. "Now, I want to look at this book with you."

There was only a brief pause before she walked over and stood beside him. "Now then," he briskly went on as Teagan's artlessly seductive scent knocked more holes into his self-control, "Let's take a look, shall we?"

She nodded as she turned her head toward the book, leaning down toward it. Mere inches away from him. Ash was exquisitely aware of every molecule of the woman standing beside him. Her luscious lips, the gorgeous freckles scattered across her features, the way her chest rose and fell as she breathed. He couldn't help test the atmosphere between them. "This time, Teagan," he said in a tone that flared with sudden heat, "we really should keep our hands to ourselves."

Her eyes shot back to his, wide and startled. Their deep mocha color darkened even more the longer he looked at her. Before he could censor himself, Ash added, "For now, that is."

The silence between them quivered with the implication of his words.

She swallowed visibly, staring back at him with an expression that both spoke volumes yet said nothing. All he could sense from her was that she was as keenly attuned to him as he was to her. Seeming caught between a desire to flee or faint, she finally broke the moment by abruptly turning her head and reaching for the book.

Biting back a small kick of disappointment, Ash's gaze caught on her hands. Ah. They trembled slightly. This time, however, it wasn't from fear. He bent his head close to hers. "Let's start with the most recent page you made repairs on. We'll simply flip through the pages after that until I find what I'm looking for."

A light waft of her spicy-sweet scent drifted to him as she nodded, then very gently opened the book. Her voice was only slightly shaky when she spoke. "What are you looking for exactly? I've already looked through the entire book when I was first cataloguing the places that needed repair. I might know where to start if you can describe what you need to see?"

Mild frustration gripped Ash as he blew out a sharp breath. Teagan glance at him from under her eyelashes, but he noted she didn't dare look at him all the way again. At that, he felt another small flash of satisfaction. She felt the odd little connection between them as well. "Unfortunately," he said, "I can't describe to you precisely what it is that I need to see. I don't know what it is," he admitted with a quick frown.

He caught her arched eyebrows out of the corner of his eye, although she still appeared to be studiously involved in carefully turning the pages of the book. "Really? Well, then, okay. This project is going to be super easy, huh?"

The unexpected sass in her tone caught him off guard. He huffed out more laughter. Teagan responded to it with a slight curve of her lips, though she kept her eyes on the book. The sight of her full lips smiling sent another bolt of pleasure through him. Despite the thick, languid tension surrounding them, she clearly was relaxing in his presence.

The Book of the Near Hills—Ash snorted yet again at the innocuous title—contained ancient Gaelic words penned in loose, flowing script on some pages, tightly cramped on others. The color of the ink appeared as vibrantly crisp and fresh as it must have looked when it was first written. Teagan occasionally pointed out the beautiful penmanship, remarking on how miraculously well-preserved the book was. She paused very briefly on each page so that Ash could do a quick scan, looking for the unknowable something he needed to see.

If only she knew that it was dragon shifter magic making the book seem as fresh as it would have been the day it had been made over seven hundred years ago. He couldn't tell her, of course. Aside from the fact that she would think he was completely insane and would probably slide out of the room to run screaming away, there were varying laws within aspects of the shifter world that forbade telling humans about their existence. Some shifter types were far more severe about the sharing of such knowledge, all the way up to the pain of death. Among dragon shifters, while there existed ancient formal accords that sharing the knowledge of their existence was something that was for the most part not to be done with humans, both magic and practical realities did more to forbid it.

First off, despite the immense strength and power dragon shifters possessed, there were far fewer of them in the world than there were humans. Mere tens of thousands worldwide, compared to the billions of humans that crammed the planet. A dragon shifter uprising, the thought of which made Ash's lips twitch at the absurdity of such an event, would be too easily quelled by humans due to sheer numbers. No, dragon shifters were more than happy to exist as they did, amassing their wealth, living well, enjoying long lives, and operating well below the radar of most humans.

Second, most human eyes could never see a dragon shifter in dragon form. Magical enhancements meant they were invisible to all human eyes with the exception of very few, such as members of fealty families.

And mates.

His dragon restlessly moved in his mind, startling Ash with the amount of edgy awareness and colossal protectiveness also present.

Teagan turned the page yet again, the heavy sound of the old vellum whispering through the room. Then a spot of dark red ink on the lower left of the first page caught Ash's eye.

"Stop. Wait." His voice rustled through the room, freezing Teagan's hand just as she reached to turn the next page.

Sounding almost breathless, she said in a low voice, "What is it? This page looks just like the ones before it."

Ash felt the scars on the right side of his face pull as his excitement abruptly tightened across his muscles. Yes, to Teagan's eyes, the page looked like it simply held more tightly squeezed writing, with an intricate border bracketing each corner of each page.

But that was because she was human. To Ash's dragon-enhanced eyesight, which he knew would be slitting vertically because of the close presence of his dragon, which in turn made him very careful not to look directly at Teagan, he saw more. Gently rippling beneath the words, as if hidden beneath another translucent sheet that molded to every billow and wrinkle on the page, a scene played out. The figure of a man standing on a craggy mountain, arms lifted to the skies as if in supplication. In the distance behind him, dark figures barreled through the sky toward him.

Slightly above, the unmistakable figure of a dragon hovered in midair, its wings pinioning down, the spare lines on either side of him indicating the backdraft their movement created. The dragon's eyes glowed a rich emerald green as fire shot out of its mouth.

Yes. Ash felt the shock of actuality wash over him in a shivering, shimmering eddy that raced up and down his body much like his scales did when he was in his dragon form. For a stomach-dropping split second he feared he was close to shifting, but a quick check assured him that his dragon simply was excited by the possibility revealed in this plainest, simplest of old books.

Teagan moved very slightly on her feet as she leaned closer

to the page, obviously trying to understand what about it so entranced Ash. The spiced cream of her natural fragrance mingled with the mysterious allure of the book itself. Together, the scents enticed him with a dizzying intoxication. They went well together, he mused, casting a quick sideways glance at the stunning redhead beside him. She was frowning intensely at the book, her lips moving very slightly as she no doubt read the ancient Gaelic to herself. Her thick, shiny hair was smoothed behind her, caught at the nape of her neck with a large silver clasp.

The contented hum of his dragon gently chimed its way through Ash's senses at the sight of her so engrossed in the book. Her work clearly deeply intrigued her. And it fit her too, he thought, recalling the ferocious passion with which she had attacked him in the parking lot. The same passion with which she had touched him. She was fascinated by the ancient stories and people and events of ancient Ireland.

Just as he was.

Feeling the odd yet welcome tingle throughout his body that meant his dragon was still very alert and very content in this moment, Ash said, "Will you keep turning the pages, please?"

Teagan gave him a perplexed look, one of her thick eyebrows scrunched down over her eye. He simply peered down again, so she did too.

"I still don't know what you're looking for," she said, confusion lacing her voice as she did as he asked. "It's still just records of one long-lost small town—"

"There's more here for me," Ash heard himself saying. What the hell? It was almost as if he *wanted* to tell her that he could see more. That there was a deeper truth magically hidden beneath the words she could see.

Apparently, she intrigued his senses yet dulled his sensibility.

He firmly held back another overly revealing comment,

instead making himself examine the hidden underpinning of the page for the next image. Again the mountain was there, and the man standing atop it, but this time he was turned around, looking at the shapes that had been approaching behind him. They were now much closer, almost on top of him. Three large dragons, two with inky black hides and one flame red. Their expressions boded no good for the man on the mountain. On his other side, the other dragon that he'd been supplicating on the page before now spread its wings back in a stance that indicated attack mode.

This time, Ash noticed something new. Deep in the heart of the mountain, something very small faintly glowed. He couldn't make out what it was. Very interestingly, there was a faint tingle from the book that he could actually feel. It was similar to the power he could feel humming off the sword, although that was ten times stronger than this.

His excitement growing, he said in an urgent, clipped tone, "Turn the page."

This time, Teagan didn't protest, nor did she even give him a funny look. She carefully turned the heavy vellum page, revealing yet more closely packed script describing the endless details of the petals of a certain flower that grew on the slopes of the near hills in the early spring.

Yet Ash barely noticed what the words said. His eyes widened as his dragon reeled back in his head, the comforting hum suddenly splitting into something sharper. Something worried, and wary.

The hidden page beneath now displayed a bloodbath. The man on the mountain had his sword out, valiantly swinging it at one of the attacking black dragons while the other one was mid-dive, heading straight toward him. The red dragon that had come with the black ones streaked with deadly intention toward the other red one on the man's right. Deep within the mountain, the hidden object glowed more brightly, almost pulsating. Ash could see now that its glow was golden. Its shape was taking place, shadowy lines becoming more delineated.

It almost seemed as if it was a—

"Next page," he said, his voice curt now with trepidation.

Teagan, her hands now trembling as she seemed to catch his abrupt worry, turned the page. This time, Ash couldn't contain his sharp inhale as the scene beneath the words sprang into his view with an almost painful clarity.

The first black dragon attacking the man had been met by a deadly sword swing that had gutted the creature and left it tumbling wing over claw to the ground, its entrails spilling out behind, glistening in the air. The second black dragon had almost reached the man, its mouth opened wide as an enormous burst of jagged flame raged toward him.

In the sky above the man, the two crimson dragons had met in battle, all teeth and claws and flame and fury. Deep within the mountain, the glowing gold light had grown even brighter, pulsing in a rhythm Ash now realized was like the beating of a heart.

This time she didn't even have to ask. Carefully, hand still trembling even though she still frowned down at what he knew she could only see as cramped text, Teagan turned the next page. In this scene, Ash saw that both black dragons seemed to have been vanquished, the first one having fallen almost entirely out of sight, just its wingtips and claws and one final, angry blast of flame appearing from the bottom of the page. The other one also fell, blood flowing from the sword strike to its heart, although its eyes still blazed with bright fury as it plummeted from the sky. The two red dragons, however, were still locked in battle, fighting furiously in the air above the man's head. The man had staggered, dropping to one knee as he clearly struggled to stay upright.

What caught Ash's attention immediately and with the most impact, though, was the glow of the object hidden inside the dark mountain. It now took up enough space that it could be seen.

It was a dragon rune.

As the contents of the hidden page flared up, Ash actually jerked his head back. Teagan jumped slightly beside him, casting him another sidelong glance. He forced himself to breathe steadily, pushing himself to stay calm. Glowing so brightly the light seemed to jump off the page, the carefully stylized lines that made up the rune were sharply delineated.

The same unknown rune that appeared on the sword.

The image of the ancient Irish Gaelic inscription carved into his heavy old library doors flashed into his mind. *To find the key to a dragon's treasure / From the fiery mouth of the clouded mountain / The scorched carmine dragon must emerge / To battle in fearless resolution for his stolen gold / And to claim the heart of his eternal true mate.* The words had been emblazoned on his memory since he was a boy visiting the old Connolly estate in Ireland. As a grown man, he'd had the doors shipped to the United States, more for their historical value to his growing collection than from any belief in what was a silly old family superstition that the words on them were an oracle, meant for each descendant to puzzle over on his quest to find to his mate. Ash had always snorted at it. After he was burned, he ignored it. But at this moment, the shocking correlation made his entire body sizzle with epiphany.

The images in the book matched the oracle just as the rune in the book matched the one on the sword.

He felt abruptly light-headed, a wondrous spin of daring hope leaping through him. The vanilla bean scent of the old pages spiraled into the air to dance with the spiced cinnamon scent of the stunning woman beside him. Slowly, letting his dragon peer out of his eyes, he looked at Teagan.

She stared with a disconcerted expression at the very same page he looked at, her freckles standing out in sublime clarity against the paling of her skin. As if she'd seen something. No.

Impossible. Absolutely impossible. She couldn't—no, it simply couldn't be.

Then she shook her head, furiously blinking her eyes and even dragging the back of her gloved knuckles over them. As if to banish a vision she didn't believe. She laughed, somewhat unsteadily.

Ash's voice whipped out in his own startled shock. "Did you see something there, Teagan? Tell me." His voice sounded too loud in the stillness of the office. "What did you see?"

Teagan shook her head in disbelief, giving him a sheepish look. "Nothing, really. I thought I saw a glimmer on the page, which was kind of strange. But then look here."

She pointed to the upper left corner of the page. Ash let his sight refocus back to its usual human strength—which was to say, not nearly as keen as his dragon's—and looked again. Aha. A minuscule speck of colored ink, likely unintentionally sprinkled from a monk's errant quill that had been used on the previous page's artless rendering of one of the dubiously acclaimed near hills.

Ash relaxed as Teagan laughed self-consciously. "I'm not completely awake yet, I guess. And you're so interested in these pages I thought I saw something interesting, too." She shrugged, seeming somewhat abashed. "Sorry."

The moment lengthened, washing over Ash much as Teagan's scent did. His mind spun in different directions. The mysterious glowing rune. The unexpected tie between the book and the sword. His dragon's intense curiosity and greater flash of alertness in the presence of this book.

And then there was Teagan. The entire time he had been acutely aware of her presence beside him. Even as he mulled over the images and the meaning of the rune, his vivid aware-ness of the wildly sexy warrior queen just inches away from his side distracted him with the incredible pull he felt toward her.

Inside, Ash's dragon bugled with yet another burst of

possessiveness that sent more shockwaves through Ash. *To find the key to a dragon's treasure*, the words whispered through him.

In that instant, he simply committed the rune to memory, knowing that taking a photo of it would be useless since the image would not show up on an electronic device. Then, very gently, he reached out his hand over Teagan's fingers that nervously yet quietly drummed on the desk beside the book.

The movement stilled beneath his hand as she drew in a quick breath. Finally, she turned her head to look at him. He turned his to look back at her, realizing that less than a foot of space separated his mouth from hers. It was entirely possible she had the same thought, because that sweet rosy flush of color flooded her face again. A long beat that held an almost booming silence seemed to surround them.

Her eyes, velvety dark and questioning, met his. He realized she was only looking at his eyes, not the ruin of the right side of his face. But it wasn't in a way that said she was deliberately trying to avoid letting her gaze fall onto the scars. No, it was more that she simply saw *him*. She saw Ash, who he was, and that was all that mattered to her. *To find the key to a dragon's treasure.*

In a surging flash of confident hope, driven by his dragon's fearless assurance about her, Ash took the bold leap he once thought he never would again. Tempering a surge of desire, yet hearing it come out anyway in the deep register of his dragon underscoring his voice, he said, "Are you free tomorrow night, Teagan?"

She blinked back at him, clearly not having expected that. "I—yes?" Her full lips rounded the words in a way that had Ash forced his right hand to clench where he held it down by his side to that he didn't let his left hand travel up her arm to caress her smooth neck, her soft cheek.

"Good. I want to see you again. Properly. I'll pick you up at seven. I'll have Eamon get your address from you." In an even lower voice, he added, "We won't be out in public. That is something I do not do. But I want to see you dressed up, Teagan. Wear something that will take my breath away."

Her jaw slowly dropped as her eyes darkened even more. He didn't miss the pulse quickening in her throat, or the wave of returned desire he scented coming off of her.

Inside, his dragon bugled again with a proud insistence.

Ash let his hand slide off the back of hers as he forced himself to step away from her. She inhaled a long, unsteady breath as his fingers glided over the backs of her knuckles. Nodding at her, he quietly said, "Thank you for the work you're doing on the book, Teagan. You have no idea how important it is to me. And I hope you won't take it as being presumptuous of me," he added, perfectly aware that it was extremely presumptuous but he didn't care, "but I'll be requesting that Sebastian bumps this project up to the top of your list. You won't work on anything else until it's done."

With that, he glanced down at his watch. Damn it. He was about to be late for another practice session with Eamon. Yet it had been well worth it to spend the past moments in Teagan's presence. And, he thought with immense satisfaction as he looked at her stunning face, to have procured a date with her.

A *date*. Marveling at that fact, Ash just stared at her for a moment longer. He had all of tomorrow night to impress the hell out of this most fascinating and amazing woman, and he intended to make sure everything would be perfect for it. Because something deep inside told him that she was exceptionally important to him. So important that it terrified him. His dragon roared. Yes, yes. Teagan also was so important that he didn't dare ignore that again.

One way or another, he intended to find out what this woman meant to him. His dragon would never give him a moment's peace again if he didn't.

10

Savannah smacked Teagan's hand as she once again raised it up to her head, half in curiosity, half in abject terror of what her friend had done to her hair.

"For the last time, don't you dare touch it until I'm done. Don't touch it even then, because that will mess it up. I swear," Savannah said, making a tsking sound between her teeth, "you are the worst fidgeter ever. I almost poked out your eyeball when I was putting on the mascara."

Teagan groaned. "I can't believe I'm letting you do this to me. Mascara. Eyeshadow. And an upsweep, do-up, whatever it's called—"

"Updo," Savannah interjected, sounding exasperated. "Seriously."

"—updo," Teagan continued, literally sitting on her hands so they didn't reach up to her hair again without her permission. "I'm terrified of what I'm going to see when I look in the mirror. I never do this. This is crazy. He's not even going to recognize me," she ended, making a slightly horrified face.

With deep satisfaction in her voice, Savannah said, "Exactly, my dear. That is exactly the point. Okay, let's get you into your new dress. No!" she cried out when Teagan made as if to turn toward the mirror. "Not until you're totally ready. You need to see the finished product so you can be appropriately wowed by Auntie Savannah's mad makeover skillz."

Teagan gulped. Privately, that was exactly what she was afraid of. Auntie Savannah's mad makeover skillz. Obediently, she followed Savannah over to the closet without looking back at the mirror. Savannah had practically destroyed her closet, flinging pieces of clothing left and right onto Teagan's bed and chair in her room, much to the fascinated amusement of Mouser. He'd been having a grand time leaping after the flying blouses or skirts or dresses as they went sailing through the air while Savannah muttered about things being to dowdy, too big, too plain, or, Teagan's favorite, "What in god's name were you thinking, girl? This style went out about a decade ago."

The outfit Savannah finally had chosen was hanging on the inside of the closet door. Teagan's sister had bought it for her to celebrate her new job at the Center, but Teagan wore it only once, at the family dinner thrown in her honor before she left for L.A. She'd never worn it in public.

She'd definitely never worn it in front of a guy. Especially not a guy who interested her. A guy who'd been in her thoughts twenty-four-seven since the amazing morning yesterday that still stunned her every time she thought about it. Wow. How had her life turned around in less than a week so that she was suddenly going on a date with a guy who was like none she'd ever met before?

Eyes sparkling, Savannah ordered, "Strip. He'll be here in half an hour."

Stomach fluttering, Teagan obeyed. She stepped into the dress, pulling it up and allowing Savannah to zip it in the back and fuss over the fit. Teagan looked down at her chest. "You sure this looks okay? I don't really have that much down there to show off."

She heard Savannah's dangly earrings tinkle behind her as her friend probably shook her head. "Trust me, this dress was made for you. It doesn't matter if your assets up top are on the smaller side. You've got those sexy hips and a nice caboose, girl. I say work 'em." She smacked Teagan's butt, causing Teagan to gasp and then giggle. She had to admit it was fun having a friend like Savannah, who slowly but surely had been teaching Teagan to have more self-confidence.

Even so, this was an awful lot of confidence perfume she was going to have to wear tonight. At least Ash had said they would not be going out in public. Although she knew it was for him because he wasn't ready for it, she couldn't help also being relieved. Because this was showing off a lot of herself in this dress, which ended just above her knees, snugged close over her waist, then squashed her small boobs and almost gave her cleavage.

Cleavage. That was a word she'd never thought of about herself before, she thought with another nervous giggle.

"Shoes," Savannah ordered next, her hand coming out from behind Teagan to point at the cute low heels she'd picked out. Because Teagan was already six feet tall, she'd never seen the need to wear needle-thin stilettos that would make her tower even more above most men, not to mention probably make her trip and twist her ankle or crack her head open. But at least the shoes her sister had gotten to go with this outfit—which also had been worn only once—had only half-inch kitten heels. She should be able to walk in them and not fall on her face.

After she slipped them on, Savannah grabbed her hand and pulled her back to the mirror. Then she put her hands on Teagan's shoulders, grinned, and gently spun her around

Teagan gasped at the woman in the mirror looking back at her. A woman, definitely a woman. Her eyes looked smoky and alluring, like she'd never seen them before. Her mouth looked—she blushed as she thought it, but it was true—down-right kissable as they glistened light pink from the fancy gloss Savannah had applied. Her hair had been swept up and pinned into place with just a few tendrils coming down one side of her face. The diamond pendant and small diamond studs her parents had given to her as a gift when she graduated from college sparkled.

Then there was her body in the dress. Holy freaking crap. She was actually—

"Hot," she breathed in disbelief, still staring at her reflection. "I actually look kind of hot, Savannah."

Savannah tossed back her head, her laughter echoing in the room and making Mouser glance up from where he was delightedly kneading one of Teagan's sweaters on her bed while purring like a freight train. "Hell, yeah, you look hot, girl. That's the whole point. Sexy, mysterious billionaire asks you out on a date, you dress up for him and show yourself off. Besides," she added, squeezing Teagan's shoulders and dropping her chin down by Teagan's neck as she grinned back at her in the mirror, "you *are* hot, Teags. You've just never seen it about yourself. You're gorgeous and you don't know it." She smiled kindly. "Trust me, that's probably something he really appreciates about you, too."

"What do you mean?" Teagan spread her hands down the front of her dress as she stared, bemused, at what seemed to be the miles of her legs extending out from it. Wow. Who knew?

Savannah moved away to flop down in the easy chair in the corner of Teagan's room. "He's a billionaire. And you said he's one of Mr. Bernal's closest friends. They move in a different circle than we do. He was surrounded by gorgeous supermodels and socialites his whole life, oh, and wanna-be starlets, too. The type of women who knew they were gorgeous. Man, the photos were just sad sometimes. Desperate women clinging to him. You? You must be like a breath of fresh air to him."

Teagan paused in her nervous assessment of herself and looked over at Savannah. "Photos? What photos?"

Savannah rolled her eyes. "What, you thought I was gonna let you go out with someone I didn't check up on? I looked him up online, Teags. I also asked about him around the Center, too."

Teagan was horrified. "You did a—a background check on him?" Her cheeks heated.

Savannah sighed in exasperation. "Of course I did a background check on him! Hey, you're the one who thought he was going to smack you over the head and drag you off to his dirty basement to do evil things to you when he startled you in the parking lot that first night, remember? I needed to be certain that that wasn't his evil plan from the start. I knew you would never dream of checking up on him yourself, so I had to do it for you. Sword lessons are great, but you need more real world self-preservation skills," she added in a scolding tone.

Mouser meowed plaintively from the bed, his purr rumbling through his voice. Teagan went over to him, stroking his head and scratching under his chin, which intensified his purrs to practically the level of a jet plane rumbling through the air. She shook her head. "It never occurred to me to check up on him," she admitted.

Savannah snorted. "That's your sweet, naïve Midwestern upbringing talking. You need to be little more careful out here in the cutthroat City of Angels, girl."

Teagan nodded. Savannah was right, of course. But at the same time, she knew that wasn't the only reason she hadn't thought about it. Something deep inside her knew she could trust Ash. Without a doubt. Believing that wasn't just simple naïveté, either.

Although it might seem dumb to think it, every fiber of her being told her that Ash Connolly would never hurt her. In fact, she somehow sensed that he would protect her with his life if necessary.

Okay, okay that sounded pretty dramatic. But deep in her heart, she still knew it was true.

Was this some sort of love at first sight thing? Teagan lightly shivered just thinking about it. Probably not her luck, but who knew. Her life had taken a decidedly odd turn. Right now, she was just going with it all.

Savannah's face became somber, "And then there was the accident."

Teagan bit her lip as she thought of Ash's face. "I didn't ask him what happened." Her voice was quiet.

"Of course you didn't. That would be rude, and you're too nice for that. I looked up what happened." Savannah shook her her head, her face bleak for a moment. "It was a car crash. Horrible. He was lucky to get out alive. The news stories said he was burned really badly, but there never were any photos." She shrugged. "Obviously, he just locked himself away so no one would ever see him again. I can't really blame the guy," she added sympathetically.

Teagan nodded as she thought of the hard, brittle mask that so easily dropped over Ash each time she'd made him feel uncomfortable. She understood the desire to hide from people, to never again let them see one's face. It was an easy out.

"Oh, crud, the time." Savannah jumped up from the chair and hurried over to Teagan. Reaching out to hold her shoulders again, she looked very seriously into Teagan's eyes. "I've got to go, he'll be here soon and I know he won't want anyone to be here except you. Now," she said firmly, "listen to me. Auntie Savannah knows what's what. From everything I heard, I'm pretty sure he's totally fine and is not going to dismember you into twenty-five pieces and scatter them in the Angeles National Forest."

Teagan snorted a half giggle.

"But," Savannah continued, holding up a warning finger as she narrowed her eyes. "You let him know that I know you're going out with him, that your phone has a tracking app in it, and I'll be tracking it the whole time. And that I expect you to call me at the end of the night. If I don't hear from you, I'll be calling the police and letting them know exactly where you are. Damn straight I will. And they will handcuff his ass and drag him off to the slammer. And hopefully they'll rescue you in time before he makes you into a skin suit or something like that."

"Savannah!" Teagan protested, still half giggling. "You said he's safe."

Savannah shook her head, smiling now. "He is, I'm sure of it. But I'm just looking out for you, my sweet Midwestern friend. Now, for the fun part." Her eyes sparkled in that slightly devious way. "When you're ready to get down and dirty with mister mysterious sexypants and start ripping off one another's clothes—"

"Oh, my god," Teagan said, the giggles immediately dying. She stared at Savannah, utterly aghast.

Savannah took one hand off of Teagan's shoulder to gently shake a finger in her face. "No matter what he says, you're the one who calls the shots."

At the thought of Ash and ripping off clothes and the implications therein, Teagan felt scorching heat slam through her entire body. From the way Savannah gently smiled as she started to shake her head, Teagan knew she had turned the color of an overly ripe tomato.

"Honey," Savannah said gently, "just remember it's only if you want it. If you're not ready, that's okay. Got it?"

Teagan swallowed. This sounded suspiciously like a lecture. One very similar to the slightly red-faced yet quite firm lecture she got from her mother back when she was in high school. In fact...

"Oh, my god," she said again, this time in a whisper. "You know, don't you?"

Savannah's smile wasn't remotely pitying, only understanding. "That you're a virgin? Yeah, I kind of suspected it. Either that, or you'd had some sort of horribly fumbling first experience years ago and not much else. But it's definitely that you're a virgin, huh?"

Feeling abruptly miserable, Teagan nodded.

"Hey." Savannah leaned in to give Teagan a light, quick hug, then stepped back. "Trust me, I understand. I have to admit that most of the biggest academic geeks I know were the same. Late to the sexy times game. Including," she added an arch tone as she started to walk out of the bedroom after glancing at her watch again, "me."

Startled, Teagan followed her out. The unaccustomed sound of her heels clicking on hardwood floors echoed, followed by a light thump as Mouser jumped off the bed and followed them in what he probably hoped was the direction of the kitchen.

"You?" She stared at her definitely sexy and self-possessed friend, who had her own hot date that night and was dressed for it.

Savannah nodded as she gathered up her purse and cute jacket from where she'd dropped them on the small side table next to the door. "One and the same. I didn't discover my powers as a woman until I was halfway through grad school and dressed up as a sexy witch for Halloween on a dare from my roommate. Man, I just destroyed the boys in my department that night. Destroyed them. Took the cutest one straight home and had my wicked way with him. Even though it wasn't the best night ever since it was my first time and all that, it was a heck of a lot more fun than I'd thought I could ever have with a guy. I learned a lot since then." That devilish glint came back into her eyes as she winked at Teagan. "Ever since, I've cut a swath of longing and heartbreak through the academic world."

Savannah burst into laughter at her own words almost at the same time Teagan did. They laughed together for a good long minute. After they were done, Savannah smiled in satisfaction as she shrugged on her coat and reached for the door handle. "Excellent. Laughter is good for the soul. Feel more relaxed now?"

Somewhat surprised, Teagan nodded. "Actually, yes. Thanks, Sav," she added, giving her friend a genuine smile. If it weren't for Savannah, she'd likely be going on the date dressed in sweats with her hair braided behind her.

Savannah just blew her a kiss, smiled again, and left.

Now all Teagan had to do was wait. For her date. With Ash. The most amazing, gorgeous, sexy, fascinating man she'd ever met.

The man she somehow knew was the most important person in her life she'd ever meet, even though she still had no clue why.

11

As Ash maneuvered his volcano red Aston Martin Vanquish through the winding streets leading to Teagan's house, he had to smile as he heard the engine purr when he shifted the gears. He'd stood in his garage for many long minutes earlier in the evening, debating which car to take to impress his warrior queen date. Having once been a gentlemanly yet dedicated tomcat—his dragon rumbled at that, though it was only a light snort at the mild insult—who liked to impress the ladies, Ash still possessed several ridiculously overpriced but thoroughly kickass cars. After he'd gotten over the worst of his injuries and could drive again, he'd first had Eamon get all the windows tinted as dark as was legally allowed in the state. Then he'd taken to going on long solo drives with no particular destination, either up the curvy mountain roads or northward along the spectacular coastline, exorcising his personal demons as he drove fast and played loud music.

The Aston Martin, though, he hadn't driven since before the accident. The small, sexy, low-slung sports car had been one of his favorites, but after a single outing when he was first able to start driving again, he'd put it back in the garage and hadn't touched it since. The memories of a more glittering time in his life had hit him too hard, and he had been too aggrieved to take it out again.

Rather, it was that he'd been too hurt, he admitted now as he sat in the custom leather seat and stroked the wheel. Eamon had kept the beautiful vehicle in excellent running condition, for which Ash was now grateful.

Tonight, however, was different. Oh, it wouldn't be quite like it was in the old days. Those were over and he knew it. Besides, as he'd stood next to Teagan yesterday morning in the stillness of the office at the Center, letting her scent suffuse him as they bent their heads together over the ancient book and tried to puzzle out its secrets, it also hit him hard that he didn't want another male on the planet to look at her and see the same intoxicating beauty he did. He wasn't about to let another man go out with her. More importantly, he had no desire to even consider going out with any other woman.

The existence of the stunning Teagan Lambert easily made him push aside all thoughts of any other woman in the world.

Letting the car slide to a smooth, easy idle at a light, he snorted at himself. Not that any other woman would even look twice at him anymore. But that wasn't the point. Those days were over not only because of the scars, but because of Teagan. Something hot and warm bloomed in his chest, sending an excitement and vibrancy through him he hadn't felt in a long time. Laying his arm on the open left window of the car, letting the warm evening air come in and touch his skin, he breathed in the night and smiled. It felt damn good to be going out again. Especially when he knew he was about to end up on the doorstep of a most incredible woman.

"Incoming call from Eamon the All-Knowing," the soothing voice of his phone told him via the car's speakers. Grinning, Ash replied, "Answer." He'd had a lot of fun programming all of his friends' numbers with playful monikers. "I'm on my way to pick her up right now," he said when the call connected. "Is everything ready?"

"Yes, of course," Eamon answered. Ash's grin turned even bigger. Of course he expected Eamon would have everything under control. It would not be like his fealty man not to. But then Eamon's tone changed, setting the little hairs along Ash's body, where he still had the nerve endings to feel them, to an uneasy attention. "I just received a call from the auction house."

The internationally famed auction house from which Ash gathered much of his personal collection had two façades. One was a very human one, which dealt in human artifacts and was open to the public. But the other one, the one Ash used more often, dealt primarily in shifter artifacts. One of the major dealers on the hidden shifter side of the auction house had Eamon's number on speed dial since Ash bought so much from them. Anyone who knew about dragon shifters and fealty families would know that Eamon worked for Ash, so it would be no secret that any dealings Eamon had with the house most likely meant that Ash Connolly was the buyer. But only the house itself would know, since Ash always bid privately. His acquisition of artifacts from them was not open knowledge to either the human or dragon shifter public.

Eamon's contact always got a hold of him when something interesting came in. But he would never call this late in the evening, well after regular business hours, without a damned good reason.

Ash instinctively knew something was wrong.

"What is it?" he asked, hearing the sudden grim snap of his voice. His dragon, already aroused by his nearly constant thoughts of Teagan, snorted a muffled warning roar as Ash's thoughts abruptly turned to the sword and both books.

Eamon's somber tones made a shiver of dread ruffle along Ash's spine. "Apparently, someone has decided to nose around your recent acquisitions from the house. A man called there earlier today. He said he's in search of a rare manuscript known as," Eamon paused for an agonizingly long moment, *"The Book of the Dragonborn."*

Ash's skin tingled even more. His foot twitched on the gas pedal, causing the Vanquish to emit its own roar as it briefly throttled up.

"He claims he's in the middle of a research project." Eamon's disapproving tone conveyed what he thought of that flimsy cover story. "Says he wants to be able to get in touch with the new owner so he may study the book himself, if possible."

There was a dark silence as Ash began snaking along the winding streets to the address Eamon had given him earlier. He could hear low background music and the bustle of preparations for his evening with Teagan as he thought about the shady underground world of dragon shifter antiquities trading. Dragons valued their gold hoards above almost anything else, since their power was inextricably linked to their glittering collection of riches. Even in modern times, fighting, treachery, and outright theft were very common. Some of the less upstanding citizens of the dragon shifter world always attempt to wrest power and strength from others by amassing more gold in ways that were illegal by any standpoint.

Ash drummed his fingers on the steering wheel as he turned up another street and then slowed, looking for the front house that sat in front of Teagan's place. The worry in Eamon's voice and his own return concern were for the same reason. If someone was looking for the ancient Gaelic text of *The Book of the Dragonborn,* it was for only one reason. The book was utterly obscure as far as the human world were concerned, and few in the dragon shifter world knew about its existence either.

For someone to be seeking it meant they'd done some historical research and had found the name of that book as being one holding some shifter magic power. Power that would increase any other dragon's hoard. They didn't know that the

Dragonborn book was merely a fancy masquerade for the other book with real power, but they knew it existed. That was bad news. For someone to inquire about both the book and the sword at the same time meant that they knew of their existence. That they understood their inherent power.

This was a direct threat against Ash's own powers.

It was clear to him he needed the sword if he were ever to regain more of his old powers, even though it didn't seem to be responding quite yet to his touch. And while *The Book of the Dragonborn* appeared to be the proxy dupe for the far more significant *Book of the Near Hills*, the former was potentially just as important to him. The books could be magically linked in a way they simply had yet to discover. He couldn't afford to lose any of the objects. Not if he were ever to have a chance of regaining his own powers to a greater degree.

Not if he were again to be more of the strong, whole man he wished Teagan to know. Although he would admit it to no one else living, seeing her right now was an epic feat for him. It was only the certainty that his scars did not horrify or disgust her that had let him even entertain seeing her on a formal thing like a date. That, and the insistence of his dragon that she was an exquisite treasure to be guarded from all others.

"Very well," he said as he cut the engine and sat in the car for a brief moment in front of the charming little back bungalow in which Teagan lived. "A dragon forewarned is a dragon forearmed." His own dragon's warning rumbled out in his tone as he spoke. "Thank you, Eamon. Keep me posted. We should be there in about twenty minutes," he added, deliberately shrugging off the thoughts of underhanded dragon dealings and refocusing on the sublime redheaded woman he was about to see again.

Eamon's own tone lightened in return. "I should certainly hope so. You wouldn't want to keep one of the best chefs in the country waiting."

Ash managed to chuckle as they disconnected. One thing

at a time. Right now, that thing was the stunning, mysteriously alluring Teagan Lambert. Feeling simultaneously soothed and energized at the thought of seeing her within mere seconds, he strode up to the little door and knocked firmly.

She immediately opened the door. Ash immediately lost his ability to speak. A sky blue dress, short but still tastefully elegant, hugged the sweet hips Ash longed to grasp with his hands, cinched snugly around her waist, molded against the breasts he longed to reach out and touch to discover their softness. Her legs, long, shapely, and strong, flashed through his head as being tightly wrapped around his waist. A soft white jacket draped over otherwise bare, soft shoulders. The fickle fall weather had turned its usual warm again, meaning the evening temperature was pleasant.

By the care she had taken making up her face and doing her hair, he was immensely glad he'd worn a nice suit. For a long moment, he abruptly wished he had the strength of self to take this stunning woman publicly out on the town, proudly giving her his arm while making sure all the attention went to her deserved beauty instead of his own shockingly beastly appearance. Yet he had to admit he wasn't quite ready for that. His dragon huffed in his mind, but Ash couldn't quite tell if it was in agreement or denial. Besides, Teagan didn't seem the sort who wanted to flash herself about in public either. Although he didn't know why, since she was so damned intelligent, strong, and beautiful. She should attack the world like a warrior queen she was, he thought, still drinking her in with an almost dazed admiration.

But that didn't matter right now. What mattered was that he had an entire evening with this woman and her agile mind, her stunning body, and hopefully many chances to hear the gorgeous burst of her laughter.

Finally managing to compose himself, he managed to speak. "You look absolutely stunning, Teagan." He extended his arm to her. With a quick grin to ease the slightly awkward moment, he said, "Would you care to be my date this evening?"

She seemed as struck dumb as he had been. But she nodded, stepping forward and putting her right hand on his proffered left arm. Briefly turning her head back to the house, she called out, "Behave, Mouser," before looking back to Ash and nodding at him with a small smile.

He raised his eyebrows at her. "I certainly hope that's a pet and not a child with a horribly unfortunate name."

There. There was the quick smile, the burst of unrestrained laughter that he'd wanted to hear. Her face opened with it, unaffected and stunningly beautiful. Good. So far, the evening was off to an excellent start.

"My cat." She smiled fondly. "He doesn't approve of me being gone a lot, so he lets me know about his displeasure by playing with a shoe and leaving it destroyed on the living room floor, or knocking the napkins off the table. Naughty stuff like that." Checking that her door was locked before she firmly pulled it shut behind them, she added, "He'll probably be really mad at me tonight. I'm almost never out on weekend nights, so he'll probably think I've abandoned him." Sunset hues abruptly blossomed in her face, making those beautiful freckles burst out even more. "Wow, way to go, Teagan," she stammered. "Now you know I don't have much of a life outside of work."

She worried her lower lip between her teeth, nearly causing Ash to stumble at her completely unrealized eroticism of the motion. "On the contrary," he said, turning his head to look at her with what he knew was a glint of major appreciation in his eyes. "I like knowing that. What it means is there's no one else I'll need to fight for you."

She blinked at him, her color deepening even as a faint smile touched her lips. "Oh. Um, thank you."

Ash smiled as he escorted her to his car. He'd wait to tell her that it wouldn't have mattered even if she'd had any other men in her life. He cheerfully would have fought and beaten each one for the privilege of spending exclusive time with her.

Although her eyes widened at the obvious luxuriousness of his Vanquish, she clearly strove to play it cool as she let him open her door and gently close behind her after she slid into the passenger seat. When he got into the driver's seat and turned on the engine, his only worry was that the ruined right side of his face would be on display for Teagan the entire way. It was only a ten-minute drive from her house to their destination, but he knew it would feel much longer.

His dragon rumbled at him. Ash forced himself to take a deep breath. This woman had already accepted him up until this point. He owed it to her to trust she wasn't suddenly going to change her mind. Looking at her, he relaxed. She wasn't looking at his scars. She was casting him sideways glances, yes, but not the type that meant someone was getting a good look at his ravaged face while trying not to be caught staring. No, Teagan glanced at him just as a nervous first date would.

His dragon bugled with a quiet triumph. Yes. This was a real date, indeed.

During the brief drive, they chatted companionably. It was as if they'd known each other their whole lives. His dragon snorted, the sound seeming somewhat exasperated, but Ash pushed it aside. He could only deal with one thing at a time. Right now, all he could grapple with was the fact that he was taking beautiful Teagan, stunning warrior woman, on a date.

That, and the growing knowledge that despite the easiness between them, an undeniable frisson of attraction sizzled and sparked as well. He caught her once or twice glancing at him with an expression that straddled the line between sensuous and skittish. Each time she caught him catching her, the color notched up in her face, and she swiftly blurted out something about the passing scenery.

When they pulled up to their destination, Teagan fell utterly silent as she stared at the small yet über-hip facade of the building. A single doorman waited, immediately heading to the passenger side to open Teagan's door. As Ash exited his side, he exchanged a brief nod with the doorman, who was a member of the fealty family who served the owner of this exclusive, trendy restaurant.

A restaurant of which Ash had paid the owner, also a close friend, a hefty sum for him and Teagan to be the only patrons for the night. Everyone working in there this evening was from a fealty family that worked for either the owner or one of Ash's own family, and Ash knew each one. It was still hard for him to let them see him so close up, even though they'd each seen him at some family functions after he'd been burned.

But for the chance to spend an evening with Teagan Lambert and hopefully impress the hell out of her, he'd already realized he was willing to be on display at least this much.

Teagan, who'd somewhat awkwardly accepted the hand of the doorman to help her out of the low-slung car, stood staring at the restaurant's sign above the entrance that stated with subdued class, ALCHEMY. This was one of the hottest spots in the city, due to both its stellar menu and its movie star owner, who occasionally graced the dining room with his mega-wattage presence. Ty wouldn't be here tonight, but he'd been more than amenable to Ash renting the place out in order to woo a girl. "'Bout damn time," his famous friend had muttered over the phone last night when Ash had called in his big favor. "For you, I'll even put up with my manager bitching and moaning about the canceled reservations she'll have to soothe and cajole into coming back with the carrot of some free stuff thrown in for their next meal there."

Teagan nibbled her lower lip as she took in the name of the place. "Alchemy?" she said, sounding a little confused. "Is this a restaurant?"

"Yes," Ash said, gently guiding her in behind the doorman, who'd hurried ahead to open the large glass door for them. "It's very good, too. This is a famous one, owned by a famous friend."

She glanced at him as they stepped inside, nervously raising her eyebrows. "Famous?"

Ash tossed her an easy grin. "Yes. Ty is one of my oldest friends. You've probably heard of him. Typhon Kade."

"Oh. Um, wow." Ty was famous enough for even a driven academic like Teagan to have heard of. He saw her eyes widen a bit, but she just nodded. She might be taking it all in stride. Or perhaps he was overdoing it? Before he could think more on it, though, she gave him a tentative look.

"I thought you didn't want to go out in public?" She was so breathtaking in that sexy outfit, he could hardly center his thoughts.

He smiled again as they entered the main dining area. "I don't. And we didn't." He gestured around the place, which was utterly empty with the exception of the doorman, who'd stayed outside to stand guard and graciously yet firmly turn away any hopefuls who tried to get a seat for the night. He knew Eamon and the chef's staff were all still bustling around inside the kitchen. "For tonight, it's all just for us. For you," he added softly.

She stared around the open, empty dining room, her brown eyes wide as she realized what he was saying. "You...there's no one else here tonight?" She blinked as she stared. "The whole restaurant is closed just for us?"

"Just for you, Teagan," he said with such emphasis that her gaze snapped back to him. He almost groaned at the sweetness of her lips, the smoothness of her skin. "Now then," he added after another long moment filled with that crackling electricity between them. "Let me treat you to the amazing evening you deserve."

12

Teagan felt like an ugly duckling firmly set down in the midst of the palace of a glorious, gold-plated swan. This place was the swankiest restaurant she had ever been in. It didn't boast chandeliers or butlers wearing long tails or anything like that, no. The place was instead totally hip, from its cute tables to its sleek wood floors to the exceedingly well-stocked bar that ran the entire length of the room. But it still screamed money.

Lots and lots of money.

Then again, since it was owned by a bona fide movie star, she supposed it had to scream money. She swallowed down her nerves. Even she had heard of sexy ladies' man Typhon Kade. Savannah liked to swoon over his picture every time she logged into some Hollywood apps she had loaded on her phone, and she sometimes regaled Teagan with his latest exploits involving this or that starlet. Besides, he'd starred as an ancient Viking warrior storming the shores of Ireland in that one movie Teagan had watched, um, a dozen or so times. She might know nothing else of pop culture, but she did know who he was.

She had to admit, deep down beneath her very slightly

snobby academic side, she was sort of fangirl impressed that a superstar of his stature was an actual friend of Ash's. This definitely was a whole different level than she was used to. Taking a deep breath, she walked inside, giving the sexy man beside her another sidelong glance as they walked toward a set table near the windows. It was one thing to have been at his mansion and recognized that both it and his collection of rare books were worth fortunes. That didn't actually faze her all that much, considering that she was surrounded by hundreds of millions of dollars' worth of priceless books and artwork every single day at work.

But him picking her up in a super-fancy sports car, then casually telling her he was friends with one of the world's biggest movie stars? Yeah, no. That was another thing entirely. She was definitely awed. This was not the circle she moved in. Ever. At all.

While Ash pulled out her chair for her, she gave him a suitably wide-eyed look. "Okay. Wow. You can get one of Hollywood's most famous actors to close down his entire restaurant for you on a moment's notice? Okay, fine. I'm impressed." She felt her lips curve into a smile. Wait, was she flirting with him? Huh. She was. Maybe Savannah was right. A makeover did wonders for a woman's self-esteem. She felt sort of bold. Almost kind of close to confident.

As she seated herself, Ash leaned in close enough that his mouth was by her ear. "I simply want you to enjoy your evening." The velvet darkness of his voice rolled over her senses. Little goosebumps shivered along her skin as the delicious fluttering somewhere south of her stomach tightened in what seemed like anticipation.

As he walked around the table to his chair, he let his left hand do a lingering slide over her shoulder, across the bare skin below the back of her neck, to the end of her other shoulder. The goose bumps turned into an outright flock of geese dancing down her arm, then fluttering wildly across her entire body. She swallowed hard, watching as he seated himself. She knew he still was keeping the left side of his body angled toward her, but she honestly didn't care anymore. Yes, her very first glimpse of his face that night in the parking lot had startled the heck out of her. Of course it had, because her nerves had already been ratcheted up high by the misinterpreted danger she thought she'd sensed. Now, though? Now, even though she saw the melted scars on the right side of his face, the shiny patches of burned skin on the back of his right hand, burns that she suspected might even cover the entire right side of his body, they truly didn't bother her.

Which was kind of crazy, considering she'd only had two real interactions with the man so far. Just like she'd thought to herself when Savannah had jokingly warned her about the possibility of his being a serial killer, she knew that not only did she genuinely trust him, but also that she had been allowed what she suspected were rare glimpses into the real man beneath the awful scars.

That man was stunning, fascinating, and definitely more sexy than anything a marred exterior package might otherwise suggest. His easy smile had a lightness in it that made his gorgeous face shine in a way that tripped up Teagan's heart. Just looking at his rusty-brown hair, those deep green eyes that sucked her in each time, the light scruff of beard that still made her want to rub her face against it, all made her feel sort floaty. Tingly, and super aware of her body. For some reason she still didn't understand, she felt incredibly—comfortable with him. Familiar. As if she'd already known him forever.

"What do you think of the view?" Ash gestured toward the wall of windows.

She'd been so engrossed in the overall atmosphere of the room that she hadn't paid much attention to the view outside. When she looked, she gasped. The city spread out below them, a rumpled blanket of black sprinkled with an outrageous abundance of sparkling lights. "Wow," she breathed again. She really needed to step up her vocabulary around this man. "It reminds me of the country, like the farm my grandmother grew up on," she said slowly. "Way out there, on a night with a new moon and far away from the lights of people. But this is even better because it *is* the big city. Also because you brought me here to see it with you," she added somewhat shyly, glancing at him again.

He smiled at her, the bright pinpoints of jade in the deeper forest green of his eyes seeming to heat her from the inside. He drew breath as if to answer her, then paused as he glanced behind her. "What has the chef prepared for us tonight, Eamon?"

Swiveling around, Teagan was pleased to see that it was indeed the same Eamon who worked for him. She'd really liked him. He gave her a courteous bow, nodding with equal gravity at Ash. "A feast. You'll begin with mini sweet peppers that are filled with lightly herbed goat cheese and roasted asparagus."

Teagan's jaw unhinged slightly even as her stomach told her that sounded amazing. Hoping the faint growling from it couldn't be heard by either one of them, she just nodded.

"Then," Eamon continued in an unruffled tone, "comes the main course, which tonight is a pan-seared duck breast accompanied by creamy truffled polenta, lightly roasted black salsify, and pears and grapes draped in a green peppercorn sauce. To balance the meal," he added with a definite sparkle in his eye, "we have a crisp sauvignon blanc crafted by one of the top vineyards in Italy. It's a vintage that should be excellent on the palate."

Teagan couldn't help the small moan that escaped her as Eamon finished. "I didn't understand half of what you said," she admitted, "but it all sounds absolutely amazing." Even though it probably wasn't the cool thing to say, she couldn't help adding, "I'm starving."

She looked back at Ash, ready to laugh away her gaucheness with a nervous giggle and some explanation about how lunch had been too long ago, which was true. But the words died in her throat as she saw the expression on his face. Dark, hungry, focused solely on her. A taut, delicious silence stretched out before he quietly said, "Thank you, Eamon. We will enjoy the wine to begin."

Even though it was super classy, this whole being treated like a princess in a fancy restaurant thing, Teagan barely noticed Eamon's murmured "As you wish," then the light pad of his footsteps as he retreated. All she was aware of was the dark intensity of Ash's gaze.

She shifted on her chair, which caused one of those small spasms between her legs that let her know things down there were ready to go. Whoa, okay, then. She reached for her glass of water and took a long drink. It was mostly to settle her nerves, but also so that she had something to do with her hands and mouth. Otherwise, she was half afraid she'd either say something that was more intimate than called for during dinner, or worse yet, try again to touch the man in front of her.

Because for some reason, he just begged to be touched by her seemingly crazy hands.

Ash's mouth curved up in a slow smile filled with promise and knowing. Well, crap. Her expression must be giving away the somewhat salacious direction of her thoughts. Her face heated. And now she had to be a dead giveaway to him. Yet she didn't want to hide herself from him. He looked at her not as if he needed to ignore her freckles, no. He looked at her as if he thought they were actually beautiful.

As if he thought *she* was actually beautiful.

Ash seemed about to speak, but then Eamon quietly returned, easily and gracefully carrying a tray with a bottle of white wine, two glasses, and a corkscrew. He deftly set everything on the table with a practiced flick of his wrist.

Raising her eyebrows, slightly desperate to start a casual conversation that could lighten the suddenly intense moment and the physical feelings running amuck inside her, Teagan said, "Is there anything you can't do, Eamon? You manage Ash's house and everything for him, you also understand ancient Gaelic, and you know how to do this sort of thing, too?" She gestured at the wine, the beautiful set table, the entire situation here. "I've met the assistants of other collectors before. You go about a hundred miles above and beyond any of them."

Ash and Eamon exchanged a quick look she didn't miss. As Eamon expertly pulled the cork from a bottle, poured a small taste, and handed it to Ash, he gave her an unperturbed nod. "My family has served the Connolly family for centuries. An unbroken line that can be traced back for a thousand years. It's a family tradition of which we are very proud."

Teagan's eyebrows just about hit her hairline. "A thousand years, really? You're a genealogist as well?" She let her nervousness blend with her excitement into a babble. "Oh, my mother would love to meet you. She's traced the lineage on her side really far back, too. She's really into it and has helped me with my own work sometimes. Although we weren't very grand, my family, I mean. There were a lot of peasants in my family tree." She said that a touch self-consciously. It was hard not to, surrounded as she was by every obvious trapping of Ash's immense wealth.

Ash, however, was quick to interject. His smile warmed her inside and out. Especially, uh, yeah. That one spot between her legs that was still tingling. "On the contrary. The people who were neither royalty nor learned helped create the history of their countries on their backs due to the literal blood, sweat, and tears of their labors. Having a working-class background is something to be equally proud of, Teagan."

She blinked at him. Uh, okay. Was he the perfect guy, or what?

Ash nodded approval to Eamon after the wine apparently met with some exacting standard or other, given the way he sniffed and swished and tasted. That, at least, didn't faze

Teagan. She'd been to hundreds if not thousands of academic gatherings over her lifetime, and wine tasting was part and parcel of many of them. She relaxed somewhat.

After Eamon handed her glass to her with a courtly flourish, she graciously inclined her head at him, then took a deliberately long, slightly ostentatious sniff of her wine as well. "There's a nice complexity of kiwi and passionfruit," she said as casually as she could. "Some flinty hints of lemongrass and maybe gooseberry. All very nicely balanced, though. I might have a lot of common blood," she smiled at the obvious surprise on their faces, "and I suppose it is something to be proud of. But I've also been exposed to a lot of wine in my lifetime, so I picked up a couple things here and there. This vintage is an excellent choice for impressing me." She let a mischievous grin dance on her lips.

Flirting, it turned out, was pretty fun.

Ash burst out into equally delighted laughter, joined by Eamon's more decorous but just as approving smile. "That was unexpected. You are quite the treasure, Teagan." A bare whisper of a sensuous interest underlying Ash's voice tugged at Teagan's senses and made that spot between her legs go into little mini-explosions of tingles again.

Oh, jeez. She worked hard to keep her face impassive, but she knew it flamed again with color.

"Indeed she is," Eamon agreed, paying attention to the bottle of wine as he nestled it back into a stylish little silver bucket filled with sparkling ice cubes. "I'll be back in a few minutes with the appetizer." He quietly left, but Teagan thought she caught a pleased expression on his face.

Ash eyed Teagan now with some speculation. "So. You actually know more about me than I know about you. I would really enjoy hearing more details about your life." The intensity of his green-eyed gaze told her he meant it.

Feeling a little flustered again, Teagan took a long moment

to savor another luxurious sip of the wine. It was so superb, she couldn't help another small moan.

Across the table, Ash's hand convulsively tightened on his own glass. "Careful there." His low, dark voice blazed along her nerves with a bolt of eroticism that startled her. "'That's your second moan so far and we haven't even begun our meal. It's giving me ideas."

Teagan snapped her eyes open, almost choking on the wine. Ash's eyes were deadly serious. "Oh. I didn't mean to, ah, create other ideas in you." Her nervousness abruptly returned in full force.

"Oh, but you have. You have, Teagan." Her name was a whisper on his lips.

The air between them coiled with a sensual attention that really took Teagan's breath away. Their gazes locked across the table. She could virtually feel the sizzle spark between them. So this was what real attraction felt like, she thought somewhere in the very back of her brain. This was what the books and the movies all meant. Sure, she had had a few crushes in her life, and yes indeed, one or two very fumbling, brief encounters before. But they all paled into insignificance in the face of the enormous depth of feeling racing through her now.

She suddenly imagined that her moans came from tasting him. Tasting Ash with her mouth, her lips, her tongue. Drinking him rather than this wine. Holy freaking whoa.

He leaned slightly across the table, an intent look on his face as the bright pinpoints of light in his eyes added an almost tantalizing gleam to them. His thick index finger circled around of his wineglass, tracing it with such a delicate certainty that Teagan's face flamed so hot she put the backs of her hands against her cheeks to cool them.

What would that finger feel like, swirling around her flesh?

She thought her face might be about to burst into literal flame.

His expression said he knew exactly what she was thinking. "I definitely planned to enjoy this meal with you," he said, not taking his gaze from hers. "Now I suspect I'll enjoy it far more than I thought."

Teagan swallowed against the dryness in her mouth, managing a tiny nod, hands still against her cheeks. She didn't trust her voice or her words right now.

Ash suddenly grinned, sitting back and breaking the nearly unbearable intensity of the spell between them. But the heat in his eyes still slid up against her, warm and inviting. "You were about to tell me more about yourself before I distracted you." The wicked tilt of his lips told her how much he'd enjoyed that distraction. "Please, go on."

Teagan removed her hands from her face and wrapped one around her wine glass instead, willing it to stay steady. Waiting until she was sure she could speak without her voice coming out a croak, she finally said, "All right. What exactly would you like to know?"

After a low, thoughtful humming sound in his throat, Ash spread his hands out to either side. "Everything, Teagan," he said simply. "I want to know everything about you."

Apparently he wasn't going to beat around the bush. Lightly clearing her throat, Teagan took another sip the incredible wine before she started. "Well, I'm not sure how much there is to know, actually. I grew up in a small college town in Illinois." She smiled, relaxing more as she thought of her cozy, safe hometown. "My parents were professors at the local college. I have one sister, and several cousins living nearby we grew up with. We're all pretty close. No pets, though. Dad's allergic." She heard the old tinge of childhood sadness in her voice at that and laughed.

Ash didn't take his gaze from her, although she thought his eyes might be sparkling even more. "I see. So Mouser was your first rebellion against your sadly petless upbringing?" Laughter edged his words.

Teagan managed to chuckle in return, feeling herself relax

again. She found herself stupidly happy that he'd remembered Mouser's name. "I suppose. I got him while I still lived in Illinois, after I moved out of my parents' house when I graduated from grad school. I stayed with them till then because it was cheaper." She shrugged. "Once my unpaid slave labor"—she smiled at her joke—"at the museum turned into a paid internship, I could afford to move in with my sister and one of her friends. Her roommate had a cat, so me bringing home a kitten wasn't a big deal."

He smiled at her, nodding a thank you to Eamon who appeared with the appetizers.

"Ah. The feast begins," Ash said. This time, she caught another bit of intensity from him, but it felt different now. One that almost bordered on—a hint of unsureness?

She smiled back at him a little uncertainly herself, waiting for Eamon to place her plate in front of her. When she took her first bite of the whatever-it-had-been, peppers with goat cheese or something, she did it again. She moaned out loud. As soon as she could politely do so, she burst out, "Oh, my god, this is so good. Thank you so much for this, Ash." Okay, yes, it was another gauche response, but she didn't care. This food was darned good, and she wasn't fancy enough to be casual about it.

Ash smiled. Sitting back in his seat, a quick flash of relief crossed his features, rippling over the one side and moving more slowly across the burned side.

Oh. Right. He was relieved that she liked their date. He really did want to impress her. Maybe he was actually a little nervous, too. He just hid it better than she did. Well, then. She kind of liked that. Digging into the fancy meal, she decided to just totally relax and enjoy herself, as well as this spectacular, fascinating, mysterious man.

"Your turn," she said, gently bumping her chin toward him. "Tell me about you and your background."

"Hmm." He let the dubious hum linger, causing her to

smile again. Now he was playing with her. She liked this date more and more with each passing second.

Reaching out to gracefully stab a small red pepper with his fork, he raised his eyebrows at her and said, "I was born with a silver...fork in my mouth." He popped the pepper into his mouth with the fork, wagging his eyebrows up and down at Teagan as she gaped at him for a moment.

Then she laughed, totally delighted. He had such a great sense of humor. It still amazed her that she was on a date with such a sexy man. One who was gorgeous, rich, and funny. And, she could tell simply from being around him, from seeing how he treated Eamon, or the doorman, he was kind. Ash was a kind man. Although, she thought more speculatively, he was also a hurting one. Almost unaware, she let her fingers drift up to her throat for a moment, splaying them over her freckles. His gaze moved there. She froze her hand.

He swallowed, took another sip of the wine. The levity had dropped away from him again. Very quietly, he said, "Move your hand, Teagan. Your freckles are beautiful. They are a very intriguing part of you."

Teagan looked at him. The sincerity in his voice was unequivocal. Heart thumping out of control, she very slowly peeled her protective hand away from her throat. Ash's smoky green gaze darkened, even as the odd little flecks of emerald in them brightened. Teagan felt something emanating from him, strong and sure. Powerful. It was something she couldn't quite understand, but she knew one thing.

Something deep and true zinged hard between them. Something incredibly real.

Guided by that funny depth of knowing she'd felt around him almost since they'd met, she carefully, deliberately looked at his scars. Ash caught her gaze and reflexively winced. He drew his head back, stiffening. Teagan sensed his protective mask of indifference begin to shutter down over him. Suddenly almost angry, she shook her head. "Don't do that."

Her words came so quickly she had no time to censor them. She sharply inhaled at her own vehemence.

Ash seemed just as surprised. He cocked his head to the side, automatically angling the right side away from her. The funny little wave of anger blew over Teagan again. "Stop it," she said softly. "Don't hide from me. Not before we even really know each other."

The light in his eyes flared brighter. It was totally weird, and also totally cool. And it didn't scare her at all. "I'm not hiding." His tone was so defensive that Teagan almost snorted out a little laugh, but she caught herself. Instead, she swerved the subject a little.

"What—what do you see when you look at me?" she asked in direct, if somewhat shaky, honesty. It was a little terrifying, but she had a point she wanted to get across.

The gorgeous, haunted man seated across from her stared, momentarily caught off guard. But he promptly answered, "I see a beautiful woman. No," he corrected himself, "a stunningly beautiful woman. One who doesn't realize it. One who believes her freckles are what people see first about her, rather than the beauty that is truly inside and out." His voice was quiet but firm.

She let the old smack of pain, the pain that agreed with his last sentence, whack into her. She let herself feel its old, nasty tentacles. Then she shook them off. "And I see a man, an amazing gorgeous man, who thinks his scars are what people first see about him."

Shadowed green eyes held hers, not letting up. She almost thought she could hear her own heartbeat. Or his. "It sucks, doesn't it," she whispered through a throat that suddenly felt tight. "Having people look at your face and make a judgement right away. A decision about who they think you are, even though they don't have the first clue about you. Even though they don't know a single thing about you."

A thunderous silence wrapped around them. Teagan felt

stark naked as Ash looked at her like he could see right through her, even though she knew she was looking at him the exact same way. It was so quiet she could hear the murmur of voices and low clangs from the kitchen area.

Finally, not taking his gaze from hers, Ash said in a low, rough voice, "Then it's a good thing you and I both understand what that's like. Because I do see a lot more to you, Teagan. A hell of a lot more. And..."

His pause was long enough, his face open enough, that she could see how hard it was for him to continue. His expression see-sawed back and forth between unease, defiance, and stark doubt. What she liked most, she realized with an internal jolt as she sat very still, waiting for him to go on, was that she could see those emotions at all. He was letting his mask drop and stay dropped. For her.

Finally, he sighed, as if in relief. "I'm glad you can see more to me than just a burned, scarred man. It means more than I can express."

She nodded, fingers tight on the stem of her wineglass. "I know," she whispered.

Another beat, his eyes searching hers. "It was an accident. My getting burned." His voice was slightly hesitant, but his gaze didn't waver. "I know you probably wondered why. Everyone does."

Teagan stared at him, her heart simultaneously breaking and expanding so much she thought it might explode. "What I thought was that it was none of my business," she whispered back. "My friend looked it up, and told me what happened." She swallowed hard at his slight flinch. "But it's your story to share with me if you want. I already know everything I need to know about you, Ash. You just showed me, right now. And that's enough for me."

It was so quiet it seemed loud, like glass chiming or the air itself breathing with heavy pressure. Teagan stared back at

Ash and his dark forest eyes with those fascinating bright points of green in them shining through.

"Thank you," he finally whispered.

Slowly, the silence loosened into something comforting. Relaxed. Still charged with intensity, but a strong, shared, safe intensity. Teagan breathed, just watching Ash watching her.

He shook his head, as if to clear his thoughts, then smiled at her. "Well, then." He voice had the smallest hint of a ragged edge. "I am very glad you agreed to come to dinner with me, Teagan Lambert. Now. Shall we continue to enjoy every moment of it?"

Smiling back at him, feeling a bright, bold wave of confidence crash over her and seem to wash her clean of doubts and fears, Teagan nodded back. She definitely wanted to enjoy every darned minute of her time with this stunning man.

This stunning man who tugged at her heart in a way she'd never thought possible.

13

Ash felt both immense satisfaction and immense relief as they left the restaurant. He'd wowed her. He also, he had to admit, had been utterly wowed by her as well. More than that, he'd been slain by her. He'd been opened by her. This woman was beyond remarkable. She was a treasure he hadn't known he needed.

Once they were back inside the Vanquish, Teagan stroked the buttery soft leather seats, a smile on her face making her already luscious lips all the more enticing. Then she took a breath, started to speak, stopped, and took another breath.

Ash steered the sleek car out of the circular drive, nodding a thank you toward Eamon from where he stood to see them off. Glancing at Teagan, he firmly said, "Whatever it is, say it. Dinner wasn't good enough?" He made his tone teasing. He watched with appreciation as the smile spread on her succulent mouth. "You're upset there was no background music? Ah," he snapped his fingers with one hand, "I know. I wasn't enough of a gentleman."

There. Once again, the rich peal of her laughter filled the car. That made Ash smile like a ridiculously puffed up peacock. He was the one responsible for that amazing sound. He liked that. A lot.

Teagan shook her head, a smile still lighting her features. "No, it's been an amazing evening. The best one of my life," she added, tossing a quick, more serious look at him. Shyness edged her expression now as she watched him to see what his reaction would be.

He nodded back just as seriously. "You might not believe me, Teagan," he said quietly, "but it was the same for me. However, that's not what you wanted to tell me, was it?"

He adored the sweet flush on her face as she admitted, "No, that wasn't what I wanted to say. Just—ah, this is going to sound pathetic and geeky." She flapped her hands, drawing his attention to her long fingers. As his mind imagined them touching him, he firmly directed himself to focus on something else. Anything else, before he entirely threw caution to the wind and pulled her body to his.

Teagan lightly cleared her throat and went on. "The wine is making me do it." Her flush was deeper now. She rushed out her next words. "It's just that—a week ago I didn't know you existed, and now," she paused again. This time, her hands nervously drummed on her thighs.

Ash let the car idle in the driveway before turning into the street. Knowing no one was trying to get out behind them, Ash took a bold chance. Reaching out to her chin with his fingers, he gently turned her head toward him. He skin was unbearably soft. So tempting. Chocolate dark eyes met his. "And now?" he said quietly, holding her gaze fast with his.

She swallowed again. Softly, the words tumbled out of her mouth. "And now, there's one person in the world who can make me feel so special. So interesting, even fascinating." Her pulse beat in her neck. "In a way that no one ever has before," she whispered.

Ash shook his head at her, feeling wonderment spread throughout him. "It should never have been a question of how fascinating you are, Teagan." His dragon rumbled beneath his tone, lending an even deeper quality to his voice. "The true fascination for me is how you've made me feel. Alive again. And attractive to a stunning woman," he said, his voice barely a murmur now, but rich enough to fill the car. "I haven't felt like that since before this happened." Taking another risk, he gestured to the burned side of his face.

"I can hardly believe that." Clear honesty shone in Teagan's eyes, her voice. "You're the sexiest man I've ever met. Even scarred," she whispered, letting her gaze touch on his burns for a moment. She looked back into his eyes.

Ash believed her. The delicious tension between them coiled, thick with energy and sensuality. Tamping down the side of him that basically wanted to ravish the hell out of her sweet curves, bury his face into her to pull in her wildly compelling scent right this second, he forced himself to behave like a gentleman instead. He just smiled, letting a slight hum of appreciation vibrate in his throat, then deliberately turned his attention back to the road as he eased the Vanquish onto the street.

They chatted lightly on the drive back to Teagan's house, which Ash made as long and scenic as he could by taking winding side streets and back routes he knew. When finally they reached her place again, though, the sight of her long legs as he helped her out of the car cracked at his control just a bit. That, and the dark pool of desire in her eyes as he quietly walked her to her door.

"Ash," she said when they reached it, stopping and turning to him. Her face was nervous, curious, hopeful, and just so damn sexy.

He reached his hand out to touch her cheek, then slowly stroked it down to her neck. Keeping his gaze on hers, he canted his palm just to the side of her neck, threading his fingers through the silky mass of her fiery hair. Gently, he tipped her head toward his. Pausing for the briefest second, giving her an out should she suddenly change her mind, he looked at her. Teagan nodded, seeming to barely breathe. Ash needed no further invitation, finally claiming her luscious mouth with his own.

A small sound vibrated from her lips to his, heightening the tension and excitement. Ash feasted on her mouth, reveling in the soft plumpness of her lips, the cinnamon spice scent that flooded him. Inside, his dragon bugled in joy, echoing the sheer masculine pride that swept Ash as this breathtaking woman allowed him to kiss her. After long, sultry moments of moving his lips over hers, he delved into her mouth with his tongue. Her right hand slipped up, curving over his shoulder and wrapping around the back of his neck. Her left hand traced his collarbone through his shirt.

Ash sucked in a harsh breath at the tingling bolts that raced over him as she touched his body. Her left hand moved over the burn on the right side of his neck. He stiffened, stilling completely as she touched the scar on the right side of his neck. He still had enough sensation there to know she explored with gentle fingers.

She paused. "Is this okay?" Her voice was a hesitant whisper against his mouth. Not waiting for him to answer, she lightly butterflied her fingers up his neck and onto his cheek, reminiscent of how she'd touched him in the library the second time they'd met.

He groaned against her. She touched him not in curiosity, but simply in the way a woman touched a man who was kissing her. She didn't care that he was burned. Teagan honestly accepted him the way he was.

"It's more than okay." His voice came out as a growl against her mouth. "I crave your touch. I've been longing to feel your hands on me again ever since the library."

The look in her eyes was no longer tentative. Instead, it was dead certain. "Me, too," she whispered, sliding her fingers over his cheek, then cupping his face both her hands. This time she sought his mouth with hers. Ash murmured with approval, his dragon roaring inside his head. Teagan's soft, pliable lips moved against his mouth even as her hands spread to the back of his head and gently pushed him closer to her.

After another long, singing moment of kissing her, Ash silently swore at himself. He knew he wouldn't let himself go inside with her. Despite Teagan's height, her strength, her fearlessness with her sword, there still existed an overall guilelessness to her, a hesitance that made him want to move slowly. He wasn't about to rush things with the first woman he'd kissed in a very long time.

The first woman, he realized with a stunning thunderclap of recognition, he'd truly *wanted* to kiss in an even longer time.

He simply allowed himself to enjoy the silken brush of Teagan's mouth, feel the fire that whipped through his veins and stiffened his cock. His entire body trembled in sheer excitement. Finally, slowly, he pulled back, difficult as that was. Her eyes, which had been closed, slowly fluttered open. Their chocolate depths now looked like black espresso with slight hints of caramel. He realized it was her arousal that darkened her eyes.

His fierce warrior queen indeed.

She sighed in pleasure. "That was really nice." The words were firm. Certain. A lingering coil of that dark arousal wound through them.

Ash felt his chest swell. He had created that in her. That arousal he sensed smoldering beneath the surface. He knew his sudden deep attention showed in his expression as that sweet rosy flush he so enjoyed seeing fanned over her face. Reaching out a forefinger, he gently circled a large cluster of her freckles, once again marveling at how exquisitely beautiful she was. "I enjoyed this evening more than you can know," he said, his voice low. The stark sincerity of his voice made her eyes widen. "But I'm going to leave now, and let you wonder just how much better this evening could have been."

Teagan's pulse fluttered wildly in her throat as her gorgeous mouth opened, the spike in her pheromones tickling at Ash's senses.

"This way," he said with a lazy smile, "I'm pretty sure that when I ask you out again, you'll say yes right away."

After she swallowed, a smile of quiet delight broke across her features. In a surprisingly firm voice, she said, "I like that plan. You're onto something there." Her voice turned more serious as her eyes searched his. "This has been the most amazing night of my life, Ash. No man has ever treated me like this. Like I'm special." Her voice was soft.

Ash growled deep in his throat. "Then no other man has ever really seen what a stunning catch you are, Teagan. They've all been fools." He almost startled himself with his own vehemence. "This is how you should be treated every day for the rest your life. Like the incredibly deserving woman you are."

She stared at him, suddenly looking a touch doubtful again. Ah, she was so unaware of how gorgeous she was. He found that almost as appealing as the intensity of her beauty. Actually, he realized, his dragon rumbling in pleased fashion inside him, he found it even more appealing. Teagan Lambert was the most genuine woman he'd ever had the pleasure of getting to know.

He planned to get to know her far better.

As if caught in a spell, they stared at one another, the silence lending even more weight to Ash's words. Finally, she shook her head and blinked, as if to break it. "I've got a lot going on at work next week," she said in a soft voice. "Long hours, day and night. But I'll have your book finished by Friday."

Ash nodded. "I know you will. You're very dedicated to your job." Abruptly, he caught her hands, brought them to his mouth, and grazed the knuckles with a kiss. Her sharp inhale gratified him as he straightened up again.

"Good night, Teagan. I'll call you again very soon." Forcing himself to turn and leave, he'd barely gone two strides when her voice stopped him.

"The answer is yes, by the way."

Startled, he swung back around to look back at her. She faced him directly, her chin tilted up a bit, her eyes sparkling. "Yes?" he said, drawing the word out a bit as he wondered what she would say.

She nodded once, decisively. The motion set tendrils of coppery red hair whispering along her cheeks. "When you ask me out again. The answer is yes." A ridiculously big smile spread across her face.

Ash heard the deep bass of his dragon in his voice as he replied. "I'll very much look forward to it."

He could see her pulse hammering in her throat. "Good night," she breathed, one hand gently coming to her throat, as if to calm herself, before he once again turned and walked away.

This time, though, Ash had a huge smile on his face as well. Two weeks ago, he'd never heard of Teagan Lambert. Tonight, he knew something deep down inside him without a shred of doubt.

Teagan, the beautiful, powerful, strong, fascinating modern warrior woman, was his mate.

She was his *mate*.

And he would do everything in his power to prove to her that he was worthy enough to call her his.

14

Teagan floated into work with a stupid, silly grin she couldn't get rid of. She smiled an exuberant greeting at everyone she saw, flinging out *Good mornings!* and *How are yous?* with wild abandon. Most people responded politely, some of them giving her slightly puzzled looks. She wasn't exactly a social butterfly here. They probably wondered what she'd had to drink that morning, or if she was a brand-new employee they'd never before seen.

She didn't care. She, Teagan Lambert, was on the highest high she'd ever felt in her entire life, and nothing but nothing could wipe it away. The memory of Ash's lips on hers, his big, strong hands sliding around her hips, curving over her back, pressing her close to him, had stayed with her during the restless hour it took to fall asleep last night. The memories had been there first thing this morning when she opened her eyes, causing a blushing pleasure that surrounded her in a glow of happiness. Even Mouser had seemed to notice her ridiculously cheerful mood, glancing up at her several times while eating his breakfast and purring with abandon..

The only thing that was too bad, she thought as she

entered her office and lightly dropped her satchel at her work-station, was that Savannah was out of town for a few days on a business trip to San Diego. Teagan had texted her last night, a simple *You are a genius! Project Teagan Makeover was magical. He's the most amazing man I've ever met. Tell you more when you're back.* Naturally, Savannah had responded with an excited flurry of texts, the gist of them being *Told ya you're a knockout bombshell, about time you realized it. Go git you that sexy man.*

Teagan's smile stayed on her lips throughout the day, even through the long in-service training her entire department had to attend in one of the conference rooms. Even though it kept her away from working more on Ash's book, and even though the speaker was fairly dry and droned on a little too much, she allowed nothing to punctuate her happy bubble. Not even Celia, who cast her several perplexed, probing looks throughout the day. Even when once one in passing Celia hissed at her, "Don't smile so much. It makes your poor face blotches stand out even more," it honestly didn't affect Teagan. She simply returned a peaceful smile and whispered back, "That's okay. My freckles are beautiful."

She turned away after the satisfying moment of seeing Celia's jaw drop in total shock. That's right, her freckles were beautiful. Ash's voice, his hands, his mouth, the genuine way he'd looked at her had shown her that he really and truly liked her and found her freckles beautiful. She believed it. His kiss stayed branded on her lips the entire day, and a sad little person like Celia couldn't take that away from her.

Ash texted her just before lunch. *I can't get you out of my mind. Very much looking forward to seeing you again soon.* The simple words sent Teagan's heart soaring and her mind to wandering again. She got through the day on a cloud of excitement, smiling at everyone she saw.

After work, Teagan drove straight to the Institute for class.

She floated through the class as well, parrying every thrust by her opponents with grace and elegance. Well, okay, not quite grace and elegance. She still face-planted a few times, once tumbling over her feet as she was outmaneuvered. Even so, the instructor, Nick, nodded approvingly at her, a funny little smile on his face. Heck, if she could get the hang of this sword-fighting thing, and also be kissed by a guy as amazing as Ash Connolly, maybe she was finally getting the hang of this life thing. She basked in that happy little dream all the way home after class.

Not long after she walked in the door, Ash called her. "So how is the warrior queen tonight?" His deep voice sent shivers rocketing throughout Teagan's body.

"Warrior queen?" She laughed, feeling slightly giddy. "I'm definitely the farthest thing there is from a warrior queen." As she spoke, she pictured fierce Queen Boudica. She hadn't yet told Ash about her secret idol. She wasn't quite ready to completely embarrass herself around him.

A rumbling chuckle rolled out through the phone, setting her nerve endings aflame and ratcheting up sweet shivers through her body. "That night in the parking lot. You were a warrior queen facing me down. You were terrified, Teagan, but at the same time you were fearless."

"Oh. Um. Okay, thank you." Her face heated with the pleasure of being complimented.

She could almost sense Ash's smile through the phone, but he changed the subject without missing a beat, asking how her day went. They settled into conversation as easily as they'd had at dinner the night before. Teagan found herself smiling again at how familiar he seemed, how easy it was to talk to him.

Just at the end, before they said good night, his words sent another delicious shivered tingling through her. "That kiss was the most delightful way for our evening to end last night, Teagan. I intend to make it happen again very soon."

She nodded like an idiot before remembering he couldn't see her. "Yes. Yes, I'd like that very much."

"Good." That dark, sensuous zip rolled through his voice. "I'll be thinking about your gorgeous mouth till then, Teagan. And that beautiful laugh of yours."

"My laugh?"

"Your laugh. It's beautiful, strong, bursting out loud with exuberance." She heard the sincerity in his voice. "You're not self-conscious about it. I lo—I enjoy hearing it."

A very slight pause held them after his slightly stumbled words. Had he been about to say he...loved her laugh?

Quickly, smoothly, Ash said, "Until tomorrow, Teagan." Despite the little stumble, there was no mistaking the erotic promise in his voice.

Blushing from her hair roots to her toenails, Teagan managed to wish him a good night. She spent yet another restless hour before she could finally fall asleep, but in the morning she felt refreshed and eager to tackle the day, even though she still had to attend the in-service all day, although thankfully this time it featured a different speaker.

Once again, Teagan floated through the day with thoughts of Ash highlighted in her mind. Even so, she did her best to focus on the details of what they were learning in the training. She decided to be the slightly bold one today and texted Ash during the midmorning break. By the time her phone buzzed with the returning text about twenty minutes later, she was back in her seat in the conference room studiously taking notes. She slipped out her phone to look at it, then almost gasped out loud.

My dreams last night were about you. Detailed dreams. So detailed that I've been tempted all morning to go get you out of your training and keep kissing you senseless.

Oh, hello, instant tingling bomb of feelings exploding inside her. Teagan could barely focus for the next several moments, so completely stunned and dazed did she feel. Also, um, lusty. Yeah, lusty. And did she mention, very lusty? Finally she managed to drag her attention back to the training to get through the rest of the day, though her face stayed deliciously heated for long minutes.

As soon as the work day was over, she raced home to feed herself and Mouser and take a quick shower. Feeling refreshed, she headed right back to the Center. She was geeky enough to enjoy in-services and trainings, but they did take away from her core work. She had a lot to catch up on now. When she got settled back in her workspace, the long table covered with her restoration instruments, she gave a small sigh of contentment at the sight of Ash's books. She'd carried *The Book of the Near Hills* back here herself after Ash's surprise visit to Mr. Bernal's office the other morning—which now seemed like a century ago—and left it carefully nestled on its stand. The other tome, romantically titled *The Book of the Dragonborn*, had been waiting for her on its own stand, ready for her to take a closer look at what it might need in the way of repairs.

She caught her breath, newly amazed and quietly proud at the thought that Ash had entrusted not just one but two of his prized ancient manuscripts to her for repair. She wouldn't let him down. She'd do the best repairs in the history of book conservators.

Carefully, she busied herself with the light, the tools she planned to use, and of course her favorite music tracks to play through a small desktop speaker she used when nobody else was around. She was ready for a long night, but the memory of getting kissed almost breathless by a man with chestnut hair and forest green eyes as well as the knowledge that she would be working on his books kept her more than energized.

Had she already mentioned that she felt a little lusty? Smiling a silly little smile, Teagan let her cheeks flame away. No one else was here to see it happen.

A few long, painstaking hours later, she finished the

minuscule repairs to the last page she and Ash had looked at the other morning. She'd closely examined the tiny slash of crimson ink left in the corner of one page, trying to determine if it was original and could be left alone, or if it was from some later careless reader and needed attention. That nervous flutter tickled across her mind again as she remembered how she'd thought the ink drop had actually glimmered up at her for a second. Muttering a low "hmm" at herself, she blew out a self-deprecating breath. Being around Ash fried her brain and made her think she saw things. He excited her so much that her strictly-trained scholar brain went all softly romantic and imaginative.

She smiled suddenly, feeling that dreamy sensation tingle through her. Okay, fine. Having a romantic brain was fun. For now, though, she had to focus on work. Shaking out her hands, she stretched, took a sip of water from the spill-proof container sitting on the desk, glanced at the clock on the wall, then bent her head back down to look closely as she kept gently leafing through the book to see what new repairs awaited her.

The rustle of the heavy page turning whispered through the silent air during a break between music tracks. The next sound she heard was her own voice shouting, "Holy crap!"

In the ancient, dryly textual book before her, the page abruptly displayed an incredible scene filled with vibrant, colorful drama that seemed to leap up at her.

A black mountain, smoking and dripping with red lava, almost seemed to thrust the scent of brimstone into her nostrils. Her eyes were drawn to the figure of a man on the mountaintop, dropped to his knees, shoulders bowed under what seemed an unimaginable weight and hollowness that hurt her heart. Up in the right corner of the image, a reddish-gold dragon tumbled through the air, the right side of its body a charred mass even as defiance glowed out of one eye and his left wing futilely beat in an attempt keep him from falling. Above that dragon, another large, black one spread its wings in victory, head flung back, smoke drifting from its nostrils, its mouth open in a fearsome grimace. Angry shots of flame roared from its mouth, tracking after the path of the falling red dragon.

Teagan's shocked gaze snapped to the center of the black mountain. Something warm and bright, almost hopeful, gleamed from deep within it. Was it a—rune? Maybe, though it was hazy and hard to tell. It had a golden light that made her think, for some bizarre reason, of love. Yet a dark shadow trickled over that light, threatening to obliterate it.

What the actual freaking crazy heck was going on? She blinked her eyes, hard. Then again, and again. Abruptly, the pages showed only dark, cramped text, like every other page that she'd carefully flipped through when she first received it.

Exactly. Because there were no images in this book. None. No paintings, no drawings. The entire book contained nothing but text. She knew that for a fact, she'd even logged it as such before she began work on it.

Very carefully, she blinked again. The vibrant painting leapt up at her again, filled with color and life and definitely real. Teagan literally jumped back, as if the painting had reared up and smacked her.

"Holy freaking crap on a stick." Her voice loudly echoed in her own ears as the next music track suddenly began. She jumped, startled, then reached out to turn off the mini speaker. Then she stared down at the book again.

Yes. The painting was still there. Carefully, her hand trembling, she reached out a gloved finger to very lightly touch the page. She didn't quite dare touch it with her bare finger, since the natural oils of her skin would cause more damage to the pages, but even through the glove she could feel the texture of beautiful heavy vellum.

Vellum that was as clean and untorn as it would have been the day this book had been made, nearly a thousand years ago.

Teagan blinked again, about ten times in a row. The painting stayed.

Okay. She had to be overtired. That was it, right? No, couldn't be. She'd gotten enough sleep the night before, and it was barely nine p.m. right now. Perhaps she was on some sort of candid camera, a terrible prank show? She cast a paranoid glance around the room before she managed to laugh at herself.

Okay, no. That was just as ridiculous as—as seeing a painting appear in a book that had had none there before. Closing her eyes, opening them again, she stared down at the undeniably real painting on the undeniably fresh paper that looked like it had never had any need for a conservator's healing hand.

If Savannah were here, Teagan would have called her right now to be talked her down off the ledge of insanity on which she apparently perched. But Savannah wasn't here. There was no one else Teagan trusted enough to share this crazy experience.

Except maybe there was.

Something told Teagan that Ash wouldn't laugh at her. He wouldn't think she was crazy. There was even a remote chance he knew what was happening here. After all, it was his book. He must have known something about it, wanted something from it, to go to the trouble of bidding and paying for it in the first place. n fact, when he was in here the other day looking at it in Sebastian's office, wouldn't he have—

Teagan suddenly went very still as the memory of that morning meeting washed over her again. Ash had looked at the book with an intensity so deep it had almost alarmed her. She'd assumed he'd simply been reading something in the text that meant something to him, but...

What if he, too, had seen pictures? He might have thought *he* was the insane one. He wouldn't have wanted to say that to her. Teagan scrubbed the back of her hand over her eyes, willing away any errant tiredness that might have influenced what she'd thought she'd seen. Or maybe she'd just watched too many movies, read too many books, about the ancient myths and legends of Ireland. Her imagination was finally getting the better of her, sent into overdrive by the white hot kiss by the very man who owned the book.

Either way, she wanted to talk to him about it. Right now. Before she could talk herself out of it, she picked up her phone and called Ash.

He answered almost immediately, pleasure deepening his voice. "Teagan. It's very nice to hear—"

"I need to see you," she rudely interrupted, hearing the unsteadiness in her own voice. An uneven, ragged edge that said she might be hovering right on the brink of serious crazy town. "Right now. I have to talk to you about something. Something that hopefully won't make you think I'm crazy. Because I think I might be crazy. But I hope I'm not." Right, babbling. Cut to the chase. "May I come over?"

His voice immediately filled with a low, dangerous concern. "What's wrong? Are you okay?"

Despite her worry about her sanity, she couldn't help but feel a blast of very feminine pleasure at the sound of his deep voice as well as his instant protectiveness. "I'm fine. Well, I think so. Well, I'm not sure. But I want to talk to you about something. About your book. I think there's something sort of —strange about it."

The silence on the other end of the line was deep and long enough that she ventured an uncertain, "Ash? Are you still there?"

There was another beat before he answered. "Yes. I'm here. Why don't I come to you, though," he began, the edge of that dangerous *something* still in his voice, but she interrupted him again.

"No, I'll come to you. I just—I need to get out of here."

The barest pause, then, "Very well. And Teagan—" He

paused for a very long moment before his next words shook her even more. "No, you're not crazy. I can assure you of that."

Teagan stared at her phone for more long seconds, even after she heard the empty air that meant he'd hung up.

Okay. Right. He knew something. So she wasn't crazy. Win, right? Teagan cast a long look at *The Book of the Near Hills,* trying to control her trembling. She briefly glanced at Ash's other book, the far more beautifully intact and valuable *The Book of the Dragonborn,* also sitting on her desk, still waiting to be worked on. Oh, god. Did it have moving pictures in it, too?

Nope. She wasn't going to look. She was just going to flee for now. Flee to see Ash. Swallowing hard, she forced herself to take a few deep breaths. She was fine. Everything was going to be okay.

Flipping out the lights as she left the room, she turned the corner around the door and almost collided with a small figure. Celia, just walking in. "Oh, I'm so sorry." Teagan offered a somewhat apologetic smile as Celia stepped around her. Her mind still whirled, but she did her best to make her expression bland rather than give away the wild spinning of her thoughts.

Naturally, Celia couldn't let the moment go by without a dig. "I thought you were behind on your work, weren't you? But you're already going home?" She shook her head in mock concern, obviously ignoring the fact that it was already past nine p.m. "You can't lose pace here. They don't reward slackers at a company like this." Celia's smile dripped with saccharine sweetness, but a hint of ugliness beneath it made Teagan bite the inside of her lip. For some reason, the woman's usual nastiness seemed even more pronounced. Teagan pulled her jacket around her more tightly. Her confidence from yesterday seemed to be wavering.

"I'm tired after the training," she hedged, sidling out the door. "I'd prefer to get a fresh start tomorrow." Prompted by a quick stab of her old feelings of inferiority, for some stupid reason wanting to prove to Celia that she was indeed working on projects, she gestured vaguely in the direction of her desk in the workroom. "I have another book right there that my client is waiting for me to start working on, see? I just want to begin it after I get some sleep." Okay, why was she explaining herself to this woman? Time to toughen up and just go. She pasted on a bright smile, still edging toward the hallway and escape.

Celia's mouth barely stretched into a tight, mocking little smile as she gave Teagan an epically disdainful look that really should be patented. Mean Girl's Kill-You-Dead Stare, or something like that. "Well, if that's what you think you need to do." Her voice singsonged a bit as she glanced toward their work stations. "As for myself, I'm beginning a brand new project. Tonight," she emphasized, as if trying to show that she was a much more dedicated employee than the apparently slothful Teagan. "A big one I just landed. I intend to go very, very far in my career. I guess you just don't have the same goals," she finished with a little sigh as she shook her head.

Teagan swallowed her sigh. No, dang it. She wasn't going to rise to the bait. She just wanted to get to Ash's house, have him tell her in person that she wasn't crazy, and not have to deal with any more drama tonight. By sheer force of will, she merely smiled, wished Celia good luck and good night, then turned and fled down the hallway to her car without looking back. Even so, she could feel small eyes boring into her back as she hurried away.

As she drove away from the Center, Teagan threw off thoughts of mean coworkers and office politics and the possibility of her impending insanity. Instead, her pulse quickened with something a lot more exciting. She was about to go see drop-dead sexy, intriguing, and amazingly good kisser Ash Connolly again. Ash, who rocked her world, who made her believe in something amazing, who somehow touched her very soul. In person.

This time, she meant to get some answers. Maybe, the

thought tickled at her, making her shift a bit as she drove because of the abruptly heavy, sweet pressure between her legs, she'd also get another kiss. Or even more. Swallowing hard at the dirty direction of her thoughts, she drove as fast as she dared to his house.

15

Ash restlessly paced his house, waiting for Teagan. His wire-tight nerves twanged at him. He strode up and down the main hallway by the front door, letting the ceaseless movement soothe his equally restless, agitated dragon. Red-gold wings stretched out in his mind, the one strong and sure, the other contorted and weaker.

Taking a breath, Ash continued pacing to burn off his troubled energy. Before Teagan had called him so unexpectedly, he'd been in his training room, practicing with the sword of his ancestors. It still refused to unlock its secrets to him, stubbornly holding onto the potent magic he sensed hidden deep within it. The golden runes etched into its silver blade taunted him with their familiarity, their meaning stubbornly just out of his grasp. He'd been heading back into the main house when Teagan called. Quickly setting the sword down on a random nearby table the second he'd heard her tense voice, at first he'd wanted to recklessly leap into his car and drive like a madman straight for her, protecting her from whatever danger she feared. But when he realized she must have seen the images in the book, he'd frozen in place, unsure of how to handle it. She would have to know the truth. He could never lie to that incredible woman who was his mate.

He simply hoped she didn't flee in abject dread and shock when he told her. He had to admit he was also very interested in knowing *why* she was able to see what had to be the images in the book. Those images should be invisible to any human eyes. Teagan Lambert, amazing as she was, was quite definitely human.

The second she knocked and Ash opened his door, his dragon bugled in sheer male possessiveness. This was his mate. *His.* Struggling briefly to keep his dragon in check, Ash took the moment to drink in the sight of the gorgeous woman on his doorstep. The woman he'd kissed till they'd been almost out of breath the other night, until she'd been shaking with arousal. Frankly, she seemed to be doing the same thing right now—remembering the kiss. A sweet, rosy flush spread on her face, her own interest in him broadcasting loud and clear to his dragon senses. There was also an underlying hint of nervousness that set him on edge, making him feel protective. He scanned the outside as he let her in, but of course nothing was out there other than the quiet of wealthy suburbia. It was just her nerves, the rational part of himself knew, which came from her wondering about what on earth was going on. Firmly closing the door, he automatically checked the wards. Nothing was amiss outside. He and his mate were perfectly safe.

"Did you give Eamon the night off?" Teagan cast a glance at Ash, a hesitant smile tipping up her lush lips. "I thought he would be the one answering your door."

Ash smiled back. "Eamon is with his lady love tonight. He won't be back until the morning." As they walked, he let his hand rest on the small of her back, reveling in the warmth and strength he felt emanating from her body. Also harshly willing his cock not to spring to life, eager and unrestrained, much as it seemed to want to do around his flame-haired, beautiful warrior queen.

"Go ahead," he said softly. "I know you have questions."

Teagan gave him a long look, catching her lower lip between her teeth. She seemed slightly skittish, like a half-wild animal that wasn't sure it could trust him. Ash's dragon huffed and murmured in his mind, completely focused on Teagan. On not scaring her. The longing to sweep her up into his arms for another soul-spinning kiss was close to overwhelming, but first things first. He had to tell her the truth about who and what he was. He decided to start slowly by tossing the ball into Teagan's court. "Tell me why you called me. What was it in the book that has so shaken you, Teagan?" He scrutinized her with a keen watchfulness as he awaited her answer.

She visibly shored herself up before speaking. "Well. Even though I don't know you very well yet," she spoke slowly, eyeing the book for another long moment, "I have a feeling you won't judge me for what I'm about to say. I hope."

Ash waited, breathing in her succulent scent while forcing himself to stay motionless in case she startled, like a deer.

"I—I'm afraid I might be going crazy." Her voice was so soft that mere human ears might not have caught it. "Please tell me I'm not?" She lifted those mocha eyes back up to look at him, the freckles standing out even more against the paleness of her skin. Her expression waved between partially imploring and partially terrified.

He gently nodded his head at her, mutely encouraging her to go on.

"Ash." Her voice dropped low. "Ash, I trust you. I barely know you, but I trust you." Pure honesty resounded in her tone. "That's why I came here right now. The only other person in the world I would dare tell what I saw is my work friend, Savannah. But she's out of town for a few days, and this isn't the sort of thing you can talk about on the phone." Teagan's eyes were serious as she studied him. "This is your book, anyway. I know you won't make fun of me for what I'm about to say."

Ash quietly watched the progression of thoughts across her stunning face. He longed to reach out and touch her, but he firmly kept his hands to himself for now, letting her finish.

She took a deep breath, blew it out, took in another. "I saw something in the book earlier that wasn't there the last time I looked. Something colorful, beautiful. Even wild and stunning." Despite the nervousness in her face, her voice, he also heard the intrigue there. "I need to know if you saw it, too."

Stark silence held them as they looked at one another. Finally, Ash quietly exhaled the breath he hadn't realized he'd been holding. Time to out with it. "Yes, Teagan. I can see it, too. There are images in the book. You're not crazy," he said softly. "Tell me about the scene you saw depicted."

Her eyes widened as her mouth dropped open. The breath she washed out was one of pure relief. "Thank god I'm not crazy." Sudden laughter bubbled out. "Unless we're both crazy."

Ash snorted, smiling back at her. "I promise you, we are not crazy. But tell me exactly which one you saw," he gently urged.

In a rush, she told him. The mountain, the glowing heart of it, the dragons, the battle.

The hopeless defeat of the man.

When she finished, Ash's hands tightened, the right hand twinging as usual. Striving for calm, he held her gaze as he replied. "Everything you saw is real." He looked directly into her eyes as he said that, pushing as much clarity into his tone and expression as he could so that she would believe him.

She gave a tentative nod back. Still trusting him. "But I don't understand. How is it possible? Magic?" She giggled. But as he simply looked back at her, his face quiet, her attempt at levity dropped off. "Oh, my god," she whispered, staring at him. "Wait. *Magic?* Like for real, honest-to-god magic?"

He paused for a bare second, then plunged on, still looking at her carefully. "Yes. The book does have magic to it. Magic is real, Teagan." He held her startled gaze. "And there is a great deal of it locked inside that inconspicuous little book."

Teagan stared back, her eyes boring into his as if trying to see his very soul. His dragon bugled in Ash's mind, brought alive by the nearness of his mate, so much so that Ash knew his dragon wanted desperately to show in his eyes. He checked his dragon's insistence. First, he wanted to be sure Teagan wasn't in an unmoving shock at the words he'd so casually dropped.

The sweet flush rose again in her face, lending it a dusky hue that contrasted nicely with her beautiful freckle design. She quietly said, "I really do believe you. Wow." Wonder touched her voice. "I knew I could trust you, no matter what. I felt it deep inside me, somehow. I know without a doubt you wouldn't lie to me." She slowly shook her head she spoke, a wondering smile playing on lips. "It's like I somehow know it deep in my soul. Is that even possible?"

Another beat held them. As a light pattering sounded outside the window, their heads turned as one to look at it. Rain, dashing against the window. Ash looked back at Teagan. Throwing caution to the wind, he plunged ahead. "You don't seem nearly as shocked as I think most women would be. Then again," he conceded, still studying her, "nearly this same thing just happened to one of my closest friends. A woman fell in love with him." He hesitated for the briefest pause before quietly adding, "A human woman."

This time, Teagan's eyebrows raised. "Human?"

She didn't look scared, though. Instead, she looked—curious. Alert. On the edge of fascinated.

She could hear the truth from him. The truth that she was *his*.

His mate. The one who was ready to know.

"Teagan." The rumble of his dragon beneath his voice, deepening it, toughening it, widened her eyes a fraction. "You truly do trust me?"

She nodded, her eyes never leaving his.

"Then let me show you what I really am," he whispered.

With that, he let his need burst into his eyes, allowing them to change from human to completely dragon.

———

TEAGAN COULDN'T HELP the small yelp that escaped her as Ash's eyes changed. The pupils elongated, similar to a cat's but, she instinctively sensed, much more powerful. They slit vertically, the green around them turning a dazzling emerald, bright and multi-faceted like a rare jewel. Just like the pinpoints of light she sometimes saw in the usual darker forest color, Ash's eyes were now all pure, brilliant green. Stunning, mesmerizing, evocative.

Not remotely human.

Teagan felt the weight of the silence in the room bear down on her so heavily, so excitingly, that she felt dizzy. Spinny. Completely aware of this moment.

Completely aware of this man, who looked back at her with an expression she suspected mirrored the wonderment on her own face.

"Teagan." Ash's face was calm as he spoke, though his eyes seemed to glow as he looked at her. No, they *did* glow. There was a wild hunger in them, a hunger that promised to come leaping out at any moment.

Despite that, she felt totally unafraid. This was Ash. He was showing himself to her. What he was.

Which was—what, exactly?

"What—what are you?" She barely breathed the words, so caught up in the amazing display of his changed eyes. Whatever he said, she could take it. And believe it.

Ash's face, the gorgeous, strong left side oddly balanced by the ravages on the right side, didn't move as he answered her. "I am a dragon shifter, Teagan. I can shift my form into that of a dragon."

Just the rain tap-dancing on the windows, the rustle of the increasing breeze outside, and the muted ticking of a clock somewhere filled the room as Teagan digested that. Finally, she gave him a faint nod. "Okay." Her voice sounded a lot steadier than she'd thought it would. "Your—your eyes right now. Those are, uh, dragon eyes?"

Said eyes glittered bright green at her, somehow awesomely chilling and wildly alluring at the same time. "Yes." The stark simplicity of his answer, the pure honesty pulsing through his voice, seemed to throb into her bones.

Huh. His eyes also reminded her of someone else's. "They're like Nick's. My swordmaster. And—oh, my god." She pulled the inside of her lip between her teeth as she carefully watched Ash for his response. "Mr. Bernal's eyes, too. No way. Are—is he like you?" Her own eyes were wide now. "Both of them? There are more, uh, dragon shifters, in the world?"

Ash looked at her steadily. "Yes. Sebastian is a shifter, as is Nick. Nick sometimes has a hard time hiding his eyes when he's fighting, or teaching others how to fight. But we all do. High emotions call our dragons close to the surface. You," he added softly, a dark, sensuous thread abruptly rippling through his voice, "call my dragon to the surface, Teagan."

A sudden flood of heavy, needful tension flowed between them. Teagan's heart raced as she slowly let her lips peel open, breathing a little faster. Ash's eyes, glowing bright green and fissured vertically, perfectly fit into his gorgeous human face despite their near otherworldliness. He looked at her with a deeper intent. A natural, purely female response spread all over Teagan's body, like tiny cat feet tiptoeing all over her.

Or was that like heated dragon's breath tingling over her skin, raising teeny goosebumps and sending an excited antici-pation through her entire body?

"Come here." His voice as he said those two words was a whisper, yet the room was already so quiet that the sound of it boomed in Teagan's ears. It wasn't a forceful demand, not high-handed or cocky. No.

It was an invitation.

The sensuous spark it kindled within her roared up into a fuller flame. She let a slow, full smile spread across her face, shine forth in her eyes. This was what she wanted. *He* was what she wanted. Dragon shifter, man, scarred, hurting—none of that mattered.

She just wanted *Ash.* Body, heart, and soul.

"Yes, Ash," she said simply, walking toward him and his glowing eyes. "Yes."

16

Teagan's legs almost buckled as Ash let out something that sounded like a growl, moving toward her at the same time. They met in the middle of the grand room, Ash pulling her toward him as naturally as if they'd been doing it their whole lives. He searched her eyes one last time, as if to be certain. In answer, she deliberately reached up her hand, smoothing it over the ravaged right side of his face, then behind his head to gently push it toward hers. "Yes," she insisted again, almost laughing as their lips met.

The second their lips touched, her laughter disappeared. Wild heat swept through her. Moaning against his mouth, Teagan felt her knees literally shake as his lips moved against hers and his arms wrapped around her. As he held her against his long, hard frame, she eagerly melted into him, a lifetime of self-doubt falling away before the dedicated onslaught of Ash's lips.

There was absolutely no question that he wanted her. Every inch of her, just as she wanted him. Their mouths collided, intensifying the kiss. Ash roved one hand up her back while smoothing the other across her waist, then lightly down one side of her hips. She moaned again at the sensation, letting him devour her mouth at the same time.

The long, rapturous kiss felt like the one they had shared the other night, but now it held much more promise. The promise of a wild letting go. The promise of something intense, amazing, unknown.

A promise Teagan was desperately excited to have fulfilled finally. Not just from years of wondering what it would be like to finally feel a man's hands on her, but for what it would feel like to have this particular man touching her. Ash. He'd awakened something deep within her that she still didn't quite understand. All she really knew was that she craved him, and only him. She also felt completely safe with him. He was the one for her. It didn't matter that she had never done this before. Every step of it felt natural, as long as she was with Ash.

She wasn't afraid at all. His touch was rousing something within her that knew exactly how to respond. Running her hands down his strong arms, to his back, stroking his waist, and daring to dip down and stroke his ass, she felt bolder than she ever had before. Pulling her head back from him just enough so she could speak, she whispered firmly, "Ash. I want all of you. Right now."

"Not in here," he growled against her mouth, pulling back enough that she could see his eyes clearly. They were still a bright green, but they'd reverted to being the eyes of a man. "In my bed. Where you deserve to be. Where you damn well belong." This time, there was nothing but pure male possessiveness ringing through his voice. She heard the dark, deep notes of what had to be his—his dragon—echoing in there as well.

Every centimeter of Teagan's lady bits tightened and tingled at that display of sheer masculinity, now making her gasp. Without warning, Ash slid his strong left arm beneath her legs and hoisted her into his arms. He grunted, his right arm dipping a bit under her weight. Alarmed, she flung her arms around his neck, giving him a brief worried look. But he shook his head at her, a small smile touching his lips.

"I won't drop you, Teagan. Trust me." He said it with a pure sincerity that she believed with every fiber of her being.

She nodded back at him. "I trust you. Take me to your bed, Ash." Her whisper seemed to ricochet around the room.

He didn't need any more encouragement. With a strength that still surprised her even as it delighted her and, yes, definitely turned her on, he turned and strode toward the stairs. He didn't bound up them, but he didn't flag despite her weight or any potential lack of strength from his old injuries.

As he carried her, Teagan nuzzled her face into his neck, kissing and licking, even lightly nibbling. He tasted like salt and ridiculously sexy man, felt like rough velvet beneath her lips. Ash shivered under her touch, another sexy groan working its way from his throat out of his mouth. "Dammit, woman, if you keep doing that, I might fall down anyway."

She breathed out a slight giggle. "No falling down until we're in your bed." Teagan almost swallowed her own tongue as she said that. He apparently made her feel very, very confident. Very sure of herself. Even so, it was true.

Ash almost stumbled, turning his head to glance at her. His eyes almost seemed on fire now, while another wondering smile filled his face. "My sexy warrior queen. You continue to surprise me, gorgeous." The casual ease with which he called her that, *gorgeous,* now made Teagan shiver.

"Hurry," she urged, leaning forward and nipping at his neck again. "Please."

His only answer was practically to race down the hallway before turning and entering a large room. He barely paused to kick the door shut behind them. "As I said, Eamon won't be here tonight," he said as he strode across the enormous room with her in his arms. "But I just want you to feel completely at ease in the privacy of my room. To know that no one can see us in here."

Teagan melted more against him. Then, she abruptly was tossed into the middle of his huge, plush bed. Laughing and half shrieking, she managed to rise up from its softness to prop herself up on her elbows. Looking from side to side at the enormous bed, which was covered in satiny golden brown sheets, she realized it was bigger than her entire bedroom at her house. She laughed again.

"I do feel like a queen here," she admitted. "You make me feel like a queen." She looked directly at Ash. Her laughter dissipated as they shared another deep, serious moment. The energy between them swirled in a sizzling power that startled and aroused her at once. This must be what all the books and movies talked about. What her married sister and experienced Savannah had told her about. This was what it was like, the sexual energy burning between her and this incredible man. She was about to have a glorious experience with him. No wonder the moment was alive with a buzzing, shimmering, enormous electricity.

There was not a single other man on earth she wanted to share this moment with. Quietly, eyes locked on his, she echoed his words from earlier. "Come here." Something dark and hot billowed under her words.

She watched the abrupt change on Ash's face with fascination. Renewed surprise whipped across it in nanoseconds, immediately followed by the hunger, so raw that she almost seemed to feel it leaping across from him to her. Her pulse started banging in her ears as her breathing got rapid.

Slowly, Ash nodded at her, the light catching on his chestnut brown hair as he did. He reached up to the top button of his shirt, carefully, and undid it. Then, a wicked grin rippling across his features, he simply ripped the shirt apart down the front. Buttons popped across the room as the tearing sound filled the air. He yanked the shirt off of him, struggling only very slightly when he pulled with his right hand.

Teagan saw his convulsive swallow, knew he was nervous. But holy freaking crap, the man had nothing to be nervous about. Ash Connolly was gorgeous. Yes, the right side of his body was scarred just like his face, and those scars were terrible. She felt that flash of pain again at what he must have gone through. Yet the man clearly had taken good care of himself since he'd been burned. He obviously worked out. This was who he was.

And it turned her on like crazy.

Teagan looked at him with pure appreciation. "Holy crap, you're freaking gorgeous," she couldn't help saying, half embarrassed by the fervent desire in her voice and half not caring.

Ash gave her a long look, standing there with his arms down at his sides, letting her examine him in the soft lighting of his room. "Is that so?" A smile played around his lips again, though she could still see the faintest hint of hesitation on his face.

Teagan pushed herself up into a sitting position, even though her skirt hiked up. She didn't miss Ash's eyes, which darted down to it before he looked back up at her with a pleased smile on his face. "Yes," she said very firmly, nodding her head. "You are."

Ash stared at her for another moment before nodding. Abruptly, she realized he felt the same level of trust in her as she did in him. He knew she meant it.

"Ash," she whispered, worried she'd strangle on her own boldness. But although low, slightly shaky, the words came out clearly. "Take the rest of your clothes off. I want to see all of you."

First, Ash's jaw dropped slightly. Then he reached down to the waist of his jeans. He flicked his eyes up once, looking at her from beneath his eyebrows, that wicked grin curving up those lips again. He yanked the jeans off, kicked them aside, and stood entirely naked and sexier than hell before her.

Teagan was pretty sure she was about to swallow her tongue. And possibly faint. And get wildly, wonderfully buffeted around in the tornado of desire whistling inside her.

Ash was a thing of glory. The right side of his body was hard her to look at, for his sake. The scars were as terrible as the rest she had seen so far, and for another brief moment, her heart thumped hard for what he had gone through. But as far as she was concerned, she honestly didn't really notice. This was *Ash*, standing before her, eyes open and unafraid as could be. Her Ash.

He let every inch of his body be on display for her, allowing her to look at him. She heard the awe in her voice as she murmured, "You're the one with the body of a warrior, Ash." She licked her lips, almost unconsciously, which snapped his gaze down to her mouth. "Come here."

Ash didn't wait. That rumbling sound coming out of his mouth, the one she now knew must be his dragon, reverberated through the bedroom as he prowled forward onto the bed. He moved toward her on all fours, then paused with his body stretched out above hers, their faces inches away. Teagan let herself nestle back into the bed, her eyes locked on his.

The rough thrill of his voice curled over her skin, whispered across every nerve ending. "I'm going to do my best to hold myself back, Teagan." His voice was a delicious sandpaper rasp. "Knowing you're right here, in my bed, is going to make it very hard for me to not want to just ravish the hell out of you."

Teagan felt a zipping shiver of delight seem to explode from between her legs and race across her body. Swallowing a couple of times before she could speak, unsure if the words would come out as anything more than a croak, she finally managed, "You have my permission to do anything to me that you want. If," she paused, suddenly as diffident as Ash had been moments earlier. She forced herself to continue. "If this is really what you want. If I'm really what you want."

Ash threw his head back, the thunderstruck look on it making Teagan want to both giggle and gasp at the same time. "You really need to ask me that question right now, woman?" The broad depth of his voice was nearly as incredulous as his expression. "Believe me, I want you, Teagan. I'm going to prove to you how incredibly stunning, beautiful, and desirable you are. Right now."

With that, he surged forward and claimed her mouth again. This time, though, he also laid his body down so that it stretched out onto hers, covering her with every inch of his hard length. She gasped into his mouth, returning the kiss as feverishly as he gave it. Slipping her hands up and down his back, one hand softly grazing over the smoothness of his unblemished skin and the other traveling with just as much wonder and sensuality over the scarred part, she paused when they both came to the slight dip just below his hard, tight ass. Smiling against his mouth, she roamed her hands down over that incredibly sexy part of his body and firmly pressed him into her.

Ash groaned against her mouth. He started to murmur something against her lips, but she shook her head, pushing up against him to kiss him more firmly even as she urged his hips down harder onto hers. She was thoroughly slick between her legs. Trembling all over. Her nipples peaked against the mate- rial of her shirt, the friction making them even harder and sending more tendrils of desire spiraling through her. Ash pulled back, just enough so he could see her face. "Teagan." His voice was unsteady. "I'm about to rip every scrap of clothing off of you. Is that okay?"

She gasped out a laughing "Yes! Do it. Please," she ended on a ragged whisper. Her entire body alternated between shiv- ering and sizzling, taut with expectation.

Without waiting another second, Ash swept his left hand

down the front of her blouse, ripping it open much as he had his own shirt. Teagan gasped at the sensation, feeling deliciously vulnerable and exposed, excited and turned on in a tumultuous whirl of excitement. He groaned again as he looked down at her breasts, encased in a lacy pink bra. Then, that wicked gleam shining in his eyes again, he reached down with his mouth, caught the front clasp with his teeth, and ripped it off as well.

"Oh!" Teagan cried out, unable to keep it in. Ash flicked a look at her, pausing as if to be sure she wasn't crying out in fear or pain. Almost frantically, she shook her head. "Don't stop," she said in a nearly breathless order. "Don't you dare stop. This is amazing."

In response, Ash dipped his head down and lightly caught her nipple with his tongue. He swirled around it, and Teagan once again felt racked by delicious explosions of pure sensation. They spiraled within her, seeming to race straight down to the sensitive nub between her legs. Ash gently nibbled her breast, then lightly bit the nipple, drawing a ragged moan from her mouth. She flung her head back onto the softness of the bed as she simultaneously pushed her breast into his mouth. She felt him smile against her bare skin. Then he switched his mouth to the other one, using his hand to play gently with the one he'd just left. Between his fingers and his lips, Teagan felt herself turn into a writhing mass beneath him. She felt like nothing but enflamed nerve endings and wanton flesh.

Ash began lightly sucking on the other nipple, circling with his tongue, occasionally gently biting with his teeth, while stroking and kneading and fondling her other breast with his hand. Then, his lips still on one breast, he moved his other hand down her stomach, shifting himself to the side so he could easily touch her. He curved his fingers around her smooth skin, gently tickling around her bellybutton beneath her skirt.

"This," he whispered, fingering the waist of her skirt, "has to go too." His voice was so deep it was as if she could feel it thundering in her very bones. She managed some sort of assenting noise, still totally caught up in the sensation of his lips and tongue doing some sort of crazy, wild magic on her breast. Just like that, his hand slipped around to the back of her skirt, finding the hook and zipper. He fumbled with it for a second, then lightly swore, making her huff out a giggle even in the middle of the deliciousness.

"Over you go, gorgeous." Before the meaning of his words could even register, Ash sat back and easily flipped Teagan over so that she was suddenly on her stomach. She gasped again—which was pretty much all she seemed able to do for the last several minutes, but holy wow was this all too incredible for words—then stilled as his hand busied itself with the hook. Now that she lay on her stomach, she knew he would find it easier to rip her skirt off of her. Yet once again he surprised her.

"Lift your hips up for me." The soft, dark words were an order.

She shivered and did as he asked, reaching up her hand to swipe her hair out of her face so she could try to see him from her position. From the corner of her eye, she could just catch the gleam of a smile playing on his mouth. Instead of ripping her skirt down, he gently shimmied it over her hips and off of her. His fingers lingered, stroking down her skin. The difference between the wild roughness with which he yanked off her top compared to the gentleness as he carefully slipped her out of her skirt sparked the firestorm within her even higher. Heat seemed to pool and melt and explode all at once in the entire region generally below her hips and above her thighs.

Teagan hardly knew what to do with all the sensations, other than soak up every bit of them in a haze of pleasure.

It was when he reached his head down to slowly, deliberately lick his way up the back of one leg, starting at her ankle and working his way up over her trembling calf, along the delicate hollow behind her knee, and up the back of her thigh until he reached the dimple of her ass, his teeth lightly nibbling at the silky, sexy underwear she'd thankfully put on, that she seriously wondered if it was possible to orgasm just from that.

She'd never felt more turned on in her life. Even all the times she'd played with herself, even in the past several weeks, with Ash's sudden existence in her life, his near constant presence in her mind, she hadn't realized she could be so aroused that she literally couldn't think of anything else in the entire world except for this extraordinary man and what he was doing to her right now.

He murmured in that dark, velvety voice against her skin, "Teagan. You're so damned beautiful you're taking my breath away."

She felt his teeth lightly clamp around the edge of the silky underthings she wore. His breath seeming white hot on her already heated skin, he gently tugged the fabric down over her hips, past her ass. She felt him reach over with his other hand to pull down the other side. Between his teeth and his fingers, he shimmied her underwear off of her as he had her skirt, flicking them down past her feet and tossing them somewhere.

Teagan froze for a long, worried second. She felt exposed. Completely exposed. It wasn't just her nakedness. Her freckles covered practically every inch of her body. She practically stopped breathing, lying there suddenly all tense. This might have been a mistake. Maybe she shouldn't be letting things go this far. What if he looked at her and decided she wasn't—

His large hand, warm and rough at the same time, curved over one ass cheek, followed by his other hand on the other one. Teagan sucked in a sharp breath as the sweet burn of his touch whipped through her.

"You are so incredibly beautiful." Dark desire lanced Ash's voice. "Ah, Teagan," he groaned, sounding like a drowning man who saw his salvation.

His mouth gently landed at the nape of her neck, instantly drawing a ripple of goosebumps across her skin. She made a small noise, which intensified as he slowly began kissing his way down her spine, his hands still stroking her ass and curving over her hips.

As if he worshipped something of incredible beauty and importance. He was worshiping *her*.

Tiny fires seem to spring up in each place he touched, combining with the heated storm already flaring throughout her entire body. She felt tingles race across her skin, extending out from his kisses and the touch of his hands, traveling every-where. Down her fingers, her toes, heck, even to the top of her head.

This was more incredible than she had ever thought it could be, and she knew they weren't even at the good stuff yet. Just as she thought that, the good stuff began.

"Lift your hips up again for me, beautiful." Ash's voice rasped with his soft, dark need. She obeyed him, heart thumping hard. He slipped a pillow beneath her hips, tilting her up so her ass was even higher in the air.

Ash's hands stroked around her hips again. "Beautiful," he muttered, his voice deep with a bass note that had to be his dragon side. "So beautiful. I can't wait to taste you, Teagan."

Taste her? Wait, how was he—

"Roll over, Teagan," he said, his voice so deep it seemed to scrape against her deliciously taut nerves. "I want to see all of you spread out in my bed. Just for me. And open those sweet legs for me, beautiful. I need to taste you right now."

Oh.

Trembling, shaking, still a little terrified of him seeing her freckles that nestled even on the insides of her thighs but defi-nitely more desperate to feel his lips on her, Teagan turned over onto her back so Ash could see her entire naked body, spread out before him like some sort of feast. Being so exposed to his hungry gaze made her feel—hot. Needy. Excited. He smiled at her, then tugged her over so that her hips still lifted into the air, propped up by the pillow.

Completely, utterly exposed to his gaze. A gaze that was hungry and worshipful at once.

Then he lowered his head down to her aching pussy and blew a hot breath over it.

Oh, holy crap, yes. Oh, yes, please, yes, please, yes please. From the approving half groan he made in response, his ragged, "Anything you want," she realized she must be breathing those words out loud. She didn't care anymore. The only thing that mattered now was sensation—the exquisite sensation of Ash tasting her right there. Tasting her pussy, the juices from it. She closed her eyes, her mouth opened as little gasps fell from it, and arched herself into him.

His hot breath blew into the slick, needy spot nestled between her legs, where her clit throbbed. As his hands very gently pushed her thighs apart, she heard rustling sounds, felt the bed move as he apparently positioned himself. Then his tongue, oh god yes that was his actual tongue, very gently dipping in to her sweet, heated folds down there.

Teagan cried out, an inarticulate sound of sheer pleasure. "Ash!" she managed to gasp out, snapping her eyes open again, reaching her hands down to press against his head. Her voice sounded strangled.

He simply lapped his tongue in broad strokes up and down her wet, trembling flesh. Sweet, wild tremors shocked through Teagan, making her arch her hips hard against him, offering all of herself to him. Holy freaking crap, this felt crazy wild hot good. She thought her head was about to blow off her shoulders. She'd dreamed about this, dreamed about a man's tongue, specifically Ash's tongue, doing these things to her. But the spectacular reality of it blew her expectations out of the water. Up, down, swirling and twirling, his tongue relentlessly assaulted that needy, aching, desirous little pussy of hers, shameless hussy that it was.

Teagan's breathing got harsher, her fingers clenching hard on the bedsheets. "Ash, I—I need something. I don't know what I need." Her mind felt chaotic, whirling and swirling just like the motion of his tongue on her.

Ash pulled his head away, causing Teagan to cry out with renewed, disappointed shock. "No, I didn't want you to stop—"

His rumbling chuckle sounded dark. Hot. Desirous. "We're not over, gorgeous. Not by a long shot. I need something, too." His voice whispered, dark and promising, its rasp setting her nerves on fire. "I need to be inside you, Teagan. Right now."

17

Ash had felt his rapidly slipping control dissipate another notch as Teagan did as he asked and turned *her* onto her back. Then, when he said he needed to be inside her, her expression undid him. Her hair spread in a beautiful red cloud around her face on the pillow, her luscious body displayed for his ravenous gaze, the ache of desire in her eyes leaping over to him. He stayed where he was for a split second, sitting back on his legs, hands spread before him, her juices still dancing across his tastebuds. He knew he probably looked like a feral beast stalking his stunning prey, but that was fine by him. She was his, and they both knew it. His dragon bugled an agreement, urging Ash toward the one thing he wanted to do.

Claim his mate.

Ash took a long, trembling breath. Teagan's eyes had darkened to rich mocha, her beautiful breasts heaving as she breathed. The vigorous explosion of freckles, like a veil of stars, spread over the front of her just as they had over her back, wrenching another groan from his lips.

"So damn beautiful," he muttered again. His words opened

her face into a radiance that caught somewhere in his chest with a squeeze.

It had hit him in a rush, earlier, that they both feared the same thing: judgment by the other due to the physical differences that set them apart from most of the rest of the world's population. Yet he knew one thing with all his soul: they were made for one another.

He smiled down at her again, his wonderment and desire mingling together. "Perfect, Teagan. You," he leaned down over one breast, "are," gently, he touched it with the tip of his tongue, "perfect."

Her bottom lip slowly fell away from her top as another sweet cry fell from her lips. They glistened, as did the sweet, delicious lips nestled between her legs.

Teagan's eyes now looked like charcoal as she gazed up at him from the bed. They were half-lidded, her mouth open in a slight pant. Ash reached forward, gently dragged his thumb over her luscious mouth to wet it. Her breath hissed through her teeth as he traced a path from the corner of her mouth with that thick digit, curving around her neck, then behind it with his whole palm to gently clasp. Moving his face down to hers, he traced her beautiful freckles with his mouth, dropping light kisses along the way. Her hand reached up his back, stroking down and up, her fingers touching his with a wondering exploration that felt somewhat tentative yet excited.

"Ash," she murmured, the mere sound of her voice igniting his blood even more.

He gently shook his head. Moving his lips to hers, he gave her a long, lingering kiss that stoked the flames of desire in him ever higher. Return his kiss an equally ardent manner, Teagan pressed up against the hard length of his body with her lush, softer one. The sensation threatened to make him lose control.

Not quite yet. Pulling his head back from her, he let a wicked smile edge his face. Pushing his hand beneath her, he wrapped his arms around her, holding her close to him. "Hang on to me," he murmured.

Teagan obeyed, lacing her hands behind his back. Ash reached down, guided his straining cock to the entrance of her soft, slick heat. She went completely still at that touch, sucking in a gasp. It was Ash's turn to groan as her eyes turned the color of black licorice, desire written across her entire face. Allowing his lazy grin to fall away, feeling his expression tauten now in focused seriousness, he slowly began to slide inside her.

She gasped again, her coppery hair tumbling wildly around her gorgeous face. He desperately wanted to grab her hips, pull that sweet, wet pussy of hers onto his cock, and drive himself deep inside her. His dragon roared encouragement in his mind, but Ash managed to hold on to the last shreds of his control. He wanted to draw this out by every agonizingly delicious second that he could.

Her next words, however, almost stopped his heart.

"I—wait," she gasped.

Ash froze, suddenly scared he was hurting her. That she had changed her mind at the last second.

"This is rocking my world," she said, her darkened eyes scanning his as if searching for an answer. "I'm not scared at all, Ash. But I, uh, have a confession to make."

She swallowed convulsively, suddenly biting her lower lip in a sign of nervousness even amidst the erotically charged haze of her expression. "I've never done this before." She gave him a hesitant little smile. "I don't really know what to do. Not for sure, I mean. I just don't want to disappoint you." Her last words barely vibrated out of her throat, lower than a whisper.

Ash felt his world tumble end over end. She—was she saying that she was a—?

"Teagan. Are you a virgin?" His voice seemed almost hoarse to his own ears.

Her eyes suddenly wide, she slowly nodded. "Yes," she

whispered, the sound flowing over his overheated nerves like raw silk. "You're the first man I've ever been with." She hesitated, then boldly plunged on, "You'll be the first one to ever touch me this way. To ever, um, be inside me."

He would be the first man ever to touch her this way.

He would be the first man ever to be inside her.

Something huge swelled in his chest, sending a shudder of pure male possessiveness roaring through him like a freight train. His dragon trumpeting, Ash snarled, "And I'll be the *only* man to ever touch you this way, Teagan." A wondering smile burst over his face as he said her name. He said it again, savoring the sweet strength of it. Of her. *"Teagan."* But even so, he waited for her to let him know it was okay to go on.

Teagan firmly pushed down on his back with her hands, slipping out one leg to hook it behind his. Her eyes, dark and heavy with her arousal, caught on his. "I want this, Ash. I want you." Her words whispered, shivered over his skin and down into his bones. "I want to feel every inch of you inside me. I trust you. You won't hurt me. Please, Ash." He voice begged him, as did her eyes. "Please be inside me. Now?"

The sweet tip of her tongue came out to wet her top lip. Ash felt every fear he'd had about the ruined side of his body, his strength as a man, vanish in the face of the pure, eagerly accepted eroticism of the moment with her. He felt his last bit of control dissipate into the furnace of his need for this woman.

For his mate.

"Yes," he growled, dipping his head to nuzzle her neck, then graze it with his teeth.

Without another warning, he slid his heavy cock the rest of the way into her, letting her fervent cries urge him on.

TEAGAN'S WORLD exploded just from the feeling of Ash's

huge, hard length sliding the rest of the way into her. He was so big, so thick. She'd been a little afraid it would hurt, and there was a stinging sensation, but she was so turned on, so wet and ready for him, that he fit inside her just right.

Like they were made for one another.

His eyes, bright green, looked at her with the barest whisper of a question. She simply nodded, lifting her hips up to his. Tilting herself up made it feel even better, causing a sighing gasp to fall from her lips. Bracing himself slightly more on his left leg and arm, Ash slowly pulled back, then slid forward again into her. Back, almost leaving her entirely, then forward again. Back, then forth. It felt so good, seemed to flip on the switch in so many of her nerve endings, that Teagan felt jolted sideways, swirled with wild, delicious sensations as he did it.

"Teagan," he groaned, his thrusts becoming longer. Harder. "You feel so damned good. I can't," he gasped along with her as he thrust into her again, sliding them over the sheets, "I can't hold back."

"Don't hold back," she said in a breathless, immediate order as she tightly gripped his back with her arms, letting her legs slide up and down his with his movements. "Take me," she whispered, looking directly into his feverish eyes. "Take all of me. No holding back. I want all of you," she whispered.

A rumbled snarl of possessive joy whipped out of Ash, the sound of it echoing around his bedroom, slamming into Teagan's heart. He pulled back, then thrust deep into her. Hard. There was a single flashing throb of beautiful pain, which quickly became a rising blaze of frenzied ecstasy. Something white-hot, shaking in the spiral of excitement that seemed about to combust, blazed through Teagan's entire body. It felt like a thousand tiny points of sensation, teetering just on the verge, raced over every inch of her skin.

Ash plunged in and out of her, his cock seeming harder than steel yet encased in a velvet softness that wrenched rhythmic cries from Teagan with each mind-spinning thrust. He swelled inside her even more with each stroke, his face hard and strong yet open and vulnerable all at once. She felt unmasked, stripped bare, willing him to come inside her with not just his body, but his entire being. The bright cedar and wild mountain wind scent of him surrounded her. She felt delirious with need.

"Mine," Ash roared, his fingers threaded in her hair, the sweet pain of the individual strands being pulled only adding to the incredible rush of hot joy that suffused her. "You are *mine*," he snarl-whispered. His mouth came down to her neck, breathing onto her, seeming to send a blast of molten lava spreading through her body. The hum of his name, *Ash*, somehow vibrated throughout her skin and blood and bones, touching every molecule within her.

Somehow, she knew with an unshakeable certainty that overwhelmed her in shattering joy, Ash was making her his. *Claiming* her as his, and his alone.

With a keening howl, she felt the inferno erupt within her, cracking her apart into sheer bliss. She screamed his name out loud, shocked by how intensely good this felt, by the primal scream of her voice, the shuddering wave of her release as it throbbed over every inch of her body. Clutching at his shoulders, his back slick with sweat, she stared into his eyes, her mouth open as her body rocked with the fierce storm of her orgasm.

Ash drove his enormous cock into her again, this time shuddering out his own release with wild abandon and a bellowing roar of exultance. She felt his hot spurts deep inside her, watched the savage, feral expression on his face as he loosed himself into her, her name on his lips as they both rode the sweet explosions. Together.

Timeless moments held them together in ecstasy, wiping all thoughts of anything else in the world out of her mind except this man. Her man. Her gorgeous dragon shifter man.

Slowly, slowly, she eventually spiraled back down to earth, her body wrung out, feeling dopey with a sweet languor. Her muscles felt like jelly, her brain a mush of serene knowing that didn't need the usual spiky jumble of nervous thoughts. The entire world was sweetly hazy yet also crystal clear.

"Teagan," Ash murmured, his voice as wrung out as she felt. "Mine," he added in a soft rumble. "Mine."

The sound of their breathing mingled in cadence, slowly dropping off to quieter rhythms. Ash moved himself to the side, then gently collapsed on the bed, off of her but still pressed to her and holding her close. He unwound his fingers from her hair and wrapped his arms around her. Sighing in relaxed pleasure, Teagan curved herself around him, nestling her head into his chest, into the hollow just below his throat. His heartbeat sounded loud and steady against her ear. The sound soothed her. It gave her the deep assurance that he had done *something* to her, something deep and marvelous that bound them together.

It felt like the safest, most comforting knowledge she had ever had.

Long moments passed with her cocooned safely in his arms, his spicy scent all around her. Slowly, she became aware again of the faint battering sound of the rain outside, the quiet creaks and soft hums of the house around them. The bedside light cast a soft glow into the room, leaving the edges of the form of the amazing man beside her bathed in a soft golden glow. She ran light fingers down his back. "Thank you." Her voice was low, a little scratchy from the vocal exercises she'd just put it through. She blushed.

His lips brushed the top of her head even as his arm squeezed her once. "For the most amazing experience ever?" A soft tease gilded his tone, but seriousness and surety sounded in there as well.

She nodded, then lifted her head and pushed herself onto one elbow so that she could look into his eyes. They were still green, although now closer to their usual darker forest shade. Curious, she said, "Your eyes. Do they always do that when your—your dragon is close to you, or something?"

A smile lit his face as he stroked the back of his hand down her cheek. "Do they do what?"

"Turn bright green, like they did before." She sighed in pleasure at the feel of his gentle hand on her skin.

He nodded. "Yes. That means my dragon is aroused, very close to the surface of me. It's when that side of me is more prevalent than my human side. Such as," he cured his fingers down her chin, stroked her neck, "when I'm around you."

She nodded again, still trying to puzzle everything out. Wrapped in his arms, the soft nighttime rain outside adding to the protective sanctuary, she felt thoroughly safe. "Ash, what you did. When you—well, I'm not even sure what you did." Slowly, encouraged by his steady gaze and slight nod for her to continue, she went on. "It was like you put yourself into me, somehow. Not the way we just did, I mean. I mean," she blushed so hard her face must be brighter than a ripe cherry. "Oh, my gosh. Not that. I'm just shutting up now."

Ashe laughed in sheer delight. "I never want you to shut up. You're very cute when you stammer and stutter and then blush like the sunset." She lightly smacked his arm, then giggled in return. Being gently teased by him felt—amazingly good. As if she belonged.

"As for what you meant," he went on more seriously, looking right into her eyes, "I can tell you exactly what that was. That was me claiming you as my mate, Teagan." The strength of those words seemed to vibrate in the air. "You are my mate."

She felt another delicious tingle slide up and down her body as he said that. Yes. She'd been right in what she'd felt when he did it. *Mate.* She still didn't know exactly what it meant, but she did know that it felt completely right.

Ash's eyes got a little harder. "This way, all other dragon

shifters who ever meet you will know that you are my claimed mate. It helps keep you safe."

Her eyebrows skyrocketed. "Safe? From what?"

Such a dark, feral possessiveness dropped over his features that she almost gasped. "From any dragon who would think he might claim you as well."

Well, then. That sounded a bit—barbaric. And old-fashioned. Before she could say so, though, Ash's face slowly melted back into hunger. Hunger just for her.

"There is an entire other world you will get to know, Teagan." He pulled her back down against him, then reached out to shut off the light beside the bed. "But for now, my beautiful sexpot"—okay, that was cool—"let's get some sleep. I have plans to wake you up in the middle of the night and ravish you all over again."

Why, yes, please.

"I like all of this so far." Ash's lips found her neck, nipping and kissing. Teagan let a shiver of delight tickle up and down her body. "But now I don't think I can fall asleep thinking about what those plans will be like," she admitted. Of course, she promptly ruined it by yawning.

Ash laughed against her neck, wrapping his entire body around hers and breathing in her scent or something. "We have all night ahead of us," he promised. "Sleep for now, my beauty."

"Mmm," she murmured back, snuggling deeper against him. That sounded like a perfect idea.

1 8

When the harsh ring tone of his phone sounded practically in his ear, Ash muttered incoherently beneath his breath, heart hammering as he was jolted from deep sleep. Teagan started beside him, murmuring something unintelligible. He slapped his hand around in the dark on the small bedside table until he found the offending instrument of hellish noise, pressing around on it with his fingers until he managed to decline the call. The phone went silent mid-ring.

Sighing, Teagan snuggled closer against him. He pulled her toward him, nuzzled at her ear. His cock, seemingly eager for a repeat of the three glorious times during the night it had spent buried deep inside her, pressed hard against her sweet, lush ass. Sucking in a sharp little breath, she wiggled against it. Ash groaned into her ear. His only desire right now was for yet another round of exquisite lovemaking with this most amazing woman.

The phone promptly and noisily rang again. "What in the hell," he snarled. Teagan murmured, but he ran a soothing hand down her arm before turning slightly on his side to grab the phone again.

Dammit. Sebastian. At this time of night, he had to answer. "This had better be good," Ash snapped into the phone.

Rage emanated from the phone almost before Sebastian's voice sliced through it. "The Center security just notified me. A thief broke in."

Abruptly, Ash sat bolt upright in the bed. "Impossible." The Bernal Center was one of the most secure places in the country. Millions of dollars' worth of irreplaceable art insured that.

"Yes, it should be impossible." Sebastian's voice was almost blank with fury. "But it gets even worse." His harsh inhale sounded very loud in Ash's ear. "They took your books. The ones Ms. Lambert was repairing. They're gone."

Ash snapped on the light and thumped his feet to the floor. Alarmed and abruptly wide awake, Teagan sat up behind him. He shot a brief glance at her, the tousled red hair falling over her face, her sweet breasts hidden as she clutched the sheet to her in some sort of automatic defense against whatever bad thing she could tell was happening somewhere. "What's going on?" she asked in a low voice. "What's wrong?"

Already standing, reaching down for his jeans that had ended up in a heap on the floor, Ash shook his head at her. Struggling for a moment to both pull on his jeans and hold the phone to his ear, he swore, then placed the phone on the floor. He put it on speaker so Sebastian's voice spilled into the room.

"I am not in Los Angeles at the moment." Ash vaguely recalled something about some gala event on the other side of the country. Sebastian traveled a lot. "I need you to get to the Center as quickly as you can. Whoever broke in is still somewhere inside the premises."

Ash swore at that. Teagan gasped, then lightly thumped her own feet down onto the floor. Despite his alarm, Ash couldn't help but admire her curves as she darted to a filmy heap of cloth crumpled on the floor. She snatched her skirt up from the throw rug it had landed on and shimmied it up her hips. Ash watched her dress, simultaneously enjoying the sight while also grappling with his growing anger at what had just happened.

Somebody had stolen not just from the Center, but from him personally. From his hoard. His dragon roared inside him, filling Ash's head with fury—and worry. Ash needed his hoard items. He had his mate now, but he still needed what little remained of his decimated hoard.

"Who possibly could be able to get into the Center and steal something?" he ground out. "Why my books?" Ash's gaze snagged briefly on Teagan's.

But even as he thought it, he knew. Another dragon shifter.

"A shifter." The same dark rage Ash felt rippled beneath Sebastian's voice. "One who thoroughly understood the value of those objects is behind this. One who knows they are a part of your hoard."

"No one there knew the value," Ash retorted. "We kept that very quiet for a reason." Glancing around for the shirt he'd ripped off himself last night, he was briefly rewarded by a view of Teagan's delectable ass as she bent over, apparently searching for the rest of her clothes. He allowed himself a brief smile of awed gratification once again that she was here with him.

"Someone obviously did," Sebastian said. "Someone who has to be one of us." A dragon shifter.

Ash tightened his jaw as the rain gusted outside. He stalked over to his closet, searching for a shirt that still had intact buttons. "You vet everyone who works there. Particularly anyone from the shifter world. Even so, how could they possibly have guessed the value of the books?" Books were rarely a part of a dragon's hoard.

Sebastian swore creatively over the phone. "I can only surmise that the underground operation run by our old friend Malcolm still exists. Whoever's in charge of it now must have had access to all the pieces he was keeping an eye on over the years."

Malcolm. Ash bristled at the memories of the duplicitous shifter who had dealt extensively in the shadowy black market of stolen antiquities. Teagan glanced from the phone to Ash, her eyebrows raised in question. Ash grimly shook his head and quietly mouthed to her, "Later."

"Not to mention that the books were already warded," Ash added out loud. Beyond the Center's impressive amount of security, the protective wards he himself had placed on the books should have kept them safe from any nefarious intent.

Sebastian's grim tone sounded through the room. "Indeed they are. Which is why, I suspect, the thief has not yet been able to get them out of the Center."

Ash stopped dead, his shirt hanging from his hand as he stared at the phone.

Rage beating hard in his chest, he said very quietly, "You mean someone dared to steal my books, part of my own hoard, from one of the most secure places in the entire country, but they weren't smart enough to have thought out their plan and are still inside the building?"

"What—" Teagan started to ask, but Ash gently held up his hand, making her swallow her words.

"Who is with you?" Sebastian immediately demanded.

Ash savagely yanked his shirt over his head, making a button pop off from the roughness with which he did so. Apparently tonight he was being hard on his buttons. "Teagan," he answered in a short tone, although he shot her a quick smile.

"Ah." Sebastian's voice was equal parts knowing and pleased, making Ash quirk his lips and shake his head. But Sebastian's voice quickly turned grim again. "I already talked to Eamon. I didn't realize he wasn't at your house tonight."

"What did he think?" Ash asked, hunting beneath the bed for his shoes. When he turned around, Teagan was dressed.

Despite the tenseness of the moment, he strode to her, put his hands to her face, pulled her toward him for a hard but quick kiss on her silken lips. She sighed into his mouth.

"Eamon thinks," Sebastian said, his tone now positively glacial, "that it obviously must be an inside job."

Ash and Teagan simultaneously broke their kiss, staring first at one another and then down at the phone. "What?" Teagan said, her voice mixed parts of affronted and angry. "Someone who works there would dare do that?"

Ash reached down to sweep the phone up off the floor as he turned to open the bedroom door and head downstairs. Teagan was hot on his heels. He left the phone on speaker so she could still hear Sebastian.

"Unfortunately, yes. It's something we screen for very carefully, but we can't hope to catch every liar who might want to work there." Sebastian's voice said exactly what he thought of such people. "Teagan, I'm glad in more ways than one that you're there."

Ash snorted, reaching out his hand to touch the softness of Teagan beside him as they hurried down the wide staircase.

Puzzled, Teagan said, "I don't understand?"

A deep rumble boom outside startled them both. A flash of light outside the window, then a sudden increase in the rain, said the storm was getting more intense.

"I know you would have only recently become aware of the importance of these items," Sebastian continued. "I trust that if you are Ash's mate, you would never betray him."

"Of course not," she immediately protested.

Ash started to snarl at the phone, but Sebastian heard him and raised his voice. "I was not implying such a thing. However, is it possible you may have just let something slip, completely unintentionally, to anyone at the Center? Anyone at all." Frustration sounded in Sebastian's voice. "You do not yet understand the intricacies of dragon shifter society. You don't yet know those employees of the Bernal Center who walk in two worlds."

From the expression on Teagan's face, she had not considered that possibility whatsoever. "Well," she said thoughtfully as she and Ash reached the ground floor, "if the other dragon shifters there are anything like Ash or you, Mr. Bernal, no. Now that I understand what to look for, I can't think of anyone like that who's there. Um, anyone who's a dragon shifter."

She stumbled slightly over the words, but her glance at Ash was calm. The concept was new and strange to her, but she accepted it.

"No," Ash said, "you wouldn't. There are very few shifters who work at the Bernal Center. The ones who do hold not only extremely high positions, they were required to enter into a blood pact in order to be allowed there. They are utterly beyond reproach. What he's talking about, Teagan," Ash looked at her beautiful eyes, feeling his heart lurch again, "are those employees who are from fealty families. Humans who know about the shifter world. Like Eamon, but aligned with a shifter who is inclined to thieve. There is an underground trade in dragon shifter antiquities. It thrives, unfortunately."

"Power is quite the aphrodisiac," Seb ominously agreed from the phone. From his tone, it was clear what he would prefer to do to those who sought such illicit gains.

Teagan's wrinkled brow of confusion was so sexy that Ash had to lean over and kiss her again. She smiled at that. "But wouldn't you know who they are?"

Ash looked at his mate, marveling again at her beauty, her calmness under the whirlwind of recent events and her life-changing discoveries. He shook his head, feeling a simultaneous snap of regret and anger. "Not if they wanted to keep it hidden. It is easy for us to know who shifters are. But fealty family members are not necessarily recognizable."

Sebastian's curt voice said, "Teagan. Does anything odd

come to mind? Any interactions with anyone who had as much an interest in Ash's books as you did?"

Teagan helplessly shook her head, watching as Ash reached into a closet in his overly grand hallway to pull out a rain jacket. "No one." Her voice was pinched now, troubled. "Only you, and Walter. Um, I mean Mr. Ainsworth," she added more nervously.

"He is beyond reproach." Sebastian's tone took on levity for a brief moment. "Not to mention I do believe the man would be perhaps the worst bumbling thief if he ever decided to take it up as a profession. Ash," he switched gears quickly, voice again going hard, "Get there as soon as you can. Keep me posted."

With that, Sebastian disconnected the call, leaving Ash in a flurry of wide awake rage and concern reflected back at him from Teagan's eyes.

TEAGAN WATCHED Ash rustle through the hall closet by the main door, drawing out a rain jacket in response to the lashing storm outside. She looked in there too, wondering if there was something she could wear. She didn't mind getting a little wet, but it sounded like it was getting epic out there now.

Ash shrugged on his black slicker and reached for the door. "I'll be back as soon as I can. Don't move. I don't know what's going on at the Center, but the house is warded. You'll be safe here."

Wait, what the what? Teagan stared at her sexy dragon man mate. He couldn't be serious. "I'm coming with you! You can't make me stay here. Those are my books, I was working on them. I'm responsible for them, Ash." She felt a flurry of remorse rise in her at the thought of it. She also felt something unexpected: a sharp blaze of anger. Anger that someone would try to sabotage her work, or steal from Ash. This sort of raw, slightly rage-y emotion was new.

She kind of liked it.

Ash narrowed those dreamy eyes at her. She noticed that the points of green in them were getting brighter again. "You will stay here. This is dangerous, Teagan." He reached out to lightly grab her shoulders in his large hands, staring hard at her as if to impress her with his seriousness. The scarred part of his face was just as grim as the unblemished side. "You don't know enough about our world yet. I need to know that you will be safe. Stay here."

She drew breath to protest again, but he silenced her with another hard, lingering kiss, pressing his body close to hers for an electrifying moment that was too short. Then he pulled back and whispered, "My world can be very dangerous for you. I will be back soon."

Then he broke away, opening the door to the whipping wet and cold outside. Teagan shivered as her skirt fluttered around her bare legs.

Ash's face was hard, yet his mouth softened as he looked at her for a last brief moment. "Stay here, Teagan." His eyes glittered bright green. "We just found one another. I'm not about to lose you."

With that, he firmly closed the door behind him, leaving Teagan alone and feeling utterly useless in the house.

Uh-uh. Nope. No way was she going to stay here. She stared at the door for a long moment, but her mind already was made up. She wasn't about to stay behind like some woman tending the home fires or whatever. Sure, she may not know anything about the dragon shifter world, but Ash was her—her mate. She still didn't quite understand it, but she was positive of at least one thing.

She wasn't going to let her mate go by himself into danger. She wasn't about to lose him, either.

Then she cast a critical look down at her woefully inadequate clothing. She needed to find something else to wear. Racing back upstairs, pulling her clothes off again, she rifled through Ash's closet and managed to find a pair of jeans that she cinched around her waist with a dark brown leather belt. Then she grabbed a long-sleeve white shirt and yanked it over her head. Giving the bed a quick glance, blushing as an image of all the delicious things they'd done in it just hours before flashed across her mind, she looked down and despaired of her footwear. Despite her height and feet that were bigger than most women's, there still was no way a pair of Ash's shoes would fit her. At least she wore flats.

Racing back downstairs, just as she was about to go out the door, a glint caught her eyes. Glancing over, she stopped short and made an *oh* with her mouth as she spied a sword lying on the table there. She hadn't paid attention earlier, either when she'd arrived at the house or just now, so caught up she'd been in—well, everything else.

The sword was absolutely gorgeous. Silver with gold and jewels set into it, and beautiful ancient Celtic runes, she could immediately tell that although it clearly was a special sword, it also had been made for battle. Huh. Okay, fine. She may not know what she was getting herself into in the dragon shifter world, but she'd finally picked up one or two things about fighting with a sword. Instructor Nick—another dragon shifter, so weird, but she'd have to find out more about that some other time—had even said she was getting to be pretty decent. If she was about to charge off half cocked, it might be a good idea to take a weapon with her.

Did dragon shifters gone bad even use swords for fighting?

Without letting herself think about it more, she grabbed the sword off the table, gasped as the heavy weight of it briefly made her arms sink toward the floor, then reached for the door handle, ready to drive as fast as she dared to the Center and help Ash.

Swinging the door open, she almost had heart failure at the sight of a man's figure looming on the doorstep.

Looking not a bit disheveled despite it being the middle of the night and that he'd clearly been summoned away from the arms of his lady love, Eamon crossed his arms over his chest and narrowed his eyes. "Where exactly do you think it is you're going with that sword, Ms. Lambert?"

The hallway Ash strode down was dead quiet. He'd never been to the Bernal Center in the middle of the night. Seeing it almost devoid of people was eerie.

Ahead of him, bright lights spilled out into the hallway. A security guard, looking both aggrieved and trigger-happy, startled as Ash approached. "State your business," the man snapped reflexively, then relaxed as he recognized Ash. "I'm sorry, sir, we're all jumpy here at the moment. Mr. Bernal told me you would be coming."

Ash gave a harried nod to the man, whom he knew was a well-vetted member of a fealty family just like every other night guard who worked for the Bernal Center. He got straight to the point. "Any ideas on where the thief is?" He felt buoyed by two things right now: hot rage at whoever thought they could dare steal not only from him but from the Center, and the new lightness that seemed as if it would carry him through anything.

His amazing, incredible, stunning mate waited for him at his house. Just knowing that she was there lent him strength.

The guard shrugged in frustration. "We checked the immediate area around the conservators' work space when the alarms went off. We haven't found anything yet. But we will," he added in a tone that made clear his certainty about that. "I was told to take you to the spot the books were last located, on their conservator's desk." Teagan's desk. "Mr. Bernal thinks you might be able to sense them from there."

It sometimes was possible for the owner of a hoard to sense the objects closely enough to be able to locate their where-abouts, although not always. It sure as hell was worth a shot. "Take me there." Ash could feel his dragon pushing at him. Angry, ready to find the enemy and deal harsh consequences.

The guard nodded grimly. He turned to head down the hall at a fast clip, throwing words over his shoulder. "Your wards, combined with the usual protective wards used here on any shifter objects, are enough to make sure that whoever took the books can't leave the premises with them, sir. The wards will not allow passage out through any of the doors unless taken by the rightful owner. Also," he said in grimly satisfied tones as he led them down the maze of hallways, "the wards set on them make sure that the thief will leave his mark on the books. Even if he just leaves them somewhere inside the build-ing," Ash's dragon rumbled in rage at the thought of Connolly artifacts being handled so dismissively, "and escapes by himself, we will know who it is."

Ash nodded without responding out loud, even though the guard wasn't looking at him. Dragon shifter wards could be imbued with as much or as little power as the shifter wanted. Combining the energies of his own personal wards with the powerful wards that were set for each dragon shifter object in the Center made for a virtually unbreakable system.

Yet someone had had enough incentive to want to try. Incentive, or insanity.

Stifling the rumbling growl that sought to escape him, he kept on the guard's heels. They came to a fork in the hallway. The right hand turn led to a Renaissance painting collection; the left curved toward the rotunda and the rest of the sprawling complex. Ash suddenly staggered forward as though he might fall.

A burning sensation spread throughout his body, but it was not unpleasant. In fact, it made him feel abruptly energized. Strong. And it beckoned him. He turned, looking around for the source of the odd call.

"Sir?" The guard was in a wary stance, on high alert as he scanned the empty hallways in the quiet museum. "What is it?"

"I can feel them." Ash heard his own voice like the ringing of a bell. It had never sounded that clear before. "They're calling to me." The sensation was so strong it felt like he might literally be pulled along.

The guard had put his hand to his holstered weapon, intently staring down each hallway. Although a gun would not do any good against a dragon shifter, it would stop a human. Even a human tightly connected to the shifter world. "Which way?" The guard's voice grated with dark focus.

Ash shook his head, confused. "I'm not sure. It feels like it's coming from every direction." He frowned, also looking down each long, echoing hallway with their muted nighttime lighting. "It feels like it's coming from everywhere." He hadn't felt a connection to any of his hoard this strongly since before he was burned. The power source crackling around him from seemingly everywhere yet nowhere in particular was nearly overwhelming. It made him restless.

Taking a guess, Ash spun around and stalked down the hallway, the guard closely following. Then he stopped, confused again by the maelstrom of pushing and pulling he felt. "Damn it! It seems to come from everywhere."

The guard's phone abruptly dinged. He glanced down at it, swiped something, then snapped his head up at Ash. "Activity reported in the south wing, sir. A disturbance in the wards. I'll head over there. You continue on this way, sir. Whatever you find, I'm certain you'll be able to handle it." He nodded respectfully at Ash, his gaze never once showing an ounce of pity for Ash's scars and obvious limp. Ash appreciated that more than he could say. "I will keep Mr. Bernal apprised of any news through the phone."

Museum security had their own app through which they could communicate. It was installed on every security member's phone as well as each cell phone belonging to the top administration officials. Ash's mouth briefly quirked at the cleverness of it. "Excellent. He will contact me if you find anything." Seb had been texting Ash with curt updates from the other guards in the building, each time with it being no news yet.

"I'll head to the rotunda," Ash said. The guard nodded and peeled off in the other direction, almost jogging. Ash plunged toward the rotunda, hoping he was heading the right way.

The hallway was filled with less valuable yet still priceless paintings and other artwork. Stern or playful visages of people dead hundreds of years seemed to glow faintly from their spots recessed into the wall and lit by the special lights. He barely registered any of it, mind blasting back and forth from his books, his roaring dragon, and his beautiful mate with her mane of red hair and the fierce warrior queen attitude he'd sensed last night might finally burst free from her self-imposed constraints.

Just like his own dragon was ready to burst forth, enraged and ready to take on the world to defend what was his.

The hallway zigged and zagged en route to the grand rotunda in which the Center had begun to host hoity-toity weddings and other fancy gatherings. As Ash approached another corner, the bizarre yet welcome feeling of strength and clarity intensified.

He drew to a halt, listening intently. Nothing.

On soundless feet, he moved forward. Every amplified sense Ash possessed he sent questing in front of him. He couldn't tell if anyone was up there, around the corner. The fine hairs on his neck prickling, his lip curled as he thought that he damn well would surprise anyone who might be hiding along the way. Hardly breathing, he reached the very edge of the hallway.

Suddenly, far down it, he heard a voice yell, then an odd clanking sound. Like the sound of swords meeting.

Then came another sound. One that froze Ash's blood.

Teagan's voice.

Screaming.

"I feel like I'm breaking and entering," Teagan whispered as she pushed open the employee entrance door.

Eamon quietly chuckled. "You are entering with your own official employee pass, Ms. Lambert." As they entered the silent building, Ash's fealty man added in an arch tone, "I must say, I have yet to decide whether you are either incredibly foolish or incredibly brave." He gave Teagan a stern look. "You display characteristics of both."

With a small shrug, Teagan said, "I guess that makes me complex?" Eamon snorted at that while Teagan turned around to softly shut the door behind them. As she did so, the sword case slung over her shoulder softly thumped into the wall.

"Careful there." Eamon raised his eyebrows at Teagan's horrified *whoops* expression. "It's a truly valuable sword in more ways than one."

Teagan let a wan smile barely lift one lip as she gingerly felt the sword through the carrying case Eamon had provided for it once they'd had a little discussion back at Ash's house. It was a lot heavier than the practice sword she often took home with her. "Tell me again how it is that I'm not supposed to be able to handle this sword, but somehow I can, even though it's all wrapped up with a bunch of dragon magic stuff?"

Eamon was already looking down the dimly lit hallway,

clearly on high alert. He carried a sword as well, which he'd told her he felt more comfortable using than a gun. She'd definitely had no reply to that other than wide eyes and a nervous swallow. Shrugging now, he replied, "I can't tell you more than what I already did. It has to be entwined with the fact that you are his mate."

Teagan nodded. "Well, okay then. Dragon shifter mate magic stuff. Right. I've got this." She tried to sound confident even though she still had no idea what was going on.

Eamon's eyes crinkled as he abruptly swung his gaze around to give her a very fond look. Taken aback, Teagan just stared. "Ms. Lambert. While we really do not know one another very well yet, I can say this with utmost confidence." He leaned a little closer, his expression suddenly serious. "Let me assure you that while not only are you the best thing that has happened to Ash in quite some time, it clearly is true in the reverse." Eamon smiled gently at her. "He makes you shine."

Teagan rocked back on her heels.

He makes you shine. Yes, it was true. Ash really did do that for her.

Wow.

She looked at Eamon, feeling abashed but warm pleasure at his very unexpected compliment. On the drive over from Ash's house to the Bernal Center, during which Teagan had clutched the precious sword to her chest, Eamon had given her a down and dirty sketch of various aspects of dragon shifter history, modern political maneuvering, what it meant to be a dragon's mate, and the essentialness of a gold hoard to a dragon shifter's power. He'd briefly skimmed over the importance of the books and the sword as well. He'd also had a brief phone call with Ash, during which Teagan had stayed very quiet. Ash had specifically charged Eamon with watching over Teagan, and Eamon had readily agreed. But he hadn't, Teagan noticed, told Ash exactly *where* he would be watching over her.

That was just fine by her. She had a feeling Ash would be

worried if he knew she was in here, skulking along the corridors carrying his sword and ready to use it. Well, sort of ready. If she had to be.

Her mind had slipped in circles as she tried to understand everything Eamon had told her about the definitely complex dragon shifter world. One important realization she had was that she wasn't even questioning the existence of dragon shifters anymore. Or the existence of Ash himself in her life. She still had that deep knowing that everything Ash told her, and by extension everything his trusted fealty man told her, was true. She simply took it all in stride now.

She also felt a burning desire help her mate. To rain fury down upon his enemies.

Well, that might be sort of ambitious. There was no way that she, clumsy, geeky Teagan Lambert, could rain anything down on anyone. It would be good enough just to find Ash, get him his sword, and help find the books. Then let her badass dragon shifter take care of everything else, such as the bad guys. That sounded like a great ending.

She smiled a genuine thank you at Eamon for what he'd said, then focused on the matter at hand. "Okay. It's doubtful the books would still be near the work area. Whoever took them probably tried to find a way outside. Obviously they haven't yet, because that would have set off the alarms."

Eamon nodded. "They wouldn't be able to leave with the books anyway, due to the wards set upon them."

"Right." Teagan nodded, though she still had only the haziest idea of what exactly a "ward" was. All she really got was that it was some sort of magical protection put onto an object by a dragon shifter. In this case, by Ash. "And the security cameras were disabled. So they have no record of what happened."

"The indication of a professional job." Eamon's voice rippled with anger.

Abruptly, Teagan was filled with a strong sensation of

warmth. No, more than simple warmth. She suddenly felt a tingling heat she'd never experienced before.

It pulled at her. Literally pulled, like a cord tied to her was being tugged on the other end. And she was supposed to follow it.

She stared at Eamon, who looked back at her with a sharp gaze. Abruptly turning, Teagan headed straight down the hallway that led toward the medieval wing. "This way," she said with a surety that came from her gut. "I don't get it, but I just know that I need to go this way."

He silently padded after her. "You should trust that gut instinct." Drawing his own sword, he added in a low tone, "You should also allow me to be your guardian in the event we are walking into an ambush."

Icy hot fear washed through her at his words, but she didn't stop walking. Ash was in here somewhere. Sure, he was a big dragon shifter who could breathe fire. But she had his sword, lightly banging against her side in its case, which she knew he needed. She had to get to him despite the assured presence of bad guys somewhere inside the Center.

Teagan followed her oddly beckoning heart. It felt like a warm leash, gently tugging at her. As they swiftly walked, Teagan continued to talk out the tangled thoughts in her head to help her focus. Fear wouldn't do her much good. "Okay. So whoever took the books is also someone who has access. There's absolutely no way someone can break in here without the entire security team knowing it."

"Correct." Eamon walked on utterly silent feet, his sword casually held beside him although his entire body posture was tensely alert.

"And they definitely were alerted when someone tried to leave with the books, which is how we know someone tried to take them."

Eamon nodded as he silently prowled beside her, sending sharp glances into each passing wing.

"It has to be someone who knows about the hidden world of shifters," Teagan went on. The more she talked about it, the more natural it was seeming to her.

Eamon nodded silently.

"I mean," she went on, "first off, the Center's entire security team are all vetted and took some kind of blood oath to Mr. Bernal. And the senior department heads who are shifters, they had to do the same thing. An actual, really-their-own-blood oath," she added, feeling awe at that. It was so—ancient.

But Eamon just nodded again. "A blood oath binding one's trust and loyalty is very common in our world."

"Our world?" Teagan gave him a surprised look. "But aren't you...ah, human?"

Ash's fealty man smiled as he looked at her. "Yes. Rather like an enhanced human, however. I, too, have given my blood oath," he added softly. "To Ash, and the entire Connolly family. It is not something that can ever be broken. Whoever took the books *never*," the word slammed out of his suddenly snarling lips, "offered any sort of oath of loyalty to anyone here. Although they may be bound to other shifters."

Teagan shivered again. Wow, this was intense. And complex. And totally, wildly crazy.

But also very real.

As they turned down another hallway, Eamon went on in a more casual tone, although he didn't lower his wary guard as they moved along. "The thief must be someone completely unsuspected." He gave her a sidelong glance, eyes narrowed in assessment. "You, Teagan, worked most closely with the books. Who here had an unusual interest in them? Perhaps ever asked you about their provenance? Maybe even referred to the black market antiquities trade?"

Teagan shook her head in frustration, fingers tightening around the strap of the sword case. "No one. I've asked myself the same question ever since we left Ash's house. Nobody even knows they're here—oh!" She stopped dead in the hallway and snapped her fingers. "Someone did know. Sort of."

Eamon stopped short as well and gave her a sharp glance. "Explain."

Just as abruptly as she'd had her lightbulb moment, Teagan deflated. "No, it can't be her. Darn it. She's not a very nice person, but I don't see her being involved in outright theft. She wants to move up in the ranks here, not go to prison. I think she's a coward, anyway. Bullies always are."

Eyes back to checking the galleries that branched off the hallway, Eamon urged, "Tell me anyway. I might know something you don't."

"My coworker." Teagan shrugged and started to walk forward again. "I was all excited, thinking I solved it, but no. It can't be her. She's obnoxious and bossy, but she's not a shifter. You all would have known that and told me already."

"What is her name?"

"Celia Hearne?" Teagan looked at Eamon somewhat hopefully as she said it, just in case it did mean something to him. "Does it ring a bell?"

Eamon frowned, shaking his head. "No," said, sounding as frustrated as Teagan felt. "But you said she knew the books were here. Who else might she have told, even in very casual conversation?"

Before she could answer, the warm tingling in her chest suddenly flared brightly. Teagan gasped. Decisively, she turned her head to the left. "It's this way," she breathed, staring down the hallway that led to current exhibitions and the great rotunda. "I don't know why I know, but it's definitely this way."

Eamon nodded as he paced alongside her. "That the feeling we are following, the gut sense you have, has not yet changed very likely means that the books are stationary. Meaning that whoever tried to take them did indeed flee, realized they could not take the books from the Center, and in desperation put them down somewhere and simply fled by themselves."

"So whoever took them is gone?"

"Maybe. Maybe not." Eamon's tight voice and still carefully probing looks into every corner they passed said that he suspected the latter.

Suddenly very grateful for his protective presence, Teagan felt a little chill dance down her spine. She didn't really know what they were getting themselves into. For a geeky academic, a book conservator, a girl who just loved ancient Irish history and had fallen for an amazing someone who was part of a magical world she knew nothing about, this was a heck of a lot more drama tonight than she'd already had. She blushed as she thought of the earlier part of the night. All she wanted right now was to see Ash's smoky green eyes, his stunning smile. Just all of him. She wanted to kiss him again. Be held by his strong, comforting arms.

Ash, she thought hard in her head, not even feeling dumb for doing it. *I'm here.*

Naturally, there was no response. But it didn't matter. She felt soothed anyway.

As they rounded another corner and headed to the airy expansiveness of the great rotunda, Teagan began thinking out loud again. "So it isn't anyone I can think of off the top of my head." Her feet now fell as silently as Eamon's on this carpeted section.

Eamon nodded, gliding along, his sword carried lightly at his side. Glancing into another quiet gallery off the hallway, he said in equally thoughtful tones, "We are missing something. There is someone with access to the Center who not only knows about shifters, but also understands the value of Ash's books. Hmm."

His last grunt was quiet, but Teagan sensed he was not happy. As they entered the great rotunda, she looked around at the shadowy corners, feeling slightly unnerved here for the first time in her life. Eamon's words reassured her. "So now all we need to do is—"

A soft thunk from somewhere ahead in the large room startled both of them, Teagan shying to the side while Eamon raised his sword and moved forward with grim intention. "Stay here," he said quietly. His voice was razor sharp and deadly.

Teagan stood completely frozen, her heart suddenly rat-a-tatting against her ribs. She wasn't about to move. She didn't think she actually could move, to be honest. The fear surged over her again, uncontrollable and nearly overpowering. Eamon slid like a shadow into the rotunda, which was lit decently but not very brightly given the hour of night. Only the galleries and rooms containing museum pieces were well-lit after hours. The rotunda held a few nice items, but they didn't need to be under virtual spotlights as were some of the museum's far more valuable holdings.

If Eamon was so willing to charge forth into potential danger, she, too, ought to be better safe than sorry. Very carefully, she slid Ash's sword from its case. Although its heft was heavy, it somehow felt light and alive in her hand. Almost like it was trying to dance. A light, silvery tingle of energy seemed to zip up her arm from where she held the hilt. Gazing down at it, she cautiously wondered what kind of magic it might hold.

This was crazy, but the sword—it fit her. Like she was supposed to handle it.

Well, then. Blinking hard into the dimness, trying to keep Eamon's figure in sight as he glided into the spacious room, Teagan also felt the warmth blossoming in her chest even more. It wanted to tug her to the side of the great rotunda, thankfully not in the direction of the sound Eamon was investigating. Well, that was interesting. Were the books just in there? Her brow wrinkled as another thought whipped across her mind. Wait, what if they were there? And what if they were still with the person or people who had tried to steal them?

Alarm choked her as she tried to call out Eamon's name, dryness making her tongue stick to her mouth. Then a low, ugly chuckle sounded from behind her. Teagan whirled around so fast she almost did a full three-sixty, nearly slicing herself on her own blade, but she managed to stop herself in time.

Holy. Freaking. No. Way.

She gaped at the sight before her.

"Well, hello there, freckle-face. I'm quite pleased you made it." Celia stepped out of the shadows to face Teagan, her expression one of such chilly arrogance that Teagan felt punched in the stomach by shock. She'd never seen such a look on the woman's face before. Celia looked—like a different person. Cool, disdainful, controlled. Worse yet, she lofted both *The Book of the Dragonborn* and *The Book of the Near Hills* in one hand, a deadly-looking sword in the other. Her sword didn't look light at all. It looked dark, sharp, and very ready to shed blood.

Teagan's blood.

Holy freaking crap.

"How very clever of you to bring that sword. You've just aided my quest immensely." Celia's words were spoken with such deep menace that Teagan's jaw dropped in shock. Who was this calm, assured, deadly woman, and what had happened to the rotten but basically harmless person who was her coworker? This Celia was like some sort of evildoer from a movie. "Well, then. Let us just see how little you have learned in your sword-fighting classes, you pathetic fool."

With that, Celia leapt straight at Teagan and flashed her sword down in a deadly, singing arc, knocking Ash's sword right out of Teagan's hand.

Leaving her utterly defenseless.

2 0

Ash's heart threatened to explode in his chest as he desperately tried to follow the sound of his mate's screams. The raging cry of his dragon shattered through his mind, then burst out of his throat in a half-human, half-dragon bellow of shock and rage. His inhuman side pushed at him to shift, feeling hot and molten just beneath his skin. Lunging down the hallway, eyesight crystal clear from his dragon's vision, Ash could almost feel himself take flight. Almost feel himself beat the air with his wings, strong down-strokes propelling him toward the woman who held his soul entwined with hers.

He could not fly. First off, he was inside a building that would not accommodate his much larger dragon shape. Secondly, he simply could not fly. Not anymore.

But he could run. Faster than a human could, with his dragon side shimmering just below the surface to lend speed to his stride. He sprinted down the hallways of the Center, aiming toward the location of his mate's terrified voice. Every other thought was shoved out of his head as he hurtled toward her. His only goal was to get to her and save her. His terrified rage simmered as he bolted along. Someone was attacking her because of him. Those were his books, part of his dragon's power. Teagan had nothing to do with any of it except for being in the wrong place at the wrong time. Clearly, she had fallen into the ugly morass of constantly shifting tides of dragon politics.

Speaking of which, what the hell was she doing here anyway? He had charged Eamon with watching over her. As he burst into the spaciousness of the enormous rotunda that was the central part of the sprawling museum complex, Eamon himself came tumbling out of the darkness there, a sword lifted before him as he also barreled toward the sound of Teagan under attack. Barely sparing a glance for Ash, his fealty man snapped, "Distraction and ambush. Took me away from her. She is the target. For some reason, Teagan is the prize."

His stark words sent Ash's heart catapulting around inside him again. His dragon raged and strained, so wildly desperate to get out and protect his mate that Ash was half afraid he would be forced to shift right here. His dragon body could fit inside the great rotunda, but just barely.

"I'm sorry," Eamon panted as they pounded down the corridor.

Ash heard the genuine fear and self-reproach in his fealty man's voice. But then Eamon added in a voice jolted by their flat-out strides, "Your mate is very strong-minded. Smart." Determined optimism underscored his words.

Sudden yelling ahead startled them both. "Stop! Don't do this, please."

Teagan. Terrified.

A female voice Ash didn't recognize responded. "You do not have the strength to fight me, Teagan. So go." The voice snapped with a cool, ruthless intent. "Take them outside. Now."

A sudden gasp of real pain nearly stopped Ash's heart.

Teagan. Somebody was hurting her. Somebody was hurting his mate.

Eamon kept pace with him for a mere few strides before Ash passed him like a hell-bent freight train. Or like a dragon on the verge of flight. His dragon hummed just beneath his skin, close to controlling all of Ash's movements and decisions, lending his far greater speed and strength to Ash's human body. Even so, he could not move as quickly as he wanted. The hitch in his gait, the drag of his right leg, slowed him down just enough that he feared he would be too late to save Teagan from whatever fate she'd just encountered.

He dodged a statue of some bygone Roman deity, then managed to leap over a cordoned-off display of an ancient stone tablet with cuneiform writing on it. Miraculously, he didn't land in a clumsy, sprawling heap. But his leg twinged violently, the tight, shrunken muscles shrieking in protest despite all the training he'd been pushing himself through.

Ahead, another small scream burst out of Teagan's throat, echoing tinnily in the large room. Sheer terror made Ash force himself on, gasping for breath. He wouldn't make it in time. His damn scars, the twisted, damaged portion of his body, would fail not only him but his mate.

Now he could see the two figures ahead. One was sprawled on the ground, the muted light of a nearby display catching on her red hair. Teagan. Overhead, another figure stood with a sword held aloft, as if just about to slice it downward in a killing blow. Ash opened his mouth, trying to yell Teagan's name. All he did was nearly strangle on it from both his gasps of exertion as well as the ugly jangle of fear that seemed to dry him from the inside out.

"Now." The figure standing over Teagan, a small woman who clearly knew how to use the weapon she held, abruptly flicked her head over her shoulder as she heard Ash's approach. Her teeth flashed in a dangerous smile, but she ignored him and turned back toward Teagan. "Now!"

With that, the woman with the sword whipped it down through the air, blade whistling. It whispered along Teagan's forearm, instantly leaving crimson blossoming through the white sleeve of the shirt she wore.

Ash bellowed, forcing the noise through the dryness of his throat, hearing his dragon's roar rip through as well. He was about to lose the battle and shift into his other being, but he didn't care. All the better with which to destroy the evil woman hurting his mate.

Behind him, Eamon yelled out some sort of warning, but Ash couldn't hear, his body caught in the dizzying swirl of the shift between man and dragon.

Teagan cast a brief, wild glance toward Ash, terror in her face. But he saw something else there as well, enhanced by the multifaceted sparkle of his dragon's eyes. A fierce, unstoppable determination. She reached down to grab the books he only now noticed lying on the museum floor beside her. His stolen books. Then she swung up a sword of her own. Blade flashing bright silver, it seemed to hum with a beckoning draw.

Ash stared, thunderstruck. That was his ancestral Connolly sword, crafted by the hand of an ancient dragon shifter king. It had been calling to him, drawing him here along with his books. Their combined power shimmered through the air, slipping over his red dragon hide and enlivening his entire being with strength and hope.

Clutching the books to her chest, the sword in her hand catching the light, his beautiful mate rolled over, staggered onto all fours, then pushed herself upright. Lunging toward the exit door, she flung back over her shoulder to the woman behind her, "Then come and get them from me." Her voice rang out with such conviction that it seemed to vibrate through the room. "I dare you."

With that, Teagan launched herself through the door, taking Ash's books and sword with her.

TEAGAN BUSTED through the door to the inner gardens like a champion door-smasher. Luckily her employee pass had already unlocked it so it wasn't like she actually smashed through glass or anything crazy like that. Although she was already bleeding.

Bleeding. Because Celia, *Celia* of all people, had cut her with a sword. An actual sword, which Celia wielded like a pro. Clearly, this day was going to go down as the strangest one in Teagan's life.

If she lived through it, that is.

Rain immediately drenched her. She instinctively hunched over the books. In sheer desperation, she stuffed them under Ash's shirt, hoping it would be enough to protect them. Wiping rain from her eyes, hunching again as lightning cracked in the sky, she looked around. Although mostly dim, the garden was still lit well enough that she could see. She was familiar with it since she'd often come out here for lunch to get some fresh air during a long workday. But she didn't usually frequent the place in the dark, in the rain, being chased by a maniac with a sword. Frantically, she swiveled her head around, trying to decide which direction to go.

Behind her, the door banged violently. Then it exploded outward in a shower of glass.

Teagan launched forward as if shot from a cannon, blindly running. She lunged across the brief expanse of open space, one hand tightly clutching Ash's precious objects to her bare chest beneath the shirt and his sword in her other hand, before veering right to begin zig-zagging down the labyrinthine pathways through what was a Zen styled garden.

Behind her, a mocking yet frosty call filled the air. "Run, idiot, but I will find you." It sounded nothing like the Celia she knew.

Really, that was almost more terrifying than anything else happening right now.

A booming roar filled the garden. Her rather freaked out mind couldn't parse what it was. Whirling around, she stupidly tried to see through the bushes toward the door she'd just left. Right, that didn't work. Apparently being a dragon's mate and finding out about cool things like magical books and whatnot didn't mean that she suddenly had x-ray vision. Turning back, she bolted toward the maze of hedges and flowers, heading in a pattern that hopefully should drop her right at the little sitting area in the middle garden space. It was wide open there, with numerous other pathways leading off from it. She had to get there. She had to flee crazy Celia and her sword.

Wait a minute. Teagan stopped so short she almost tripped over her own feet. Ash's sword, clumsily held by her as she ran, lopped off the heads of several beautiful pinkish-purple azaleas. Pulling the sword close to her, sending a mental apology to the flowers now lying in beheaded states on the ground, she took a deep breath. Focus, she sternly admonished herself. What would her instructor Nick say? Right. *Panic and disarray is a sure way to lose the upper hand to your enemy. You must pause and find the flow of your battle sense.*

Huh. Dragon shifters sure were a sensible lot.

Cocking one ear toward the horrific sounds coming from inside of the building, which basically sounded like some enormous creature was trying to smash its way out of the walls, as well as listening for the approaching steps of the woman chasing her down and trying to kill her, Teagan forced herself to assess the moment.

Celia had thrust the books at her, back inside the rotunda, and ordered her to take them outside. She'd seemed really pleased that Teagan had brought Ash's sword, too. She called it the cherry on top. Why? What was so important about the books, the sword? She somehow understood that taking them outside the building was something Celia hadn't been able to do.

But Teagan would be able to, and Celia clearly knew it.

Teagan's academic mind stubbornly mulled this over, while her instinctual mind urged her to keep fleeing the enemy. The voice of her sword master drifted through again, nudging her to stop and assess before meeting the enemy in combat. Not, of course, that the Institute of Ancient Battle Arts really thought she'd ever have to use their training in a real-life skirmish.

Wait a minute. Had they?

In the next split-second, mulling academic mind found itself overridden by instinctual mind, firmly bent toward keeping her whole and in one piece, as Celia burst around the corner like a silent creature of the night world. Startled, Teagan half screamed again—really, she had to stop doing that. So girly—whirled, and again began racing pell-mell toward the center garden.

"I'm right behind you," came the dark slither of Celia's voice. The sound chased Teagan along, both the menace and poise of it still stunning her.

How was this happening to her? How had her life ended up with her being chased by a woman with a sword while her newfound dragon shifter lover was probably being eaten by some giant monster back inside the Center?

Just run! Teagan's gibbering instinctual brainstem shrieked at her. *Stop thinking, and run!*

She ran.

Further behind her now, a sudden enormous shuddering sound like an explosion rent the air. It sounded like an actual bomb had gone off, scattering debris into the garden. Teagan felt tiny pellets of concrete and other building bits rain down on her head and back and shoulders as she ran, sharply twisting and turning through the delicate garden hedges and trees.

What the actual heck was going on? Oh, right. Didn't matter. Time to just run now.

Faltering briefly in one corner, she tried to remember if she was supposed to take the left fork or the right. A pouncing step behind her, then a sharp, hot prick on her back that left a line of fire along her spine made her shriek and lurch forward again.

"Oh, don't stop now. Keep running." Darkness wrapped around the horrifying chords of Celia's voice. Lightning crackled again, as if to underscore the menace.

Teagan jolted forward, brain scrambling over the fact that the woman had sliced her again. With a real sword. Real metal. It had really just cut into her flesh, just like it had earlier.

Holy freaking crap.

Teagan ran. Hard, and fast, and terrified. She heard her own breath going in and out, harshly echoing inside her ears. Her feet slapped the ground. Her stupid work shoes were thin enough that the occasional pebble or twig, or simply rough patch she stumbled over, raked pain through her soles. Yet she forced herself onward. Celia clearly had no qualms about slicing her to pieces. Teagan spared the briefest glance over-head as she ran, but she could see nothing except the shadows cast by the graceful willow trees that draped the pathways. Sopping wet, the trees scattered more rain onto her as she ran.

She just had to make it to the open grassy space in the middle of the garden. Once there, she could find the little hiding spot behind a statue that was virtually impossible to notice. All she had to do was gain a couple more lengths ahead of Celia, who despite her determination still had far shorter legs than Teagan. She was falling behind. Putting on a burst of speed, doing her best to ignore the bite of pain as her feet slammed down on something particularly hard and spiky, to ignore the heaviness of her arm holding the sword in one hand

and still clutching the books to her chest with the other, Teagan made herself race onward.

There. She saw a lighter spot ahead. The soft glow of the lamp stands that circled the inner garden. In seconds, she burst out into the clearing, only to find herself once again pummeled with rain as the skies heaved and banged with more thunder before sending a new flooding burst of water down everywhere. Then her feet touched down on the grassy center. She immediately slipped on the wet, manicured lawn and promptly went down. Twisting her body, wrenching her sword arm out to one side to keep from chopping off her own head while also trying to keep the books safely held to her beneath the shirt, Teagan landed face first, grass shoving up into her mouth and nose.

Then everything happened at once. Celia burst out halfway behind her, darting toward Teagan, sword raised, something like an actual snarl splitting apart her lips. Lightning cracked again, brightly illuminating everything for a split second.

Illuminating the enormous dusky gray dragon that hovered in the sky overhead. Massive wings, deadly claws, scales and everything. Not to mention a huge mouth opened wide, the razor-sharp blades of its teeth aiming right for Teagan where she lay on the ground.

Girly or not, newfound determination or not, she shrieked at the top of her lungs in terror at the monstrous vision coming right at her.

A mighty roar seemed to shake everything. It was followed by another thunderclap. Then another blast of lightning revealed another dragon. This time, a magnificent crimson one that was so stunning, so flat out freaking majestic, that Teagan swallowed her scream as her breath caught in her throat. Gleaming ruby scales shimmered along its sides and back, so breathtakingly grand that Teagan just stared. Huge, serrated ridges rippled down its back, the colors a shifting blend of onyx and carmine.

The dragon's huge, splendid left wing beat hard to keep it aloft. The right wing valiantly tried to stretch out as well, but it was hampered by the twisted, blackened flesh there. Glowing green eyes looked at Teagan with a blast of comforting familiarity. It reminded her of the dragon she'd seen depicted in the hidden images in the book, only way, way cooler.

Holy freaking crap. Teagan's breath whooshed back into her, filling her with such clarity and wonder that she laughed with incredulous joy. It was Ash. Ash was actually a mother-freaking dragon, flying in the sky above her. Soaring like a spectacular creature of power and strength, like a gorgeous winged god of the sky. Her Ash, a magnificent dragon, *flying*.

No. Teagan's body shivered with sudden cold dread. Not flying any longer. Hurtling toward the ground.

Falling. Ash was falling, because his one good wing simply couldn't support the rest of his huge body.

A sh knew it would hurt like hell when he hit the ground.

It did.

He landed with a mighty whomp that almost knocked the breath out of him. Maddened by terror for his mate and fury at the one who would try to steal from him, Ash had battered his giant dragon body against the inside of the Center, unable to follow Teagan and the small woman with the sword through the door, too crazed by fear and fury to shift back into his smaller human shape. He'd roared and bellowed and howled, flinging himself against the wall, ignoring everything else. Ignoring the shouting behind him that came from Eamon, yelling at him to stop.

Ash ignored everything. He had to get to his mate. He had to protect her.

His huge dragon body finally smashed its way out of the Center, destroying the wall and the door in a violent burst of rubble. He'd have to pay Sebastian for its repair later. But first things first. So attuned to his mate that he could actually sense her as she fled along the pathways beneath the canopy of bushes toward the center of the beautiful gardens, Ash launched himself into the air, the forceful spring of his powerful hind legs and pure desperation driving him into the sky to fly.

To *fly*.

He thrilled at the joy of being able to swoop upward under the power of his good wing and the half strokes of his bad one, feeling the air rushing past him while rain pelted his hide. The ozone in the air from the storm seemed to electrify his hide, adding more fuel to his fire dragon abilities. His wing flapped. One stroke. Two strokes.

There! An enormous clap of thunder followed by a bright flash of lightning revealed his redheaded mate hurtling into the open center of the garden. He exulted at seeing her, an exultation which was immediately turned to a new fear as the small shape bearing a sword burst out after her. Ash roared a warning.

Then Teagan slipped. Fell to the ground, body curling and rolling until she ended up in a heap, the sharp blade of Ash's ancestral sword barely missing slicing off her ear. As she lay helplessly on the ground, the thief with her own deadly sword raced toward her, weapon raised in what was clearly meant to be a killing stroke meant for his mate.

Ash bellowed in rage and fury, one that was answered by a mocking roar from above him. He whipped his head up to see a dark gray dragon in the air, one he immediately recognized as being from the Kerberos clan up north. He swore even amidst his terrorized fury. Seb had been right. All this had been an organized, calculated attempt to greatly increase the powers of another dragon. The gray one above was related to Malcolm Kerberos, one of the most despised, now thankfully dead, dragons in the entire country. Opening his jaws again, Ash bellowed out a warning to the gray dragon, then turned his attention back to his beleaguered mate.

It was at that moment that Ash's ruined body failed him. His one good wing simply wasn't strong enough to keep supporting his entire body, despite the valiant effort of his other wing. Bellowing again with frustration and anguish, Ash plummeted to the ground. His landing whomp drew a groan from him and anxious cry from Teagan, who still lay sprawled on the ground nearby.

From the sky above him, the gray dragon roared as it dove downward, claws extending forward, ready to grab. Behind Ash, the thieving women said in a cold, ruthless tone, "Excellent. You've both done an excellent job delivering exactly what it was that we needed. We can't thank you enough." Her last words were sticky with sarcasm.

The dragon in the sky above them abruptly slowed to a hover, its giant wings flapping gusty drafts throughout the garden and spraying around yet more rain. Thunder clapped and cracked again, another bright flash of white momentarily illuminating everything. Teagan's wide-eyed, white face, her mouth open as her gaze darted around. The small woman striding toward them both, her sword now held to the side rather than in an offensive posture. The oddly delicate, sweet scent of unknown flowers reached Ash's sensitive nose just as the brightness from the lightning flash disappeared again.

He could see quite well even in the dimmer light from the tall lamps situated around the garden. Opening his fearsome mouth, Ash let out a hissing snarl at the woman as she came closer to his mate. Struggling up onto his haunches, he extended his good wing over Teagan, blocking her from both the woman and the marauding dragon in the sky above. Lifting his head up, his eyes glared at the other, darkly laughing dragon Ash bellowed out his warning again. *Stay away,* his booming snarl said. *This woman is mine, and I will protect her with all my power.*

Eamon abruptly skidded into the clearing, his own sword drawn. He immediately halted as Ash flicked him a glance, standing quiet and wary as he quickly took in the scene with his eyesight that was much better than that of the two human women there. Ash knew his glowing eyes were visible to everyone anyway. He tightly nodded his large head at Eamon.

Eamon spoke in a deliberately casual tone to the woman, projecting his voice through the loudness of the sluicing rain and lingering rumbles of thunder as the storm slowly passed over them. "Who are you to dare think you can steal from this place and this dragon?" He gestured at Ash.

The woman laughed. The mocking edge to it matched that of the booming, dragon-ish laughter that occasionally came from the sky above them.

"I," she said in a cold, stark tone, "am but the messenger. This," and she flicked her fingers to indicate them all, "is a message to all those shackled dragons and their servants who obey all the laws and never experience real freedom. The freedom of creating your own power in this world."

Ash rumbled deep in his chest at her dismissive tone. Beneath his wing, he felt Teagan moving and shot a glance down. She was sitting up, then pushing herself to standing. He kept his wing steady over his mate as she situated herself.

"Shackled dragons?" Eamon's tone was just as coolly dismissive as the woman's. "I think you mean just, fair, and honorable dragons. Unlike the ones you serve." He jerked his head skyward toward the hovering gray dragon, though his eyes didn't leave the woman. Eamon was keeping as close an eye on her as Ash was.

"An antiquated, completely useless old system in these times," the woman snapped back, her cool façade cracking for just a moment. "Why should dragons be allowed to receive power only from their inheritance or acquiring artifacts only on the legal market, rather than from all possible venues? It takes far too long, and it places a very unfair advantage on some dragons while disadvantaging many others."

Ash felt another rumble vibrate through his frame. Beneath his wing, he sensed Teagan rustling about, his sensitive dragon hearing able to pick it up even through the sheets of rain.

Eamon slowly shook his head at the woman. "There's always been inequality in the world," he said, still watching her closely. "That does not mean that rules and laws should be broken because of it. But what of you? You're not a shifter. And I did not recognize your last name from any fealty family. Celia Hearne," he added, glancing at Ash. Ash rumbled an irritated snort. He did not recognize it either.

Celia laughed. "The name I use is my grandmother's maiden name. There is no way to connect it to the fealty family that has served the Kerberos clan for centuries. I still serve them with great pleasure." Genuine pride rang in her voice, although it had an odd touch of bitter despair.

Ash let smoke and fire billow from his mouth as anger raced along his ridged spine. All the corrupt shifters of the Kerberos clan were diabolically clever at times. It made sense their fealty family members would be as well.

Eamon simply grunted and stayed focused on the matter at hand. "What is your gain in this scenario?" His eyes stayed watchfully on Celia. "It is clear that you must work here at the Center." He gestured with one hand in the direction of the building that surrounded them. "But after this stunt you have lost your job, any standing you had within the antiquities community—the aboveboard antiquities community, I may add. Not to mention you'll certainly be facing prison time. For what gain?"

Above them, the gray dragon gave his wings an angry beat, slicing out another roar into the storm.

The coolly assessing look back on her face, the woman let a sardonic grin stretch over her mouth. "The same gain many dragon shifters seek, through whatever means deemed necessary. Power," she said in a voice that was low yet somehow rang through with strength.

Ash froze as he stared at the woman, slowly blinking his

eyes a few times in the dragon equivalent of narrowing them at someone. She was human, yes, but her voice only could carry around the small inner clearing that way due to dragon shifter magic. Teagan would never have been able to sense that, of course. Nor would anyone in the shifter world on a casual inspection, since she could not carry the magic with her at all times. She could only use it on occasion, such as now. This accounted for how the woman had been able to slip into the employment ranks here without being known to associate with shifters. Dirty, dark, underhanded dragon magic infused her.

It made her even more dangerous.

He snapped out a low, sharp bellow. The woman flicked her gaze up at him. "And now we have all the pieces right here that we need in order to gain even more power." She looked under Ash's sheltering wing, her gaze now subtly contemptuous. "I didn't realize how important Teagan was in gaining these particular artifacts. I thought it was just another simple snatch and grab, as I have done before."

Teagan stepped out slightly from under Ash's wing, despite his instant protective warning rumble at her. He could see that she had tucked the books beneath her shirt, doing the best she could protect them from the rain. Sudden pride swelled within him yet again. His glorious, conscientious historian mate was doing her best to protect the pieces of his own history she held close to her. His sword still gripped in her hand, she said, "You've done this before, Celia? You've stolen antiquities?" Her voice was a mixture of combined horror and disgust.

"Naturally." Celia gave Teagan a steady, cool gaze. She clearly was well trained. "Never from the Center before, of course. Even I have to admit that the security is far beyond anything we could ever penetrate. But I learned the routines of the guards, and the weakest areas of the Center. Tonight's guards have been either incapacitated, or distracted over to the far southern wing where I planted a dummy ward, set to ding the alarms about ten minutes after you arrived. It will take them too long to get here."

Her stance was still easy, light, as she shrugged at Ash's irate roar at her clever subterfuge.

"Once I figured out the importance of these particular artifacts, we realized we had to get them no matter the cost. So," she flashed another cool smile, "we devised a way to have them come to us. All of them," she added with an oddly focused look at Teagan, her glance flickering down to the sword in Teagan's hand. "This garden is still accessible by air. We just needed to get the books out of the building. I knew if we lured you here because of it, Teagan would be sure to follow. She takes her job so, so seriously." Celia's laugh danced on the edge of derisive, but it was calculated. She was goading Teagan.

Ash rumbled his warning again, but Teagan, his still clearly nervous yet magnificent warrior woman, took another step closer to Celia, likely caught up by the story as well as the baiting. "I still don't understand why the books are so important to you."

Above, the gray dragon slapped his wings again and huffed into the storming wind. The stink of sulfur suddenly mingled with the ozone in the air, causing Ash's hide to tighten reflexively.

The diminutive Celia let another mocking smile slide across her face, although her voice was still coolly possessed as she answered. "They are everything, you silly fool. The book that seems interesting but actually isn't. The dull but far more valuable other book. The powerful sword of Ash Connolly's ancestors, although having that here tonight is quite the unexpected bonus." Her deep knowledge of everything sent a chill rippling down Ash's enormous frame. "Then, of course, there was the final key to releasing all the locked up magic within the books. The key I didn't realize until tonight was the only thing I had missed."

She took a deliberately casual step toward Teagan. Eamon

took a deliberately deliberate step toward them both, holding his ground when Celia lifted her sword in a defensive position. It was obvious by the way she held it that she knew precisely how to handle it.

"Wh-what is that?" Teagan held her ground as well despite the small shake in her voice. Her arm tightened around the books she still held close to her chest, beneath the shirt she wore that Ash knew was his own.

"Why, the true key to a dragon's treasure, or so I'm told." The sharp tang of grief suddenly coated her words as tension radiated from her. In the sky overhead, the gray dragon's snarl crawled through the echoing thunder as the smell of sulfur intensified.

Then Celia easily, deftly spoke in ancient Gaelic. *"To find the key to a dragon's treasure / From the fiery mouth of the clouded mountain / The scorched carmine dragon must emerge / To battle in fearless resolution for his stolen gold / And to claim the heart of his eternal true mate."*

Resounding silence met her words. Teagan and Eamon wore matching expressions of pure shock, which echoed the massive jolt of astonishment and alarm that slammed through Ash.

"So very romantic, your ancestors." Celia's smile at Ash was terrifyingly cold.

"What—how did you know about that inscription?" It was obvious that Teagan was desperately trying to understand the machinations of the ancient politics tumbling around her. She still bravely stood there, Ash's sword tightly clutched in her hand, his books making a lumpy shape beneath her soaked shirt.

Celia laughed. "Research, of course. A lifetime's worth. I am actually a trained book conservator, you know. I just use my knowledge to further the goals of the Kerberos clan."

"To further the goals of thieves, you mean?" Teagan's voice

disbelief was bordered by a touch of contemptuous anger. Ash rumbled in approving echo.

Ignoring the barb, Celia just smiled again with her own cool contempt. While she didn't step closer to Teagan, her entire body did subtly tense in a way that signaled an imminent attack. "'That inscription was so very important to understanding what needed to be done here. It told me that the combined magic of the books could only be released, and therefore be truly valuable, by an exact circumstance."

Despite the gushing rain and the swells of thunder that still rolled over the grounds, everything suddenly seemed to go utterly silent with sick tension.

"What sort of exact circumstance?" Teagan's voice sounded doubtful. Nervous.

A tight smile flashed over Celia's face. "'The circumstance in which the owner of the books, the one to whose hoard they belong, and the key to his treasure are in proximity to the books at the same time. The key, of course," she said in a silken smooth voice shot through with a bitter pain and regret, "is his mate."

The key to a dragon's treasure. His mate. The words reverberated through Ash's head.

Before anyone could move, Celia whipped forward so quickly she was a blur. Her sword tip neatly sliced down the front of Teagan's shirt, sending *The Book of the Near Hills* and *The Book of the Dragonborn* tumbling to the ground amidst the sound of Teagan's horrified yelp. As Celia sprang back before the quick-footed Eamon's sword could reach her, the books landed with heavy thumps on the ground, their ancient pages flying open to be pelted with rain. Ash roared in desperate fear as Teagan made as if to grab the books, shoving down his huge head to try to protect her from foolishly trying to save them. He cared a great deal more about her hide than the books, magically-imbued or not.

"Teagan," Celia said, her voice a deadly command. When

Teagan wildly looked at her, Celia was already swinging her sword. Teagan met the lunge with an automatic defensive move, Ash's bright sword moving up to strike with Celia's immediately over the books.

A shower of silvery-golden sparks loosed from Ash's sword slipped down through the rain to land on the books, which lit up with an unearthly glow that brightly illuminated everything in the small garden. Teagan gasped, falling back toward Ash again as he bellowed his own surprise. Eamon's startled cry was swallowed by the triumphant scream of the gray dragon overhead.

"Oh, my," Celia added in a singsonging, light tone, her body suddenly becoming vibrant with a sort of excitement. "The sword is really quite a nice addition. Very clever of you to bring it, Teagan."

Ash could feel his mate's anger as if it were his own.

"One last thing, of course." Celia's voice rang clear and loud through the garden.

Teagan's voice was a bare whisper now, although Ash could still hear her easily. "What's that?"

Celia's lips curved into an icily avaricious smile. "Blood."

With that, the woman vaulted forward, sword gleaming in the rain-lit night air as the gray dragon shrieked out an ugly, challenging call overhead.

Eamon charged forward at Celia. Ash roared, automatically spreading his wing out again to protect Teagan as well. But Celia unexpectedly flipped in midair, kicking back with one leg to deliver a calculated blow to Eamon's head. He dropped like a stone to the sound of Teagan's stunned cry.

Then the woman whipped herself around again, her years of training obvious as she arrowed for her goal. But her goal wasn't Teagan.

It was Ash.

She sliced her blade down onto his wing, carving into a joint so that his blood abruptly flowed out. Ash's shocked bellow of pain and surprise rent the air. "Dragon's blood is the final key," Celia whispered, her voice shuddering with a dangerous ooze of power as she sprang back.

Into the sudden hush, a huge frisson of something massive pulsed through the very air.

Power. Enormous power that was much greater than the shadowy film of magic Celia had pulled over herself. This was Ash's power. The power that had been weakened by the whittling down of his hoard, then truly handicapped after his being burned. It flared now, billowing to and through him. He felt strong. Light. Clear-headed. Confident. More so than he had in years. He felt like he had back when his power was at full strength. He'd simply forgotten what it was like.

Opening his mouth into an enormous bellow of joyous triumph, Ash beat his wings through the whipping, rain-filled air. His right one was still crumpled, charred, twisted. But it was stronger even in that second. It would still likely never heal completely, but he didn't need that. He just needed it to work right now.

He could sense without a doubt that it would.

He loosed his bellow again and again into the drenching rain and the rumbling clouds. Looking down, he saw Teagan looking at him, her gorgeous, brave face shining with both awe and power. The power was in her, too. It was part of her, it was from her, it was wrapped up with her.

The key to a dragon's treasure. Yes. *Teagan* was Ash's true treasure. Because she was his mate, she had been the key to releasing the magic worked into the books, the sword, Ash's dragon self. Her presence was the element he'd been missing.

His mate. His heart.

"Ash!" Teagan's radiant face, slicked with rain, looked up at him. "I believe in you. I believe in you!" Jubilant tears slid down her face, glistening through the rain. "I believe in both of us," she added in a whisper that carried to him as if she had trumpeted the words.

The sheer force of her belief rocked through him, adding even more punch to what was already a very satisfying moment. But then Celia shifted the stakes again.

"Quite touching," she said in that cool, trained voice that covered something bitterly ugly. "But a little premature, I'm sorry to say. You've simply fulfilled our plan to release the magic, not to mention enhanced it by having the Connolly sword here as well. Now," her voice bit out with deadly surety and grace, "it's time for us to take that magic and put it to better use."

With that, she whirled her glittering blade through the air, aiming it directly for the unsuspecting Teagan's head. Roaring, Ash lunged forward to protect his mate. But too late. The leaden gray dragon in the sky above abruptly dove down and sunk his deadly claws right into Ash's back.

22

The agonized, furious sound of Ash's shriek as the other dragon swooped out of the darkness and shoved his terrifying claws right into Ash's exposed back tore at Teagan's heart. She also quaked with fear for Eamon, crumpled on the ground. Maybe even dead. But she had no time to worry about either one of them, because now Celia was coming for her. This time, she really meant business. Her sword shrieked through the air, coming right at Teagan's face.

Oh, holy freaking crap. Teagan stood frozen there for what seemed like a timeless moment of shock, mouth open, body feeling shaky and loose and strange all at once. The key to a dragon's treasure had been found. Apparently Celia had what she wanted now: the artifacts and Ash's blood. Teagan had been the key, but she no longer was. Now she really was expendable. Celia's leap had almost reached her, seeming strangely in slow motion, a grimace across her face, her sword arm extended out to deliver the final, fatal blow.

Sword master Nick's words about strength and courage and calm floated through Teagan's head in a split second. The amazing badassery of Queen Boudica flashed through as well.

The strange, intense power she could feel whispering through her entire body bolstered her. But mostly, Ash's pained shriek scraped through her head, her entire soul, leaving a burning agony within her as well.

Abruptly, it also left a cold, steely resolve. Everything whirled around Teagan as clarity and purpose exploded over her so fully that she could feel the wild, crazy dragon magic settling into her. Into her flesh, her bones, like it belonged to her.

More like, she belonged to it now. It was Ash's dragon power, the power he had from his hoard, and somehow from his books and sword as well. She could sense it. Her entire body came alive with the sizzling burst of energy. Sheer strength and joy flooded through her. It was echoed by a deep, vibrant roar from above as Ash must have felt the power burst over him as well. Teagan felt the weirdest sensation of being buoyed by it, wrapped up together with Ash by the power. Connected to him. Bound by their mate bond, and whatever magic had just exploded into being.

Holy crap, this was amazing.

Teagan narrowed her eyes at Celia. The freaking gloves were coming off. "I said earlier, I dare you," she said in a voice so low and dangerous she almost didn't recognize it. She added with a snarl, "Bring it, Celia."

For a split second, Celia seemed startled. Her muddy brown eyes widened as Teagan abruptly swung up Ash's sword and met Celia's strike with her own fierce response.

Clang! With a ringing sound deeper and more vibrant than any Teagan had heard before by clashing swords, their blades met in midair. Huge silvery sparks again lashed off of Ash's sword, shimmering and hanging midair for a split second before dissolving. Teagan could take no time to admire the wild beauty of it. She pulled on everything she had learned in her sword classes this year, plus her sheer desperation over Ash's safety, and the other sort of deep, strange magical power that filled her as she fought for her very life.

The first hit made Celia stagger back, as unprepared as she was for Teagan to actually counter. But the small woman quickly recovered, stumbling to the side then finding her balance on the balls of her feet as she gave Teagan a calculating look. "My, my. Will the surprises never cease."

Before Teagan could think of a good reply, Celia lunged at her again. Thrust, parry, strike, dance back, thrust again. As they circled one another, swords clanging, Teagan found her body responding instinctually. Her sword master Nick had been right. Muscle memory was actually a thing. She gave in to it, allowing it to lead her in a state of clearheaded flow as she fought this crazy woman.

Overhead, the horrible sounds that were two giant dragons battling blasted the air. Teagan couldn't spare a look to see if her mate was okay. She also couldn't dare more than a quick glance at Eamon again. *Oh, please don't let him be dead,* she begged to whatever deity might be listening to her at the moment.

Then she had to shut off her worry and focus on simply keeping herself alive.

With each parry and lunge that Teagan offered, Celia met it with the cool grace that shocked Teagan more each time. She found enough breath between blows to say, "Who are you? You're nothing like the woman I've been working with all year."

Rain sheeted down Celia's face as she and Teagan warily circled one another. Teagan didn't dare take her eyes off her opponent, but she desperately listened for sounds from the battle above. She was simply rewarded with the same shrieks and bellows and occasional thumping crashes that she imagined were dragon bodies meeting in the sky. A weird, heavy stink filled the air, one that took her a long moment to puzzle out. It was accompanied by a loud hissing and sizzling sound.

She finally realized they were the smell of sulfur and the sound of flame being breathed by the awesome giants above. By her mate, her Ash. She could only hope with every fiber of her being that the flames were only coming from him, not scoring his gorgeous crimson hide even more.

Still breathing lightly despite the fact that she had to move twice as fast as Teagan due to her much shorter stature, Celia corrected her with a slow shake of her head. "No. The woman you've been working with is nothing like me. That's what you and everyone else here failed to see. So easy to fool," she said in a scornful whisper, the coolness slipping for a moment.

Teagan took in the information, let it roll around her mind for a scant second, then drew her brows together. Ignoring the rain water pouring down her face aside from occasionally swiping at her eyes so she could still see, she carefully circled around her insane, traitorous opponent. "So you were putting on an act. They didn't know. And somehow you figured out everything about Ash's books. His sword." The sword in question seemed to pulse in her hand, as if in answer. That should have freaked her out, but it didn't. It felt utterly natural, as if she had been born to wield it.

She caught the quick flick of Celia's glance down at the sword. At the runes on it.

Celia's smile was chilly. "It all finally came together and made sense tonight as I looked at those precious books of yours. That they held dragon shifter power and magic was obvious simply because of whom they belong to, not to mention the research I did. But there was something else in there. I couldn't quite put my finger on it since I'm not a shifter." Something that skirted just on the edge between heart-wrenching grief and desperate desire colored her voice. "My masters had told me enough about the provenance of the items. I also overheard your dear, sweet friend Savannah talking about 'Project Teagan Makeover.'" Her voice suddenly twisted into the snippy ugliness that was familiar to Teagan.

As Teagan stared, Celia laughed, her face reverting to the cool, obviously trained fighter she was. Whoa, creepy.

"I knew the instant I saw you the other day, when you actually managed to stand up to me, that you were Ash Connolly's mate. It had given you strength and presence of self. I know what love can do to a woman." The twist of pain flared in Celia's voice for another brief moment. "But most importantly, that meant you were the key to unleashing his power. The magic."

Head swimming with the overload of new information, Teagan latched onto the thing that seemed the weirdest. "Your masters? What—wait, do you mean dragon shifters? They're your masters?"

Celia laughed before abruptly darting forward and just managing to nick Teagan's upper arm with the tip of her sword. She could have pressed on, but she whirled away, showing her back to Teagan in a deliberately insulting show. "You understand nothing about the dragon shifter world, Teagan." Her voice was sheer ice. "All you know is that you're in love with your wonderful dragon shifter mate. Everything in the world is beautiful. Amazing. Your future is endlessly hopeful."

This time, the note of bitterness was clear. Celia's eyes locked on Teagan's then. "My dragon shifter mate was named Malcolm. And after collecting all the artifacts that we needed to complete my transformation, I truly would have been able to be his mate. A dragon shifter just like him."

Teagan was completely confused. She didn't understand a single thing Celia was saying. Just as she opened her mouth to ask, a sudden, scratchy voice to the side jerked both of their attentions away.

"It won't work, Celia." Eamon. He was sitting up. A nasty bruise had already spread across his temple. "Dark magic, conjured by thievery and treachery, has no place in the true dragon shifter world."

The cool laugh, touched still by some desperation, snaked through the inner garden as Celia stood tensed with her sword. "The shifters in my world don't play by those rules, you old fool. And neither do I."

So thankful that Eamon was okay, Teagan let down her guard for a split second as she smiled with relief. But just as she opened her mouth, Eamon abruptly staggered to his feet, his expression shouting a warning even before his voice did. "Duck!"

Teagan's body obeyed the order without her conscious thought, swooping down from the waist and swinging to the side. The high-pitched whistle of a blade screamed a hair's breadth away from her own head. She whirled around, meeting Celia's mocking expression visible in another brief flash of lightning.

"I guess you have learned a thing or two at the Institute. But here is the real test now." With that, Celia came at Teagan again.

Teagan gave herself over to the battle, letting her body and the sword take over. The shrieks and crashing booms of the dragons overhead, Eamon's croaked warnings, her awareness of the treacherously slippery footing beneath, all coalesced into one moment. She flowed into her sword, and it flowed into her. For the first time, she finally truly understood what her instructor was always trying to drum into her head. *Do not lose your concentration, but do not dwell on it, either. Your sword is an extension of your body. It is not a separate object from you, but it is a part of you. Dance with it, and let it lead.*

Fighting with fierce grace, feeling as if something possessed her body, she battled Celia into a corner of the hedges. Celia's face lost its cool, calculating expression, morphing into a more hotly desperate, frantic edge as she realized that Teagan was truly getting the upper hand.

When Celia finally slammed up against something hard and gray in the dim light of the garden, her back to it and nowhere left to go, Teagan knew exactly what it was. The statue she had intended to hide behind earlier. There was no way Celia could escape. Teagan could actually—*kill* the woman right now if she wanted to.

The knowledge of the power in her own hand shocked and stilled her at once. Her blade held still and steady, covered in raindrops, less than an inch from Celia's exposed throat.

The sound of their harsh breathing was all that Teagan could hear for a long second. Finally, Celia spoke in a low voice. "Go on." She raised her head, exposing her throat in a fearless acceptance Teagan had to grudgingly admire her for. "Finish it. Are you still too much of a pathetic, nerdy little girl to be tough enough to do it?"

There was another long beat, Teagan staring into Celia's eyes. She heard a sudden, triumphant roar from the sky overhead. It was Ash's dragon voice, she knew without even looking. He'd bested his challenger, just like she'd bested hers. Would he actually kill the other dragon? Was she supposed to —really and truly *kill* Celia?

Even as she asked herself the question, she knew the answer. She pulled her sword back slightly, still keeping it close enough in case Celia tried something. "You're right," she said softly. "I am a nerdy little girl, and I always will be. I'm also one damned badass warrior woman, and I'm strong enough to let you live so you'll have to pay for what you've done. There's no escape, Celia."

A heavy thump on the ground behind her made her jump, heart squeezing. It was quickly followed by another, lighter thump. She didn't dare turn her head, but she instantly relaxed again as she felt Ash's presence. She could actually sense him behind her. Alive and whole. Teagan felt completely *in* herself, in her body, aware of herself and who she was, for the first time in her life. It was amazing. Slowly, she backed up until her body nestled into the warm, strong body of her dragon shifter mate. Reaching her free hand behind her, she felt the incredible softness of his hide, inhaled the spicy scent of him. Holy freaking whoa, he was a dragon. He rumbled overhead, the sound equal parts awe, pride, and triumph. There was a strange shifting sensation beneath her hand, then she abruptly felt his human shape.

Ash stepped up beside her, human again. Side by side with Teagan, he cast a dark glance at Celia, then dismissed her by looking at Eamon, who nodded at him, indicating that he was okay. Eamon swiftly moved to Celia, taking her sword from her unresisting hand and guarding her now with two weapons. Teagan suspected he could swing them both at the same time. Celia wasn't going anywhere now but to jail. Or shifter prison. Or whatever it might be.

It was obvious Celia didn't mean to put up a fight. Her glance had gone behind Ash, to what Teagan guessed must be the other dragon where he had landed on the ground. Celia's face betrayed no emotion, but her body slumped in defeat. Sure, she might have some sort of magic, but it seemed to be useless without an actual dragon shifter on her side. She looked at Teagan, still expressionless, then shrugged. "Well. Perhaps tonight just wasn't my night. Another time, then."

In a sharp tone, Eamon said, "I think not. The dragon council will decide your fate, and I strongly suspect it will not allow for more misdeeds from you." He nodded his head at Celia to indicate she was to walk before him, his double sword points just behind her back, toward the Center.

As she inclined her head and acquiesced, Celia gave a final glance at Teagan, her expression suddenly stark. "If you really love yours as much as I loved mine," she said in a quiet, ragged voice, "can you blame me for what I did?" Then the detached, cool smile slipped back over her face, and she waited for Eamon.

Eamon awarded a respectful nod of his head at Teagan. "This has been an extraordinarily challenging experience. But you handled yourself remarkably well. Welcome to our world, Teagan." He nodded at Ash, then took Celia away.

Teagan stood for a moment longer, trying to collect her wits. Nope, that wasn't going to happen just yet. She turned around and looked at her dragon shifter man, then shook her head in wonder as she took in the fact that he was wearing clothes, disheveled as they were. At this point, nothing more would surprise her. She simply said, "Dragon magic?"

Ash's chuckle, warm and safe, wrapped around her. She laughed with him, feeling a bit giddy and lightheaded from everything. Then she looked at him. Really looked at him. Her hand flew to her mouth, her eyes wide. "Ash," she said through her fingers, "Your scars. Is it—is it just the light, or are they really less there?"

His smile nearly split his gorgeous face. "Dragon magic," he replied, quirking an eyebrow at her. Softly, he added, "I still won't ever heal completely, Teagan. Magic and gold hoards only go so far. But it's more than I thought I'd ever have again." Wonder touched his voice looked at her, emotion brimming in his eyes. "It was you, Teagan. You were the key that changed everything."

Teagan thought she might suddenly choke from the crying welling up in her throat, the tears spilling out of her eyes.

Then Ash said, still smiling in bemused delight as if he'd never seen her before, "But actually, you're not the key to my treasure."

She wasn't?

Ash reached forward to take her face in his hands, gently stroking his thumbs over her skin. "You *are* my treasure, Teagan. You have my heart," he whispered.

Oh. Holy freaking emotion attack. Teagan wasn't sure she could speak, but she tried anyway, feeling her chin shake from her happy tears. "And you have mine, Ash." The next words just spilled out of her, as naturally as breathing. "I love you, Ash Connolly. I don't know much about anything that

happened here, but I know enough to know that I love you."
Astounded joy made her entire freaking body feel light as her
gorgeous dragon shifter man smiled with an exultation she
knew she was reflected on her own face.

"I love you, too, Teagan Lambert." Even in the dim garden
lights, she could see his dragon fully present, tears playing at
the corners of his glowing green eyes. Then he pulled her into
him for a long, deep kiss, one that melted Teagan's entire body
and made her sniffle with tears and relief and an unshakeable
knowledge.

Her entire freaking world had just changed like crazy, but
Ash was hers and she was Ash's. That was all she needed to
know, and it was definitely more than enough.

Ash pulled back and added in a firm voice, "My powerful
warrior woman. My incredible, badass mate." His smile
engulfed her with stunning joy. "That is who you are, Teagan."

Swallowing the knot of emotion in her throat, hoping her
voice wouldn't shake, she said back as firmly as she could,
"You're pretty badass yourself, Ash. We make a good team,
don't we? Mate," she whispered, tasting the word on her
tongue and feeling how right it was. "My amazing dragon
shifter mate."

"Mate," he agreed through the huge smile that cracked
open his face, his voice deep and rich and joyous as it echoed
through the air. "You are the eternal mate of my heart, and
treasure of my soul."

The End

Thank you for reading *Burned!* Ash & Teagan's story was
challenging yet ultimately so very rewarding to write. Dragon
shifter characters make for very intriguing tales.

ABOUT J.K. HARPER

J.K. Harper lives in the rugged, gorgeous canyon country of the southwest, which is a great place to let her imagination run wild.

For more information about her books, please visit her website: www.jkharper.com.

READ MORE BY J.K. HARPER

Silvertip Shifters
Hunter's Moon: Quentin (*Black Mesa Wolves crossover*)
Mountain Bear's Baby: Shane
Taming Her Bear: Beckett
Rescue Bear: Cortez
Ranger Bear: Riley
Firefighter Bear: Slade
Superstar Bear: Bodhi
Christmas Night Bear: Wyatt

Black Mesa Wolves
Guardian Wolf
Alpha Wolf
Hunting Wolf
Wild Wolf
Solstice Wolf
Christmas Wolf
New Year Wolf
Protector Wolf
Fire Wolf
Rogue Wolf

Dragon Mates
Dazzled
Thrilled
Burned

Wicked Wolf Shifters